T0178878

WHISPERS MOST FOUL

WHISPERS
MOST
FOUL

Emma MacDonald

This is a work of fiction.

Cover art by: Kelly deVos

ISBN: 978-1-64710-147-3

First Paperback Edition. October 2024.
1 2 3 4 5 6 7 8 9 10

An imprint of Arc Manor LLC

www.CaezikSF.com

CONTENTS

1

WITHIN THESE HALLOWED HALLS

THERE was something quite lonely about the library on the edge of autumn. Browning pages crinkled beneath Rose's fingers, the stale scent of old parchment and the fluttering of snoring books her only company amid these empty, echoing halls. No hushed whispers hung in the vaulted ceilings. No quiet laughter hummed between the towering shelves. Not another soul lurked here in the dim glow of early evening. At least, not yet.

If she looked closely enough, she could almost count the cobwebs hanging from the furniture. Tidy rows of mahogany desks and chairs sat tucked between the looming shelves, almost aching in the loneliness of the last days of summer.

But the illusion shattered as a shout of muffled laughter floated in through the window beside her. With a sigh, Rose glanced out at the courtyard beyond, where her fellow students milled around below the roiling gray sky and Dunhollow Academy's towering spires. Some idled at the edges of the courtyard, casting shimmering shields over their heads, their collared coats wrapped tightly against the autumn chill. Others were scurrying out of the rain, charmed bags floating behind them and familiars close at their heels as they fled toward the steps of the university's main hall.

Most bore a warm, sun-kissed glow, the remnants of languid summer months spent away from Dunhollow. Rose leaned back in her chair, which groaned in response. Some part of her wished she too could escape this place for a few months.

Gallivant off to the furthest corners of the world and forget all about her degree. But these hallowed halls of magic were her home, and there was a quiet tranquillity to them that she wouldn't trade for anything. Or, at least, there used to be.

The hairs on the back of her neck pricked beneath an unseen gaze, and Rose tightened her grip on her book. She knew, somewhere in the back of her mind, that she shouldn't look. That she should keep her gaze fixed on the pages before her and let everything else slip away.

But slowly, surely, her eyes were drawn back to the window.

There, across the courtyard, lingered a figure that did not fit among the rest, nearly lost in the haze of fog and the dim glow of perpetually golden leaves. It was gaunt and pale and Rose's eyes almost slid right past it, for it was more shadow than solid form.

Aveline.

The girl's face had been plastered all over campus for months, flaxen hair and blue eyes staring out from faded Missing posters. Even the stains of Dunhollow's abysmal weather couldn't drown out her bright smile and rosy cheeks. So much life captured in a small, unchanging image. But there was nothing lively about her anymore.

Blond hair twisted around her throat in tangled clumps; emaciated skin stretched taut across her thin face. Rose's stomach flipped as the girl's pale eyes fixed on her, cold and dead. Yet filled with an anguished fury that burrowed into Rose's heart as Aveline's form wavered. And then, before Rose could even blink, the girl wisped away, only soaked, barren stone left in her wake. The books fluttered and snored around her, punctuating the silence.

A chill skittered across Rose's skin—a warning born almost out of instinct. Hardly a second later, the window before her shifted, a wan figure bent upon its surface. Rose's heart leaped into her throat, but she sat rooted to the spot.

Raindrops pattered against the panes, curling around Aveline's reflection, spilling down her skeletal cheeks like tears. Slowly, silently, she reached out a marred hand, the glass splintering around her fingers in spidery tendrils.

For a moment, Rose almost wished she would say something—*anything*. What she wanted, why she was here, what had happened to her. But she remained silent, as she always did. Until her cracked lips parted and a terrible shriek ripped from the abyss of her unhinged jaw.

Rose cried out as the scream clawed at her skull—piercing from within almost as much as from without. Squeezing her eyes shut, she clasped at her ears. But Aveline was everywhere. Clinging to her thoughts, aching in her bones. She tore through each beat of her fearful heart.

The shatter of glass rang out against the stone walls, shards stinging against Rose's cheeks, scattering into her hair. Then, as suddenly as it had begun, the shrieking stopped and the library settled into startling silence once more. Rose counted her breaths. One. Two. Somehow, the quiet was almost worse.

Until all at once every sound returned. The fluttering of books, the patter of rain on the windows. The raging beat of her own heart. Rose ran a hand over her face, her hair. But there was nothing there—no wounds, no glass shards to even speak of.

She sucked in a steadying breath, burying her head in her hands. When Aveline had first appeared, Rose had thought her nothing more than a dream. Dim whispers that hung on the edges of nightmare—a cold face seen only in the dead of night. But then the shadow had started following her, lurking in mirrors and windows, creeping constantly into Rose's waking thoughts.

Yet there was something about Aveline that had only grown stronger as the summer came to a close, no longer bound to mere reflections. Bile crept up Rose's throat as a memory burned at her mind. It had only been a few weeks ago when she'd first taken full form. A perfectly ordinary afternoon at the local pub shattered by the girl's choked, rasping wheezes as she dragged herself across the floor, grasping at Rose's ankles. And not another soul had seen a thing. She shivered, shoving the thought back.

Even in a place built on the bones of magic, there was no good reason for seeing ghosts. It was only her silence that kept Rose from being forced before the imperial mentalists or put on trial for practicing necromancy. Never mind that the idea she could cast such powerful, forbidden magic was almost more unbelievable than a ghost stalking her in the first place. *Almost.*

"Thought I'd find you in here." A hand curled around Rose's shoulder as a warm voice sliced through the stillness.

She jumped, chest tight with a strangled scream, as if a fist had closed around her lungs. With a sharp gasp, she whirled around, meeting a pair of familiar eyes framed by thick glasses.

"Fen?"

Her friend beamed down at her, laugh lines crinkling in tandem with his dimpled cheeks. "Jumpy, aren't we?"

He stood there with the softest gaze, welcoming and windswept, looking for all the world like a ray of sunlight in this dreary place. Before Rose could think better of it, she launched herself into his arms, breathing in the warm scents of his cedarwood perfume. He staggered back, but his arms still curled around her and she sunk eagerly into his embrace.

"Good to see you too." A choked laugh reverberated through his chest. But his smile slipped as Rose pulled away. "Are you all right?"

She glanced back at the window, which stood unmarred, as if she'd imagined the whole horrid thing. Perhaps she had, for the only shadow that remained was the outline of gray clouds. Rose swallowed a shudder. Aveline was gone—for now.

Clearing her throat, she forced a smile across her lips. "Fine. Just glad to see you."

Fen stared at her a moment longer. If there was any part of him that doubted her, he hid it well, leaning against the table with a wry grin.

"I bet." He jerked his head toward the open book beside her. "Doing a little light reading on necromancy, are we?"

She followed his gaze to the ghoulish illustrations of ghastly figures and decrepit undead. With a weak chuckle, she hurriedly closed it and tucked the book under her arm.

"You know me." She slid an auburn curl behind her ear. "Just getting a head start on coursework."

It wasn't a complete lie, at least—she *did* have a history course on pre-imperial magics on her roster this term. But the weight of it still sat heavy on her tongue. She'd been trawling through the library for nearly a month now, desperate for any shred of an explanation for Aveline. Beyond just that Rose was slowly losing her mind, of course.

It seemed to fool Fen, though, for he only shook his head. "Did you leave the library at all? You look like you haven't seen the sun in weeks."

Unlike him. Rose's eyes traced the sharp lines of his jaw, his russet skin sun-kissed and glowing even in the dim candlelight of the library. His dark hair was a bit shorter too, falling in soft waves around his shoulders. She could practically smell the sea salt that clung to his freshly pressed blouse and burgundy vest. No doubt he'd spent the summer lazing about at his family's seaside villa, indulging in fine wines and breaking hearts up and down the coast.

His full lips quirked into a sly smirk, making Rose's stomach twist. Once, she might have counted herself among his dalliances, as short-lived as it had been. When they'd been giddy first-years, hiding away in Dunhollow's dark corners and sharing stolen kisses. But Fen wasn't one to be tied down, and their friendship had always been far more important to her. Even if his beauty still sometimes caught her off guard.

Thrumming her fingers against the spine of her book, Rose turned away. It was almost too easy to get swept up in the intensity of his gaze and the warmth of pleasant memories. Staring into those soft, brown eyes felt like coming home in a way, even if they pierced straight through to her heart. She could have told him everything in that moment—wanted to, even.

But doubt pricked at the back of her mind, tangling the words around her tongue. Throughout this ghoulish summer, Fen's was the only voice she'd truly missed. It was perhaps a bit conceited of her, she supposed, but her heart swelled at the thought that hers was the first voice he'd sought too.

Standing here with him was the first time she'd felt safe in months—one last place Aveline's presence had not touched. Some selfish part of her longed to hold on to that for just a while longer, even against reason.

So, she shrugged. "How was your break?"

"Without you? Frightfully dull. There's only so much peace and quiet one can take."

Rose almost laughed. Every year, he invited her to join him, and every year she declined. Socializing with the upper echelons of Na

Qisan nobility over charcuterie and crudités wasn't her idea of a relaxing vacation. Though this summer it might've been preferable. She fidgeted with the pages of her book.

"Sounds like a nightmare."

"Say what you will, but it's nice to be back." He plucked the book from her hands and tucked it into the folds of her leather satchel, which rested on the seat beside Rose. "Now come on, or we'll be late for the start-of-term feast."

"So?" She ducked as the book came screeching out of her bag, whizzing for a nearby shelf. Rentals could be so touchy. "It'll be nothing but dull speeches we've already heard."

"If dull speeches are the price to be paid for the open bar, so be it." He extended a hand to her. "Plus, maybe your mother will have some news on Aveline."

Rose's notes slipped from her fingers as she reached for them. "Wh-what?"

"Aveline Goarsbel?" He frowned, scooping the papers off the floor and handing them to her. "You know, the first-year who disappeared last spring?"

"Yeah, I remember." She gritted her teeth, shoving her notes into her satchel. "What about her?"

"She's still missing. With the gossip flying around the capital, I'm surprised your mother hasn't said anything."

Rose scoffed. "Well, that would require her to talk to me."

That, at least, was true enough. Though chancellor, her mother had barely been at Dunhollow all summer, traipsing off to board dinners and galas across the empire. Not that it would have made a difference. Though there had been an inquest when Aveline had first disappeared at the end of last semester, her mother had kept its findings quiet, and had been doing damage control ever since.

Fen had the decency, at least, to look mollified by this, tugging at his ascot. "Well, maybe she'll make an announcement tonight."

"I wouldn't get your hopes up."

"Aren't you the least bit curious?"

Rose stilled, her spine rigid. There was a part of her that would have liked to believe she would have been, were she not being haunted by the girl at every turn. But she knew it wasn't true. If those gaunt, lifeless eyes hadn't been following her like a shadow, she never would have paid attention to Aveline past the first headline. She'd have buried her head in her books and let the rumors slip right past her.

Even now she didn't think she truly wanted an answer. The official story was that Aveline had run off, but that was a hollow lie, even without her ghost. Yet, if Aveline was dead, then why could only she see her restless spirit? If she wasn't, well …

Rose clenched her jaw tight. She didn't want to think about that. "It hadn't really crossed my mind."

"Of course not." Fen shook his head. "Well, if not for gossip, then at least come and get a few drinks with me. Please?"

Her eyes narrowed. Drinks meant staying for the feast, which also meant dealing with her peers. And probably her mother too. Still, the idea of spending the remainder of her evening here in the looming shadows made her blood run cold. And Fen, with his pleading eyes, had always been impossible to say no to.

"Fine." She straightened to her full height, which was still barely up to Fen's chin. "Just a few."

His smile brightened. Handing over her satchel, he slung an arm across her shoulder and dragged her off through the maze of shelves. Most of the books were quietening now; they shuffled low overhead instead of whizzing past. She and Fen had to skirt around a few that flew into their path but managed their way through the library in easy silence.

Rose ducked her head as they approached the exit, careful not to look into the small glass windows carved into the great oak doors. She'd gotten quite good at it over the summer, avoiding any reflective surface, as if it might curse her.

Mirrors, windows—even puddles. Facing her own pale skin and the dark circles etched beneath her eyes each morning was bad enough without Aveline's emaciated face appearing over her shoulder. But it was a useless habit now, for Aveline no longer seemed content to be contained by mere shadow and glass. Nowhere was safe anymore.

The cool autumn air brushed against Rose's cheeks, laden by a damp chill that crept along her skin as she and Fen stepped out into the colonnade. Her eyes darted across the courtyard. Golden leaves trembled and twisted upon a breeze, fluttering into the puddles beneath their feet. Ancient gargoyles glared down at her from the gutters, rain spouting from their snarling mouths. But no sign of Aveline—yet.

The Missing posters had all but disappeared from campus now. Or rather, her mother had removed them, Rose was sure. It wouldn't do for the chancellor of the most illustrious university in the empire to admit she'd lost one of her students. Better to pretend she had run off—just another girl drowning beneath the weight of this place.

Which was, perhaps, only another reason to keep quiet about it all. Telling Fen would be hard enough, but the moment she admitted it was real she'd have to report it to her mother too, and that was a conversation she dreaded more than Aveline's ghost. Or the capital inquisitors.

Besides, it wasn't as if the girl had told her anything useful. Grating shrieks and horrid visions offered her nothing about where Aveline's body might lie, or what had happened to her. No proof that what Rose saw was even real.

Shaking the thought aside, she followed Fen up a flight of slick stone steps, trading the misty drizzle for the imposing heights of the main hall. The room hummed with excited chatter, shouts and laughter bouncing off the aged wooden walls, ensconced in flickering candlelight.

Long tables stretched out across the hall, though few people sat at them yet, instead crowding around the makeshift bar at the back of the room. But the sea of faces only made Rose's skin crawl.

Students clustered together in packs, some swirling iridescent wineglasses between their fingers while others cast bursts of magic about the room. Slowly, sourly, their eyes turned upon her, the lively chatter fading to a low hiss as they shed their spells and closed ranks. Rose pulled her bag tight against her chest. Assemblies were the worst.

She jumped as Fen's fingers linked through hers. "I'll grab us some drinks before your mother starts her speech. My treat."

"It's free."

"Well, then, I'll get you two." He grinned before weaving through the crowd of bodies with practiced ease.

The line for drinks idled along, but no one seemed bothered as Fen cut ahead of them. Instead, they clapped his shoulder, all smiles as they asked about his break. Rose hung back, leaning against the far end of the table.

"Out of the way!" A shrill voice cut through the crowd.

Rose turned, a sneer already curling her lips as a streak of red hair and milky pale skin jostled toward her. Arden Osiander. Pretension clung to the boy like the pomade caked into his curls with its greasy sheen—foul and easy enough to spot from a mile away. Not that he made any effort to hide it.

A smug grin seemed permanently stuck to his face, and everything about him was sharp, from his angular features to his bony elbows, which he used all too eagerly to shove his way through a group of nearby first-years. His constant shadow, Ewan Elaegius, followed behind him with a bored expression.

They only lacked their third member, though they were rarely seen apart—like some unholy trifecta. Rose winced as one of the first-years failed to get out of Arden's way in time, and he twisted around them, crashing into her—hard. Pain shot through her shoulder, but she fought to keep her face even as the boy straightened.

"Thenlif." Arden's lips curled around her name as if it were foul and distasteful. "What are *you* doing here?"

Rose met his sneer with an acrid smile. "Well, I do study here."

"Though one does wonder why," Ewan drawled.

With their blue eyes and shock of gold streaks through their raven hair, Ewan always looked as if they belonged on the cover of a magazine one might find in the capital's wealthiest salons. That was probably where they'd spent their summer too, if the glow of their warm brown skin was any indication. They were beautiful, Rose had to admit. At least, so long as they never spoke.

"Bullying first-years again, Arden?" An icy voice cut through the air. "Doesn't that ever get dull?"

Sylvie Belliaris. A chill ran down Rose's spine. She should have known the woman would be lurking somewhere nearby. Their trifecta was hardly complete without her, after all.

Her jaw tightened, and she turned to face her classmate, a frigid smile pulled taut across her lips. Except Sylvie's face was anything but cold. Warm and inviting, a soft smirk tugged at the corners of her mouth, amber eyes bright and a soft flush blooming across her tawny cheeks. Her sleek black hair framed her face in smooth waves, tucked around the collar of her dark turtleneck and long houndstooth coat.

"Oh." She glanced down at Rose, the kindness falling flat in her eyes like a spell snuffed out. "It's you."

"Hello, Sylvie. I trust you had a nice summer?"

The pleasantries rolled off her tongue, bitter as poison. Arden and Ewan exchanged a glance before shifting back into the crowd as if they were mere summonings Sylvie had cast away. Not surprising—she hardly needed their aid. Her wit wielded blades theirs would weep to witness.

"Lovely." She glanced Rose up and down. "I am shocked to see you managed to crawl out of the library though. I thought you'd taken up residence there."

Rose fought to keep her smile even. Such barbs were like a game to Sylvie—a cat toying with her prey. It wouldn't do to let her draw blood so early. She bit the tip of her tongue. It seemed unusually cruel that someone so vile could look so perfect. Beautiful, yet venomous as a serpent.

"It's called studying. You might try it sometime."

Sylvie's eyes darkened. "Yes, well some of us prefer to focus on our natural talents. How are your attempts at casting going, by the way?"

Rose's fingers curled at her sides, cutting into her palms. Harsh words twisted around her tongue, though none of them were quite sharp enough. Sylvie's smirk only widened at her silence.

"Sylvie, darling!" Fen's voice floated over Rose's shoulder. "How are you? Playing nice, I hope?"

Rose's lip curled in a sneer as Fen handed her a drink before leaning in to kiss Sylvie's cheek. *Traitor.* Sometimes, his ability to make friends with absolutely everyone made her want to throttle him.

Sylvie threw Rose a coy glance. "Always."

"I doubt that." Fen laughed. "Can I get you a drink?"

"No, thank you. I was just leaving." She squeezed his shoulder before brushing past them. "See you in class, Thenlif."

Rose glowered at her back as she disappeared into the crowd. With any luck, they wouldn't have any classes together. But the universe would never grant her such a fortune.

Fen chuckled beside her. "Only you could walk into a crowd of people and bump into your archnemesis."

"Please, she's not my nemesis." Rose took a sip of wine, wrinkling her nose. It definitely tasted free. "She's barely even a rival."

"Mhmm." He bit back a grin. "Sure."

Rose squirmed under his gaze. He wouldn't understand—he loved the witty insults and hidden meanings that came with politicking.

They rolled off him like water off a duck. But they didn't for Rose—especially when they came from Sylvie.

The woman had a singular ability to get under Rose's skin, never letting her forget that she hadn't earned her place here. That she would never belong. Never mind that she had the highest marks in their class. For people like Sylvie, the fact that she couldn't cast a practical spell was all that would ever matter.

"She's just ... awful." She glared into her wine. "And she thinks she's better than everyone."

"What, you don't? You hate pretty much everyone here."

Rose opened her mouth to protest just as the candles flickered twice and a hush fell over the room. Her eyes flew to the dais at the front of the hall where her mother stood twirling the flames under her charmed grasp and tapping her cane against the floor.

As if drawn by her hand, students filed into their seats at the long tables stretching across the hall. Most fell naturally along the divisions of their years, while some crowded around those from their chosen schools of study. She and Fen settled at the end of a row of their fellow third-years, who whispered welcomes at him or waved across the table.

Few of their greetings extended to Rose, of course. But that was always the way. He fitted in everywhere and she hardly anywhere. The only place they shared was with each other.

Her mother cleared her throat. Ink-black hair coiled in a neat bun at the nape of her slender neck, glimmering in the soft glow of the room, while a crimson gown stood out like a shock against her alabaster skin. She was insidiously elegant—mesmerizing in her perfection. Though Rose couldn't say whether that was due to magic, luck, or just sheer determination to never have a hair out of place.

"Welcome," she called out, her voice rich and deep. "Welcome, everyone. I am so happy to be starting another term at Dunhollow. I know you're all eager to indulge in revelry, so I will be brief. First-years will have their orientation tomorrow—the rest of you have had your course lists sent to your dormitories."

Rose leaned against her palms, watching the platters whizz by. As she'd predicted, it was all drivel they'd heard before. Fen was going to owe her a lot more than two drinks for suffering through this.

"For those of you planning any nighttime frivolities this evening"—her mother's eyes followed the rest of the crowd's directly to Fen, who shrugged—"please bear in mind that curfew is midnight and no later. Drunken spellwork will not unlock the gates, I promise."

The room broke out in nervous chuckles, and her mother paused with a brief smirk. She did love a captive audience.

"Now, a few announcements. First, the welcome breakfast will begin at eight o'clock tomorrow morning, and I expect to see you all there, even hungover and near death. Second, I'd like to remind you all of a few safety rules."

She droned on for a bit, skimming over regulations and protocols that everyone but the first-years seemed happy to tune out. Eyes began wandering toward the floating trays while the din of quiet conversations grew louder. Rose tried to drown them out, but there was one thing that echoed in hushed whispers—one name on everyone's tongue. The same name that plagued her own mind.

Aveline.

As if summoned by the thought, the shadows behind her mother began to shift. Pale and wavering, Aveline hovered just over her shoulder, her clouded gaze cracked by grief. Rose's breath caught in her throat, fleeting and fragile, like a loose thread snagging on a jagged edge.

No one else in the hall even batted an eye. Every student at Dunhollow, every rank of caster, and not one of them could see her. Only Rose.

In the space of a moment, she'd never felt more alone. Here she sat, trapped in a sea of bodies, and all she could do was stare at the one form that wasn't there. Or perhaps just the only one that saw her too.

She winced as Aveline's aching eyes met hers in the candlelit glow. Slowly, she pointed a trembling hand at Rose, as if it took all the strength in the world. And then she was gone, faded into shadow as her mother stepped into the space she'd left behind.

"Lastly, enjoy your evening, and welcome once again to Dunhollow." Her eyes locked directly on Rose, sending a shiver straight down her spine. "I'm sure we'll do great things this year."

2

LIKE SO MUCH ELSE

SWEEPING ink letters stared up at Rose, their looping curves and small flourishes almost laughing at her. Her head pounded with the mistakes of the previous night, her throat dry. Why had she let Fen talk her into an after-party, of all things? Her stomach heaved at the thought of how late she'd made it back to her dorm, only to find the unpleasant surprise that now mocked her.

Rose glared at the neat script of her course list, somewhat hoping the words might have changed. But they remained, as bold and damning as they'd been last night.

SMT: *Casting in Pre-imperial Societies, 9:00–10:25, Menier/Wenore/Fenvier*

SDA: *Strategy and Source Level 3, 10:45–12:10, Menier/Wenore/Fenvier*

CUA: *Advanced Alchemical Functions, 11:00–12:25, Tenier/Torier*

SPS: *Practical Spellcraft and Sorcery, 15:25–16:50, Tenier/Torier*

She sighed. At least she was sober reading them this time—not that it made them any easier to swallow. She took a sip of her steaming umber telka, grimacing as the bitter taste hit her tongue. Normally, she'd have savored it, but this morning she needed something a little softer to dull the ache in her head. Sprinkling a bit of sweetened cream into her mug, she took another sip. *Much better.*

Still, the buzz of chatter wasn't helping any, though the main hall had quietened some after the initial breakfast rush. Now, only a few dozen students remained, lounging at the long tables with mugs of steaming telka or roll-ups they'd dared to smuggle indoors for a smoke. Platters of food floated around the tables, though most had nearly been picked clean of pastries, pies, and tarts.

Even the trays that circled the professors' table at the head of the room lay mostly empty, though the fare they held was still finer than what was given to the students. Rose's mother stood idly beside the sage-haired Professor Burroak, wearing her usual crimson gown and a bored smile.

Rose's headache flared back to full strength. Though the shields at the doors were charmed to keep out the dampness, it still weighed at her temples. She sank closer to the table, rubbing at her brow.

"Good morning." Fen's voice reached her over the din, and she slid a sharp glance toward him. "Ugh. What's the matter with you?"

Her scowl deepened. He looked surprisingly awake for someone who had been downing wine like water last night. His long dark hair framed his sharp face in luscious waves, and his brown eyes were bright and alert, though it was rare for him to be awake this early. His outfit was even less tarnished, his linen blouse crisp and his sapphire vest freshly pressed and tucked over a pair of pleated trousers. She wrinkled her nose as he plucked a pastry from one of the roaming trays, reaching for a savory tart herself.

Biting into it, she slid her course sheet over to him. "This."

Fen's thick brow furrowed. "Didn't you say you applied for all theoretical courses this term?"

"That I did." Her fingers tightened around her mug, eyes sliding to her mother. "*Someone* must have decided to change it."

"You don't really think—"

"Yes," she cut across him. "I do."

"*Dia vhal.* Good luck with that."

14

She didn't answer, her gaze locked on her mother as she moved away from Professor Burroak's side. Rose leaped to her feet, making Fen jump as she took off between the tables.

"Chancellor Thenlif!" Her mother's gaze darted toward her, eyes widening before she veered left, heading straight for the exit. "Chancellor, wait. Chancellor—*Mother!*"

Finally, her mother stilled, her cane hitting the stone floor with a sharp thud as the hall fell silent. Rose's cheeks flared as her mother turned, a terse smile plastered on her painted lips.

"Rosera, darling. How good to see you."

Rose shoved her course sheet in front of her nose, in no mood this morning for the saccharine tone of her mother's voice. "What is this?"

Her mother's gaze slid pointedly from the paper to the other students watching their exchange with marked interest. "Why, that looks like your course list, my dear."

"No, my course list was supposed to include Botany and Stratagem, A History of Magical Law, and Theoretical Alchemy, not Alchemical Functions." She bit out the words. "This? This is just cruel."

Her mother fell silent for a moment before grabbing Rose's elbow and pulling her into the corridor, out of earshot of the other students. Drawing herself up to her full height, she glared down the bridge of her nose.

"It wasn't cruelty—it was necessary. You cannot take a random handful of courses simply to avoid casting."

"I *can't* cast, Mother." Rose's nails drew harsh marks along her palms. "And since you won't let me pursue a degree in Magical Theory, what do you expect me to do?"

"I expect you to *try*." Her mother's tone was sharp as glass.

"But—"

"Enough, Rosera!" Her cane struck the floor with enough force to shake the stones. Around them, the sconces darkened, casting the corridor in an ominous shade. "You *will* learn to cast this year, and you *will* choose a degree field that won't see you stuck in some archive for the rest of your life. Do you understand?"

Shadows flickered in the arched windows, a cool contrast to her mother's wrath, but a warning, nonetheless. Rose turned away from the stained glass. Shapes swirled behind the panes of emerald and sapphire— sallow cheeks and clouded eyes that she could not bear to see. *Not now.*

15

Clenching her jaw, she met her mother's gaze. There was no use in arguing—as always, her mother would get her way.

"Yes, Mother."

"Good." She straightened Rose's ascot. "Now, get yourself to class. Tardiness is so unbecoming."

With a soft *tsk* she turned away, leaving Rose alone in the corridor as the bell chimed to mark the hour. Tears burned at her eyes, but she refused to let them fall. Not in front of everyone, at least. Rushing back into the main hall, she snatched her bag from the table, ignoring Fen as he called after her.

The courtyard grew blurry around her as she raced out the front doors. But Rose kept her head down, ducking into the nearby toilets off the main colonnade and locking herself away in a cubicle. Sagging against the door, she unclenched her fists, examining the harsh red marks across her shaking palms.

Some part of her wished to feel the warmth of flame burgeon within them—something to match the pain that seared through her veins. But if she were capable of that, she wouldn't be here. Tears streamed freely down her cheeks now, and she sucked in ragged breaths, trying her best not to blink and ruin her makeup.

If there was one thing she'd become good at over the years of dealing with her mother, it was knowing how to cry without leaving a trace. Well, besides perhaps a slightly red nose, but, pale as she was, that was rather hard to avoid. She reached for some toilet paper to wipe the snot from her upper lip, swallowing another sob. Breaking down in the toilets was one thing—letting anyone hear it was a whole different beast.

As if drawn by the thought, the main door swung open, carrying with it a gaggle of voices. Rose hiccupped, pressing herself tighter against the wall. She hoped they'd be too absorbed in their own conversation to pay much notice to her occupied cubicle.

"I just find it odd," said one. "You'd think the chancellor would've at least mentioned it."

Their heels clacked against the white marble floor, and Rose peered through the crack of the cubicle door. She could just make out as one of them stopped before the mirror to check their lipstick. The glass shimmered, spilling out compliments before another figure stepped in front of it.

"I'd be more shocked if she *had* brought it up. Imagine how that would look."

Brought what up? Rose frowned, studying their faces, though she couldn't make out much at this angle. Still, she didn't recognize them. Second-years, maybe? They didn't have the deadened eyes of most fourth-years, nor did they have the fresh-faced look of first-years.

"Better than it does now, at least."

The second student leaned against the counter. "Aveline was flighty on the best of days. She probably just ran off to 'find herself.'"

Aveline. The name sent a shiver crawling across Rose's skin.

The first student shrugged. "Maybe. She *was* on about some village boy after she and Arden broke up."

Arden? He hadn't exactly seemed cut up when Aveline disappeared. Or even now, given his attitude at the welcome feast last night. Then again, he was likely too self-absorbed to notice she was gone.

Rose shuddered. *Poor Aveline.* If Rose had had the poor judgment to date such a cloying waste of space, she might have run off too. But matted hair and wan features flickered at the edges of her mind, and the thought curdled in the pit of her stomach like sour milk. *No.* If what she saw of Aveline was true, then something far more sinister had happened to her.

"See? They probably ran off together."

"Or Arden made her disappear."

"I doubt that," said the second student. "He doesn't have the gall for it."

Rose brushed her thumb against the sore marks on her palm. As much as she detested Arden, she couldn't help but agree—she doubted he'd risk getting his own hands dirty. The boy was an entitled ass, but even he wasn't foolish enough to go after another student for something so trivial as heartbreak. Such things were like currency here at Dunhollow. He likely would've only been looking to cash in on sympathy and gossip.

Still, he'd been a third-year when Aveline disappeared—why had he been dating a first-year? Her lip curled. Actually, that didn't shock her too much. Most likely everyone in his year saw right through him, but a malleable first-year might have been an easier target. Rose swallowed a gag. Even so, it was odd that his name hadn't come up at all in the initial inquiry in spring.

"Well, it's still strange that Chancellor Thenlif didn't say anything. I hear Aveline's parents are offering a reward to anyone with information."

The second student scoffed, the door creaking as they shoved it open. "Yes, but they had to make a sizable donation just to get her accepted into Dunhollow—they wouldn't want to accept that she'd gone and wasted that."

Rose chewed the inside of her lip as the pair made their way out of the room, their chatter fading with them. Well, that explained why her mother had had such an easy time waving away the rampant rumors around Aveline's disappearance.

There were only two types of students at Dunhollow: those born with influence and connections and those who could buy them. If Aveline's parents were the latter, they were likely capital merchants who went through money like water but had little of the pedigree the more established noble families clung to like a lifeline.

It would have been all too easy for her mother to shut down an investigation into Aveline's disappearance if she'd convinced the titled nobles that their wealthy brethren were getting a little too uppity again.

Not that it mattered. The fact that her mother had ignored the issue said more than enough. Perhaps that was why Rose saw Aveline's ghost now—she was paying the price for her mother's apathy.

The thought left a bitter taste on her tongue. Jiggling the latch, she slipped slowly out of her cubicle and made her way over to the sink. What did it matter anyway?

For months, it had been easy enough to pretend the girl was a mere figment. Nothing more than shadow bent upon glass, or some fear-fuelled wisp dreamed up by her slumbering mind. If nothing else, it served Rose with the perfect palatable excuse for her silence. Who could she tell in these empty halls beyond her mother, who had made it plain that she had no interest in the truth?

And, if Aveline really was dead, then whatever had happened to her was a secret she'd taken to her restless grave. Even if she could tell Rose something useful, how could Rose pass that along to the authorities without putting herself in the line of suspicion? *No.* There was no solace to be found in the truth now—no peace. Only questions that Rose had no good answers for.

She sighed deeply, her throat tightening. Perhaps it wasn't her mother's apathy that had prompted her haunting but her own complacency.

The mirror loomed overhead, but it spilled no compliments for her and she didn't dare look into it. Instead, she kept her gaze fixed fiercely on the tap as she turned it, pressing cool water to her raw cheeks. Even so, a shiver stole down the back of her neck, trailing down the soft hairs on her forearms.

Not now. She gripped the edge of the counter until her knuckles turned white. But it was no use. No amount of wishing or willing would wash this stain away.

If she did not look, the girl would only remain longer, hanging over Rose's every breath. Whatever message she meant to impart, she clearly wanted it to be passed through suffering.

Bile bit at the back of Rose's throat as she lifted her head. But it was not a milky gaze or withered flesh that greeted her now. Blood pooled from Aveline's sunken eyes, bright, startling blue against the crimson. Bulging veins of sickly gray climbed up her throat, as if the shadows swirling around her had etched themselves into her emaciated skin.

She didn't reach for Rose, didn't shriek or cry out. She didn't even move. Instead, she was utterly still, almost as if she was just as trapped by this form as Rose was.

"Please." The whisper fell from Rose's lips, dry and heavy as lead. "What do you want from me?"

Aveline's shape wavered upon the smooth panes of the glass. Shadows pulsed around her matted curls and her mouth fell open. But it wasn't words that emerged. Pools of liquid shadow spewed forth from her lips, swallowing the girl up in a shower of cracking glass and—

The door swung open with a great bang, echoing off the marble walls. Rose screamed, stumbling as she spun around.

"*Dia vhal,* it's only me." Fen held his hands up. "Are you all right?"

Rose steadied herself against the sink as dark spots danced across her vision. Squeezing her eyes shut, she sucked in deep breaths. The air was cool and pure against her aching lungs, but it did little to soothe her.

When she opened her eyes, Fen's gaze was fixed solely on her. Not on the mirror nor any of the horrors held within. *Just her.*

How must she have looked to him? All too much like Aveline, she supposed. A pale reflection of herself, only moments away from shattering.

Forcing a small smile, she straightened. "I'm fine."

He took a step closer as he reached for her. "Rose ..."

"I said I'm fine." She brushed his hand away.

"You don't look fine."

"He's not wrong, dear," the mirror whispered.

Rose glared at the shimmering surface, now free of any haunting visage. Only her own red-rimmed hazel eyes stared back at her, tear-stained tracks tracing haphazard paths down her pallid cheeks. No, she had to admit, he wasn't.

Fen's eyes softened. "I take it the talk with your mother didn't go well?"

She faltered. *Oh, right.* Her mother's words had seemed so far away for a moment, but now they came flooding back.

"You could say that."

With a sigh, Fen reached for a towelette, running it under cold water before blotting it against Rose's reddened skin. But it was no use, for his gentle touch and warm smile only brought fresh tears to her eyes.

He stroked them away with a soft brush of his thumb. "I'm sorry."

There was something in the way his brow creased that turned Rose's heart. It cut jaggedly across his forehead, so at odds with the laugh lines at the corners of his mouth. Almost as if his features did not naturally lend themselves to the expression. But then, her mother had that effect on people.

Fen's hand stilled, and his dark gaze dropped ever so slightly as silence fell over them, fragile as glass. Rose's breath caught in her throat. For a moment, he looked as if he were about to say more, fingers curling gently around her chin. But then he simply smiled, draping her auburn curls over her shoulder and fluffing up the collar of her blouse.

"We'll need to do something about your eyes. Can't have the wolves sniffing around for blood."

Without warning, he ran a warm hand over her face, his magic casting his signature scent. Beyond petrichor, the smell of worn leather and red wine hung on the air, melding with his perfume of cedarwood and caraway. In spite of herself, Rose almost smiled. Each caster wove a bit of themselves into their spells, a small trace. Negligible almost, but still there.

Turning, Rose blinked at her new reflection. Though her face was still tight and raw from tears, bright eyes now stared back at her, the only redness remaining in her flushed cheeks.

Grinning at his handiwork, Fen leaned closer to the mirror, tousling his hair and fixing his smudged eyeliner. A pang of jealousy twisted around Rose's gut. He cast as if it were as easy as breathing—no more than a trifling thing. She glanced down at her empty palms, but all they held were the marks of bitter disappointment.

Though Fen would deny it in a heartbeat, there was a cynical, caustic part of her that somewhat believed he only hung around her for his own reputation. Appearances were everything here, and what better way to maintain his image as Dunhollow's golden boy than by taking pity even on the academy's resident casting defect?

She gritted her teeth, the thought sinking in her heart. Fen didn't deserve that. And she perhaps didn't deserve him.

Dunhollow was forged by deceit and betrayal—it had no use for anything so mundane as sincerity. But Fen ignored that rule. Or rather, threw it out the window entirely. He cared deeply about everything and everyone. Even her.

Beside him, she didn't feel the sharp edges of her mother's words as keenly, nor the looming weight of Aveline's ghost. Though both still lingered at the back of her mind like a creeping fog in the early dawn. And what comfort had she offered in return, save the unfounded ignorance of deceit?

The thought hollowed out a pit in her stomach. Would the truth really be so terrible? A small part of her knew that he wouldn't turn away, no matter what she told him. Somehow, that scared her more.

Shaking her head, she sucked in a sharp breath. "Fen, I—"

With a great clamor, the second bell rang out, a last warning before the start of classes. Rose startled, though Fen hardly looked fazed.

"What?"

"I—" The words fled from her lips, any courage she'd mustered failing alongside them. "Nothing. Never mind."

She scurried out of the door before he could say anything more, melting into the bustle of students in the corridor. Hardly any even looked up as she joined their ranks, just another soul lost in a sea of argyle and tweed. Stepping out into the cold drizzle of the perpetually gray Dunhollow skies, she could almost pretend that she belonged here. That, even if only for a moment, there was hope she might somehow make it through this year unscathed.

But hope was cold comfort, and it seeped away from her with each step, vanishing with the rain, like so much else.

21

3

NO LESS DEADLY

THE School of Magical Theory had always been Rose's favourite. It was tucked away in the old quarter of campus, and the crisp scents of old books and aging wood hung on the air, mixed with the intoxicating aroma of freshly roasted telka and a faint hint of pipeweed. Most of the other halls held the cloying stench of petrichor that came with casting—but not this one.

Here, no stray spells flew about in the vaulted ceilings. No bubbling cauldrons and backfired charms choked the corridors with smoke. Here, it was only books, philosophy, and debate, traded about by those who cherished the magic of the mind.

Most importantly, this was the oldest of the halls. Carved from wood that had seen the birth of the empire, it lacked the looming glass windows the rest of the university boasted. What few did exist perched just below the ceiling like half moons and brought in just as little light.

Some perhaps would have been deterred by the dark pall this cast over the lecture hall. But not Rose. For the first time in months, she stepped confidently into the room, letting the darkness wreathe her like a shield. Yet the feeling was cold and fleeting. Once, it might have kept Aveline's ghost at bay, but now it made no difference. Nowhere was safe.

Rose clutched her satchel tighter, nearly stumbling on the low stairs. The lecture hall sprawled out before her, curved benches in tiered steps surrounded by panelled walls that creaked with great age and secrets. Students filtered in slowly, shuffling toward open benches, still blurry-eyed and hungover from last night. In the center of it all, Professor Sylverfir leaned against a great oaken desk, surrounded by a gaggle of eager students.

Thin, ink-black braids hung midway down his back, half held in a low bun, and a few framing his face. His lips quirked in an easy smile, his umber skin marked by laugh lines and scars in equal measure. It was almost odd to see him without a glass of whiskey in his hand, stretched out before his hearth and debating ancient history late into the night. He and Rose could both whittle away hours on the subject, and there was precious little else to do in the long evenings of the summer months.

He was one of the few who cared for the history of magic over practical casting. The theory, the potential—the artistry of it all. Of all her professors, he never made her feel lesser for her lack of magic. In some ways, he almost reminded her of Fen. Not the golden-boy social-ite side of himself he usually presented but the Fen that could ramble on about the intricacies of alchemy or bury himself in ancient texts for hours on end. Though she couldn't quite see him as a professor. He had far grander plans than that. In all fairness, however, Sylverfir didn't always seem much like a professor either.

If one looked beyond his world-weary cloak of tweed and truly awful puns, he could almost blend in with the students around him. He claimed to be the same age as her mother, but he hardly looked a day over twenty-five. Rumors abounded that he'd been cursed with immortality and that each scar marked a death he'd cheated. Rose wasn't quite sure about that, but it certainly didn't stop her peers from fawning over him.

With his soulful brown eyes, warm smile, and overabundance of cryptic charm, she couldn't really blame them. As if sensing her entrance, he glanced up, eyes brightening as she stepped into the amphitheatre.

"Morning, Rose."

"Morning, Professor."

The formality sounded strange to her ears. Growing up, he'd always just been Soren to her, but she'd rankled under such familiarity as a student. There were enough jokes cut at her expense for being friendly with the teaching staff—she didn't need to give them anymore fuel. Sylverfir was a happy medium they could both agree upon, but "professor" always rolled off her tongue more as a snide remark than an acknowledgement of his title.

A few of her peers tittered at their exchange, already whispering behind their hands. *Wonderful.* Rose's cheeks flared, and she ducked onto the nearest bench with a creak. She busied herself with unloading her bag, pointedly ignoring the hushed laughter and sidelong glances.

But as quickly as they'd begun, the whispers cut off sharply. Rose steeled herself before lifting her gaze, only to find herself blinking up at the last face she'd ever expected to see here.

"Thenlif." Her name fell from Sylvie's lips as if it tasted foul. "I should've known you'd be here."

Rose gaped, words failing her. For all her skill as a caster, Sylvie had no patience for theoretical courses. They were the only place Rose had always been able to avoid her—where she'd always been able to shine without the threat of her shadow looming.

"I—why are you here?"

"Believe me, I'd rather not be." Sylvie rolled her eyes. "The chancellor thought I needed to 'branch out.'"

With a huff, she plopped down in the seat directly behind Rose, and a small smirk curled at Rose's lips. If she had to suffer Sylvie's presence, at least she could take comfort in knowing Sylvie would detest every moment of it too. And it gave her no end of petty pleasure that she wasn't the only one who'd had her schedule forcibly switched to a more "acceptable" curriculum.

Wait. Her smirk slipped. No—even her mother wouldn't be cruel enough to force them into the same classes intentionally ... would she? Rose shook her head. Of course she would.

The thought left a faint taste of dread at the back of her mouth as Sylverfir got to his feet. A hushed silence fell over the room as he rolled up his left sleeve, revealing a golden tattoo carving its way up his forearm. It writhed for a moment before coming alive in the shape of his familiar, a small golden dragon named Nora. Yawning loudly, she flapped over to Sylverfir's desk, where she curled up for a nap.

Rose's arm burned along the edges of her own familiar's bond, and her stomach sank. She didn't think they'd be casting today.

"Don't worry about summoning your familiars," said Sylverfir, as if reading her mind. "I simply wanted the boost."

Rose let out a small sigh. Even the presence of her familiar didn't give her anymore ability to cast, and she'd been hoping this would be the one course she wouldn't humiliate herself in.

"Now, before we begin, I'd like to take the opportunity to remind everyone that this lecture is on casting in pre-imperial societies." Sylverfir paced before the curved benches. "If you've found yourself in the wrong class—or perhaps even the wrong college—you may want to correct that now."

He grinned as one student darted up from the front, their milky skin flushed pink as they raced from the hall. Behind her, the sounds of shuffling and wooden thuds told Rose a few other students may have found themselves with the same misfortune. If only Sylvie could've been one of them.

"Now that we're all where we're meant to be, let us get to the interesting bit. Forbidden magics. Necromancy, dreaming, and divining. The very bane of our empire, if some are to be believed, but who can tell me the regulations that were in place on them in pre-Calamity societies?"

The room fell quiet once again as her classmates glanced around at each other. Rose ducked her head over her notes. The answer burned at her tongue, but she could already hear Sylvie's snide teasing if she were to give it too eagerly.

"Any volunteers?" Sylverfir's dark gaze roved over the room. "If it helps, this isn't a quiz—just a discussion."

Rose sighed, unable to contain herself any longer. "There weren't any. Pre-Calamity societies didn't limit magic."

"Correct." Sylverfir's grin widened. "Magic weaves through this world like a song, and each culture shapes it to its own tune. Ancient civilizations didn't limit magic, but only because they already practiced a more rigid form."

Rose leaned back in her chair, flashing a glance at Sylvie, who rolled her eyes. Rose's gaze caught on the notebook before her, which lay empty, save for a sketch of a tree. How Sylvie expected to pass this class without taking any notes was beyond her, but Rose wouldn't mind seeing her fail for once.

"But *why* was theirs more rigid?" Sylverfir's voice drew her back to the lecture. "Some would argue this has to do with magic's source. According to some theorists, magic simply had a more rigid nature then. By other accounts, magic has always abounded in various forms. Here in Na Qis, we practice magic from all over the empire."

"Well, *some* of us practice anyway," Sylvie muttered softly.

Rose's jaw tightened, but she refused to turn around. Instead, she bent low over her parchment, her pen nearly tearing it beneath the force of her grip as Sylverfir carried on.

"Alchemy from the northern reaches of Ir Taril, botany and herbalism from the southern forests of Arbelis. Even dangerous source magic from the heart of Tol Qilius." He relaxed against his desk, crossing his legs. But his casual pose could not hide his eagerness. "And yet there are some we deem too dangerous—too wild. But why? Is flame less dangerous than jumping through dreams? Are warping time or divining the future truly so deadly? Is healing someone from the brink of death worse than pulling them back across that threshold?"

"Those magics are rarer." Sylvie's voice rang out across the room. "We know less about them, which makes them harder to defend against."

"And why would you assume we'd need to defend against them?" Sylverfir's dark brow raised above his glasses. "Could they not also benefit us?"

"Maybe." Sylvie's shrug was almost audible. "But history tells us they didn't, and magic that can't be controlled is a dangerous thing."

Rose swallowed a scoff. Coming from the woman who wielded her magic like a blade. Control was no less deadly than chaos in some hands.

Still, for once, she almost couldn't disagree with Sylvie. Aveline was a mere ghost, and already she'd latched on to Rose like a parasite, sucking all life and light out of the world. If history was to be believed, ghosts were the very least of a necromancer's repertoire, and the entire Qisan empire had once been brought to its knees by the divining of a sole rebel queen.

"Precisely." Sylverfir's familiar shimmered as if charged by his excitement. "Control is the key here, but why these magics? People have spent entire theses arguing the danger of source magic, and yet we have precious few laws to regulate it. Meanwhile, we have the whole

Edict of Ardalis to protect us from dreamers, diviners, and necromancers, of which there were only a few to begin with."

A few within the empire, he meant. Rose fiddled with her pen. There were plenty beyond its borders, in the far older places of the world. Not that most Na Qisans cared. Though their empire made up only one of three continents, most liked to act as if it were the center of the world. Of course, to them it was. And the empire liked nothing less than things beyond its reach.

"Because we don't control them," she said. "The lands they come from aren't within the empire."

"*Yes*, thank you, Rose." Sylverfir beamed at her. "And, as Sylvie pointed out, we don't like things we can't control. Our illustrious officials are more than happy to incorporate new magics as our empire grows. But the forbidden arts are far older and far beyond the lengths of the empire's control, and so they exert it where they can."

Several yawns cut across the room, but Sylverfir hardly seemed deterred by his lagging audience. Pushing off his desk, he waved his hand and a glowing, ancient map of the three continents appeared behind him.

"Now, starting with necromancy, who can tell me where the earliest forms of it were recorded?"

That was easy. A cacophony of voices filled the air as her classmates clamored over whether it was the Queendom of Pelanghe, the Pellagius of Ilaura, or the earliest progenitors of their own empire. They were all wrong, of course: it was the Pentarchy of Etanhe, far on the coast of the westernmost continent, Allian, though saying so only earned her another glare from Sylvie. *Good.*

The class flew by as Professor Sylverfir carried on with question after question. Hardly any of them even made it into Rose's notes, and she wondered how this class got marked at a third-year level. She could recite most of this lecture in her sleep.

Her eyes began to droop as she leaned against her hand. It would break Sylverfir's heart if she, of all people, fell asleep in his class. But weeks of poor rest pulled at the back of her mind, the darkness of the room curling around her like a blissful cocoon.

The windows above almost seemed to darken, as if further tempting her to slumber. But something flashed across her eyelids. A sliver of light—a wisp of form that jolted her awake.

Her breath caught in her throat as the room came back into focus. It was still dark and dreary, while Sylverfir carried on in front of his map and a few heads sank low over the benches before her. At least she wasn't the only one.

The tightness in her chest loosened, just a bit. Straightening, she turned to sneak a glimpse at Sylvie. If Sylvie had caught her dozing off, she'd never live it down. But it wasn't Sylvie's piercing gaze that greeted her.

It was pale skin and hollow eyes, stretched, gaunt, and looming only inches away from hers. It was cool breath brushing across her skin and the musty scent of moss and stone reeking from every pore. It was thick, darkened blood, pooling on the bench beside her, inching ever closer.

A scream burst from Rose's lips as she scrambled back. But Aveline was already gone. The bench beside her was clear, the room around her brighter. And every eye was now fixed on her.

"Rose?" Sylverfir's voice made her jump. "Are you all right?"

His dark eyes glinted in the shimmering light of the map beside him, swimming with concern. Even his familiar was awake now, her golden body trembling. *No.* The thought pounded through her head, but she forced herself to nod.

"Yes, Professor." A fierce heat crept up her cheeks. "Sorry."

The trilling of a bell split the air, sending the other students into a flurry before Sylverfir could say anything else. Rose's outburst momentarily forgotten, they grasped at books and bags, darting for the door as Sylverfir shed his glimmering map with a flick of his wrist.

"Don't forget the reading for next class!" he called after the retreating students. "We'll be covering the shift away from elemental magic in the post-Calamity period, as well as the rise of spirits in early Ilaurian society."

Rose slowly tucked her things into her bag. She could feel the other students' eyes probing her as they passed. Some questioning, some mocking—none of them concerned. Sylvie's gaze was the worst though.

It wavered somewhere between disdain and something kinder. Something Rose had barely thought she was even capable of. *Pity.*

It prodded at her like a stray thorn, festering in her mind. Sylvie had fixed Rose with the same look once years ago—just before she turned the whole academy against her. Rose's jaw tightened. She could keep her pity. Or, better yet, choke on it. Sylvie lingered a moment longer before getting to her feet, but Rose waited until she had well and truly disappeared to follow her.

"A moment, Rose?" Sylverfir's voice stopped her in her tracks.

Damn. With the threat of her classmates' overhearing them gone, the pretense of formality would fade all too easily into familiarity. Sylverfir had known her since birth—he'd be able to see through her lies in a second. It was only by some small miracle that she'd been able to evade him most of the summer.

Clearing her throat, Rose turned, forcing her expression to remain innocuous. "Yes, Professor?"

His warm smile set her at ease, his familiar morphing back into a golden tattoo as he stepped toward her. But his eyes were hard—piercing.

"Are you sure you're all right?" His voice was softer now, losing its professorial edge. Not that he had much of one in the first place.

"Yes, I just—" Rose faltered, rummaging through which lie to force out this time. "I haven't been sleeping well recently. Nightmares."

"Dozing off?" He raised an eyebrow. "That's not like you."

None of this was like her. She swallowed hard. Last semester, she would've made it to class early to pick Sylverfir's brain for term paper topics. She would have relished every opportunity to show up Sylvie ,and her notes would have been immaculate and detailed.

Aveline's presence had stolen so much more than just her sleep and sanity, it seemed. It sapped at her thoughts, her energy, her passions. As if Aveline were draining the very life from her.

But she didn't say any of that to Sylverfir. She merely hugged her books closer to her chest. "Sorry."

He stared at her a moment longer, as if there was something more he wanted to say. Instead, he pulled his glasses off with a small sigh, tucking them neatly into the pocket of his burgundy vest.

"Your mother mentioned that you intended to declare your degree field this term."

"Did she?" Rose's eyes narrowed. Of course she did.

"Yes, and I"—he wrung his hands—"I wondered if you had considered the School of Magical Theory? You'd breeze through a history degree, I'm sure—or even an anthropology degree with a focus on ancient cultures."

Rose's heart skipped a beat. It sounded like a dream, no longer having to worry about practical exams and snide remarks when her casting backfired. But if this morning was any indication, her mother wouldn't hear a word of it—not when she could pursue a more prestigious degree.

"I'm afraid my mother wouldn't allow it." She tucked the last of her notes into her satchel. "What would people think if she had a casting-deficient archivist for a daughter?"

He sighed deeply, the wooden desk creaking as he leaned against it. "Let me speak with her again. I might yet convince her."

"You might try." She slung her bag over her shoulder, turning for the door. "But I wouldn't hold your breath."

4

STRATEGY AND SOURCE

THE crisp autumn air billowed gently against gray skies as Rose approached the training field. No one knew why the sun rarely shone in Dunhollow. Tucked away in its isolated, mountainous corner of the empire, some believed that the university and its surrounding village did not hold to the boundaries of the waking world, instead lingering somewhere between there and the dreamlands of old.

Others claimed that so much casting over the centuries had clouded the skies, just as the amber trees seemed to be perpetually aging. Rose inhaled deeply the ever-present aroma of petrichor. That theory seemed more likely, at least. The scent of magic hung so thick on the air she nearly choked on it.

The clouds too were cast low today, a thick fog creeping across the field. It seeped out of the looming tree line like a slow breath. Ancient gnarled trees reached out toward the sky, a tapestry of muddled leaves and bristling twigs. Faint screams filled the air, but Rose barely flinched. They would be worse by nightfall.

Rumors abounded of cursed creatures that lived within the Whispering Woods, shrieking from dusk till dawn. Whether there was any truth to them, she couldn't say. No one really wanted to find out for certain, after all.

Inching away from the tree line, Rose pulled her bag tighter across her chest. Filled to the brim with books, scrolls, and scattered notes, it almost weighed her down. Though none of it would help. No amount of knowledge or know-how would ever get her closer to casting source. Or any other form of magic, for that matter.

At least in the open training field there were no windows—no reflections. The river and lake were on the other side of campus, and the shock of green grass soaked up any puddles.

Of course, she could hardly trust that would stop Aveline now. She was stronger, more brutal and threatening than the mere reflection she'd once been. As if the more of Rose's sanity she drained away, the more powerful she became.

Would that be how this ended? When Aveline had consumed so much of her that Fen would one day find Rose reduced to a gaunt, shriveled shell of what she'd once been? Even beneath her long herringbone coat, Rose shivered. But why her?

If Aveline was a mere figment of her mind, then her fixation on Rose made sense. Rose picked at the raw edges around her short nails. There were treatments for that, though she doubted she'd ever see them. Her mother wouldn't even allow her to choose a "lesser" profession. It certainly wouldn't do for her to be seen visiting mentalists in the capital.

And if she wasn't? Rose swallowed hard. If Aveline truly was dead, then some form of necromancy had to be at play. Though if she'd been killed, Rose couldn't imagine Aveline's murderer would want her ghost lurking about. And that still didn't explain how *she'd* stumbled into whatever curse was disrupting the girl's afterlife.

Rose's fingers tightened around the strap of her bag. Perhaps she should have told Fen. Or even Sylverfir. Solitude had been easier to retreat to in the quiet of the summer months, but now? Still, the very thought of burdening them with that knowledge—worse yet, risking their disbelief—made her heart skip a beat. She knew at her core that neither of them would turn her in to the capital inquisitors, but their silence would damn them as surely as it would Rose, were the truth ever to come out.

No. Easier instead to never speak of it. To bury it away until it festered and fermented into a fine wine, or else ate away at what little remained of her soul. That was the Dunhollow way, after all.

Shaking her head, she took her place with the other students at the edge of the field. Mostly fellow third-years, she guessed, and all better casters than she. Rose flexed her fingers, willing some element of source magic to curl into her palms. Fire, lightning, ice—anything.

But they remained empty. It was no use. She sighed, flinging her bag down beside her.

Scanning the field, it didn't take her long to catch Sylvie's familiar features in the crowd. She scowled. If Sylvie really was in every one of her classes, she was going to kill her mother. A spiral of ice curled idly between Sylvie's fingers as she chatted away to Ewan and Arden, but she paid Rose no attention.

It figured that ice would come naturally to her—her heart was probably carved from it. Memories burned through Rose's mind. Of dueling circles drawn before eager students and her mother's overbearing gaze. Of Sylvie's sickening smile and the chill of her ice against Rose's skin. How ready she'd been to impale her just for a shred more influence with their peers.

A soft nudge sent Rose stumbling and she glanced up at Fen in surprise. "What are *you* doing here?"

"Last-minute schedule change." He shrugged, though the familiar spark in his eye told her there was more he wasn't saying. "But you owe me for roping me into such an early class."

"It's eleven o'clock."

"Exactly."

She threw him a disparaging glance. Was he really so worried about her? She supposed that wasn't unfair. To his eyes, he'd returned from break to find her a frail, sunken mess who jumped at her own shadow. She'd be worried too.

Still, it wasn't like him to rearrange his schedule. Though he excelled in fire source, alchemy was his passion. Not that many people knew. Most saw only the charming facade he presented—the seductive, kindhearted, charismatic heir of his fabulously wealthy mothers.

They never saw the person beneath who could recite calculations in his sleep or showed up at Rose's dorm in the middle of the night for sleeping teas because his mind just wouldn't stop. She had no talent for magic, but plants were her forte, just as questionably explosive experiments were his. She hated to tear him away from that.

Rose opened her mouth, but closed it promptly as Professor Troidilis strode onto the field. Their emerald robes clashed starkly against the dim skies, their tanned skin a bit weathered, despite the little amount of sun they got here. With their short, dark hair and their piercing brown eyes, they had always reminded Rose a bit of a hawk, ready to pounce on unsuspecting prey.

Those eyes alone called the field into silence, students rushing to line its edges as they straightened their clothes. Not Sylvie, of course. She glided through the grass as if she had all the time in the world, her sleek black hair coiled in a neat bun and her tawny skin glowing. Her eyes found Rose's as she took her place directly across the field and smirked.

Rose bit back a groan, suddenly immensely grateful for Fen's presence. At least there was one person in the course who wouldn't use her as target practice.

"Good morning, everyone." The professor's sharp voice made her jump.

"Good morning, Professor." A chorus of mumbles rose from the students.

"I know many of you are likely quite excited about this course." They raised a thin brow. "Source is the flashiest form of magic—and the most dangerous. Which is why this course is focused on strategy and not shooting fire at your enemies. Anyone who takes issue with that may leave now."

Nobody moved, though eyes darted rigidly about the field to see if anyone would dare.

"Very good." Professor Troidilis gave a curt nod. "Now today we will take a moment to review the fundamentals. Being able to cast infernos, blizzards, and gales is impressive, but you'll be dead before you can if you don't first master a proper barrier."

"Apologies, Professor," said one intrepid voice. "But aren't barriers a bit elementary for this level?"

Rose rolled her eyes. *Arden.* Of course he would think he was too good for this class. Though, as a fourth-year in a third-year level, she wasn't sure why. She glowered at his flaming red hair, combed and coiffed atop his head with enough pomade to choke him. Some days she wished it would.

The professor's eyes narrowed. "If survival was considered too basic for your skills, Messere Osiander, perhaps you wouldn't have needed to retake this class."

His face went bright red, nearly matching his hair, as a few of the other students snickered. Rose herself bit back a grin.

Lips curling, Arden whispered something to Ewan, who stood idly beside him. They looked like a stain of ink against the tree line, from their woolen turtleneck to their long, black trench coat billowing in the morning breeze. Sylvie, by contrast was radiant, a sun amid lesser stars.

The three of them stood inches apart, silently mirroring each other's movements. She wasn't even sure if they were aware of it, or if they were simply cut from the same cloth, ever threaded together.

Perfectly beautiful and utterly rotten. As if some petty deity had poured all their malice into such lovely forms. They were, at their cores, everything Dunhollow could want in its students.

At least, as far as appearances went. They came from the right families, had a talent for casting, and always looked like they'd come fresh from a photo shoot. And, in a few years, Rose was sure she would read an article somewhere about Sylvie and Ewan's engagement—the match of the century. But scratch the surface and it all quickly fell away.

Arden only stayed enrolled by the grace of his parents' diplomatic status, while Ewan had the misfortune to be spawned by the haughty chief board member of Dunhollow. Even Rose's mother detested the man, and she willingly spent time with politicians. Sylvie didn't throw around her parents' weight like the others, but she was more than happy to use her own reputation to terrorize her way to success.

That said, at least she had the skill to match her arrogance, and Ewan could apparently be quite charming when they tried. But Arden? Rose shuddered. What could Aveline have possibly seen in him?

She couldn't imagine anyone finding him alluring, at least not once he opened his mouth. In fact, next to Ewan's gold-streaked dark hair and Sylvie's piercing amber eyes, he almost looked plain by comparison.

Perhaps it had just been the draw of an older student with connections? Or Aveline had hoped his parents' diplomatic roles would somehow further her own standing. It wouldn't be unusual here.

Prestige outweighed anything as fleeting as sentiment. Fen was the only one she'd met here who chose his lovers for enjoyment rather than social gain. Everyone else treated love like some insidious game, wearing their conquests and subsequent heartbreaks like badges of pride.

Rose pursed her lips. Sometimes, she was very glad she didn't partake in any of this school's social frivolities. Loneliness wasn't nearly so painful as betrayal. And Aveline had perhaps fallen victim to both.

With a sharp jolt, Fen moved from Rose's side, and she blinked. "What's going on?"

He raised an eyebrow. "We're practicing barriers."

Her stomach sank, eyes flitting across the field to the other students pairing off. The scent of casting filled the air as they called forth their familiars, and Rose swallowed hard against the growing lump in her throat.

"Here." Fen took her by the arms. "I have an idea."

Rose's eyes darted between him and Professor Troidilis, who marched around the field judging the other students' casting. "Is it going to grant me the ability to cast?"

A wry smile curled at the corner of his lips. "Go on. Cast your familiar."

She wasn't sure what that would do, but she rolled up her sleeve nonetheless. The dark outline of a crow stood out against the pale skin of her forearm, and she winced as it burned around the edges. Her flesh stretched and shifted, the ink upon it sharpening into iridescent ebony feathers that fluttered and pulled away from her. Prea stared up at her with keen, intelligent eyes before hopping onto her shoulder.

Most casters forged their own familiars, choosing the form when their magic bloomed and branding the bond into their skin. A piece of magic made manifest, so they could always call upon it to lend strength to their casting.

Rose had picked out her form when she was only seven. Dunhollow had been a lonely place for a child, and she used to doodle little crows on her arms and legs to copy the older students. As she'd grown, the drawings slowly faded, and her mother forbade her from getting the real thing until she learned to cast.

It had been Sylverfir who'd taken her, in the end. An early birthday present before the start of her first semester, he'd had to lend her a piece of his own magic to bind the familiar. The pain of it hadn't burned nearly as much as her mother's fury afterwar. But it hadn't mattered anyway—she'd never once felt the boost to her magic other casters talked about, and two years later, she still couldn't cast.

As if to prove her point, Fen loosened the cravat around the collar of his cream blouse, easily calling forth his familiar, Fideus, from the tattoo around his neck. The little shadowsnare stretched its wings. Its long, snakelike body remained wrapped around Fen's shoulders as it buried its little bat nose into the nape of his neck with a yawn. But its presence granted a glow to the magic pulsing around Fen's palm that hadn't been there before.

Rose pursed her lips. "How is this supposed to help?"

"Hold your hands out." Fen took hold of her wrists.

"And what, concentrate really hard?"

"Have a little patience."

Rose gasped as, with a flick of his hand, a soft green barrier fell over her. It tingled against her skin with a gentle warmth, protective and sure, even with a few stray holes and jagged edges.

"Did you have to make it look so scraggly?"

"Such a critic." Fen rolled his eyes. "It would hardly be believable for you to cast a perfect barrier."

Rose tested the edges of the pulsing source. "And how are you going to cast your own source to counter 'mine?'"

"Well, luckily for you, I took a page out of your book over the summer and brushed up on my skills."

Rose gaped at the flames that curled down his arm. "You learned to double cast? How?"

Fen's grin widened. "I met some fourth-years who were *very* keen to teach me."

"Messere Thenlif!"

Rose stiffened as Professor Troidilis approached, lips pressed in a thin line. "Yes Professor?"

"Is this barrier yours?" Their eyes narrowed, roving over the thin, green shield.

"I—yes?"

"You don't sound sure." They traced their fingers along its pulsing edges. "I was under the impression casting would be a struggle for you."

A fierce heat crept across Rose's cheeks. The thought of lying to a professor made her mouth go dry, though Fen's eyes offered only reassurance.

"I, uh, practiced."

"Hmm." The professor sniffed. "Well, do go on, Messere Hathorin. Test it."

Fen's throat bobbed, but the flames sparking around his fist brightened. Though his source magic was strong—perhaps even stronger than Sylvie's—it must have been an incredible strain to cast two spells at once. What if he failed and they were both made to look like fools?

Rose struggled to keep her hands steady, a cold sweat stealing across her brow as Fen released his flames. They slammed into the barrier harmlessly, arcing across the shield in smoking tendrils. The hairs on the back of her neck pricked as the magic cooled and the barrier fell.

Fen's russet skin went a tinge pale, but Rose bit back her concern as he sucked in steadying breaths. There would be no use in calling further attention to it under Professor Troidilis's eagle-eyed gaze. But the only thing that flashed in their eyes now was the faintest hint of satisfaction.

"I'm impressed." They nodded. "But let's see how you do against a foe who has no fear of harming you. Messere Osiander!"

Rose's heart leaped into her throat. *What?* Arden would happily fry her to a crisp on the professor's orders. Already, he was sauntering across the field, his magpie familiar perched on his shoulder. Sylvie and Ewan followed close on his heels, bringing with them a larger crowd of students. All keen to see her demise, she was sure.

Prea let out a coarse warning rattle, fluttering her wings. There were times Rose wished she could fuse with her familiar and see the world from great heights. Now, she might have just settled for the ability to sprout wings and fly away.

Arden came to a stop before them, his freckled lips curled in a smirk. "You called, Professor?"

"I'd like you to test the strength of Messere Thenlif's barrier."

"*You* cast a barrier?" Sylvie blurted out.

"A flimsy one, but yes," said the professor before Rose could respond.

"Er, Professor?" Fen cleared his throat. "I'm not sure that this is the safest pairing."

A thin smile spread across the professor's lips. "Gentleness is not required in this course, Messere Hathorin. Unless you have some reason to believe Messere Thenlif will struggle to cast another barrier?"

"No, of course not. I just—"

38

"Then I see no reason not to proceed. But you will keep your hands where I can see them"—Arden fluffed out his coat like a preening peacock—"I'll go easy on her."

"You will do no such thing," the professor snapped. "You are both students at the most prestigious magical academy in the empire—not children playing with stray magic. Act like it."

Rose's eyes widened. Surely they couldn't be serious? This was a classroom—not a dueling ring. And even then, there were rules. Regulations set down in magical law texts that were nearly as old as her bloodline. She'd read plenty of them, even if she'd rarely had reason to put them into practice.

The other students circled around the pair of them, and Rose swallowed hard. Somehow, her throat had only grown drier. Hadn't the professor themself said this class was about strategy and not just shooting fire? Granted, Arden's source specialty was lightning, though she couldn't say that sounded preferable.

To Rose's great surprise, Sylvie stepped forward. "Fen is right, Professor. I don't think—"

"I didn't ask you to think, did I?" Professor Troidilis didn't even bother looking at her. "Now kindly step out of the way."

Sylvie fell silent, her expression unreadable. Before Rose could blink, a shimmer of source curled around Arden's wrist, lightning sizzling past her head. Heat grazed against her cheek, not close enough to singe her, but startling all the same in the damp morning air.

"Don't worry, Syl." A spiral of smoke plumed away from his fingers. "You can have a shot at her next."

Professor Troidilis sighed. "Messere Osiander, the point of this exercise is not to frivolously cast source about. You must at least give her a chance to summon her barrier. Now, go again."

"Of course, Professor." Arden's grin widened. He was *enjoying* this.

The source formed more slowly around his hand this time, lightning spreading across his skin in delicate webs. Rose braced herself. At least if he injured her, she could sit out of class. But a small part of her mind rankled at the thought of giving him the pleasure.

Had he been so cruel with Aveline? Had he taken joy in her pain—in small tortures that wouldn't readily meet the eye? She couldn't see him getting his hands dirty, but she could easily believe he'd driven her to whatever fate she had met.

His bolt whizzed a hair's breadth away from her ear, so close that its acrid stench filled her nostrils. Rose's pulse pounded loud enough that she could barely hear beyond it. She exhaled softly, catching the singed lock of hair that drifted into her outstretched palm.

"How curious, Messere Thenlif." Professor Troidilis tilted their head. "Your previous barrier was almost artfully crafted, but now you can't summon one at all. Why might that be?"

"Perhaps fear isn't a good motivator for me, Professor," she snapped before she could think better of it.

Professor Troidilis's eyes narrowed, and Rose bit her tongue. She'd never talked back to a professor before, let alone raised her voice at one. But her nerves trembled beneath her skin, pushing her to bolder and more foolish action.

"Again," the professor barked. "And you'll be losing marks for that snark, Messere Thenlif."

Fen took a step forward, dark brow creased. "I really must protest, Professor."

"Agreed," Sylvie drawled with a bored sigh. "If she can't cast, leave her on the sidelines and let the rest of us learn something useful."

"Your concerns are noted. Now both of you step back. I won't tell you again."

Rose tucked her marred hair behind her ear with a frown. Fen's objections made sense, but she rather thought Sylvie would be cheering Arden on. This was nothing she hadn't done before, after all.

The looming, dark walls of the assembly hall pricked at Rose's memory. A duel to determine the top student at the end of their first year. Back before Rose's lack of casting had been well known, and she'd secured the position through marks alone. Back when her and Sylvie's rivalry was little more than lighthearted competition in class.

An end-of-term tradition, her mother had called it. But it hadn't felt like tradition to Rose, only cruelty. And Sylvie had been all too happy to participate then, casting shards of ice and frost at Rose with gleeful aplomb. It had only been a technicality that saved her.

One foot out of the dueling ring had called the match in Rose's favor, much to her mother's relief. Not for Rose's safety of course. More so because she wouldn't lose face over her loss. Though Sylvie had wasted no time crowing to the other students how the duel was fixed by her mother. Never mind that her mother had been the one to force

Rose into the duel in the first place—the damage was all too easily done. Rose may have won, but Sylvie had come out on top. *As she always did.* Yet now, Sylvie's eyes danced with depths Rose could not fathom. Not that she wanted to anyhow.

Turning back to Arden, Rose sucked in a long breath, releasing it slowly through her nose. Lifting her gaze, she met his with every ounce of defiance she could muster. She had no power to stop him, but she wouldn't give him the satisfaction of cowing her.

His blue eyes sparked, as if this was nothing more than amusing for him. But then they faded, bright and bold one moment to cold and dead the next. Bile crept up Rose's throat as Aveline's features flickered over his.

Her chest tightened, dark spots dancing across her vision as it narrowed. There was no field now, no students. Even the threat of lightning no longer held any warmth for her. It was just her, Aveline and the breath ripping through her lungs.

Falling to her knees, she braced for the searing impact of Arden's magic—anything to break Aveline's choking grip. But none ever came. Instead, a soft warmth fell over her, shielding her in a gentle green glow.

All at once, colors filtered back into Rose's view—the verdant grass beneath her, Arden's shock of red hair. Then the clamor of her peers filled the air, her pounding heart echoing in her ears. Then, finally, warmth. And a field free from any trace of death.

Aveline was gone, faded behind the thread of source that tingled against her palm. Rose blinked up at the barrier, singed and waning, but still strong. Her gaze slid from her hands to Fen. But he stared right back at her, eyes wide and brow furrowed. Had he not ...

The scent of the cast stole over her with a pang. That wasn't Fen's. His was a blend of red wine and worn leather. Warm and spiced, it reminded her of stolen kisses and reading side by side on lazy weekend mornings, lipstick stains still faint upon his collar from the night before.

This, though, was a heady mix of plum and lilac. Sweet and rich, it was all too familiar—and so very unlike its owner. Her gaze flew to Sylvie, whose eyes remained locked on the ground, one hand tucked behind her back. *No.* It couldn't be.

"Very good, Messere Thenlif." Professor Troidilis's sharp voice cut between them. "As you can see, proper motivation is key to source casting."

Or cruelty. Rose's jaw clenched, but she said nothing as she pushed herself on to her feet.

"Now, I think that's more than enough excitement for today." The professor gave a bored wave of their hand. "You're all dismissed."

Brushing off her pleated trousers, Rose didn't even question class being dismissed nearly half an hour early. The sooner she could get away from here, the better. She barely made it a few steps before Fen was by her side.

"Are you all right?"

"Fine." She bent down to pick up her bag, refusing to meet his gaze.

"Are you sure?"

"I said I'm fine, Fen," she snapped, cheeks flaring. But her anger cooled in an instant. None of this was his fault. "Sorry, I just want to get out of here."

He squeezed her arm with a soft smile. "Are you going to report this to your mother?"

"You think she'd care?"

"I can't imagine she'd approve of this—even if it did get you to cast. Which, congratulations, by the way. How did you manage?"

She pulled up short. "I didn't."

"What?" Fen's eyes flickered from her to the field and then back again. "Then who?"

"I think it was Sylvie."

"Why would she do that?"

Her eyes darted across the field, where Sylvie was hurrying toward the toilets. Why indeed?

"That's what I intend to find out."

"Rose, wait." Fen tried to hold her back.

But she shook him off, charging across the field. Whatever Sylvie's reasons for protecting her, she doubted they were altruistic. Besides, she couldn't have Sylvie lording it over her at every opportunity. Jaw clenched tight, she almost barreled right into the toilets when a raised voice halted her in her tracks.

"Just leave me alone!"

Sylvie barged out of the door a second later, nearly crashing right into her. Rose stumbled back, all thoughts fleeing her head, save for the red rims around Sylvie's amber eyes and the tears carving paths down her cheeks.

They stood like that for a moment, eyes locked and both unmoving. Silence held between them, tense as cracked glass. She'd never seen Sylvie cry before. Honestly, she hadn't thought she had the heart for it.

But something swam in the depths of her gaze that stilled Rose. It lingered, dark and cloying, like the sweet scents of her perfume clinging to the air between them. Orchid and musk, alongside something sharper that she could never place.

"Can I help you, Thenlif?" Sylvie's taut voice jolted her from her thoughts as she furiously wiped the tears from her cheeks.

But all Rose could do was blink up at her, every thought forgotten under her piercing gaze. "I—"

"Ugh." Sylvie shook her head. "Just move, will you?"

Without thinking, Rose stepped aside, letting her pass without another word. It was only moments later, when the door swung shut over empty air and the scents of Sylvie's perfume had long faded, that her questions returned with burning intensity. Why had Sylvie protected her? More importantly, who had she been talking to?

5

THE WITCH'S BREW

ROSE glared at the bathwater below her glimmering in the glow of the candles lining the bath's edges. Warm and inviting, steam curled off its surface in smoky tendrils, filling the air with the soothing scent of lavender. Hot baths had a way of soothing scars upon the heart. Raw and aching or sewn up and sore beneath the weight of time, they all melted away in the water's scalding embrace.

But now, she could think of nothing less appealing. A shiver crawled down her spine. As horrific as the first week of classes had been, nothing pulled so sharply at the dread coiled in her stomach as this.

Her eyes flickered to the dark cloth hanging over her mirror like a shroud. A useless precaution, at this point, but a habit she found hard to break. She'd covered the lancet windows above the tub too, repositioning her many hanging plants in front of them as a protective wall of overgrowth. Still, it wasn't enough.

She knew that none of it would protect her now. Aveline was always there, no longer confined to mere reflections and growing ever stronger—angrier. Yet what choice did Rose have? She could hardly keep from bathing indefinitely.

The wind howled lightly against the windows, nearly covering the screams from the forest beyond. Pulling loose the tie of her robe, Rose sucked in a sharp breath and gingerly dipped her toes into the water. The heat crept across her skin like a warm embrace as she sank into it, but she found no comfort in it.

She sloshed the water up and down her arms, scrubbing her washcloth over her rosemary soap and then across her pink, freckled skin. She just needed to get in and out, then make it down to the pub for first-week drinks. For Fen's sake.

He hardly expected her to show up, she was sure. But, for once, she wanted to. He'd been watching her all week as if she were made of cracked glass, ready to shatter at the slightest touch. And perhaps he was right. But there was a desperate, broken part of her that wanted to pretend, just for one night.

To watch his eyes spark with delight at the sight of her, not concern, as they so often did these days. She swallowed hard, washing away the last of the soap. The weight of it all ripped her apart, but she would keep it from hurting him, if she could.

Setting her washcloth aside, Rose was reaching for her towel when the water at the edge of the tub splashed. She froze.

A few rebellious curls stuck to the back of her neck in damp tangles as a cold sweat crept across her skin. Gripping the edge of the tub, she clenched her jaw.

Seconds ticked by with agonizing leisure before the water sloshed again. This time, the candles beside Rose flickered almost in warning. The soft hair on her forearms stood upright as a chill swept over her, despite the steam still curling up from the bathwater.

All at once, the water seemed tepid and stale, what little joy it had held snuffed out in an instant. Rose reached for her towel once more, suddenly desperate for the safety of her bed.

But the candles flared again as she did, singeing her skin before they all went out at once. Rose's heart pounded against her ribs in the darkness. Fast and featherlight. Like a bird trying to break free from the cage of her chest.

Her breath coiled in her lungs, throat so tight she could barely swallow. Water lapped softly against the porcelain tub. Then, with a start, the first of the candles leaped back to life. But the light brought no relief.

Gray, bloated fingers curled around the sides of the tub. Cracked nails caked with grime screeched against porcelain, dug deep and dragging, dragging, dragging—ever so slowly. Rose trembled, tears pricking her eyes as the water parted, but she couldn't look away. Couldn't move. Couldn't even breathe.

Soaked tangles of ragged blond hair crested slowly through the suds. Then pallid flesh, marred by dark, spidery veins carved around a sparse brow. Then, finally, her eyes. Bloodshot and sunken, they fixed furiously on Rose as Aveline's cracked lips pulled free of the water.

Blood pooled at the corners of the girl's mouth, spilling down her throat. For a moment, they just stared at each other. Rose rooted to the spot and Aveline simply waiting. *Watching*.

And then she lunged. Slick fingers clamped around Rose's throat and squeezed—hard. With a cry, she wrenched away from Aveline's grip, scrambling back. Water cascaded over the edges of the tub as Rose leaped free of it, soaking the rug beneath and snuffing out the one lit candle.

She stumbled in the darkness, reaching desperately for her towel, then the counter, then finally the door. The glow of her dormitory greeted her as she flung herself toward her bed. She sagged onto it, towel wrapped tight against her bare skin and trembling in the cool air.

For several moments, all she could do was watch the doorway, but it remained empty. No bloodied eyes peered at her out of the darkness, no wretched figure crossed the threshold.

Then, all at once, the candles flickered back to life, filling the washroom with a soft, inviting glow. *She was gone*. Numbly, Rose lifted her knees to her chin, released the breath burning in her lungs, and simply wept.

Great, aching sobs tore through her, hot tears pooling into the satin duvet as she rolled onto her side. She couldn't bear this any longer. This terror, this torment. If she stayed here another moment, she would simply unravel.

Shatter into a million pieces or fade away with so much sorrow.

All of a sudden, she craved the comfort of other bodies, even if the safety they offered was only an illusion. For the first time in memory, she didn't want to be alone.

And so, dressing quickly and freeing her tangled curls from their updo, she fled from the confines of her room. It wasn't until the cool night air pressed against her skin that she noticed the heat beneath her collar. Swallowing hard, she reached under her blouse and traced five angry bruises blooming along her throat.

Rose's breath hung on the cool air, heels clacking against wet cobblestones. Even at night, the clouds around Dunhollow still clung to the skies. Low and thick, they all but blotted out the starlight. The moon drifted between their cover, casting eerie shadows upon the fog hanging low over the river.

She quickened her pace, darting across the stone bridge as the golden glow of the town beyond it pierced the fog. It was a rare thing to see Dunhollow village by night. Between the pub, the smoking lounge, and the gambling den under the florist's shop, it offered very little of interest to Rose after the sun went down. But tonight, the leaning, wood-slatted buildings drew her in like a moth to flame.

Twinkling lights hung from the thatched roof of the little stone pub, beckoning her closer. Sad-looking flowerpots hung from latticed windows and a rickety wooden sign swung lightly over the doorway. *The Witch's Brew*, it read, a colorful, bubbling cauldron dancing atop it.

A tongue-in-cheek joke of sorts, for no caster would ever refer to themselves so blithely. But it was fitting, somehow. Warm, cozy, and entirely irreverent, the pub might have been the only place in all of Dunhollow that didn't fall over itself to be taken seriously.

A strange sensation stole over Rose as she reached for the door. Cold and bitter, it soured on her tongue with a metallic tang. *Blood.* Flickers of Aveline's face flashed past her eyes, crimson stains leaking from hollow sockets. Rose's stomach dropped, but she shoved the thought from her mind.

With a steadying breath, she ducked through the threshold. A wave of warmth hit her as soon as she stepped inside, thawing the chill upon her nose and cheeks. She breathed in deeply. The buttery aroma of fresh mutton pies wafted out of the kitchen, mingling with woodsmoke from the great stone hearth at the center of the room.

Far too many students squeezed into the small space, like sardines packed into a tin. Most vied for spots on the couches around the fireplace or at the booths beside the fog-stained windows. A few mean-dered about looking for places to sit, ducking under sagging beams and around the odd array of worn tables dotting the room.

Even a few professors had joined the crowd. Sylverfir and Briony Burroak huddled in one of the booths, sipping large glasses of wine alongside Dunhollow's violet-haired librarian and Briony's wife, Delia Droosberil. Glancing up, Sylverfir gave her a small wave, but Rose only nodded, a familiar unease sliding across her spine.

Despite all the people here now, she knew none of them could save her from Aveline's wrath. But the warmth of their bodies all pressed together offered more comfort than the lonely shadows of her dormi-tory. A cold comfort though it was.

Across the room, her eyes found Fen almost instantly, drawn to him somehow, like everyone else in this place. He lounged in the mid-dle of a gaggle of students packed on one of the center couches. Shak-ing her head, she couldn't help but smile.

Most people here had a circle—a tight-knit cadre of cohorts who were carefully curated in pedigree and style. Fen, however, had an orbit. A random collection of friends, acquaintances, and even strangers who got sucked in by his charm, oftentimes in spite of themselves.

In fairness, it was all too easy to do.

It took Rose a moment, sometimes, to remember that this facade of a charming socialite hid beneath it the wonderfully quirky boy who could spend hours tucked away in the library with her as easily as he could at the pub. A palatable, pleasing second skin, as it were.

Unlike the rest of Dunhollow's inhabitants, Fen never wore this side of himself to hide or gain anything. The pretense was half the fun, though the truth was somehow threaded between the two. Like an expensive overcoat he could toss aside as needed. A part of him, but not nearly all of him.

Her chest loosened just at the sight of him. As if he alone were a balm for her haggard soul. Tugging at her sleeves, she stepped forward, only for a solid form to crash right into her.

"Watch where you're going." Sylvie's voice grated against her ears. Then, a pause. "Thenlif?"

The shock that splintered through her amber eyes almost softened her features. But it didn't ease the weight in Rose's heart. Of course she would run into *her*.

"Hello, Sylvie."

She had no mind for barbed words and careful calculation tonight. Just looking at Sylvie made exhaustion sink deeper into her bones. Sleek black hair twisted delicately over her dark turtleneck, and a plaid skirt cinched neatly around her slim waist. A glass of red wine dangled between her fingers, nearly matching the stain of her rust-red lips as she glanced Rose up and down.

"What are *you* doing here?"

"Trying to have a drink." Rose sighed. "Is that a problem?"

Something flashed through Sylvie's eyes, dark and fleeting. Gone before Rose could even decipher it. She frowned. The same thing had danced through her gaze that day on the training field, but she was burying it better now.

"Suit yourself." Sylvie shrugged, brushing past her.

The scent of her perfume lingered on her hair as it brushed past Rose's cheek. Floral notes of orchid that withered in the woodsmoke and the stale stench of ale. But beneath that lay the scent of her casting. Plum and lilac. Conjured so often that it still clung to her. As it now hung in Rose's memory.

"Why did you cast the barrier?" she called after her.

Sylvie stilled. "What?"

"In class. You protected me. Why?"

She slid her razor-sharp gaze back toward Rose. "I don't know what you mean."

"Oh, I think you do." Rose wasn't going to let her get away that easily.

Sylvie leaned in, her eyes dark and unreadable. This close, Rose could almost count the freckles dusted across her nose or trace the faint lines of the scar that cut through her upper lip. Her breath caught in her throat. The heat of Sylvie's body pressed against her, even as a cold smile crept across her lips.

"Think whatever you like, Thenlif," she said before turning on her heel. "Enjoy your drink."

Rose watched her saunter away, rooted to the spot. She should have known she wouldn't get a straight answer. Sylvie would rather die than admit she'd ever help her, she was sure. But then, why do it at all?

"You came!" Fen's voice broke through her thoughts.

Rose turned to find him towering behind her, hands filled with empty glasses and a faint line of lipstick staining his collar. But the mere sight of him made her heart leap. Tears stung her eyes as his grin faded, and she gave him a watery smile.

"Hey, Fen." Her voice was taut beneath the strain.

His eyes narrowed as he set the glasses on a nearby table. "What's wrong?"

The truth burned against Rose's tongue, but in the crackling glow of the fire and the din of raucous laughter, it fell silent. "Nothing. I just needed a drink."

Fen didn't press this time—didn't argue. There was not even a trace of truth in her words now, and they both knew it.

"All right." He nodded. "Go find us a seat; I'll grab us some."

Rose blanched. Half the open spaces would have required her to squash herself between overeager first-years spilling drinks on themselves. The other half were far too close to an uproarious game of Caster's Darts, which were well known for their habit of flinging themselves about in a tizzy or chasing after anyone who made a particularly bad throw.

She wrinkled her nose, eyes sliding to the booths by the window. But the thought of sitting that close to the glass—of pale shapes and thin shadows stealing past the corner of her eye—made her skin crawl.

"I'll just go with you."

Fen's frown deepened, but he took her hand, drawing her through the crowd. He moved through the other students with practiced ease, though their progress was somewhat slowed by his need to say hello to every one of them. Rose sighed, waiting for him to finish, when a shout rang out from the bar.

"Rose Thenlif! Is that you?"

She managed a small smile as the crowd parted, revealing a tall, middle-aged man, blue-streaked blond hair falling in waves around his shoulders. His large brown eyes sat atop rosy cheeks, lips spread wide in his ever-present smile.

"Hello, Hollis."

Standing there in his stained apron and with a mug of ale in each hand, the pub owner looked so at one with the bar. Like a piece of a puzzle that would render this place less without its presence. His family had owned this pub for generations, and he and the pub went hand in hand.

Hollis and the pub. The pub and Hollis. He just fitted here. Save, perhaps, for the low-hanging beams, though he never seemed to mind ducking under them.

During term, Rose rarely visited here, and Hollis was always far too busy to stop and gossip as long as he'd like. But when summer came and all the students abandoned this place, she loved to sneak down here and get the bar all to herself. Hollis never seemed to mind. In fact, he probably enjoyed the company. Though the whole village was there to serve the academy, the pub felt most hollow in the students' absence.

"*Dia vhal*, you're the spitting image of your mother." He whistled as she and Fen approached the counter. "For a moment, I thought time might be playing tricks on me."

Rose eased herself on to one of the velvet-capped barstools with a sigh. Well, that was hardly true. Her mother was the picture of graceful severity—a sharp contrast of alabaster skin, jet-black hair, and piercing green eyes. Equal parts brutal and mesmerizing, she drew in praise and envy in the same breath.

Rose, meanwhile, was a lesson in mediocrity. With dull, auburn curls, hazel eyes, and pinkish pale skin that freckled all too easily in the sun, she stood out to no one. Pretty, yet unassuming, like prey that had learned not to draw attention to itself.

She tugged at her collar. Hollis knew better than to bring up her mother, anyway. Most of her summer visits here had been to get away from the woman, and Hollis had always been happy to let her stay as long as she needed to avoid her.

"Please, Hollis. I came for drinks, not insults."

"Insults?" He quirked an eyebrow. "My dear, that was the highest of compliments. In her day, your mother had run of this place."

"And what's changed, exactly?"

Soft lines folded around his eyes as he chuckled. "She's a bit tamer now. Back then, she was a force of nature—not a soul could outcast her. Save perhaps her sister."

Rose blinked. It was rare to hear anyone mention her aunt Astoria. She'd died decades ago, but her death had cast a long shadow, and her mother rarely spoke of it. The only remains of her life were bound up in fragile memories and old photos. Rose used to look upon them as a child—gray, smiling faces framed by dark wood and the browning stains of age. The picture of youthful innocence, captured on cold, lifeless paper.

"I didn't realize you and my mother were close."

"Of course. Old schoolmates and all that. But that was a long time ago …"

The man's eyes darkened, almost glassy as he gazed off over Rose's shoulder. Suddenly, she was quite sure she didn't want to know *just* how well he'd known her mother. Trading glances with Fen, she cleared her throat.

Hollis's head snapped up. "Right—sorry. What can I get for you?"

Rose chewed the inside of her lip, mulling it over. "What reds do you have?"

"How about a glass of Valé Doir? We've just had a shipment in from this lovely little vineyard in Telemestra."

Fen's favorite. Though he wasn't exactly picky. "Sounds perfect."

"A woman of good taste." Hollis winked, turning to Fen. "And for you?"

A wry grin tugged at her friend's lips. "Why stop at a glass? Bring the bottle."

"As you wish, Messere." Hollis dropped in a flourished bow before whisking himself away.

Rose leaned against the counter, scowling as her arm landed in some vague, sticky substance. "You don't have to do that."

"I'm sure you'll pay me back later."

Her scowl deepened. He always did this, and there was never any use in arguing. She wasn't even sure how much coin she owed him anymore. But there was a part of her that felt guilty letting him spend so much money on her, even if he could afford it.

Technically, she could too, but every coin of her allowance had to be accounted for with her mother. To the point that the pleasure of anything bought was lost simply in having to explain it.

She gestured to the bottle as Hollis set it before them. "I hope you plan on finishing most of this then."

"I might." Fen shrugged, pouring two full glasses. "Provided that you tell me what you're really doing here."

Rose's heart leaped. "What do you mean? You invited me."

"I always do, and you never come." He leaned against the counter, downing half his glass in two sips. "You show up at my dorm in the morning with a full breakfast and a stack of books to help me through the hangover."

Damn. He knew her too well. She took a slow sip of her wine, savoring its heady aroma, the smooth warmth of it tingling against her tongue. And she should have known better than to think he would just let her waste away before his eyes. He was too good for that. Still, that didn't make the truth any easier.

"I—can we not do this now?" She glanced around at the crowd. "Not here."

"Rose—"

"Just leave me alone!" A cry cut through the din of the pub.

Rose jumped, turning toward Sylvie and Ewan, who no longer sat huddled in the corner booth. Instead, Sylvie was pushing through the crowd, Ewan close on her heels.

"Sylvie, please, just listen." Ewan caught her hand as the other patrons quietened their chatter to stare.

But Sylvie yanked her arm away, stumbling back to lock eyes with Rose, whose heart fluttered. The soft curves of Sylvie's ovaline features almost mocked her, so effortless in their perfection that it turned her stomach. Sylvie's lips parted in a small gasp, her tawny cheeks flushed as she turned and dashed out through the door.

Rose stared after her, lifting her glass dazedly to her lips. In the last two years, she'd rarely seen Sylvie upset. Yet that was twice now that she'd lost her composure in the same week. She scowled.

Leave me alone. The words rang in her head. It was what she'd said in the toilets too. Could it have been Ewan she'd been talking to?

But they'd been across the training field at the time, and Rose hadn't found any trace of anyone after Sylvie had left. A jolt of dread shot straight through her, cold and sobering. What if Sylvie was also seeing forms that weren't there?

What if Rose wasn't alone?

The thought pulled at her, almost drawing her to chase after Sylvie. But then the din of chatter resumed, the disturbance already forgotten by their peers. Save Ewan, perhaps, who slumped dejectedly staring at their own feet. After a moment, Arden appeared beside them, guiding them over to the bar.

Rose tugged at her collar as Fen poured a second glass. "What do you think that was about?"

"Don't change the sub—" She flinched as Fen caught her hand, eyes narrowed at her throat. "Rose, what are those?"

Shit. The bruises. Her cheeks flared as she scrambled to tug her blouse back into place, but it was too late.

"I—it's nothing."

"It doesn't look like nothing." His voice softened. "What happened?"

Cupping a hand around her chin, his brown eyes bore into hers, pleading. His thumb stroked softly over the red welts, almost as if he didn't realize he was doing it. But it brought tears to Rose's eyes all the same. He could see the bruises.

They were real.

Which meant Aveline was too. The thought hit her like a brick, and she nearly fell from her stool. Pushing Fen's hands away, she slid off it, gripping the counter until her knuckles turned white.

"I can't—" She sucked in a wheezing breath. "I need to get out of here."

"Hey, it's all right." His voice was low and soothing. "Just breathe."

Rose nodded, forcing her breath to slow. It took a moment, but when she opened her eyes all that met them was Fen's warm smile. He pulled her close, pressing a gentle kiss to her forehead.

"Thank you," she whispered into his chest.

"Anytime." His lips curled against her skin. "Why don't you wait outside while I sort the tab with Hollis?"

Any other time Rose would have argued. Told him not to waste his night, to stay here with his friends. But tonight, she was too fragile, and there was nothing she craved more than him. Not his body—not like that, at least. Just the warmth of his arms, and the steadiness of his heartbeat beside her. Nodding numbly, she grabbed her coat from the barstool beside her and fled into the cold.

The frigid air pierced Rose's skin as she stepped out of the pub, and she sucked in sharp, steadying breaths. She'd barely been there an hour, but already the temperature had plummeted, her breath puffing around her in small clouds. It was sobering, if nothing else.

Stepping away from the pub, she made the short walk back to the bridge, pacing beneath the flickering lamps just to keep warm. *Aveline was real.* The thought ran through her mind in hollow echoes. *All of it was.*

She breathed into her hands to warm them. What did that mean for Aveline? Dead, likely. The thought hit her with startling acridity. It had been so much easier to pretend she was a figment, but the truth of it was harder to brush away.

Soft crinkling sounded above the river coursing beneath her, and Rose frowned. A ragged piece of parchment fluttered in the light breeze, clinging to one of the lampposts. A sharp gust tangled past her curls and sent the paper flying into a half-frozen puddle.

It shriveled in the water's grasp, but the harsh ink lines still screamed back at her. Rose leaned in, blinking a few times before the words straightened.

MISSING, it read in large, bold letters. *AVELINE GOARSBEL, AGE 19*.

Rose's throat went dry. She'd thought her mother had had these posters removed from campus. Underneath, it continued on about where she was last seen, including the promise of a reward for any information. And a picture.

It stared back at Rose, blue eyes and shimmering blond hair the only things about the poster that remained undimmed. Charmed, likely. A ghostly reminder of what was lost.

Behind her, a door creaked, and Rose jumped. *Finally*. She turned, ready to chide Fen. But there was no one there. Besides the muffled ruckus coming from the pub, there wasn't a soul around. She stilled, all her hair standing on end.

Rose's heart thudded dully in her ears, nearly drowning out the river. Yet, all at once, she could hear every sound in the tree line, as if amplified by the fear racing through her veins. Every snapping twig, every flutter of wings. Every hollow breath.

Slowly, reluctantly, she turned, already knowing what she would find. But it wasn't Aveline's emaciated face that greeted her this time. Instead, a lone figure stood at the far edge of the bridge, their back to her and shrouded in fog.

"A-Aveline?" She took a hesitant step forward.

If she was real, perhaps she had been trying to tell Rose something all this time. But she didn't turn now. Didn't charge. Didn't move at all.

Her matted yellow hair shimmered in the lamplight, coiled around a ragged blazer. A dark stain ran down the back of it, as if she'd been standing out in the rain for some time. But it wasn't rain that dripped from her fingers now.

Thick and crimson, it oozed from her hands, dripping onto the slick cobblestones beneath her. Rose covered her mouth, stifling a scream as she traced the path of the blood up the girl's collar. A deep, angry gash glared at her from the back of Aveline's head, clotted around the edges and staining her hair a rusty pink.

What horrors had she already suffered that death would not release her? Slowly, Rose reached out a trembling hand. Why, she couldn't really say, but a small tapping stilled her.

Soft at first, as if distant. Then closer. And closer still. Until there was no mistaking it for what it was—footsteps.

A jolt ran through her, begging her to return to the pub. To the warmth of glowing fires and the safety of Fen's presence. But her feet remained rooted to the ground, almost as if Aveline had cast some spell to bind her there. A chill skittered down her spine, knees buckling as the girl turned, gaunt eyes fixed on her.

"Run."

A scream of the forest split the air, shattering through Rose's muddled mind. In a heartbeat, she spun around, racing for the pub. Her breath burned in her lungs. Piercing cold stung her skin.

But the only footsteps now were her own thundering beneath her. When she reached the door, her fingers curled around the handle when it burst open, revealing Fen.

He blinked down at her, pushing his glasses up the bridge of his nose. Rose stared back at him for a long moment before she launched herself into his arms.

"Steady on." He stumbled back. "What's wrong?"

"There was—and I was—" She broke off, gasping for breath. "Where *were* you?"

"Sorry." He rubbed the back of his neck. "Hollis was stuck down in the cellar trying to find a cask for some second-years and paying the tab took a little longer than expected. Are you all right?"

She backed away, wrapping her arms tight across her chest. Despite her racing heart, the street looked almost welcoming now, the fog caught in a warm glow from the lamps. Yet she couldn't shake the feeling that the footsteps belonged to something sinister.

No—*someone.*

Someone even Aveline had feared. She swallowed hard, nails biting into the delicate skin of her palms. Suddenly, she couldn't stand to be here a moment longer.

"I ... I have to go."

"Rose, wait!" Fen reached for her, but she dodged out of his grasp.

Her feet pounded against the slick cobblestones as she darted back up the street. Freezing rain splattered against her cheeks, but she couldn't stop. Not for Fen, not for Aveline. Not for anyone.

In the dim glow of the moon, the swaying shadows of the branches curled toward the street, as if to pull her into the forest and swallow her up. But still, she ran further into the fog, leaving the warm glow of the streets behind in stone-cold silence.

6

A FOOLISH HOPE

ROSE stared down at the full plate of food before her, mouth dry and stomach roiling only with dread. In the gray, early hours of the morning, there was nothing she longed for more than solitude. But her mother had summoned her, as she did every week, and any courage Rose had to refuse had long fled her.

She prodded listlessly at her poached eggs. She wasn't sure why they still bothered with this charade. It wasn't as if they ever actually spoke, or even much enjoyed one another's company, for that matter.

Even now, her mother hardly paid attention to her, long nose buried in the folds of the weekly gazette as she muttered and scoffed over some scandal in the capital. But at the very least it saved Rose from becoming the target of her discontent.

Steam rose from Rose's telka as she sipped it gingerly, letting the bitter taste wash away sour words. She'd often found silence was the best cure when dealing with her mother, and she had no appetite for an argument this morning.

The dull thudding of racing footsteps against slick cobblestones pounded at the back of her mind, and a pop from the fireplace made her skin crawl. Her eyes flew to the window, but no pale reflection lingered there—no gaunt eyes or oozing, crimson wounds. But they would come. She always did.

Rose turned away, a pang of guilt coiling around her heart. *Aveline was real.* Her ghost, her essence—whatever it was that remained of her. It was all real, and she'd done nothing but brush her aside, just like everyone else.

When she'd thought Aveline a mere figment, perhaps her inaction could have been excused, forgiven against the weight of what it might have cost her—but now? She could have told Fen everything last night—finally set the truth of the poor girl free. Instead, she'd only let the lies sink deeper into her flesh, like a festering poison.

For so long, she'd convinced herself it was better this way. Lonelier, certainly, but kinder. Still, some foul whisper of doubt seeded its way into her mind. Was it really compassion that held her tongue, or simply fear? A well-worn noose that kept her in strangled silence.

Even now, she sat before her mother and said nothing at all. Her jaw clenched tight. Would it do any good if she did?

Rose took another slow sip of her telka, trying to let the soft pattering of rain against the fogged windows soothe her. But there was nothing comforting here.

Everything about her mother's upper office was meant to set the occupant on edge. The dark paneling along the walls made the space all too small, while the long mahogany table stretched from one end of the room to the other. That, at least, she was grateful for, though this morning, the distance did not seem quite enough.

The crystalline glasses and porcelain dishes floating about the room made Rose feel rather like a raging bull in a glass shop. Everything was far too fragile. As if she might shatter the lot in a single, ill-considered move. Even with the soft piano music lilting from the charmed phonogram and the fire roaring away in the hearth, there was not a shred of warmth to be found.

"Rosera, are you even listening?" Her mother's voice made her jump.

"Sorry, what?"

Rose swallowed hard. Even at this early hour, not a hair lay out of place on her mother's perfectly coiffed head. The collar of her scarlet dress drew a stiff line against her alabaster jaw, her burgundy lips pressed thin. She was, by far, the most immaculate, imposing thing in the room.

"I asked how your courses are going."

"Oh. Fine."

"Just fine?"

Rose raised an eyebrow. What more did she want? Then again, it would hardly have surprised her if her mother expected thanks for sabotaging her course list.

"If you were hoping for more enthusiasm, I'm sorry to disappoint."

"Hmm." Rose's mother lifted her porcelain cup to her painted lips. "I heard you managed to cast a barrier in your Strategy and Source class this week. Well done."

A scoff built at the back of Rose's throat. "No, I nearly got killed in Strategy and Source."

"Don't be flippant, it's—"

"Unbecoming?" She stabbed at her eggs with her fork. "So is being forced into a duel. But you wouldn't have a problem with that, I'm sure. Anything is fair so long as I learn to cast, right?"

She almost felt guilty for letting the lie pass unremarked. Solidified, even if only by omission. But the feeling slipped away before it could take root. Her mother's thirst for her to learn how to cast was what had led them here in the first place. So, if casting was all that mattered to her, let her believe it. It might even earn Rose a blissful end to her mother's snide comments. Until she failed to cast again, at least.

Her mother leaned forward in her chair. "Professor Troidilis wouldn't allow such barbarities in their classroom."

Barbarities. The thought burned at the back of Rose's mind, caustic and all too sharp. Had her mother not herself resorted to the same measures once? Did she even realize her own hypocrisy? No, more likely she conveniently wouldn't recall the incident at all. Like a woodcutter who'd forgotten how many trees they'd felled. But the lessons were carved into Rose's very bones, and she remembered every notch.

"They're the one who encouraged it," she bit out. "Ask any of the other students if you don't believe me. Even Sylvie thought they went too far."

So much so as to protect her. Though she could still hardly believe that. Her mother frowned, green eyes sparking behind dark lashes. After a moment, she reached for her telka, dabbing her cloth napkin gently over her painted lips.

"I will have a word with Professor Troidilis, then," she said finally, her voice oddly taut. "Duels cannot simply be held at whim—there are rules and regulations that must be followed. Safety protocols. They should never have put you in that position."

Rose blanched. Of all the reactions she might have been expecting, that was not among them. Denial or coldhearted apathy, certainly, but this? It could hardly be called caring, but it was *something*.

What would she say of Aveline? Rose's eyes flew back to the window as the thought gripped her. It was a foolish hope to think that she might listen. Her mother would never care. Not really. She simply was not capable of it, not in the way Rose needed, at least. Yet still, there was something in that surety that settled her.

An old scar poked and prodded, but difficult to reopen. Rose straightened. The full truth was perhaps too distant a prospect, still too heavy on her mind and bound up in fear. But a hint of it? She owed Aveline that much at least.

"I heard something interesting in the pub last night," she said finally.

Her mother scoffed. "The pub? And what trifling gossip was so interesting, pray tell?"

"Someone saw Aveline's ghost."

At this her mother stilled. "Don't jest about such things, Rosera. Necromancy is a serious charge."

"I'm not."

As if she would. Whatever else she could be called for her complacency—craven, heartless, cruel—she would never make light of it.

"And who was it that you overheard?"

"I'm not sure." The lie tangled around her tongue. "I just thought you might want to investigate."

"Investigate what, precisely?" Rose's mother brushed back a stray lock that had fallen loose from her bun. "I can hardly call in the capital inquisitors over some pub gossip. Aveline's case is ongoing, and accusations of necromancy would only complicate matters."

"Yes, but they think she's just missing. Doesn't this suggest there was more to it?"

"No, it suggests your peers have overactive imaginations or are dabbling in summonings they barely understand," her mother cut across her. "Either way, I won't open Dunhollow to further scrutiny without hard evidence. A body, a blood trail—something more than mere ghost sightings."

Rose swallowed a scoff. *Dabbling in summonings?* Necromancy was powerful magic—wrought from source that was near impossible for all but the most accomplished casters to even fathom wrangling. It was hardly the type of thing a student could conjure casually. Something her mother surely knew; she just didn't care.

Rose bit her tongue. She should have known better than to have hoped she would. "Whatever you think is best."

Her mother shook her head, straightening her burgundy collar. "Honestly, don't you have assignments you could be working on, instead of listening to hearsay? It would be a much better use of your time."

Rose's jaw clenched so tight that it was almost painful. Of course her mother cared more about her marks than the fact that a student had likely been murdered right under her nose. Appearances were everything, and she would do anything to protect her damn reputation.

"Of course," she scoffed. Grabbing a piece of toast, she got to her feet and slung her bag over her shoulder. "Always a pleasure to see you, Mother."

The whispers of ancient tomes greeted Rose in a frenzy as she entered the library. They flew overhead, flitting to and fro on their shelves, fluttering their pages as they gossiped among themselves. She rolled her eyes. Sometimes, the books were no better than her fellow students.

That said, they did fill the library with a sort of warmth that even the aging, vaulted ceilings and gray clouds outside couldn't chase away. Or ghostly inhabitants. Rose's eyes slid to the windows. Still—nothing.

Her jaw tightened, a cold, dreadful feeling stealing over her. Had Aveline given up? Imparted whatever message she needed to and moved on? *No.* It couldn't possibly be that simple. Drawing her bag tighter over her shoulder, Rose made her way further into the maze of shelves.

Though the rest of the library lay empty, there was one other person she could rely on to be here this early on a weekend: Delia Droosberil. The violet-haired librarian stood alone at the front desk, wrangling a stack of books that rather raucously refused to be tamed. Her black cat familiar, Abas, lay beside her, curled amid some scrolls and sleeping soundly. Rose grinned, gliding over to the counter.

"Good morning, Delia," she signed.

The librarian peered over her thin glasses, crimson lips pulling in a sly smile as her fingers danced over her words. "You're late."

As if to prove her point, a small clock came to life with music, nearly ringing itself off the desk. Abas leaped from his perch with a yowl, back arched and hissing. Rose shook her head. Only Delia would consider nine o'clock late on a weekend. Rummaging around in her bag, Rose set an ebony-and-gold-embossed novel on the desk.

"Hardly. And I come bearing gifts."

Delia's dark eyes narrowed as she leafed through the book. Though her expression barely shifted, the way her pale cheeks reddened as she sped through the first pages betrayed her. Rose grinned. The librarian could never turn down a good romance.

Tapping her fingers against the counter, Rose gave Abas a few scratches, waiting for Delia to finish. It was a familiar pattern, this little exchange of theirs. It had been the summer after Rose's fifteenth birthday that it started, when she'd tucked herself away in a forgotten corner of the library to finish some historical romance series she'd been enthralled by.

When the books started disappearing, she'd been perplexed. Until the end of summer, that was, when she'd caught Delia, nose deep in the third book in the series, which had mysteriously gone missing from Rose's pile only a few days before.

After that, they'd started a bit of an impromptu book club, spending hours shut away in the library they both loved. It had made a good escape after many an argument with her mother, and she found Delia not nearly as uptight as some of the students claimed her to be. Strict, sure, but only in protection of her precious books.

Once Rose became a full student, however, Delia started sharing her best books. Rare tomes on loan from the Library of Tol Qilius, ancient scrolls unearthed and transcribed by respected scholars. And, sometimes, if Rose had shared a particularly good novel, books from the Untold section, where only professors were allowed to go.

But, this time, Delia had promised her something truly special if she could locate a copy of her favorite author's newest work, some sensational royal romance that was sweeping through the courts of the capital like wildfire. All the uproar had caused quite a bit of a wait-list, unfortunately. Luckily, her mother somehow got hold of a signed copy—likely as a gift to curry favor. Though she wasn't a devout romance fan, so Rose was hoping she wouldn't notice if it went missing for a few weeks.

Leaning back on her heels, she sighed as Delia finally deigned to look up from her reading. Rolling her eyes, the librarian silently slid over a great, obsidian tome with glittering golden letters. *Ilaurian Innovation: A Study of Post-Calamity Magic and Engineering in Early Ilaurian Society*. Rose gasped. She'd been looking for a copy of this for months.

Not for idle reading, of course—she'd planned on studying the topic for her term paper in Professor Sylverfir's class. Plus, his birthday was soon approaching, and a gift like this certainly wouldn't go amiss. Rose cracked open the cover to check the copyright: 1864. Vintage, certainly, but not a first edition, so maybe Delia would be more willing to part with it.

"Thank you. I—"

But Delia only cut her off with a wave of her hand. Clutching the book tighter to her chest, Rose gave Abas a final pat and headed off back into the shelves. Almost out of habit, her feet carried her through the maze. It was second nature now, finding her way about, though that wasn't all down to her.

The shelves groaned as she passed, shifting and turning into new paths, as if guiding her. Perhaps the library was, in its way. Most students found this such an imposing place, though she'd never thought so. The books could be a bit rude from time to time, and if one didn't pay attention to the changing shelves, then it was easy enough to get turned around.

But the library simply was as it was treated. Like anyone else, she supposed. To trembling first-years, it was a daunting, frightening place, and so a terror it often became. Yet if one treated the books fairly and thanked the shelves for their guidance, they could be amenable. For

Rose, anyway. Stroking the worn wood fondly, she grinned as the last shelves parted, revealing her favorite nook.

Rose froze.

The desk sat innocently enough, lit by the warm glow of the ever-enchanted candles. But a cool light stole through the window overhead, creeping across the scarred wood. Her throat tightened as she stared up at the glazed panes.

A piercing scream clawed its way out of Aveline's throat as the glass splintered around her—

Rose squeezed her eyes shut, sucking in a sharp breath. She'd been avoiding this spot since the start of term, not that it made any difference. Aveline would come back, she knew. She always did. But the thought of being trapped alone in these halls when she did sent a shiver crawling down her spine.

For the first time, the library no longer felt quite so safe.

Tugging on the strap of her bag, Rose turned on her heel. But the shelf beside her quivered almost indignantly before shifting into its neighbor with a rather final clunk. She faltered, fingers tensing around the spine of her book.

Traitor.

With a long sigh, she slowly peeled herself away from the shelf. For whatever reason, the library clearly wanted her here, and she wasn't about to argue with it. Gritting her teeth, she moved toward the last seat at the long table, as far from the window as possible. She wasn't sure why she still bothered—but it felt safer somehow.

Rose breathed in deeply the scent of aging pages before slinging her bag over the last chair. The enchanted candle flickered but didn't go out. They blazed near endlessly, specially charmed not to burn the books and wonderfully bright amid the pressing gloom of the hall.

Easing into the chair, she rummaged around in her bag for her notes. The hair on the back of her neck pricked, and she bit her lip. She'd never be able to get anything done here.

The books in this part of the library were quieter than those at the front, though that did nothing to still her trembling hands. They shushed her as her pen clattered onto the floor. Rose's cheeks flushed, and she ducked beneath the desk to grab it. But her hands brushed against something leather instead. A journal.

Straightening, she flipped through its pages with a frown. *Property of Sylven Belliaris*, the front page read, scrawled in Sylvie's familiar, atrocious handwriting. Rose's scowl deepened.

Wonderful. The last thing she wanted to deal with today was Sylvie. She glanced around at the looming shelves, their shadows longer in the dim light filtering through the arched windows. Surely she wasn't hiding among the shelves like a child, awaiting her chance to strike. Rose eyed the journal again.

Most likely she'd just left it behind. Though it must have been here for at least a couple of days by now. Sylvie never came in here on the weekends.

Still, it would annoy her to no end to know that Rose had it—or that she might have read it. Not that Rose cared at all what few thoughts it held. If any of them were legible, anyway. Still, she tucked it into her bag. It would be enough just to see the stricken look on Sylvie's face when she returned it to her.

With a scoff, Rose shook her head. The first time she'd met Sylvie had been at this table. She'd thought her beautiful, at first, though the thought brought only a wry smile to her lips now. The minute Sylvie had opened her mouth, the illusion had broken. Haughty and cold, she'd stolen Rose's seat and then had the audacity to sneer at her as if *she'd* been the one in the wrong.

After that, it had been a constant fight for the space, though Rose couldn't even say what Sylvie used it for. It wasn't like she actually studied, after all. Still, a part of her almost wished she were here. Sylvie's sharp tongue was ultimately preferable to Aveline's dead eyes.

The thought skittered across her skin like a countered curse. She never thought she'd find Sylvie's company preferable to anyone's.

Setting the journal aside, she turned back to her notes, determined to get at least *some* studying done today. Still, after a few hours, the words began to blur, and none of them stuck in her mind. Raindrops hung on the frosted glass above her, though very little light passed through the window now.

With a sigh, she closed her book, frowning when the candle beside her sputtered out. Rose blinked as her eyes adjusted to the dim light, a breath caught in her throat. The dreary glow of the cloudy skies provided little aid, and the candlelight at the other end of the table didn't quite reach her.

An icy whisper stole between the shelves, and the other candle flickered out with a soft whoosh. Rose stilled, every hair standing on end.

Aveline.

It had to be. The library hung in utter silence now—even the books had quietened in their shelves. Only the pattering of rain against glass and the beat of her own heart dared to break it. And then a soft thudding. Cold and hard against the stone floor—and getting ever closer.

Rose sucked in a steadying breath. Her neck was stiff, made almost brittle by fear. As if it might crack were she to turn and face whatever loomed behind her. Mouth dry, her mind flickered back to the other night on the bridge. To formless footsteps and unseen gazes. To whatever Aveline had feared.

Rose yelped as a gust of wind pitched her notes across the table. Leaping to her feet, she stumbled back into the bookshelves. Her heart pounded against her ribs, a scream wound in her throat. But the papers stilled, the room falling silent just as all the candles flickered back to life.

The shadows receded in their warm glow, and Rose's breath loosened. Slowly, tenuously, she peeled herself away from the shelf. Her notes lay scattered across the table and floor, almost as if mocking her. She'd been expecting something far worse. Screaming, blood—dire warnings. But a little wind? It was almost as if Aveline was toying with her now.

Knees stiff, she bent to retrieve her notes. Most of the pages had landed on the chair, but one lay upon the floor on the other side of the table, engulfed in a thick, dark puddle. Spilled ink, perhaps?

Rose frowned. Reaching for the parchment, she traced her fingers along its edges, crimson staining her skin. *No.* A shiver crawled down her spine.

Not ink—*blood.*

7

COME WHAT MAY

THE acrid stench of smoke hung heavy in the College of Untamed Arts. It coiled upon the air, swaying over bubbling cauldrons and cloying around flickering candles to fill the room with a thick haze. Rose coughed quietly, brushing some stray sulfur from her sleeve.

As the home of alchemy majors, this hall was no stranger to the occasional explosion. Well, not so occasional, really. She eyed the swirling glass windows, offset by thick metal frames and specially charmed not to shatter. Rain pattered softly against them, but the odd pop and sizzle of thirty-odd cauldrons drowned it out.

She tucked a strand of auburn hair behind her ear, wincing as her hand grazed the tender marks upon her throat. Her bruises had faded somewhat in the last few days, but they still ached faintly, and Rose tugged at her collar. If she was lucky, any wandering eye would assume they were some trophy left over from a weekend dalliance. Though she rarely had interest in such things, it was easier to swallow than the truth.

She sighed, staring down at the listless feris sulfuria mixture before her. Could she even say what the truth was anymore? The dark outline of blood against dim stones flickered through her mind, but she shoved it back. *No.* It had been nothing more than one of Aveline's gruesome games—it *had* to be. She sprinkled a little more sulfur into her cauldron, flinching as its dust floated too close to the open flame beneath and nearly singed her arm.

A soft chuckle grated at her ears as Rose yanked her hand back, a furious heat rising in her cheeks. She turned, half expecting to hear Sylvie's lilting voice announce to the class that her mixture was a failure. No doubt her own formula was already bottled with a bow and ready to ship off to the botany department.

But the eyes that met Rose's were hazel, not amber—familiar only for the mockery that lingered in them. Rose blinked at the student, their mousy brown hair and milky skin a far cry from Sylvie's elegance. They whispered something to their friend behind them, and both descended into hushed laughter.

Rose resisted the urge to roll her eyes, but only barely. It shouldn't bother her anymore. The sidelong glances of her peers, the pitying smiles of her professors—the whispered rumors that she stayed here only by the grace of her mother. That she would never belong. They should all have slipped away from her, entirely unheeded.

After all these years, one might have thought she'd have built something of a fortress around her shame, yet still it pulled at her heart. A little tear in her chest, wrenched open so many times that it refused to heal.

One that Sylvie was adroitly adept at severing. Rose's grip tightened around her wooden spurtle. It was odd not to find her in her shadow, sneering or muttering pointed barbs under her breath. Odder still that she didn't seem to be in class at all. That wasn't like her.

Most students treated attendance as optional, as the professors rarely checked or cared. But Sylvie thrived on lording over the room, as if her presence were the most valuable thing in it. She was often fashionably late, but never absent entirely.

Rose glanced around the hazy room. How had she not noticed? Perhaps the fumes had addled her mind. Yet, now that she thought of it, Sylvie hadn't been in Sylverfir's class yesterday either. Rose had skipped Strategy and Source, but something told her Sylvie hadn't been there either. Rose frowned. Sylvie's absence should have been a balm to her haggard soul, but it pricked at her like a stray splinter—irksome, yet too small to pull free.

Her mind once again leaped to the blood in the library. To Sylvie's journal abandoned in that dark corner. *No.* She was being ridiculous—jumping at ghosts before they even appeared. And one was already bad enough.

The hiss of hushed whispers drew her from her thoughts as the room fell under the grip of sharp gasps and nervous giggles. Rose glanced over to the doorway, where a tall, handsome figure loomed in the threshold. *Oh*—of course.

Fen's dark eyes found hers almost instantly, but then flicked away, darting toward the front of the room. Her mouth went dry. What was he doing here?

She hadn't seen him since the pub. Hadn't wanted to, even when he'd come knocking on her door. She'd never turned him away before, not once. And the thought of it now ate away at something in her very soul.

For a moment, she half debated fleeing. Just dropping her spurtle and sneaking out before he could catch her. But her jaw clenched tight at the thought. This was *Fen*. If anything, she was lucky he was still willing to be in the same room as her.

Any other day, he would've sauntered over with an easy smile to tease her or fix her failed formula with a wave of his hand. But today he hardly looked at her as he crossed the lab in a few long strides, seemingly oblivious to the longing gazes that followed him. Professor Saoloris glanced up, their woven, silver hair brightening as their smile widened.

Whatever words passed between them were lost to the din of the room, but Rose couldn't tear her eyes away. Not unlike the rest of the class, she supposed, though her thoughts were perhaps a bit less lustful. Clearing her throat, she ducked her head low over her cauldron, trying to focus on her incantation. Not that it would do any good, but it was something, at least.

She could almost pinpoint the moment Fen turned around just by her peers. Whispers rose and fell with each row of desks he passed, his steps counted by their pining. Until, finally, his polished leather loafers came to a stop just beneath her desk. Rose swallowed hard, staring at his shoes for a moment before slowly lifting her gaze.

Fen peered down at her with narrowed eyes, so sharp she nearly recoiled. "Hello, Rose."

She straightened. "What are you doing here?"

"Just dropping off notes for my thesis project."

Rose frowned. He could do that at any time, and at just shy of midday, it was far too early for him to normally even be awake yet. Her stomach twisted with a truth she dreaded to utter. So, she supposed did Fen, from the way his eyes skirted just past hers, as if unable to meet them. He was here for *her*.

"You're checking up on me, aren't you?"

"Can you blame me?" He shifted his books into one arm, adjusting his glasses. "After the pub and—er—everything, you just ran off."

A stifled snort from the desk beside her made Rose's cheeks flush. Did he have to phrase it like that? Most people already assumed they were still sleeping together. After all, what else could the chancellor's reclusive daughter offer the academy's golden boy but a chance at better marks and a clever tongue? Otherwise, it was a waste, like pairing fine wine with dry, bland toast as far as their peers were concerned.

It wasn't anything that hadn't been said of them when they *had* been lovers. And it had weighed on Rose just as heavily then.

Rose swallowed hard. She couldn't blame Fen for that—or for his anger. He deserved better than secrets and lies. He deserved better than *her*. The thought sank like a stone.

Not for the first time, she wondered if he'd be better off without her. But he was her one lifeline, a steady cliffside against this abyss she'd been pitched into. Even as she selfishly dragged him down with her, she couldn't let him go. And a part of her knew she never would.

"I know—I'm sorry." The words felt sharp and jagged.

Fen folded his arms over his chest. "What, that's it?"

His brown eyes held no warmth now, his lips pressed tight. It was odd to see his features so cold—so void of his usual kindness. Her heart flipped. Perhaps it would be him that soon let *her* go.

"I ..."

"You can't keep running away from this, Rose." His voice softened, some spark of warmth returning to his eyes. "Whatever is going on, you can tell me."

Her throat tightened, any words falling dry and silent on her lips. The student at the desk beside her watched them unabashedly, two others behind them whispering quietly behind their cauldrons. *Not here.* Not now.

"I want to, but—"

"But you won't," Fen scoffed, pushing away from her desk. "Even if it tears you apart."

Before she could protest, he turned and swept from the room without another word. Rose's heart sank. Even if she gave him the honesty he craved, would he know it for what it was? Already, the bruises had faded, and even that, she knew, was hardly proof of anything.

Still, though the truth may break them both, the lies would shatter them that much faster. She dug her nails into the soft flesh of her palms. *Tonight.* She sucked in a sharp breath. Tonight, she would tell him, come what may.

8

THE TRACE OF ESSENCE

THE towering corridors of Aithwood Hall were almost never silent. Dark stone walls loomed like in some sort of dungeon, the air heavy with thick, sulfurous smoke that shimmered in the low candlelight. Rose ducked out of the way as a student charged out of their dorm, their blond hair standing straight on end and smoking at the tips.

Alchemy majors. She rolled her eyes. The hall was full of them—always tinkering away at their formulas and nearly bringing the walls down around them. How Fen felt at home in this place she'd never understood.

She breathed in deeply, fidgeting with her platter of peach tarts as she approached his door. They were his favorites, and she had braved the kitchens to bake them for him, but somehow the gesture felt hollow now. Wrestling with charmed flour and wading through the greenhouse's defenses for fresh peaches hardly made up for everything.

But the truth somehow hadn't felt like enough on its own. If he would even accept it. Rose's fingers tightened around the plate. It didn't matter—he deserved that much.

Raising her fist, she knocked twice. It was rare for him to lock his door, and rarer still for her to knock, but barging in felt like an invasion somehow.

After a few moments the door creaked open. Fen peered down at her, his long hair fallen flat against his forehead and dark circles clinging beneath his eyes. He almost looked worse than her. Yet the sight only made her smile. Glamours he wore everywhere, like a dazzling suit of armor that fended off even the sharpest gaze. At least he didn't hate her enough that he felt the need to wear one now.

She smiled weakly. "Hey, Fen."

"You have the worst timing, you know that?" He pursed his lips. "If you're going to run off, could you save us both the time and do it now? I'm very busy."

Harsh. Rose bit back a grimace. But not undeserved.

"Truce?" She held up the tarts hopefully.

Fen eyed them for a moment before drawing in a deep sigh. "Fine. Come on."

Stepping back, he gestured for her to enter, though she didn't miss the way his lips twitched. As if holding back a smile took all the effort in the world. She ducked her head, hiding one of her own. Fen never could hold a grudge for long.

"Thanks," she muttered.

"Thank me with the truth." He snatched a tart off the platter as she slid by him.

Of course. Getting in was the easy part. What came next would be infinitely harder.

She sucked in a sharp breath, nearly choking on a heady incense that filled the air with a rich haze. His room was more of a lair than a dormitory, really. The one place Fen could truly be himself. And she alongside him, she supposed.

A sanctuary for them both. Bright, cozy, and immaculately decorated, it felt more like home than any place she knew. A phonograph played soft piano music in the corner, spinning under some charm. The notes bounced playfully off the teak dresser cluttered with ornate decorations, lending warmth and life to the luxury of sapphire, satin bedsheets and golden relics he shrouded himself in.

Rose set the tarts upon his desk, her hands trembling. None of it comforted her now. She felt all too much like some gauche decoration—out of place and unwanted amid all the finery.

Floorboards creaked as Fen crossed the room and sank onto his bed with a soft rustle. He was waiting for her to break the silence, she knew. But how to even begin? Clenching her jaw, she turned to face him.

His dark brow lay furrowed, but his glasses slipped down his nose in a way that nearly made her smile for the familiarity of it all. How many times had she seen him stretched out upon that bed, laughing and smiling as he made his way through several glasses of wine? How many times had they lain within that canopy pretending the rest of the world didn't exist as they gossiped into the small hours of the morning?

Her heart lurched as their eyes met, and she swallowed hard. He didn't look so languid now. Nor at ease.

Stacks of parchment lay cluttered beneath him, crinkled and torn as if he'd shuffled through them a thousand times. Dark circles hung under his eyes, and he wore none of his usual robes, just a wrinkled undershirt with wine stains dotted along the collar. She raised an eyebrow.

"What's it on?"

"What?"

"Your paper." Rose jutted her chin at the parchment underneath him. "You only get this messy when you don't know what to write."

He glanced down at his bed, then back at her, his scowl deepening. "Rose …"

His tone was sharp—a warning. She swallowed hard, turning back to the desk. "So, what's it on? Maybe I could help."

Her fingers grazed over a few odd trinkets but stilled before a crystalline orb. A storm crackled within, lightning sizzling against the sides. She frowned, reaching for it when Fen's hand caught hers.

"Don't touch that." His grip was gentle, though his tone was anything but.

"What is it?"

"My thesis project." He took a step back. "And a work in progress."

"What does it do?"

"Does it matter?" His gaze hardened, as fierce and wild as the storm he held. "You didn't come here to talk about my thesis or a damn paper."

She recoiled, tearing her hand away. "Fen, I—"

His face fell, softening into the features she knew all too well. "At least, I hope you didn't. Please, Rose, I can't help you if you don't tell me what's wrong."

Her heart flipped, the truth burning against her lips. The end of her rope hung by a few frayed strings. If he did not believe her .... Her throat tightened. Then there truly would be nothing left. Aveline could rip away her life, but she would find it cold and empty.

Silence pulsed between them for a moment before Rose dropped her gaze. She thrummed her fingers along the rim of his desk, words stuck to her tongue. A compass spun idly beside her, never straight and never still. Supposedly, it was meant to point him toward his greatest wish, though she wasn't sure Fen even knew what that was. Rose shook her head. Did anyone in this place? Most preferred to bury what they truly wanted beneath shrouded smiles and veiled guile.

As she was doing now.

The thought pulsed at her, tangling around her heart like a cord of guilt. The truth. *That* was what he really wanted. So why couldn't she give it to him? It clawed desperately at the fear holding it at bay. But she couldn't do it.

"Rose?" Fen's voice finally broke the silence.

It wasn't sharp—nor even spiteful. Instead it fell upon her softly, like a gentle hand holding her steady. Somehow that only made it worse.

Fen reached for her, but she pulled away. Tears pricked at her eyes as she stumbled back into his desk—hard. Behind her, there was a loud clunk, and then something rolling across wood. *The orb.* Without thinking, she reached for it, catching it before it tumbled off the desk.

But it struck her like a blow. Crackling around her palm, it rooted her to the floor as if lightning coursed through her veins. Yet it did not burn her. Did not surge through her bones with an aching heat. It simply held her in its grasp, chilling her, as if ice gnawed its way through her chest. Her heart sank as the room shifted.

"Rose?" Fen's voice sounded distant—muffled. As if reaching for her through a thick pane.

And then he was gone.

All trace of him vanished—all warmth seeped from the room. All that remained were cold stones, stained by water and rot, and cast in a sickly, green glow. And a soft pattering that grated at her ears.

Drip. Drip. *Drip.*

It drowned everything out. Her breath. Her thoughts. Even the dull thudding of her pounding heart. She swallowed hard. Crimson rivulets of blood oozed down the walls, dripping onto the floor, inching ever closer. And then the walls shifted.

They closed in all around, crushing Rose between shadow and blood. A scream wound in her throat, but no sound came out. The green flames flickered, dancing over formless shapes. But a face stirred in the darkness, a gaunt visage she knew all too well.

Until it shifted. Matted blond hair faded to black and sickly pale skin bloomed to tawny brown. And when her eyes opened, they were bright, piercing amber.

Sylvie.

Rose's breath burst from her lungs in short, shallow gasps, heart thudding against her ribs as if it were clawing its way free of her chest. *It couldn't be.* She squeezed her eyes shut, but it did nothing to chase the vision away. Cool, clammy fingers stroked her cheek, coiling around her throat, and then—

"Rose!"

The orb wrenched out of her grasp with a sharp twist. In an instant, the vision faded, wisping away like nothing more than air. The room filtered in around her. The warmth, the music. The stone floor beneath her.

Rose's heart still pounded in her chest, a dull reminder of the life pulsing away inside her. But it wavered—cracked, like broken glass. As if one false move might send her swiftly into the hands of death.

Fen stared down at her, the orb crackling away in his palms and a deep scowl furrowing at his brow. *"Dia vhal."* His chest heaved with shaky breaths. "What *was* that?"

Rose blinked at him. "You saw her?"

"Her? No. I saw you." He set the orb back on his desk, running a hand through his hair. "Your eyes … they went white and your skin was cold as ice. I thought—"

He broke off with a shake of his head, staring at a threadbare spot on his rug as if it might hold all the answers. Rose sighed, shakily hugging her knees to her chest. So he hadn't seen it. Seen her. Or *them.* The thought sent a shudder down her spine.

She jumped as Fen fell to his knees beside her, taking her hands gently in his own. "Please, Rose. Just tell me what's going on."

His gaze was so earnest, so pleading, that it tore the truth right from her lips. "I saw Aveline."

Fen's eyes widened. *"What?"*

"I mean, I *see* her. Constantly. Everywhere." The words fled from her as if they had a life of their own. "In mirrors, puddles, windows—even the bath."

"I don't understand." He shook his head. "Like a ghost?"

"I—" she faltered. "I don't know. But only I can see her."

He recoiled as if she'd struck him. "Rose ... how is that possible?"

And there, in the depths of his eyes, flickered the first sparks of doubt. But they caught in Rose's chest like a blaze. He didn't believe her. A sharp breath ripped from her lungs. Of course he didn't.

How could he? An insidious voice whispered at the back of her mind. *Who would?* If she were anyone else, he likely would've assumed she was dabbling in necromancy herself. But even the simplest stacking charm was beyond her reach—the idea that she could cast such insidious, advanced magic was unfathomable, even to Fen, she was sure. Which left only the possibility that she was lying ... or worse.

"You don't believe me, do you?"

"No, that's not it. I mean, I want to, I just—" He faltered. "Just, start from the beginning."

And so she did. Through tears and broken breaths, she told him of the first whispers of Aveline's form clinging to her like a bad dream. Of apparitions in stained windows and screams echoing through cavernous corridors. Of blood-soaked visions, baths, bruises—all of it. Save Sylvie. Aveline, she knew, was real, but Sylvie? One glimpse did not a ghost make, and so she held that still in silence. A little sliver of secrecy she still clung to, even against her better judgment.

To his credit, Fen listened to every word, his features unmoving. But he held her close, stroking her hair and soothing her with little more than a gentle touch. As he always could.

When she finished, he was silent for a long moment before he finally sighed. "I'm sorry."

Fresh tears spilled down Rose's cheeks, and she leaned her head against his chest. Of all the things he could have said, that was the last she'd expected to hear. Disbelief, perhaps. Or even derision. But the hope of sympathy had long fled from her.

"Do you—do you think I'm losing my mind?"

A soft chuckle rumbled through lean torso. "Of course not."

Warmth flooded through her, loosening the throbbing ache in her chest. She hadn't realized how much she needed to hear that.

How much such a simple thing would soothe this aching chasm in her heart.

"Then what?"

"Necromancy's a good guess, though why it would be centered on you, of all people, I couldn't say." He grimaced. "I mean, no offense."

She wiped away tears with a wry scoff. "None taken."

It was nothing she hadn't thought before, and one of the many things she still had no answer for. Of all the people here, every rank of caster, why her?

"Maybe a curse of some sort." Fen ran a hand through his hair. "It doesn't sound like what I know of true necromancy. I've never heard of a ghost that could only be seen by one person. Or one that kept mum about their death."

Rose's throat tightened. Yet Aveline had given her nothing. Save the bruises fading from her neck, there was nothing real or tangible for her to cling to. Not even so much as a clue, except ...

Sylvie's journal.

Rose leaped from the floor, dashing over to her bag and rummaging through its contents. There, at the bottom of the satchel, lay the journal, forgotten and unscathed. Snatching it up, she shoved it into Fen's hands, jabbing at the dried blood staining its yellowed pages.

"Can you see this?"

"Er—yes?" He held it up to the candlelight, examining its edges. "Is that blood?"

Rose staggered back, head spinning. *It was real.* But then ...

The blood could only be Sylvie's. The thought jolted through her like a flame, and she nearly collapsed again. Perhaps it wasn't. Maybe her frayed mind was drawing connections where there were none. But there was something about it all that clung to her like a bur. Some shred of dread, some seed of doubt that would not release her.

"She wasn't in class today." Her heart sank into the pit of her stomach. "Or yesterday."

"What?"

"Sylvie." She wrapped her arms tight around her torso, as if that might somehow hold her together. "I found that beneath her study spot in a pool of blood. A-And I saw her in Aveline's eyes tonight, like she'd shifted, somehow. What if she was killed too?"

"Hey, calm down." He reached for her. "We don't know what happened to Aveline. And we don't know that anything has happened to Sylvie either. Just breathe."

Rose clenched her fists tight. Threads dangled before her in a tantalizing array, but pulling on any too hard felt all too much like tearing at the shreds of her sanity.

Fen rubbed her shoulder, then cleared his throat. "If that blood *does* belong to Sylvie, there's an alchemical formula that can be used to match samples of someone's essence. Blood, hair, skin—that sort of thing."

"You mean the Trace of Essence?"

"You know it?"

She raised an eyebrow.

"Right, of course you do," he conceded. "Well then, if we can get a sample of the blood and something with Sylvie's essence to compare it to, I could run the trace."

"You're sure?"

"Eh, reasonably?" He paused. "It works best on fresh samples, so we're already at a disadvantage. I should be able to cast a preservation charm on it until we can get something to test it against, though."

She tugged at the ends of her sleeves. "We'd have to break into the library. If we get caught trespassing, this will hardly pass as a decent excuse."

Not to her mother, anyway. Nor to Delia, for that matter. Trespassing after hours resulted in severe restrictions on library privileges. Not to mention that she'd spent years building up Delia's trust—it would be foolish to risk it for this. The thought made her stomach churn.

But Fen only grinned. "Then we best not get caught."

The halls of Dunhollow after dark held something sinister within them. Ancient and looming, shadows hung upon the stones like a cloak, swallowing up any shred of light. Rose shuddered. Even she didn't know all their secrets—nor was she sure she wanted to.

Beside her, Fen's eyes flitted to and fro like a flame, his throat bobbing in time with their soft footfalls. A lantern floated in front of him, illuminating each line of his face.

"This is a terrible idea," Rose whispered as they approached the arched entrance to the library. "We should just come back in the morning."

"No." Fen shook his head. "Every hour we wait, the sample will degrade. Who knows if it'll even be accurate now."

Frowning, she let him lead her through the entrance. Inside, it grew darker still. Books snored softly on their shelves, a few muttering in their sleep. One even yelled at them to put out the light, which Fen ignored.

A cool sweat crept across Rose's brow as she and Fen ducked between the shelves. They shouldn't be here.

She caught his arm. "Look, maybe—"

The clanging of the clock bells shattered through the air, swallowing up her words. Rose jumped, fingers tightening around Fen as the lantern sputtered and went out, plunging them into darkness. All at once, the books clamored awake, shrieking and howling about the noise. But she could barely hear them over her own pounding heart.

"Shit," Fen hissed.

"What happened?"

"I charmed the lantern. It goes out if anyone approaches."

Rose's blood ran cold. For a moment, she didn't even breathe. As if the sound of it might have somehow drawn the attention of the ranting books. Or anyone else. She pressed her lips thin, counting her heartbeats. After a few moments, the books quieted, settling back onto their shelves with muted grumbles.

In the hollow silence left behind, the lantern flickered back to life. Warm and soft, it illuminated nothing more than a low-flying book lumbering toward its shelf with a yawn. Rose's chest loosened, though her pulse refused to calm.

Disentangling his arm from her grasp, Fen shot her a wry glance. "Just a night owl," he whispered. "Though, you'd think it was four in the morning the way most of the books are going on about it, though."

In spite of herself, Rose bit back a laugh. "Most of them *are* over a century old. Ten o'clock is well past their bedtime."

"Well, then, it's best we don't linger. Wouldn't want to disturb their beauty sleep."

Or Delia's. Rose winced. Friend or no, the librarian wouldn't take anymore kindly to her breaking in. Less so, even.

Like the books, she retired and rose early. It made the library hours rather skewed, but it was safer than leaving students to their own devices when the books were at their cruelest, she supposed. Rose was perhaps the only exception to the rule. She'd learned all too young how temperamental the books could be, and Delia trusted her not to wreak havoc. Though she did like to know when Rose was there, at least.

Their shoes thudded softly against the stone floors, a broken, haphazard rhythm. Each step made Rose wince. Shadows hung over the shelves, dancing under the lantern's glow. Few of the books seemed to note their presence now, though that did little to settle her restless nerves.

She dug her nails into her palms, leading Fen over to the study nook as quietly as she could manage. It looked so empty in the darkness—untouched. Tugging Fen around to the far side of the table, her stomach sank as the lantern flickered across the floor. There, etched deep into the stones, a dark stain stared up at her in the low glow of the flames.

A shiver ran up her spine, stealing all the warmth from her veins. In that moment, she almost would have welcomed Aveline's presence. That always faded, at least. But this was real, solid. And all too likely lethal.

Her throat went dry, the library split by such pressing stillness. Somehow the silence was more unnerving. It lurked in every shadow, waiting to be broken.

"Is it enough for a sample?" she whispered.

Fen pulled a swab and a small vial from his pocket. "Possibly? It would have pooled between—"

His head shot up, eyes fixed over her shoulder. Rose frowned as his glasses slipped down the bridge of his nose, lips still caught on a stray thought.

"What is it?"

"I thought I heard something."

She followed his gaze. Shadows danced eerily in the silence—each darker than the last. Her ears pricked. Each creak, every whisper of sound, struck her pulse like a match. But nothing crept out of the darkness.

No gaunt face lurked. No decrepit fingers curled toward her throat. Still, she shuddered. There was no more safety in the shadows than there was in the light of day.

"Just get the sample so we can get out of here."

Fen nodded, scrubbing at the floor with a small swab. Rose peered between the shelves, counting the seconds. It felt like an eternity before Fen's head popped up again.

"Got it!" he whispered, just as the lantern sputtered out. *"Dia vhal."*

Rose cursed under her breath. The shadows were so thick now that her eyes could not pierce them. But she could still hear. A soft thunk—the dull patter of footsteps. Her heart leaped into her throat. *Someone else was here.*

She turned, ever so slowly, to meet a pair of glowing, yellow eyes. *Shit.* The thought tore through her mind as the lantern flickered back to life, revealing the small black form of Abas. Delia's familiar stared at her for a moment, blinking innocently before unhinging his jaw and shrieking loud enough to wake the dead.

The sound split through the stillness, and Rose nearly jumped out of her skin when Fen grabbed her hand.

"Come on—we have to go!"

She stumbled as he dragged her past snapping and snarling books, awakened by Abas's wailing. Shadows swirled in the corners of Rose's eyes, blurring as they ran. Until they caught a shape, and her heart stilled. There, across the myriad of shelves, she met a pair of amber eyes she knew all too well.

Sylvie.

9

REPUTATION WAS EVERYTHING

THE next morning dawned with a damp chill in the air. Not unusual at Dunhollow, of course, but its presence pressed against Rose's temple, slowly becoming a dull, throbbing ache. With a groan, she set her hairbrush down, rubbing at her brow.

Sleep had not come easily last night, her mind rampant and racing between thoughts. Though the stain of blood had long faded from her skin, its memory still burned at her fingertips, like some strange scar.

Amber eyes flashed through her mind, and she sucked in a sharp breath. The blood had to belong to Sylvie. No one else made sense. The thought left a sour taste in her mouth—bitter, like bile.

A part of her wanted to brush it away. Pretend that Sylvie would be whispering snide remarks in her ear in Sylverfir's class or freezing her solid in Strategy and Source. But she knew it wouldn't happen.

With a sigh, she eyed her reflection in her mirror. The dark circles were more pronounced beneath her eyes, and her auburn curls lay a bit flat, though she couldn't be asked to care much now. What did it matter when Sylvie may well be dead?

The idea pierced her more than she'd like to admit. A year ago, she might have felt some shred of sadness, or maybe even regret. Now, she covered her mirror hastily, reaching for her coat.

What if Sylvie really did become like Aveline? Her stomach heaved. The thought alone almost spurred prayers to her lips. To whom, she couldn't say. The old gods of the empire were long dead—if they'd ever existed—and any beings that now had sway over the workings of this world had proved long ago that they cared little for Rose. But desperation sent her spiraling into depths she didn't recognize.

Seeing Sylvie's face each day in class was torment enough. If it peered over her shoulder in every reflection, gaunt and lifeless, then draining her life away might indeed be a mercy.

She gripped the edge of her chair until her knuckles turned white. *No.* She couldn't let it haunt her. *Not yet.*

Fen had the sample of the blood. Now all they had to do was get hold of something belonging to Sylvie and then they would know for sure. She glanced back at the covered mirror. One way or another.

A light tapping noise made Rose jump, and her eyes flew to her window, half expecting to see Aveline's gruesome form. Instead, she found the bright crimson wings of her mother's familiar, Gwell. She stared at the falcon for a moment as he continued to tap his beak against the window, a small note tied to his foot.

Wonderful. What could she want at this hour?

Steeling herself, Rose darted around the edge of her bed. Her sage-green rug caught beneath her feet as she fought through a canopy of hanging plants to get to her reading nook and thrust open the window. Gwell perched upon the sill, his golden eyes roving over her room with a keen judgment all too similar to her mother's.

Well, he *was* a part of her, she supposed. Still, it made Rose bristle as she brushed a strand of ivy away from her brow. Her mother would say the room was too common for a caster. She would sniff at the soft, green walls and sparse decorations. If she ever bothered to set foot in here, that was.

The hanging plants that covered every spare inch of the walls were not alive with magic. They did not chatter to Rose, nor dance in their baskets. Useful only for teas and tonics, or simply for decoration. The books stacked neatly in her shelves did not snore or snap as she passed, no enchanted music floated through the room, and the four-poster bed could not make itself each morning. She didn't bother with magical trinkets or a perch for her familiar, for she didn't cast it often enough to matter. Even the mirror was silent, save for Aveline's ghoulish whispers.

It was every inch a mundane room, and none of it was deemed suitable by her mother. But it suited *her*. Provided comfort where she was likely to find little else. Or, at least, it used to.

With a sigh, she unknotted the note tied to Gwell's leg. She could almost feel him glaring at her as she scanned it.

Come to my office before your morning class.

A looping signature scrawled out beneath the paltry message. Chancellor Araminta Thenlif. The formality of it prodded at an old ache buried deep within her heart, though she wasn't sure why. It wasn't as if she expected her mother to resort to something so base as familiarity.

Crumpling up the note, she tossed it into the trash and grabbed her bag. The walk to her mother's office was surprisingly quiet, though she supposed the first bell hadn't even rung yet. Most of her peers were probably ambling through the cantina and grumbling about early classes. Her stomach growled under the cinched waist of her long woolen skirt. For once, she would actually have preferred to join them.

Coming upon her mother's tower, she sucked in a steadying breath before entering the stairwell. The spiral steps lurched to life as soon as Rose touched them, and she gripped the metal railing to keep from tumbling back down them as they carried her ever higher. Her stomach roiled, twisting around nothing more than nerves as they deposited her on the landing.

An ornate obsidian door stared down at her as she straightened, like it had been pulled from the very depths of a volcano. Clenching her jaw, she lifted her fist to knock when raised voices carried out into the corridor. Muffled, a bit, but just barely.

"I tasked you with helping my daughter learn to cast, not getting her killed."

"It was necessary to—"

"It was anything but, Revan!" her mother snapped. "This is an institution of higher learning, not a back-alley dueling club. You are here to teach students, and I expect you to follow the curriculum as laid out in your contract."

Revan? Had her mother actually made good on her promise to speak to Professor Troidilis? The thought brought a wry smile to Rose's lips. It might have been wiser to turn away, but her feet remained rooted to the floor. It was rare to hear anyone else on the receiving end of her mother's ire. And it wasn't as if the professor didn't deserve it.

"The curriculum wasn't made to suit your daughter. She'll never learn to cast if you keep coddling her!"

The room fell into a tense silence. After a moment, the muffled squeak of her mother's chair echoed through the air. Rose winced. She knew exactly the look she'd fixed Professor Troidilis with, and she didn't envy them in the slightest. Still, she couldn't say it didn't bring her the smallest bit of joy to hear her mother defending her for once, odd as it was.

"If I want your opinion, Revan, I will ask for it." Her mother's voice was low and icy when she finally spoke. "Given your years of tenure, I'm doing you the courtesy of not taking disciplinary action. But if I *ever* hear of you frivolously risking students' lives again, you will be dismissed before you can so much as cast your familiar. Am I understood?"

There was a long pause. "Yes, Chancellor."

"Good, now get out of my office before I change my mind."

Rose barely had time to move before the door flew open and Professor Troidilis came sweeping out of the room. They drew up short at the sight of her, fixing her with a hard stare. Her breath coiled in her chest. Would they make another scene? Strike her down where she stood?

But, after a moment, they simply brushed past her. Rose released a shuddering breath. Something told her she should watch her back from now on. Though she couldn't imagine why they chose her to pull such a stunt in the first place. She was the chancellor's daughter, after all. Not that her mother particularly cared for her safety, but any threat made to Rose could be considered a challenge to her authority. And her mother couldn't have that.

Shaking her head, she turned back toward the office. Whatever the professor's reasons, Rose had more pressing issues to consider than their petty plays at power. Taking a few short breaths, she steeled herself to knock.

"Enter!" Her mother's voice was crisp.

Rose hesitated a moment longer before finally stepping into the room. Like everything else her mother touched, her office inspired no sense of comfort. Scarlet flames crackled away in a cavernous hearth, almost as if to match her mother's fury.

But she herself sat still as stone at her polished mahogany desk. Framed by arched, stained-glass windows, she almost looked like something out of a painting, fair and insidious, without so much as a wrinkle in her brow to mark her harsh words only moments ago. For years, Rose had referred to that as her mother's mask. Her singular ability to smooth away any inconvenient expression without so much as a breath of effort.

It took her far longer than she'd like to admit to understand that she'd had it the wrong way around. The mask was never the lack of emotion, but the display of it. Her mother had no time to be bothered by such petty things, of course.

She didn't even look up as Rose approached. The trilling of an alarm drowned out her thoughts as her mother's calendar lit up on the wall behind her. No doubt informing her of some appointment she'd consider far more important than speaking to Rose.

A faint beeping came from a glittering globe on the mantle beside her, and a lilting voice filled the room with a report on the status of the Tol Qilius trade markets. Rose's head spun. Magical artifacts of all sorts buzzed and whirred about the room, their din carrying even up the floating spiral staircase to the dining room and lounge at the second level of the office. She pressed a nail into the bed of her thumb, trying to center herself.

Digging her heels into the plush rug beneath her, Rose measured her words carefully. She was well familiar with this play of power her mother employed. Ignoring every entrant as if they were no more significant than a fly on the wall. But today, she had no patience for it. Finally, when she could bear it no longer, she cleared her throat.

"Mother."

She spared her the briefest glance. "Oh, Rosera. Why are you here?"

"You sent for me?" Rose fidgeted with her sleeves. Apparently, her mother considered her so unimportant she didn't even remember inviting her.

"Ah, yes. I suppose you saw Professor Troidilis on your way in?" Her mother tapped on a swirling communication mirror at the edge of her mahogany desk. "You'll be pleased to know you're no longer in their class."

She blinked. "I'm not?"

"No, I don't believe their course is suitable for you anymore." She leaned forward, tenting her fingers beneath her chin. "Instead, you'll be placed in Healing Herbalism with Professor Burroak. Of course, you'll still be expected to cast for potions and tonics, but the curriculum should be more appropriately paced for you."

Rose's heart skipped a beat, giddy with the thought. To not have to attend Strategy and Source again? She nearly smiled. Even if she did have to cast, Briony wasn't the sort of professor to try and poison her in an effort to encourage her lacking skills.

"I—" she faltered. "Thank you."

"Never let it be said that I don't do anything for you." Her mother sighed, her attention already back on the papers on her desk. "Now, was there anything else?"

It was odd, the small spark of warmth that spread through Rose's chest. Hopeful, almost. For the briefest moment, the truth burgeoned against her lips. Of Aveline's ghost, of the blood still caked between the stones of the library floor. But it faded in an instant.

Whatever kindness her mother offered was like a collar—it almost always came attached to a leash. She knew better than to trust it. Rose shuddered, the warmth waning in her chest.

Whether they came from Rose's lips or the vague notion of pub gossip, her mother would still dismiss claims of Aveline's ghost out of hand. She'd made clear that her priority was Dunhollow's reputation, after all. Even the blood she might make disappear, like she had with all uncomfortable inquiries surrounding Aveline's disappearance. Deceit came easier to her than breathing—what use would she have for anything so inconvenient as the truth?

Rose frowned. But Sylvie was different. A star caster, a top student, and equally one of the most reviled and adored people in the school. There's no way even her mother could sweep her away so easily as Aveline.

"Have you seen Sylvie?" she blurted out before she could stop herself.

Her mother paused her scribbling, but didn't look up. "Sylvie Belliaris? No, why?"

"She, uh, hasn't been in class for a couple days. Do you know if she took sick leave?"

89

"If she did, that would be between her and her professors."

"I know, but it's not like her to miss class."

" 'Not like her'?" Her mother finally looked up. "Really, Rosera, I don't know why you care. I thought you detested the woman."

She did. Of course, she did. But that wasn't the point.

"Yes, but—"

"Then instead of wasting time on frivolous questions, you should get to your classes. I'm sure Professor Sylverfir won't appreciate tardiness." A great clanging of bells rang out through the room, as if to punctuate her point. Her mother raised an eyebrow. "Now, Rosera!"

"Yes, Mother."

Rose bit her tongue. Sometimes she wondered what would happen if she were to say more. Would her mother curse her? Strike her, perhaps? No, that might leave too obvious a mark. Reputation was everything to her mother—it would hardly do to make people talk. Her punishment would be far more subtle, she was sure. Pressing her lips tight, she turned for the door and fled out into the corridor.

10

IVERIN STASIA

FOR the first time, Rose could not recall a single word spoken in a class. Sylverfir's lecture had been interesting enough, but his words rang hollow in her ears. Any answers she might've had flitted away from her, like dead leaves afloat on an autumn breeze. For the only thing that filled her mind was the fact that Sylvie's seat remained achingly bare.

Rose frowned, doodling on the edges of her notebook. Dark, jagged lines etched deep into the page. It took her a moment to realize that what she'd drawn wasn't just an idle sketch. It was gaunt, dead eyes.

She jumped when the bells rang out, slamming her notebook so loudly it earned her a few odd glances. Even from Sylverfir. Cheeks reddening, she gathered up her things in haste, darting from the room before he could pull her aside.

But she couldn't shake off her thoughts so easily. They ran rampant as she made her way toward the greenhouse. All she knew for sure was that there was some blood in the library, and she had yet to explain it.

And that Sylvie was absent—again. As she'd known she would be. Already, their peers were whispering and trading in spurious rumors, though Rose doubted there was any truth in them. A bad cold, a pressing family matter in the capital, a secret dalliance with a student at Maalstrum, one of Dunhollow's rival academies. None of it explained the blood—or the hauntings.

She chewed the inside of her lip, eyeing the stone colonnade. Few students uttered her name in the same sentence as Aveline's yet, and no one had yet reported her missing, if her mother was to be believed. Once again, her ghost was hollow space left behind that only Rose saw the truth of.

But Sylvie was no timid first-year—she was a force to be reckoned with, binding the attention of any room she walked into with a caustic grip. She had connections and clout that Aveline never had. At the very least, Rose would have thought Arden and Ewan might be cashing in on the rumors, collecting sympathy like currency. Unless they'd had something to do with it.

The thought chilled her to the core. The last time she'd seen Sylvie had been in the pub, arguing with Ewan. The last time anyone had seen her, as far as her peers' speculations were concerned. Then again, she couldn't really see Ewan attacking Sylvie anymore than she could picture Arden going after Aveline.

Not that they would ever have to get their own hands dirty. Their families had money and power enough to ensure any "problem" might simply disappear. And if anyone in this place had ties to ancient magic like necromancy, it was likely one of them. Rose drew her coat tighter as a shiver crawled up her spine.

By the time Rose made her way to the greenhouse a few hours later, her headache had been revived, burgeoning behind her eyes. Not helped in the least by the fact that this was the one place in all of Dunhollow where the sun reliably shined.

A charm, certainly. But enchanted or no, the sun beamed down at her from the glass ceiling. The dirt floor warmed her toes through the thin soles of her leather loafers, soothing, in its own way. Usually she loved it here, with the great oak sprawled at the center of the room and luscious planters overflowing with magical herbs and oddities. Bees buzzed about, filling her ears with their gentle song and entirely unbothered by her presence. But she was in no mood for it now.

Rose wrinkled her nose, eyeing the cheerful room with undue judgment. Today, of all days, she yearned more for the gray skies and gloomy drizzle beyond these walls. For a brief moment, she almost turned away, and the irony of it shocked her.

Had she not wanted to be switched into this course? To be surrounded by the hand-painted bug homes and stench of compost floating overhead, sorting itself into well-coded piles? Had she not pined for the soothing sight of drying racks hanging above ivy-strewn walls? For the snarling plants and whimsical flowers that bickered and snapped in their cages?

Still, she couldn't help her stomach sinking as she caught Professor Burroak's gaze. Soft lines crinkled around the professor's eyes as she beamed at her, waving with far too much enthusiasm. Reluctantly, Rose plastered a smile on her face. Briony didn't deserve her foul mood.

A short, round woman of middle age, Briony's sage-green hair fell in tight curls around her tawny cheeks. Thick brows and a strong jaw sat in contrast to her prominent brown eyes. But her smile was what Rose had always found most compelling. Kind and inviting, it somehow felt like a warm cup of telka on a cold winter's day.

"Ah, Rose"—Briony's voice was low and husky—"your mother said she'd be switching you to this class. Welcome, welcome!"

Heat flared across Rose's cheeks as the other students glanced up from their planting. "Er—thank you, Professor."

"You haven't missed much—we've been working on transplanting some iverin stasia." Briony herded her over to a workbench.

Rose glanced around at the array of shockingly blue flowers set before the other students. Though not all of them looked quite as vibrant as they should, with dried, graying leaves scattered across the greenhouse floor. She frowned. Though she didn't possess the skill to cast healing tonics and tinctures, she'd always had a bit of a green thumb.

Her mother used to fill their quarters with dozens of plants, all of which were near death within the week. But Rose had always had a knack for bringing them back. Not magic, perhaps, just a love of all things green and growing. Something about soft soil beneath her fingernails and the earthy smell of a garden always felt like home.

But that was a long time ago. Before she'd moved out from the watchful eye of her mother and into the incessant rush of the dorms. Still, the thought brought some joy back into the sunny halls of the greenhouse. At least she could be grateful that it was far from the danger of the casting courts. Here, she didn't run the risk of dying.

A jolt of dread shot straight down her spine, shadowed images of bloodstained stones and deadened eyes flashing through her mind. They flickered between hazy blue and sharp amber, sinking into gaunt, grotesque faces. Rose's grip tightened on the strap of her bag, and she sucked in a steadying breath.

"Here we are." Briony interrupted her thoughts. "You can sit beside Ewan."

Ewan? Rose's heart leaped into her throat. She blinked down at her peer, frozen for a moment, though they barely looked up at her approach. What were they doing here?

For some reason, her eyes flew first to their hands, as if the stain of blood might still cling to them, incriminating them. But they didn't exactly look as though they'd gone about brutally murdering their girlfriend over the weekend. They fiddled with the dead leaves of their plant, looking bored and listless, as they almost always did.

Still, most days, they'd have protested about having to be in the same room as Rose. Or sneered and whined, at the very least. Now, they almost avoided her gaze as she settled uneasily beside them, leaning closer to their plant, like it was the most fascinating thing in the world, despite the fact it was half dead. *Odd.*

Briony cleared her throat, eyes flashing between the pair of them. "Now, I'm sure you know where to find your supplies—do your best to revive your iverin stasia. The student hospital at Savoissanta DeVoil has requested a large quantity for a trial next spring to research its use as an anesthetic."

Rose faltered under the professor's expectant gaze. Briony had long encouraged Rose's love of plants, ever since she was a child hiding out in the greenhouse. Any other time, she'd have shared in her enthusiasm—asked a dozen questions. Now, it was all she could do to feign a smile.

"Fascinating."

"Isn't it?" Briony practically bounced on her toes. "I'll see if I can find a copy of the study's findings if you'd like to read more about it? It would make an excellent term paper topic."

"Er—sure." Rose slid her bag off her shoulder, tucking her hair behind her ear. "Thank you."

"Excellent!"

The professor beamed at her brightly before turning for the front of the room, humming as she went. Rose frowned, picking gently at the leaves of her plant. It needed new soil, for one, and a larger pot. Iverin stasia roots spread wide, but not terribly deep.

It was in desperate need of a good trim too. Ducking under her workstation, she rummaged around for a pot and a set of shears before tearing into her sack of soil.

For a while, the pruning and repotting almost held Rose's attention. But she couldn't stop her gaze from sliding back toward Ewan as she worked. Though they never looked at her, they slowly started mirroring her choices, barely even bothering to hide the fact that they were copying her.

Rose's jaw tightened. They certainly didn't lack the audacity to have murdered Sylvie, just perhaps the wherewithal. She narrowed her eyes at their ridiculous gold-streaked hair, swallowing a scoff.

Like a good heir and scion of House Elaegius, they barely ever shared an opinion outside of what their illustrious father allowed. She doubted they could've acted without his say-so. Though, with their family's resources, leaving a pool of blood behind seemed a tad sloppy. Then again, bloated arrogance often did lead to such glaringly obvious mistakes.

"Can I help you, Thenlif?" Ewan's velvety voice made her jump.

They still didn't look at her, but their tone dripped with such acrid boredom that it made her skin crawl. Like the simple act of deigning to speak to her was beneath them. Rose bristled, burying her spade in the bag of soil before straightening.

"Yeah, where's your other half?"

They startled a bit but still didn't meet her gaze. "What?"

"Sylvie. I'd have thought this class would be right up her alley."

Well, not precisely, but she would be shocked if her mother had placed her in a class Sylvie wasn't meant to be in. The only one they hadn't had together thus far was her Practical Spellcrafting course. Plus, Sylvie wasn't actually as terrible with plants as she was at taking notes. Better than Ewan, at least, who cleanly snipped off the head of their iverin stasia. Their cheeks flushed as Rose failed to stifle a snort.

"Not here, clearly."

"Yes, I can see that." Rose rolled her eyes. "She wasn't in Sylverfir's class either."

"So?"

Rose pursed her lips. Clearly, they weren't just going to come out and admit it. "Actually, I haven't seen her since your little tiff in the pub."

Ewan's grip tightened on the plant. "Then that makes two of us."

"Really? I thought you two were glued at the hip."

"Just let it go, Thenlif."

A small warning at the back of her mind urged her to listen. But something deep within her pushed her forward. "No, I don't think I will."

Finally, they turned on her, eyes sparking and nostrils flared. "Fine, if you must know, we broke up. Happy now?"

Rose recoiled. It was rare to see them so riled. It wasn't exactly a tantrum, but Ewan was slow to ... well, any emotion at all, really, that it practically counted as such. She eyed the shears gripped tightly in their fist and swallowed hard.

"Oh." Her voice came out small and soft, like a mouse cowed by a cat.

The muscles around Ewan's jaw tensed. But something passed over their blue eyes, and they fell—dull and listless. Sighing, they sank back onto their stool, the image of bored indifference once more.

"If you want to know where Sylvie is, I'm guessing it has something to do with that."

She could've let it drop there. Should have, even. But Ewan's shoulders sagged with such surety that it stilled her. That was no lie told to save their own skin—they actually *believed* it.

Never mind that she'd once seen Sylvie drag herself to class with a fever that would've sent most folks straight to the infirmary. The idea that a breakup would cause her to even shed a tear, let alone miss class entirely, was laughable. Not over something so trivial. But then, Ewan had always had a rather high opinion of themself.

A snort bubbled out of Rose before she had the good sense to stop it. "Don't flatter yourself."

"Excuse me?"

"Courses are the only thing I've ever seen Sylvie care about, and you think she'd risk her marks for your sake?" Rose raised an eyebrow. "If you honestly believe that, you're a fool."

Ewan stared at her for a moment, their dark eyes dancing with something she could only describe as … fear. She frowned. Of all the reactions they could've had, that was the last thing she'd expected. Derision, maybe—even anger. But fear? It just seemed so out of place.

"You're right," they muttered finally, which nearly knocked Rose out of her seat.

"Pardon?"

They ran a hand through their gold-streaked hair before hurriedly tucking their belongings into their bag. "I have to go."

"Wait, what?" She recoiled as Ewan got to their feet, racing to the door. "Ewan!"

Rose's cry turned a dozen gazes upon her, but it didn't slow them at all. Her heart pounded as she stared at the empty doorway. What was *that*?

"Everything all right, Rose?" Briony made her jump.

"Yes, Professor," she said in the most composed voice she could manage. "Sorry."

Turning back to her plant, she shoved composted manure into her soil. But she couldn't stop her eyes flickering to the door. Whatever Ewan knew, they'd rather lose marks by leaving class early than spill their secrets. Rose sank her fingers into the dirt. But would they kill to keep them?

11

AMONG PALE IMITATIONS

THE gray Dunhollow skies felt almost like an insult as Rose stared up at Baer Hall. Heavy with the threat of rain, they glowered down at her, coating her in a light drizzle. Her heart pounded in her ears as a few students jostled past, their laughter fading as they fixed her with sidelong stares.

Rose pulled the hood of her coat further over her face. Baer Hall housed only School of Defensive Arts majors, and no one could mistake her for that. Tugging on the strap of her satchel, she bit back a groan. This was a terrible idea.

What if Sylvie was in there? She glanced back at the dormitory, its ancient stones cast like a dark shadow against the sky. Did it matter?

Rose's heels clacked against damp cobblestones as she paced back and forth. She shouldn't *be* here. She should have been preparing for her alchemy class or studying for her quiz in Sylverfir's class tomorrow. After all, were their roles reversed, Sylvie wouldn't be caught dead lurking outside her dorm hall.

A quiet curse brushed past her lips. In her place, Sylvie likely would've cast some banishment charm on Aveline the moment she'd seen her or reported her to the capital inquisitors, embracing rumors of necromancy with pride. She wouldn't waste away, cowering from shadows like a child. And she wouldn't give a second thought to Rose.

But it had been four days now, and still there was no sign of Sylvie. Gaunt eyes flashed at the back of her mind and her fists tightened. Already, Aveline threatened to claim her life. If Sylvie was anything like her now, she wouldn't hesitate to finish what she'd started. Rose's nails cut harsh lines across her palms. She had to know for certain.

If Sylvie was there, wonderful. If not, then all she needed was a few hairs or a toothbrush, and she and Fen could be sure whether or not the blood belonged to her at all.

Once she had proof—irrefutable proof that her mother couldn't deny or dismiss, then …. She faltered. Then what? She'd hand it over to her mother and let her sweep it all under the rug again?

A few cool raindrops splattered onto her cheeks. If there was even a chance of settling this, she had to take it. Straightening, Rose turned on her heel and marched toward the doors.

But, standing there before them, her courage faltered, and her hand stilled just above the latch. Wading through Aithwood Hall was a dangerous enough price to visit Fen. She didn't even want to know what curses the residents of Baer Hall might have laid upon it.

Sucking a sharp breath, she shoved her way quickly through the doors. But no lightning sizzled against her skin. No flames singed her brows. And there was no sign of any curse. Her breath loosened in her chest. Then again, it was the nature of curses that the bearer didn't know they'd been cast until far too late.

Rose swallowed hard, glancing down the corridor. It was oddly quiet. She'd have thought Baer Hall would be far more boisterous. Source magic didn't usually attract the studious or the meek. Still, she wouldn't spurn a turn of good luck.

Pushing back her hood, Rose made her way toward the stairs. Dorm B13 was on the second floor at the far end, if she recalled correctly. Though her own dormitory was on the other side of campus, she made sure to stay appraised of Sylvie's living assignments each year.

Easier to avoid her when she knew which paths she'd take to class. Or rather, it used to be.

She faltered as she reached the steps, trailing her fingers along the singed edge of the banister. Scorch marks littered the walls all the way up, and a stray icicle still clung to the window above her. Rose's pulse skittered. Clearly her appraisal of the residents here hadn't been entirely unwarranted.

The air cooled as Rose stepped onto the landing, her breath curling around her in clouded puffs. *Odd.* Her eyes flew to the window. The icicle was half melted, yet a thin layer of frost inched out across the glass pane behind it. She shivered. That was no source magic.

Shadows shifted in the corner of her eye, and her breath caught in her throat. Her heart hammered in her ears, and she jumped as a hiss of harsh whispers crept over her shoulder. She whirled around, eyes flying open. But there was no ghostly form.

Just two second-years who tramped down the stairs, whispering loudly behind their hands as they fixed her with sidelong glances. Rose's cheeks flared, and she shoved past them before their whispers turned to something more insidious.

Darting down the corridor, she skidded to a halt before an ornate door carved with idle sketches, rough drawings, and a glimmering illustration involving guests and poison. Rose swallowed hard. Dorm B13—*Sylvie's dorm.*

She raised her fist to knock but hesitated. It would hardly be unlike Sylvie to curse her threshold. Beyond that, what would she say if Sylvie *was* actually there? Gritting her teeth, she rapped her knuckles against the door all the same. She'd deal with that as it happened. But, as she stood there in the lonely corridor, she received no reply. Frowning, she knocked again. Still, nothing.

Another group of students passed by, eyeing her with clear disdain and huddling together in a fit of giggles. Rose shrunk closer to the door as if that might somehow hide her from view. The longer she loitered out here, the more she was sure the entire school would hear of it.

She shoved her hand into her pocket, fingers curling around a copy of her mother's master key. She and Fen had it forged in their first year, before he'd managed to learn an unlocking charm. Cast with a dampening hex, it was meant to protect the chancellor from any stray spell a student might use to guard their door. Though Rose rather pit-ied anyone foolish enough to entrap her mother in a curse.

Still, though Rose rarely needed to use it anymore, she was glad, in this moment, that she never thought to remove it from her key ring. She eased the key into the lock and opened the door, which let out a deep groan.

"Sylvie?"

No one answered.

Rose hesitated a moment longer before deciding to risk it and ducking inside. But the sight that greeted her stilled her in her tracks. For a moment, she thought perhaps the room had been ransacked. But, upon closer inspection, she recognized a pattern to the madness, though it was hardly distinguishable from the mess.

Laundry spilled out of an oak wardrobe, random notes and books scattering across the mahogany desk with overdue library notices. *Strange.* Sylvie herself never had more than a hair out of place. The picture of perfection.

But her room was pure chaos. As if every hint of havoc or mayhem Sylvie encountered had been shoved away into this dorm, far from the prying eyes of their peers. A few papers crinkled loudly underfoot as Rose stepped further into the room and she winced, holding her breath a moment.

Sylvie could come back any second now—perfectly healthy and incandescent with Rose for entering uninvited. After all, if something *hadn't* happened to her, then this was a terrible violation of her privacy. Perhaps it still was.

Yet Rose couldn't quite bring herself to leave. If she could find something with Sylvie's essence on it, she would be in and out without anyone being the wiser. And then she'd have all the answers she needed.

She tiptoed across the room, past a canopy bed draped in amber-and-crimson curtains and piled high with more laundry. Flameless lanterns hung overhead—charmed, no doubt, to fill the room with a warm, cozy glow. It seemed designed to lend a little life to the space, but the walls were remarkably bare.

A few stray sketches hung above the bed—thick charcoal draw-ings of cats and crows. But, beyond that, nothing.

The desk, however, was a different story, stacked with nail polish, a plethora of mugs coated in lipstick stains, and no small amount of makeup. Still no photos though, she noted. Nothing to indicate that Sylvie had a life outside this place. Or within it. Rose's gaze strayed to the window, which looked out over the thick forest, the trees mere inky silhouettes against the gray sky.

Trailing her fingers along the edge of the desk, she frowned. She'd have thought Sylvie would decorate every scrap of space in her achievements. She was captain of the dueling club, head of the artistic association, and a ranking member of the debate team. Awards and trophies should litter the walls and shelves, and yet the only clue that she was even a student here was the cluttered leather bag lying half open beside the desk.

Rose moved a little closer, startling when the mirror upon the desk came alive, roasting her with a slew of criticism. Of course, Sylvie wouldn't own a complimentary mirror. She scowled. How did she ever find anything in this mess?

It was enough effort just to walk through it. She could hardly find the bed, let alone anything bearing Sylvie's essence.

Glancing around, she finally landed upon a hairbrush perched precariously at the back of the desk. Curling her fingers around it, Rose tried prying it from underneath a pile of notes without disturbing them. But, of course, this only succeeded in knocking the papers loose, scattering them across the floor.

Cursing under her breath, she bent to retrieve them. Mostly, they were just random scribbles, though a small charcoal drawing caught her attention. Of a woman, it seemed, staring longingly out a window, with a caption jotted sloppily beneath.

> *So she goes*
> *A bright star among pale imitations*
> *A rose amid these thorns*

Rose's cheeks flushed. Surely the phrasing was a coincidence. And yet, she couldn't help but notice the figure's hair had a similar curl to hers, and the window she stared out of looked all too much like the one looming over their library nook …

Shaking away the thought, she paged through the rest of the notes. Random, chaotic things that only loosely resembled the outlines of class lectures. Hardly useful at all. But there, in the margins of each page, bold words drew her gaze. *The Order of Salix*, it read. Over and over again, etched in harsh, unforgiving lines.

Rose frowned. Salix? Dunhollow was well known for its student organizations and elite clubs, but she'd never heard of that one.

She flipped to the next page, which abandoned any structure of notes. Instead, it depicted a sprawling tree, with names scrawled on each branch. Beneath the roots, only one name stood out—Salix. A family tree, perhaps?

Her eyes narrowed, for under that was a single word, underlined so deeply it nearly tore through the page. *Starlings.*

Rose stared at the parchment a moment longer. She'd never seen Sylvie take such detailed notes before. Maybe it was an ancient bloodline, or some research project for Pre-imperial Casting? But it felt wrong somehow, like some cursed magic was bound to the image, reaching toward her.

She couldn't tear her eyes away as it blurred, twisting from the tangled mass of roots to harsh, insidious lines. No—*veins.* They carved around a pallid face, ink oozing from the pages like blood. Bile bit at Rose's throat as the room faded around her.

But the walls did not close in on her this time. There were no walls at all. No blood, no bloated, rotting fingers. Just trees. Gnarled and warped, they clawed their way up toward a moonlit sky. Shrieks echoed through the air, mingled with muffled chanting that filled the woods around her like a steady heartbeat.

Cloaked figures loomed against the weathered trees, circling her. Until they stopped, and the forest fell deadly quiet. One by one, they turned, their faces hidden by ivory masks that gleamed in the moonlight. Carved into hideous expressions, they fixed on her with keen interest, drawing closer. And closer still.

But Rose squeezed her eyes shut. *"No!"*

The cry burst from her with such force that she stumbled back, blinking about at the bare walls of Sylvie's dorm. *It was gone.* Her heart leaped, and then sank almost as quickly. Aveline had never released her so easily before.

But then, it hadn't felt like her either. Sylvie, perhaps? The thought made her mouth go dry. But why would she show any kindness?

Her fingers brushed over the page again. Is that what had happened to them both? This strange Order lurking in the woods? It had to be connected somehow.

Stacking the last of the notes back together, Rose traded them for the hairbrush. But no sooner had she tucked it into her bag than she heard footsteps outside, stilling just before Sylvie's door. Rose froze, rooted to the spot as a knock rang through the room.

"Sylvie?"

She knew that voice—deep and velvety, yet somehow piercing. *Ewan.* Her heart thundered in her chest. She hadn't seen them since they'd fled class yesterday—what if they'd come to cover their tracks? And what would they say if they found her in here, snooping through Sylvie's things?

"Sylvie, are you in there?" Another knock. "Look, I know you don't want to talk to me right now, but please, open up."

The doorknob twitched, sending an icy jolt through Rose's chest. She needed to hide. Eyes darting about, they landed finally on Sylvie's wardrobe. She wrinkled her nose. It was hardly ideal, but it was better than being caught by Ewan.

"Syl?" The doorknob twisted. "I'm coming in."

Hesitating a moment longer, Rose threw herself into the wardrobe, closing the door behind her as gently as she could. Not a second later, the bedroom door clicked open. Rose peered through the smallest of cracks in the wardrobe, her pulse racing.

Ewan merely stood there for a moment, surveying the room. Sylvie's clothes fell in front of Rose's face, blocking her view and assaulting her with the sweetly rich scent of her perfume. Orchid and musk. She stopped herself from breathing it in. A rare glimpse of spring in this place that only ever lingered on the edge of autumn.

Her clothes were unusually soft too, brushing against her skin with a gentility that Sylvie herself had never possessed. But it was fitting, somehow, that they should be the opposite to her. For Sylvie had always been a wolf in sheep's clothing. Soft to look at but sharp to touch.

"Sylvie?"

Ewan's voice drew Rose from her thoughts, and she caught herself idly stroking the smooth fabric of one of Sylvie's blouses. Swallowing a scoff, she brushed them aside and leaned in closer to the crack in the doors.

Ewan ventured further into the room now, running their fingers sadly over each surface. *Odd,* she thought. Rose's breath hitched as they reached Sylvie's notes on the desk. What if they noticed something out of place?

They perused through them without much care, splaying them out across the dark wood. But her eyes narrowed as they paused. For a moment, they stood still as a statue, as if their muscles had forgotten how to move.

Then they leaned in, peering at one of the pieces of parchment. Rose squinted through the crack, trying to ascertain which one had stalled them, but it was too far away. They stumbled back as if in shock, eyes darting about the room before they fled out the door.

How strange.

She waited a few minutes longer, making sure they wouldn't come back before she tumbled out of the closet. Straightening, she brushed off her clothes. Not that it would do any good. She'd likely smell like Sylvie for a week.

Grimacing, she made her way over to the desk, where she too stilled. Sitting at the top of the pile was the family tree, its dented, inky branches staring up at her like some mocking puzzle. Clearly Ewan knew what it meant—feared it, even.

Chewing the inside of her lip, she tucked it into her pocket. Whatever it was, it could be the key to Sylvie's disappearance—and all the answers Rose needed.

12

THE ORDER OF SALIX

THE library was quiet just after dark. The candlelight had dimmed to a soft glow, the arched windows offering nothing but fickle moonlight beyond their panes. With a sigh, Rose closed yet another book, coughing as a thick layer of dust spiraled into the air. Snoring tomes lay scattered around her, utterly unhelpful in their slumber.

How long had she been here now? An hour—two, maybe? Yet all she had to show for her efforts was a burgeoning headache. And all her fingers intact, which was something of an accomplishment given that most of the books were already getting settled for the night.

She rubbed at her brow, pushing away whispers of hooded cloaks and masked faces that plagued her mind. They'd lingered in her dreams last night, pulling her from her already restless slumber. This Order of Salix *had* to be important somehow? Yet the library remained remarkably bare of any record of it.

She'd tried several tomes on the history of Dunhollow student organizations and *Who's Who of Tol Qilius* magazines from the last thirty years, yet—still—nothing. She'd even tried looking through two decades' worth of yearbooks in case her vision was wrong and it was some obscure group of artists or casters' darts champions.

Leaning against the shelf behind her, Rose groaned, burying her face in the last of the yearbooks lying in her lap. The book recoiled, leaping from her hands and giving her a solid thwack before disappearing back to its shelf.

Touchy. She scowled, rubbing at her head. Still, it probably had the right idea—this whole endeavor seemed fruitless. Perhaps Sylvie's note had been just that, or else some random scribble. Something to at least give the appearance that she paid attention in class.

Yet the thought needled at her, haggard pleas hanging in her memory. That vision had felt ancient—corrupt. But then, so was Dunhollow. In its six hundred years of tenure, the academy had had more than its fair share of sordid societies and grisly guilds. Though most had petered out decades ago, so what was Sylvie doing wrapped up with one?

If she even was. Rose tugged at the collar of her emerald sweater. Besides her gruesome vision, she had no proof it was tied to either Sylvie or Aveline. Or that they were connected to each other. Or that anything had happened to them at all. Perhaps this all was nothing more than her fearful, broken mind desperately reaching for some semblance of reason.

There was the blood. She clung to the thought like a lifeline, eyes flickering to the study nook looming at the end of the row. In the darkened, abandoned corner of the library, however, it would never see the light of day. An indelible stain that would meld into the stones before another soul ever came back here. Only she and Sylvie had ever braved it. And now, only Rose.

She jumped as the bells clanged to mark the change of the hour. *Seven o'clock.* Fen would be out of class by now, likely idling in the student lounge with his usual horde of admirers or getting ready to head down to the pub to celebrate the start of the weekend. She didn't relish the thought of interrupting him, but letting him run his trace on Sylvie's hairbrush was probably a better use of her time than sitting here.

Still, something rooted her to the floor. Some old, reflexive desire that had always bound her to these halls. Rose glanced up at the dark, arching ceilings, a shiver clinging to her spine. The comfort of the library had once been a steady surety in her life. Now, it wavered—providing her with refuge one day and wrenching it away the next.

It was almost strange now to think the place had held so much peace for her once. Most every memory was stained by sunshine that had never graced these aging halls but whose warmth still lingered on her skin. The library had been her one hope—the one place magic might have ever burgeoned inside her, even if only in the depths of her imagination.

Every argument with her mother, every failed spell, every cruel whisper—the library had always been her last haven. Yet even its solace had now faded. Like everything else, she supposed. Every ounce of comfort leeched away by a girl whose name was barely uttered anymore. Left to rot in the shadows. Rose faltered. Perhaps that would be her fate too.

Her throat tightened. It wasn't even Aveline's looming threat that frightened her now, but the inevitability of it. She stared at the desks before her, caught between shadow and warm flame. The last time the candles had flickered out, she'd been frozen by fear.

Now, she wasn't sure it would faze her. Even the thought of Aveline's fingers twisting around her throat sparked little more than a shudder. A cold weight that numbed her to the core. Once these walls had been her fortress—now they seemed more like a tomb.

Tears spilled down her cheeks, quiet sobs caught in her throat. In the silence of the library, it would be all too easy for someone to overhear. The thought soured. Ever respectful, never daring to cause a ruckus. Even into death, she would fade quietly.

Warmth bloomed in Rose's veins, a pulsing, prodding urge to do something—*anything*. But it faded quickly. What more could she do?

Nothing, in the end.

With a scoff, she pushed herself to her feet, wiping away her tears. Trudging off down the aisle, she was so lost in her own thoughts that she didn't pay much attention to how the shelves turned. It wasn't until she nearly ran into a glowing barrier that she glanced up, blinking in surprise.

A stone archway inlaid with shimmering crystals bore down upon her, monstrous stone guardians wrought on either side. *The Untold Section.* Her pulse quickened.

Most of the books within held terrible curses or were plagued by murderous tendencies, even if their contents were priceless and precious. A reminder that not all knowledge was innocent, Delia would say.

Rose peered in at the chained tomes, swallowing hard. The violet barrier pulsing before her was there as much to keep the books in as it was to keep students out. Usually, only professors or visiting scholars were allowed within its confines, and even then, only with the strictest limitations.

The energy quivering through the barrier made the hair on her arms stand on end. Low chanting echoed through the back of her mind—masked faces guarded by shadow and bone.

If this Order was as insidious as it seemed, perhaps she'd been looking for answers in the wrong place. And yet they somehow seemed even further out of her grasp. Even Delia wouldn't just let her waltz into the Untold Section. Not without good reason anyway.

With a sigh, she backed away from the barrier, nearly jumping out of her skin when she crashed into a solid form.

"Oh, I'm so sorry, I—" Rose gasped, straightening to find herself staring into a pair of familiar amber eyes.

It can't be.

"Sylvie?!"

13

INTO THE UNTOLD

FOR several heartbeats, the only thing Rose could do was stare. The silence of the library hung like a shroud around her, yet her heart slammed against her ribs, loud enough to wake the dead. Sylvie was *here.* Alive and well. And gazing down at her all too smugly.

Rose was vaguely aware, somewhere in the back of her mind, that her mouth had fallen agape, her bag slipping off her shoulder. Her shock couldn't have been more evident, and Sylvie seemed to revel in it, as her smirk only grew wider.

She looked exactly as she had that night in the pub. Sleek black hair twisted delicately over her dark turtleneck and a plaid skirt cinched around her slim waist. Even her lipstick was the same shade of rusty red. She really was perfectly fine. The thought echoed through Rose's mind with a kind of hollow disappointment.

It didn't make any sense. If she was alive and well, why miss class? Why was Ewan rifling through her things? Her heart thudded against her ribs. Why did Sylvie's piercing gaze haunt her visions?

Words tangled behind her lips, but none of them quite fitted. She gripped the strap of her satchel as though it were a lifeline, her nails biting into the leather. Sylvie, however, didn't seem at all fazed, inching closer like a spider to prey ensnared in its web.

"Sneaking around in the library after hours, Thenlif?" She raised a dark brow. "I didn't know you had it in you."

Rose almost scoffed. Even now, Sylvie couldn't resist a biting remark. Aimed to cut her down as surely as any shard of ice. But they weren't foolish first-years any longer, and this was no dueling ground. Her jaw tightened. Suddenly, she couldn't fathom why she had been concerned about Sylvie at all. "I wasn't sneaking." Her eyes darted to the shelves behind Sylvie and back again. "I was … researching. Anyway, what are *you* doing here?"

She folded her arms over her chest. "Studying. Obviously."

Rose frowned. Was that a joke? "For four days?"

"What are you talking about?"

"Y-you haven't been in class since—"

"What?" Sylvie cut across her with a firm shake of her head. "I would never miss class."

For a moment, the smallest sliver of vindication leaped in Rose's heart. But then it sank like a stone. An icy shiver crawled up her spine, and she took a step back, flinching when she nearly stepped into the barrier.

"Sylvie, no one has seen you since last week."

Finally, something other than smug satisfaction flickered across Sylvie's face. Her smirk slipped, and her eyebrows inched up her forehead. And there, in the depths of her warm, amber eyes, something strange festered—cold and harsh. *Fear.* It set Rose's heart racing.

"No." Her lips pressed thin. "That's not possible."

The icy grip of dread squeezed around Rose's heart, and her eyes danced over Sylvie's outfit once more. Though missing her signature houndstooth coat, it really was the exact same outfit that she'd worn in the pub the other night. And if she was missing time too, then …

Rose's breath caught in her throat. But it didn't make sense. Aveline's hauntings had begun with quiet whispers and fleeting shadows, not lively visions in the library. If they were alike, how could Sylvie still look so vibrant—so *real*?

She watched Rose shrewdly, but her eyes were still bright amber. Piercing and full of life. No dark veins carved their way across her tawny skin, no inky blood oozed from the corners of her mouth. It was as if she were a photograph—a perfect moment captured in ageless eternity. Forever unchanging, but somehow lifeless.

Rose's stomach churned, and she stumbled back, the barrier pulsing behind her. But Sylvie didn't close the distance between them. She didn't move at all, in fact. Not even as a lagging tome lumbered straight through the back of her head.

A gasp ripped through Rose's chest, but she remained rooted to the floor, the book missing her by mere inches. Flashes of blood flickered across her mind. Dark and thick—creeping between ancient stones, pooling from the back of Aveline's head. Her knees buckled as the girl's pale face crept forth from the shadows, hanging over Sylvie's shoulder.

"No!" The whisper fell numbly from her lips.

They were exactly alike, and now nothing stood between her and their vengeance.

"Thenlif?" Sylvie reached for her.

But her touch struck Rose like a blow. Images flashed behind her eyes—brutal and cruel. The shelves caught in the dark grip of shadows, one lone light snuffed out as the crack of bone shattered through the library. Aching, white-hot pain seared at the back of her head, warm blood trickling down the back of her neck as she pitched forward. And then only frozen, empty darkness as everything drifted away. Save for the soft echo of fading footsteps ...

Rose wrenched her arm away. "Get away from me!"

"What was that?" Sylvie recoiled with a gasp. "What did you do to me?"

"Nothing, I—" Her mouth went dry, the words like lead against her lips. "Someone attacked you. *Killed* you."

All the color drained from Sylvie's face. For a moment, Rose was struck by how young she looked—how innocent. Too young to greet death. A pang lanced through her heart, filling her with a sickly feeling, but she pushed it aside.

Silence fell over them as Sylvie stared at her. *"What?"*

"I-I found blood. Beneath our desk." Rose's voice shook. "That must have been where they struck you."

"No." Sylvie backed away from her. "No one attacked me. Look at me—I'm perfectly fine."

Rose's throat tightened, every breath tearing through her chest with an aching desperation. "I don't think you are."

Sylvie looked so fragile now, so fearful—as if the truth might shatter her. But then she straightened, her eyes fixing on Rose with a piercing ferocity. "I'm not dead, Thenlif." Her voice was thin, as if she couldn't quite convince herself. "I *can't* be."

"Sylvie, wait!"

But she didn't answer, shoving past her. Rose turned to follow, but collided instead with the violet barrier blocking her path. Her stomach sank as it pulsed brilliantly before the stone surrounding it cracked and the guardians came to life.

Shit.

14

NOT EVEN A SHADE

THE odd pop of the roaring fire was the only sound that dared break the silence held upon her mother's tongue. Tense and furious—poised like a blade about to strike. The dim light of her office cast ominous shadows upon her alabaster skin, her eyes dark and heavy with ire. Rose dropped her gaze, glancing over the glass of amber whiskey and the array of notes scattered upon the desk.

Her mother's hardened stare pierced her, like some old portrait that felt both too still and far too watchful. Better than the stone guardians outside the Untold Section, at least. Thankfully, they were only spelled to entrap students, not skewer them on the spot. The alarm system they'd set off still blinked furiously above her mother's desk, though Delia had managed to placate them, for the time being.

Yet, at the moment, facing them down seemed almost preferable to whatever might come out of her mother's mouth. Banishment from the library? Academic probation? None of the options were particularly appealing.

Still, better than death. The thought cut through her mind with startling acridity. Better than lost alone in the depths of the library, an echo of what she'd once been.

Finally, her mother leaned forward in her chair, the leather creaking with insidious intent. "The Untold Section?" Her voice was low and icy. A warning. "Really, Rosera. What were you even trying to do?"

"I was—" She faltered. The truth would not pacify her. But neither would lies now. "It was an accident."

She scoffed. "An accident? Did you somehow miss the guardian statues? Or did you just stumble through the barrier?"

Rose ducked her head. What would she say about Sylvie's ghost? Would she mock her—laugh it off? Or would her punishment be worse? As it was, she was a mere embarrassment to her mother. If she ever became an inconvenience …. Rose's throat tightened. Would she turn her over to the capital inquisitors?

No. Her mother tread always upon the cracked, fragile glass of rumor and reputation. She could not bear the weight of any threat. More likely, Rose would be shipped off to their family in the Outer Isles of Ir Taril, forgotten and left to rot. Still, after everything, that seemed somehow better than letting her deception bury her beneath her fear.

"I saw Sylvie's ghost."

The words fell from her like cold, hard lead. Not the whole truth, but enough of it. It hovered over her like a great weight, waiting to crush her at the slightest whim of her mother's words.

"*What?*" Her voice cracked. "That's impossible."

Rose's hands curled at her side. "No, it's true. She was in the library."

Her mother's alabaster skin somehow grew a shade paler. But her eyes remained fixed on Rose, their emerald hue lost in the dim light of the fire. After a moment, she eased herself over to one of the windows, staring off into the darkness.

"It was you, wasn't it?"

"What?"

"You didn't overhear any sightings of Aveline's ghost, did you?" Rose's mother still didn't turn, her voice strained but ever even. "It was you that saw her."

Rose's mouth went dry. How could she know that? "I—yes."

"I see." Rose's mother folded her hands behind her back. "And did you tell anyone else about this? Did anyone else see them?"

"Only Fen, and no—just me." Rose shook her head. "But there's blood, in the library, beneath where Sylvie always sits. I can show you."

It wasn't the hard proof her mother had asked for, but it was something. Still, the cruel voice of doubt crept into her mind. What did it matter if her mother couldn't see their ghosts? This would be just another all too frequent reminder of Rose's uselessness, if it came to nothing.

But her mother didn't scoff or laugh. She merely stood, frozen, at the window. Rose frowned, heart thrumming in her ears. If her mother was going to dismiss her story—tell her she'd imagined the whole thing, or some other nonsense to keep her in line—she didn't need to drag it out like this.

"Thank you for bringing this to my attention," she said finally. "I will look into it immediately."

Rose's heart leaped. She *believed* her. "Actually, Fen and I have already—"

"But you will stay here."

"What?"

Her mother raised a thin eyebrow as she turned. "Would you prefer to be banned from the library?"

Rose hung her head. "No."

"Then you will do as I say." Her mother sighed. "I'm not doing this to be cruel—necromancy is not to be trifled with. I don't know how you managed to stumble across it, but ghosts are dangerous, especially those belonging to powerful casters. If you had magic of your own to protect you ... well, it's far safer for me to get to the bottom of it."

Rose's jaw clenched. As if she didn't know that. But two students were missing—dead, likely. And their ghosts still prowled the campus. Not to mention whomever had attacked them. Yet still, her mother could not resist the urge to undermine her.

Before Rose could protest, her mother swept out of the room. She stood, rooted to the floor, for a moment. A part of her wanted to chase after her. To tell her everything Sylvie had said—to run the trace on her blood and prove she wasn't just seeing shadows in the dark.

But what would be the point? Her insolence would be paid for with her mother's wrath, and neither would leave her unscathed. Slowly, numbly, she left her mother's office, heading back to her dorm, as if her muscles had a mind of their own. Drawn to the inevitable conclusion, she supposed. As always, her mother would get her way.

And for what? Tears pricked at her eyes. To keep her out of danger? It wasn't like she had ever cared about that before.

Besides, Sylvie hadn't seemed dangerous. She'd seemed … frightened. Vulnerable, unsure, and alone. All things Rose had never expected to see in her—or ever would again, she supposed.

She drew to a sharp halt. There was something so hollowing about the thought that her heart skipped a beat. For all that Sylvie annoyed her, the idea of classes without her felt emptier somehow. The challenge would be gone, the victory less sweet. And the thought of Sylvie haunting her, slowly decaying into Aveline's gaunt form, chilled Rose to her very core.

She frowned. When had Sylvie become such an abyss in her life? Sucking in every effort, devouring every success. Yet now that Rose no longer stood at its edge, here she was, missing the very threat of the fall.

Perhaps that was just the nature of a rivalry like theirs. To think of each other with every second breath, until it became all but part of the very nature of breathing. Even if it was wrought in sour, acrid distaste.

Though, even in the deepest recesses of her heart, Rose had never held enough hatred for the woman to want her dead. Obnoxious as Sylvie was, she simply couldn't imagine that anyone would. Then again, it could've been an argument gone wrong. Some heated, entangled thing that had slipped out of Sylvie's control.

Her mind slid back to Ewan—to that fight erupting in the pub. It was the last time she was sure anyone saw Sylvie alive. But they'd seemed genuinely shocked by her absence, and by her notes. So, if not them, who?

Rubbing her brow, her satchel slipped from her shoulder. It dropped with a dull thud, flopping over with so little aplomb as its contents spilled all over the floor. Rose cursed, but stilled when her eyes caught on a small, toothy form.

Sylvie's hairbrush.

She'd nearly forgotten about it, and there was little point in testing it now, she supposed. But still, it was something. Some small piece that only she could put into place.

Well, she and Fen. If they could run the trace and prove the blood belonged to Sylvie, then perhaps it would settle this spark searing through her chest like dry kindling.

Chewing the inside of her lip, she reached for a stray piece of parchment, scribbling a hasty note.

Urgent: Meet me in our room. Bring the sample.

~Rose

She squinted at it, reading it over. It was legible, at least, if not elucidating. Rolling it up, she tied a small piece of twine around it and pushed up her sleeve. Her forearm tingled at the edges of her tattoo as Prea's form took shape, her ebony wings iridescent and glimmering in the moonlight.

The familiar clicked her beak, a soft gurgle, almost like a purr, rumbling through her throat. Giving her a scratch, Rose slipped the note onto her foot.

"Find Fen."

Prea blinked at her a moment before unfurling her wings and disappearing into the night. Rose leaned against the stone windowsill, sucking in a sharp breath. They would figure this out. Together.

The third-floor storage closet held a strange sort of comfort for Rose. Tucked far away from prying eyes and cluttered with a host of forgotten magical artifacts, it had always been the perfect place to hide away from her mother. When she was a child, she used to let the floating carpets carry her up to the rafters, to the lonely fortress she'd built for herself there.

But the same rugs laid listless now, their charms long faded and covered by a thick layer of dust. In the cool darkness that shrouded the space, the odd squeak of enchanted, mechanical mice and shuffling of charmed furniture held a sinister sort of promise. In the far corner of the looming shelves, a clock tap-danced ceaselessly, waiting to shriek at the turn of the hour.

Favored toys and curios of generations of spellcasters now lay abandoned in this cramped little room. Rose tugged at the ends of her sleeve. This place was a repository for discarded things—it was no small wonder that she had always felt at home among them.

She paced before the sole, lonely window, cast in the pale light of a clouded moon. But it didn't feel much like home anymore.

Nowhere did. Not with Aveline's threat hanging constantly in her shadow. And now Sylvie.

She shivered. The night air was cool against her skin, but it did little to calm her mind. She couldn't think about that. Once Fen was here, they could run the trace and finally have some answers. If he came at all.

The dancing clock ticked along, seconds melding into minutes as she paced. Surely he had better things to do with his evening than gathering dust with her in a storage closet and running a trace on mysterious blood. Hopefully, he hadn't roped himself into some soirée or romantic entanglement, though she doubted she'd get that lucky.

Rose's gaze drifted from the starless night to the cauldron tucked away in the corner of the room, surrounded by empty carafes of wine. It was here that she'd first met Fen, hiding away from their peers to conduct a particularly explosive experiment within a month of their first year. She'd bristled at the intrusion at first, but no one was immune to Fen's charms, not even her.

It had taken precious little time for them to fall into a shared rhythm within these walls, he with his alchemy and she with her books. It became a haven, a hideout—even a home. A place where they'd become friends, lovers, and everything in between. Now, Rose couldn't even think of it as anything but theirs.

Finally, a flutter of wings at the window stilled her pacing. Prea stared down at her, hopping along the ledge before she flew over and dropped a small note into Rose's outstretched palm. With a final purr, she dove and dissipated back into Rose's arm. She winced. The sensation never got any easier. Shaking it off, she unfurled the note.

On my way

    ~Fen

She peered at it closer, examining the red-stained lines of the script. Was that … lipstick? *Good gods*. She rolled her eyes, casting the note aside with a scoff.

Turning back to the window, she pushed it shut and finagled the rusted latch back into place. But a thick mist cloaked the glass like a strange curtain as she stepped back, hiding the moon behind its shade.

Then it shifted.

Rose's stomach lurched as eyes crept out of the haze. They were dull—glazed. Yet full of such malice that her knees buckled. With a great crack, the glass shattered, scattering around her.

Stumbling back, she shielded her face, but it was little use. Shards pierced her skin like tiny blades. Her breath caught in her throat. Strangled, as if Aveline was already sucking the life out of her. Rose straightened, trembling as the girl glided over broken glass, feet bloody, yet never touching the ground.

But she did not reach for her. She merely watched, her eyes clouded by death, her mouth twisted in fury.

And then she lunged.

Aveline's fingers clawed at her skin, shoving her to the ground, slicing through her flesh. A scream ripped from Rose's throat, but it was no use. Aveline was no longer content with killing her. She wanted to tear her apart.

Yet her hands stilled, as if some force held them back. Her features flickered, pale skin warming to tawny brown—blond hair now sleek and ink black. The spirit's grip loosened but her eyes still loomed, so close now that Rose could count the amber flecks within. Her heart leaped.

"Sylvie?"

"Rose!"

The voice hovered somewhere beyond her, as if miles away. Not Sylvie—*Fen*. And then the air around her tingled with a shock of magic, scents of red wine and worn leather engulfing her. Warm and soothing, a barrier wrapped around Rose with a peaceful lull, cutting through the ghost with a sharp shriek.

Fen's hands cupped around her face, pulling her back. "Are you all right?"

Blinking, Rose scrambled away from him. Shallow breaths ripped through her lungs, the chill of the stone walls falling numbly upon her unmarred skin. The window stood, whole and empty, the soft light of the moon stained in hues of blue and green. It was never real, but there was always a part of her that hoped it was. That some other soul might see Aveline—or Sylvie.

Her eyes slid to Fen, who knelt before her, his face unreadable. She raised an eyebrow at his tousled hair and slightly askew ascot, a fierce heat creeping across her cheeks. She was quite sure she didn't want to know what evening plans she'd interrupted.

The thought loosened the knot in her chest, however, and she eased back on her hands with a soft sigh. "Thank you."

But his eyes only darkened, lips pressed thin. "Was it Aveline again?"

She nodded slowly. "And Sylvie."

"*What?*"

"I-I saw her in the library. And just now, it was like she and Aveline had ... melded somehow."

Fen fell back on his heels, tears welling in his dark eyes. "*Dia vhal.* I know you weren't her biggest fan, but still."

Rose's throat tightened as he pulled his glasses off, dabbing his eyes. Some hint of sorrow, some stray musing of grief ebbed at her heart, but she refused to allow it to take hold.

If their roles were reversed, Sylvie wouldn't sit here weeping. She wouldn't miss the opportunity to find the killer herself and outcast them just to gain the adulation of their peers. Either that, or she'd congratulate them for offing Rose. Still, she wouldn't shed a tear.

Clearing her throat, Rose got to her feet and pulled a handkerchief from her vest pocket. Fen gave her a watery smile as she handed it to him, pulling him upright.

"It was strange," was all she managed, after a moment. "She seemed so ... normal."

"What do you mean?"

"Aveline is angry—brutal." She shrugged. "She always looks on the edge of death, but Sylvie looked exactly like she did at the pub. She didn't even know she was dead."

Fen dabbed his eyes carefully, so as not to disturb his eyeliner. "Odd. Do you think there's a chance others could see her too?"

Rose leaned heavily against the shelf behind her, swatting away a pair of charmed gloves that were trying to braid her hair. "I guess we'll find out. My mother has gone to investigate."

"You *told* her?"

"I got caught in the Untold Section, so I had to tell her *something*. I'm only surprised she believed me."

Fen was silent for a long moment. "And if she can't see Sylvie?"

"Then we'll need something else to convince her." Rose pushed away from the shelf. "Did you bring the sample?"

"Yeah." He fumbled to pull the amber vial out of his pocket. "Did you find something to test it against?"

"Will this work?" She whipped out the hairbrush.

He raised an eyebrow, pushing his glasses back into place. "Should do, yeah. Though I'm not going to ask how you got it."

"Probably for the best."

Fen peered at the hairbrush for a moment before turning for his alchemy set in the corner. Pulling on some gloves, he produced a pair of tweezers from his pocket and gingerly detangled a single strand from the brush with delicate precision. Twirling it around, he cast some muttered spell upon it before shoving it into the vial with the blood.

In spite of herself, Rose's shoulders loosened, and she eased into one of the cushions on the floor, which sighed heavily. There was some familiar rhythm about watching him cast that soothed her, the smell of red wine and worn leather tickling her nose.

It mingled with Sylvie's perfume, still lingering on Rose's skin. She breathed in deeply as the warm notes faded. She didn't suppose she'd ever smell it again. Swallowing hard, she shoved the thought aside. What did it matter?

"How long will it take?"

"Not much longer." Fen gave the vial a final shake. "If it's a match, it should glow blue. If not, it'll turn pink."

Another moment passed by, caught in bitter anticipation. Finally, the color shifted. Not to blue or pink, but to a vibrant shade of violet.

"What does *that* mean?"

Fen frowned at the vial. "That some of the blood belongs to Sylvie—but some belongs to someone else."

15

JUST THE OCCASION

THE scent of rain hung in the library like a fine mist, falling across floating books and hushed chatter. But Rose had no patience for any of it this morning, sluggishly ducking out of the path of a wayward tome as she paused at the threshold. Her mind had danced restlessly all night, flickering over bloodied stones and ghastly images of Sylvie's face vanishing into thin air. It nagged at her even now, worming its way between each thought.

Whose blood had been mixed in with hers? Who would've had the gall to attack her? She tugged at a wrinkle in her crumpled blazer. It wasn't as if they could go running the trace on everyone in Dunhollow. And the trace they already had only provided them with more questions.

It burned a hole in Rose's pocket now, wrapped in the folded missive she'd received from her mother this morning. Pulling the note free, she scanned it once again, though she knew nothing would've changed.

Rosera,

*I have found no evidence of your claims of ghosts in the library. As such, in punishment for your attempt to enter the Untold Section and falsely reporting evidence of necromancy, you will join me at the next board dinner. It will be held this Sanier evening in the assembly hall at eight o'clock sharp. Do **not** be late.*

Rose frowned at her signature, etched into the bottom of the page. Her mother hadn't even bothered with a salutation. A rush of heat coursed through her veins.

Three days, and this was all she had to say? There wasn't a single part of her mother that doubted her conclusions, that thought for a moment there might be something more. *Typical.* Rose's pride might swallow her, but her mother's could drown the whole empire. She certainly couldn't be trusted with the results of Fen's trace.

Rose glared up at the looming halls of the library. She should've known her mother would find nothing. But Sylvie had felt different than Aveline, somehow. She *had* to be there—her blood proved this wasn't just a figment of Rose's mind. Her mother must have missed something. Or had chosen not to see it.

Some furious energy burgeoned deep within Rose's chest, pushing her forward up the steps, even as doubt crept into her mind. What if her mother *was* right? Or what if Delia barred her from entering after her stunt with the Untold Section?

She faltered. There would be no easy answer for Aveline, Sylvie—any of it. This place guarded its secrets well. She would either have to seek them herself, draw them out like poison from a wound, or else let this ravenous current swallow her up and slip away into the darkness beneath. Clenching her jaw, she straightened and marched up the final step.

A wave of cool air washed over her, an earthy scent of ancient stones and aged books that covered just the faintest hint of must. Rose breathed in deeply, glaring up at the shelves ahead.

For once, luck was on her side, as Delia was occupied breaking up some rowdy first-years when she entered. Ducking past the front desk, Rose snuck over to her studying nook. But there, with the bookshelves towering over her and the table spread out bare before her, any sense of purpose fled her mind.

The blood was gone. Bare stone stared back at her—worn by age, but without even the slightest trace of crimson pooled between its crevices. Her heart flipped. How was that possible? The only other person who'd been here was … her mother.

A sharp breath escaped her. Almost a laugh, but darker and dry as kindling. Was she really so brazen to have just cleaned it away? The thought rang through Rose's mind with a hollow sort of shock, and she shook her head. Of course she was.

She could have covered up anything. Sylvie's ghost, her disappearance—even Aveline and this Order. Perhaps she *had* found Sylvie's ghost last night and simply banished it without a second thought. A snared thread of dread twisted around Rose's heart. She should never have trusted her.

"Sylvie?" Her voice trembled pitifully, and shame burned deep in her gut. Clearing her throat, she tried again. "Are you here?"

Silence hung on the air for several long moments like a pulsing heartbeat. But her only answer was the soft flutter of pages from somewhere overhead. The familiar sting of disappointment burrowed beneath Rose's skin. She could hardly help the sigh that pushed past her lips, nor the whisper that followed it.

"Please, just come out."

She turned, heart leaping as the air shifted behind her. But it wasn't Sylvie. Milk-white eyes stared back at her, dark veins etched across pale skin. Aveline was so close now that Rose could smell the rot on her. The foul scent of decay—of death.

"What do you want?"

Rose's murmur was more of a curse. Some desperate plea for surety where none existed. Dark blood oozed from Aveline's mouth, pouring down her throat as a rasping whisper crawled out.

"*Run.*"

Rose flinched, but she couldn't move. Couldn't flee. Couldn't *breathe*. The shelves and arched windows faded. Instead, haunting masked faces stared down at her, their chanting reverberating off looming trees. The pale glow of the moon was her only light, and it too snuffed out as she was left alone in grating silence.

Short, shallow breaths burned in her chest, tears pricking at her eyes. Slowly, she reached out a trembling hand. Damp, mossy stones brushed beneath her fingers, cool and slick to the touch. The keen scent of metal hung on the air, but there was no source for it. No sound. No sight. Only darkness.

And then a whisper. A slight shuffling of pages. Rose's mouth went dry, her mind screaming at her to flee. But there was nowhere to go. Slowly, she turned, and a gasp ripped through her chest.

It was like looking into a mirror. A sallow reflection of the library she knew and loved caught behind a marred, swirling pane. Her own hazel eyes stared back at her, clouded and blank, as if no soul remained within them. Aveline stood over her kneeling form, her bloated, decrepit fingers cupping Rose's chin gently. A sickening smile spread wide upon her flaking, stained lips as she leaned down and pressed them soundly to Rose's.

"No!"

The world narrowed around Rose, her heart scrambling against her ribs like a caged bird. Some wisp of shadow slipped out of her mouth as Aveline pulled back, like a tether bound between them. Her soul? Her spirit? Or perhaps just her life, finally clawed away from her with so little resistance.

Rose's pulse hammered in her ears as she slammed her hand against the pane between them. She had to get back. She *had* to. But her fists pounded uselessly against the glass, her cries falling silently into the abyss of this void that held her.

She fell still, letting the cold shadows caress her as her head spun and her vision blurred. Until warm fingers laced around hers, wrenching her away from the shadow's grasp. The sting of shattering glass rang in her ears, a fading shriek hanging on the air. And then nothing.

Rose sucked in desperate breaths, her knees aching against hard stones. She hardly trusted her own eyes enough to believe it when the shadows receded, and she was left alone in the silence of the library. *No.* Not alone.

Amber eyes bore into hers. Bright and burning—warm and so *real*. Sylvie's chest heaved, and her gaze darted to the looming ceilings. She still wore the same dark turtleneck and plaid skirt, not a hair out of place. Rose wondered briefly, wildly, if the notes of orchid and musk still clung to her skin. But she pushed the thought away, swallowing hard.

Scrambling back, she tried to still her pounding heart. "Get away from me!"

But Sylvie didn't even look at her, staring instead at the empty space Aveline had left behind. "What in the name of The Nine was that?"

The sound of her voice made Rose jump. Breathless and scathing, it sent a jolt right through her core. But Rose could only blink at her, words spinning through her muddled mind. It was as if her thoughts were swimming through thick molasses, slow and sluggish as they creaked into place.

"Wait, could you *see* her?"

"Who?"

"Aveline."

Sylvie's eyes widened. "*That's* who that was?"

Rose grimaced, slowly pushing herself to her feet. She didn't trust herself to answer, her nerves too frayed—her wounds too raw. Instead, she turned away, tilting her head toward the shadowed ceiling to keep her tears from falling. Mercifully, Sylvie didn't speak for a long moment, and when she did, her voice was soft—gentle.

"That's why you screamed in class." It wasn't a question, just a simple fact. "You've been seeing her this whole time?"

Wordlessly, Rose nodded.

"How long?"

Rose faltered, measuring her words carefully. She wasn't sure why—no matter what she said, Sylvie was bound to find some fault in it. But lies had flowed from her tongue so naturally these past few months that the truth now seemed foreign to her. Strange, and all too difficult to wrap her tongue around.

With a sigh, Rose finally met her gaze. "Since the start of summer break."

Sylvie's eyebrows shot up her forehead. "That was *months* ago, Thenlif. Why didn't you say anything?"

"Because no one would've believed me," she snapped. "Even if they had, they would've turned me over to the capital inquisitors or a mentalist somewhere remote and far from Dunhollow."

"Please." Sylvie crossed her arms. "Like your mother would've allowed that."

Rose bristled under her sharp gaze. Sylvie really thought Rose's mother would protect her? At this rate, she'd probably feed her to the wolves herself.

"Oh, I tried telling her, don't worry," she scoffed. "She wasn't interested. Ghosts are such an inconvenience, you see. Easier all around to dismiss you and Aveline as two gruesome figments of my imagination instead." Her voice grew soft—tenuous. "And maybe she's right."

A soft sigh escaped Rose. Perhaps there was no necromancy or curse hanging over her. Perhaps Sylvie was nothing more than a product of her guilty conscience, strengthened only by the fleeting proof that she'd been harmed somehow. It would explain why she seemed stronger—more alive.

For all their mutual detestation, Rose knew Sylvie in and out. Enough at least to imagine what she'd say in most situations—her obnoxious tenacity and general air of disdain. Which was more than Rose could say of Aveline.

But Sylvie's eyes darkened, and she took a step closer. "I'm nothing like her. That was—"

"Hideous? Monstrous?" Rose's throat tightened under the threat of fresh tears. "I've seen worse."

"What is that supposed to mean?"

"Nothing you want to know."

That much was true, at least. Aveline might well be a glimpse into Sylvie's future, but even Rose wouldn't wish that upon her. Despite the dark furrow of her brow and the harsh tilt of her lips, the concern that filled Sylvie's eyes in Aveline's shadow had been genuine.

Twice now she'd protected Rose, even against all logic. It was, perhaps, that simple fact that almost convinced her Sylvie really was there. And which kept the awful truth from falling from her lips.

A thick silence crept between them before Sylvie sighed. "So, what now?"

"What?"

"I assume you came here for a reason, Thenlif." She leaned against a nearby table. "To gloat? Or dance over my grave, perhaps? Sorry to disappoint, but I seem to be missing a body."

"What? No, I—" Rose faltered. Her thirst for knowledge had led her this far, but she honestly hadn't thought much past it. What *had* she been expecting? "I was looking for you."

"Why?"

"To prove that you're real. That you're not just in my head."

128

For a long beat of silence, Sylvie said nothing. And then, to Rose's great surprise, she laughed. Gentle, yet hollow, it burst from her lips like a melody played off-key.

"You know, it figures that it would be you."

"Pardon?"

"Of all the people to be stuck with." Her laughter didn't meet her eyes, which pierced Rose like a blade. "The Nine must have a sense of humor."

The Nine? Rose frowned. She hadn't realized Sylvie was religious. Gods and spirits were such a relic of the past that it was rare to hear them invoked within these halls anymore. But her words bristled beneath Rose's skin.

"Trust me, I don't like it either," she snapped. "This all would have been so much easier if you and Aveline had just—"

"What, stayed dead?" The laughter slipped from Sylvie's lips. "Sorry we've been such an inconvenience for you."

"That's not what I meant."

But it was. Rose's heart skipped a beat. Even if she wouldn't have said it in so many words, there was a part of her that still longed for it.

"And what if we're not dead?" Sylvie leaned back, her skirt sliding up her thigh as she crossed her legs.

"What?"

"You said someone attacked me, but where's my body? Where's your proof?"

Rose folded her arms over her chest. Now Sylvie sounded like her mother. "I'd say the fact that we're having this conversation is pretty strong evidence."

"Is it? Then why can only you see me?" she asked, giving voice to the doubt already lurking in Rose's mind. "I may not be as well read as you, Thenlif, but even I know that, when ghosts are summoned, usually everyone can see them, not just one person."

She was right, of course, though Rose would never admit it. Sure, it was possible she wasn't dead, she supposed. In the same way it was possible that Rose might one day cast. But it was equally unlikely.

Still, it left Rose at the same crossroads she kept coming back to. Either she truly was unraveling, or there was a necromancer prowling the corridors of Dunhollow, and only she had noticed. Though if someone wanted to get rid of Sylvie, why curse her soul to wander? Or Aveline, for that matter.

Rose winced as the crunching of bone echoed through her memory. If Sylvie wasn't dead, then how had her blood wound up staining these very stones? Why did Aveline appear to her as a bloated, decaying corpse? The fleeting hope bound up in Sylvie's words dwindled with each thought.

"Maybe." Reaching into her bag, she pulled Sylvie's journal from its depths and set it on the table beside her. "But I wouldn't count on it."

Sylvie stared at it, her hand falling lightly upon it. Rose frowned. Strange how she could touch some things, while others slipped right through her.

"Where did you find this?" Her voice was low—hollow.

Rose ducked her head. "In a pool of your blood. Right underneath this table."

"My blood?" Her hand shook as she reached for the journal. "Did you read it?"

Her head snapped up. "I'd say you have bigger problems right now than whether I read your diary, don't you think?"

Truthfully, the thought had never entered her mind. Even when digging through Sylvie's bedroom, she'd not once considered cracking it open. As if some secret, broken piece of Sylvie might have still lingered between the pages, marking a boundary she would not cross.

Sylvie conceded the point with a roll of her eyes. "And you're sure it was mine?"

"The blood?" Rose nodded. "Yours and someone else's. Fen and I ran a trace."

"Someone else's—like the person who attacked me?"

"One assumes, yeah."

"Oh."

Her voice sounded almost pitiful now. Barely breaking a whisper, it held such defeat in a single syllable that Rose's heart cracked.

"Look, I don't know who did this to you, but"—the words stuck to her lips like a bur—"but I could help you find out."

Sylvie stared at her as if she'd sprouted a second head. To be honest, even Rose couldn't fathom what had possessed her to make such an offer. But now it lay between them like a challenge, waiting for one of them to pick it up.

"*You* want to help *me*?"

"Want has nothing to do with it." Rose shrugged. "But I need to know why this is happening to me, and the best way to do that is to start with what happened to you. And Aveline."

Whether it was a curse or they really were dead, she had to know. *Why* it happened. Why them—why *her*? And how to make it all stop.

"And how do you propose we do that?"

Rose eyed her for a moment, as if she were a skittish, feral animal. The last time they'd gotten to this point, she had fled, after all. But Sylvie didn't even flinch now, leaning in toward Rose like she'd tossed her a lifeline. Perhaps she had.

"I suppose we could start with what you remember. What happened after you left the pub?"

"I don't know." Sylvie let out a long sigh. "I was … angry, I think."

"Because of your argument with Ewan?"

"What argument?"

"*The* argument," she prompted, but Sylvie only stared at her blankly. "You two broke up over it."

"We broke up? Why?"

"That's what I was hoping you could tell me."

Sylvie shook her head, and Rose's jaw tightened. At this point, the only fruitful thing she'd gotten out of her thus far was a headache, and that might end up proving better company.

Rubbing her brow, Rose sighed deeply. She doubted Ewan was responsible for Sylvie's disappearance, or else why go searching for her? But they could still be involved. They *had* seemed spooked by that note in Sylvie's room, after all. A piece of this puzzle that still didn't fit.

Rose glanced about at the looming shelves. A mysterious Order with naught a record to be found in these vast halls? It sounded like exactly the type of place one might find stray curses and illicit dabblings in necromancy. And it was a better explanation than her imagining the whole thing.

"Could it have been about the Order of Salix?"

Sylvie's eyes widened. "Where did you hear about that?"

"There was a note in your room."

"You went in my room?"

Rose's cheeks flushed. "You missed class. I thought you might be— well, I just wanted to figure out what happened."

"I'm flattered."

"Did it have to do with this Order or not?"

"What part of 'I don't remember' isn't clicking for you, Thenlif?" Her tone was dry as sand. "I'd say ask Ewan, but I doubt they'll talk to you."

Rose's heart sank. She wasn't wrong. They hadn't exactly been forthcoming before, and tracking them down didn't sound like an exciting use of her weekend. But then, her weekend was already doomed. Rose chewed the inside of her lip, mind flickering back to her mother's note.

"Maybe not," she said finally. "But I might have just the occasion."

16

A MATCH OF WITS

LEAFY vines hung low from the overgrown ceiling, tickling Rose's nose as she frowned at her bed. Three gowns lay splayed innocently across her sheets, sent by her mother for that night's board dinner. But Rose only glared at them.

One was a rich emerald, laced with glimmering, golden leaves that echoed those falling outside as they pooled around the great train. The second was a deep sapphire, trimmed with silver stars that shone across the fabric, almost as if the night sky had been captured upon it. The last was almost somewhat plain in comparison—a muted rusty red with autumn leaves mapped along its skirt. Unlike the first, however, these leaves lay still, twisting only as she moved the fabric.

They were gorgeous, of course, but spending the entire night dodging board members while dressed in a gown her mother had picked out sounded like just about the worst thing in the world. Especially a gown cast with more magic than Rose herself would ever possess.

"Are you planning on getting dressed sometime tonight, Thenlif?" Sylvie's voice grated at her ears. "Or were you thinking of attending the gala in the nude?"

Rose glared at her as she eased back in her desk chair with a sly smirk. She took it back; spending the evening trapped with Sylvie was infinitely worse. True to her word, she'd hardly left Rose's side this last week, following her around like a sharp-tongued shadow.

Every so often, Sylvie went off on her own, chasing after other students, trying to talk to them—but none of it had worked. Rose's scowl deepened as Sylvie prodded idly at one of the plants on her desk. For whatever cruelly ironic reason, it seemed Rose really was the only one who could see her, as if some stray spell had bound and cursed them. Worse yet, she could *hear* her.

Her voice was sweet enough, she supposed. It always had been. Smooth and rich, like honey, but hiding a sting beneath. Nothing like dark whispers shrouded in reflections. Rose shivered, Aveline's shrieks piercing her mind.

Why were they so different? She tugged at the end of her curling ties. Looking at Sylvie, she could almost believe she was still alive. Her tawny skin was warm with the flush of life, her amber eyes still bright and alert. So far from Aveline's sallow cheeks and sunken, milky eyes. They *had* to be connected somehow. But then, what had changed?

With a sigh, Rose folded her arms over her chest. "I suppose you have an opinion? You always do."

Sylvie leaned forward, dark eyes dancing. Her ebony nails clacked against the chair's wooden frame, long and thin. More like claws, really.

"You should go with the blue one." She jutted her chin toward the bed. "You wear green so often that it's almost mundane now."

Rose scowled. She didn't wear green *that* often. Besides, how anyone could call a dress like that mundane was beyond her. Though Sylvie always had thought herself an authority on absolutely everything.

"Are you sure you can't haunt anyone else?" Rose tugged at the ends of her hair. "I'm sure half the school would love to get your unsolicited fashion advice."

"Then consider yourself lucky, Thenlif."

"That's one word for it."

"Anyway, the red dress will clash horribly with your hair." Her eyes narrowed. "And your skin tone, to be honest. You'll look washed out and pale as—"

"A ghost?" Rose muttered.

The glare Sylvie shot her could have cut through stone. "Which leaves the sapphire one. It matches your undertones and will catch people's attention."

Rose squirmed under her gaze. Somehow, she felt almost exposed, standing there in her nightgown and curlers while Sylvie waxed on about her undertones. Likely, she assumed she was being helpful, but every word out of her mouth sounded like she was talking to a small child who'd gotten into their parents' makeup for the first time.

"Isn't the point not to draw attention?" Rose asked. "We just need to suffer through enough of the idle chatter to talk to Ewan and get out."

Not that she trusted they would talk to her. But the gala gave her a decent enough reason to approach them, at least. Though it seemed like a ridiculous idea now.

"You're the one who wanted to go to this thing."

" 'Want' is a strong word." The words popped out before Rose had thought them through.

Her stomach sank. She'd so far managed to skirt around the fact that attending the gala wasn't by choice. The last person who needed to know of the intricacies of her relationship with her mother was Sylvie.

She eyed Rose oddly, as if she were some volatile potion with a missing ingredient. "You know the best way to avoid idle chatter?"

"I'm sure you're about to tell me."

"Look like you belong. Or better yet, outdress everyone. It makes people scared to talk to you."

"You sound like my mother."

Sylvie raised a sculpted eyebrow. "And why do you think it is that no one stands up to her?"

Because fear was a powerful tool. Rose's mother embodied that truth well enough, but it wasn't the weapon for Rose. The very idea of all those eyes on her made her skin crawl. Jaw tightening, she turned away from Sylvie.

"I'm not my mother." Her lip curled. "And you'll have to excuse me if lessons on how to go unseen seem like rather cheap advice from a ghost."

Sylvie shrank back. "We don't know for sure that I'm dead."

"Then what, Sylvie?" Rose snapped. "Surely you must have some other idea, or did you just drag me into this in the hopes of fueling your own denial?"

Sylvie recoiled, pain flickering across her face. "For a moment there, you sounded *exactly* like your mother."

Rose blinked, a sinking feeling plummeting through her chest. She had, hadn't she? A tremor ran across her skin, her stomach turning. But Sylvie only watched her with thinly veiled disdain.

"Wear whatever you want then, Thenlif." Sylvie turned away from her. "I'm sure your mother will be proud either way."

The din of the assembly hall pulsed in Rose's ears like a heartbeat. Tucked just behind the main hall, it was slightly smaller and just that little bit less grand. Though pretension still hung within its aged wooden walls like a choking perfume. An enchanted orchestra played softly at the edges of the dance floor, instruments floating in a gentle melody beneath invisible hands. Dancers twirled under their spell, faces hidden behind beautiful lace masks. All terrible, opulent, and entirely unnecessary.

Rose took a sip of wine. The crystal chalice dangling between her fingers was warm to the touch, but the sparkling white within was icy cold. Magic lingered all around her, touching everything in its path and choking the air with petrichor. From the illusory autumn scenes cast upon the walls to the many patrons smoothing out their conversations with charms and incantations, she could hardly bear the stench any longer.

Her mother certainly knew how to torment her, though at least she'd had the decency not to stop by and sneer at her discomfort. She was far too busy breezing through her guests, her dark hair spun up in an elaborate updo and an emerald gown hugging her figure. Rose wrinkled her nose, pulling her wineglass tighter. Suddenly, she couldn't be more thrilled to have picked the sapphire gown.

"Nice dress," a sly voice whispered in her ear. *Sylvie.* "I have always liked you in blue."

Heat flared across Rose's cheeks, and she turned as the woman eyed her up and down, looking far too smug for her own good. She was toying with her now.

"Thank you." She forced a wan smile. "I'm afraid you're a bit under-dressed, though."

Sylvie's grin faltered. For once, she looked so out of place. Elegant, as always, but lacking the opulence that surrounded her. Still, she held herself with such an air of pretension that Rose wondered if she'd ever in her life felt as if she didn't belong.

Yet when she met Sylvie's gaze, it wasn't arrogance or snide judg-ment that hung there, but hunger. It flashed through her eyes, bright and fierce, and just as fleeting. But then it darkened, and Sylvie tucked a lock of her gossamer hair behind her ear with a scoff.

"Yes, well, my options were limited on such short notice." She sniffed. "How's the wine?"

"Not terrible. Shall I grab you a glass?"

"Hilarious, Thenlif." She rolled her eyes.

Rose blanched. Sylvie had never conceded one of their repartees so easily before. The thought soured at the back of her mind and her lips tightened.

"How's that work anyway?"

"How's what work?"

"*This.*" Rose waved her hand over Sylvie, then caught herself and balled it in a fist at her side. "You can walk through walls, but you can also sit in a chair. You can't drink wine, but you can pick things up?"

Sylvie shrugged. "How should I know? I haven't been hungry or thirsty since I … woke up. Or even tired. As for the rest of it, it de-pends, I suppose."

"On?"

"I don't know." She gave a bored sigh, wrapping her fingers around Rose's glass, who flinched as their fingers brushed. "If I want to touch something, I can. If I want to pass through something, I do. I hadn't really thought much about it."

Rose pulled her glass away. "Can you touch other people?"

"Doesn't seem like it."

"But you can touch me, clearly."

A slow smirk pulled at Sylvie's lips as she leaned in close. *Too close.* "Why, have something particular in mind, Thenlif?"

In spite of everything, Rose's heart skipped a beat, fluttering use-lessly against her ribs. *Wretched thing.* She swallowed a gag, backing away. This was *Sylvie*, after all. And she wasn't some moon-eyed first-year. Straightening her shoulders, she fixed Sylvie with the most scathing glare she could muster.

"Ugh." She rolled her eyes. "Can't you go bother someone else? Or better yet, make yourself useful and spy on Ewan."

"I tried, but they're not talking to anyone."

Rose's gaze darted across the dancing figures, none of whom seemed to take any notice of her. Her eyes caught on a dark figure lurking in the corner, and a shiver skittered across her skin. *Aveline.* Her breath shortened as she backed into Sylvie. But then the form stepped into the soft glow of the sparkling candles.

Warm brown skin and gold-streaked black hair shone bright, and Rose's chest loosened. It was just Ewan.

"Thenlif?" Sylvie grabbed her shoulder gently.

"I'm fine." She yanked her arm away, eyeing a few drunken attendees who stumbled past them. "And how do you expect me to talk to anyone with you whispering in my ear all night?"

Sylvie's gaze darkened, any compassion within falling flat. "I'm not a rowdy child. You'll barely even know I'm here."

"Somehow I doubt that," Rose muttered into her wine.

"Messere Thenlif," a flat baritone voice crept over her shoulder, nearly sending the wine up her nose. "How surprising to see you here."

Wincing as she forced a swallow, Rose turned to meet a pair of piercing gray eyes that sent her heart tumbling into her stomach. Imrys Elaegius—Ewan's father, and more dangerous by a league. Tall and broad, he swathed himself in shimmering robes of onyx and ruby, carrying himself as if the world were meant to bow beneath him. His face was intriguing, if not conventionally attractive, all sharp angles and thin features. Almost as if he was born looking harsh and shrewd.

He had few wrinkles, and his pale olive skin was nearly flawless in a way that pricked at Rose's unease. As if the face staring down at her wasn't quite real, though her eyes couldn't find purchase in the facade to determine why. A glamour, she assumed.

The only thing it couldn't cover was the way his mouth pinched around the corners, same as her mother's. Some natural consequence of their mutual inability to ever say what they truly meant, perhaps.

"Good evening, Messere Elaegius." Rose ducked her head.

Her heart stumbled. She couldn't recall the last time he'd spoken to her—though it was never a pleasant experience. Usually, it was just idle chatter, a wry comment here or there to rile her mother. But tonight, his eyes gleamed with a purpose she could not fathom.

"What does he want?" Sylvie growled.

How was she to know? Rose fought to keep her face even, resisting the urge to shoot Sylvie a sharp glance. Imrys's gaze felt keen enough to catch any imperfection, even beneath her mask. Did he know she was here for Ewan? Her mouth went dry. How could he?

"I heard your paper on pre-Calamity magical systems was nominated for publication in the *Journal of Arcane Arts* last spring." His lips spread in a slow smile. "I must admit, I find the subject fascinating."

Rose blinked at him. *That's* what he wanted to talk about?

"Quite the accomplishment too, for a second-year." His eyes flickered over her shoulder. "Your mother must have been so proud."

She followed his gaze across the hall, the fluttering in her stomach turning to cold, hard dread. *Oh.* Her mother's gaze had fixed on the pair of them as if she could tear through them by will alone. *Of course.* He didn't care about her, or her paper. This was all a game to him. Some unspoken match of wits he'd entered into with her mother. And she was merely a pawn on the board.

In that moment, she could almost see his hand behind Sylvie's disappearance. Not in any tangible way, of course. Rather as if he had set all the pieces in place—the mind in the shadows that moved them all at his whim.

But why?

Two missing students was enough to tarnish her mother's reputation. Perhaps even remove her from her post. Was he really that petty, or was he playing at something even more sinister? Something like necromancy, perhaps? After all, if Ewan had connections to this Order and whatever secrets it held, she could almost be sure it was through their father.

Rose's cheeks heated, pulse pounding in her ears. Soon, her mother would come over to trade veiled barbs, drawn right into Imrys's trap. Their blades never quite reached each other, but Rose would be cornered in the treacherous space between them with no easy escape.

Perhaps Sylvie had been the same. Caught between forces even she wasn't powerful enough to fend off. And now they might both pay the price.

She jumped then when a hand curled around the small of her back. "Rose, darling." Fen swept in to kiss her cheek. "There you are. You look gorgeous."

Rich scents of caraway and cedarwood pressed against her nose, and she breathed in deeply, the knot in her chest loosening. He grinned down at her from underneath a crimson lace mask, a gilded goblet dangling between his manicured fingers. Dressed impeccably in a fine burgundy vest and jacket, he looked so at ease that even the likes of Imrys Elaegius could not cow him.

"'Darling'?" Sylvie snorted behind her. "How sweet."

"Shut up," Rose muttered under her breath, heat creeping up her neck.

"Messere Hathorin." Imrys nodded politely.

A feigned smile pulled at Fen's lips. "Imrys, how are you? It's been far too long since we've seen you at the villa. My mothers said you've been wrapped up in some sordid taxation bill in the capital? Dreadful."

"Quite." Imrys's lips twitched. "If you'll excuse me."

Fen beamed. "Of course. I'll tell my mothers you'll write them soon?"

Imrys gave a terse nod before gliding off. Fen's smile dropped, and he rolled his shoulders before taking a long sip of his wine.

"Dia vhal." He shuddered. "That man could give ice a cold."

In spite of herself, Rose managed a weak chuckle. "You know him well?"

"He and my mothers run in the same circles, though they're not close. I'm not sure anyone is with him."

That figured. She rubbed a hand over her arm, all her hair standing on end, as if warning her of some unseen danger. "Well, thanks for getting rid of him. What are you doing here anyway?"

"I go to every board dinner." He shrugged. "My mothers have me attend in their stead."

"And mine just lets you wander around?"

"She has more important guests to worry about, I suppose. And I never cause too much trouble."

"I doubt that," Sylvie scoffed behind her.

"Anyway, I'm far more interested in why *you're* here." He raised a dark eyebrow. "Doesn't exactly seem like your scene."

"I was forced." The gems of her dress bit into her skin as she folded her arms over her chest. Her eyes flickered to Sylvie before she lowered her voice. "My mother's idea of punishment for entering the Untold Section."

Rose was almost grateful for her mask now, for Fen's eyes nearly burned through the fabric. "Punishment?" He spat the word out as if it had a foul taste. "For an accident?"

"For wasting her time, I'm sure."

"*Dia vhal,*" he muttered darkly. "And you still don't want to tell her about the trace? It might change her mind."

Sylvie circled to Fen's side, brow creased. "Wait, you didn't tell your mother the blood was mine?"

Rose cringed. Another thing she'd neglected to mention. But Sylvie's anger would have to wait.

"Or she would just bury it. Even if she did investigate, she'd still shut us all out."

"All?" Fen's gaze bore into hers, dark and piercing. "What do you mean?"

Shit. Rose's heart flipped. She had to tell him about Sylvie eventually, but some unspoken, reflexive part of her mind still faltered. Held in fear and hardly daring to speak.

Aveline was like a force of nature, fierce and furious, desperately clawing her way back to life. But she was also fleeting. There and gone, leaving the truth hanging in her wake for her and Fen to piece together.

Sylvie, though, was a fixed constant. There could be nothing spoken between Rose and Fen that she wouldn't pick apart. Secrets and depths that she could use to unravel Rose entirely.

"Wait," Fen's dark eyes darted across the air around her. "Sylvie's not … is she *here?*"

Rose grimaced. Some days she wished he couldn't read her quite so well. Taking his arm, she pulled him away from the dance floor, ducking into a dark corner. Sylvie followed closely behind them, for once keeping blessedly quiet.

Pressing her lips thin as a few guests passed them by, Rose turned back to Fen. "Yes, she's here."

He pulled off his mask, running a hand through his dark hair. "*Dia vhal.* How?"

"I went back to the library to find her, and now she won't leave me alone."

"That's quite the interpretation of events, Thenlif," said Sylvie.

"And you can talk to her? I mean, she's not … violent?"

Like Aveline, the words echoed in Rose's mind, though he had no need to say them. "Annoying. But no, not violent."

"Charming," Sylvie shook her head.

Fen pressed at the bridge of his nose, almost as if he'd forgotten he wasn't wearing his glasses. "So, she can see us?"

"Yes."

"And hear us?"

"Every word." Sylvie sighed deeply.

"*Yes*, Fen," said Rose. "Why?"

"Prove that it's really you then, Sylvie." He jutted his chin at the empty space over Rose's left shoulder. "Tell Rose something only you and I would know."

Rose scoffed. "What could she possibly tell you? You two rarely talk."

"Talk, no." Sylvie hummed beside her. "But we got to know each other *very* well after last year's Wintermas festival. Ask him if that's proof enough."

Rose stared at her in abject horror, her heart thudding dully in her ears. Fen and Sylvie. Fen and *Sylvie*. Heat flared across her cheeks. That traitorous bastard.

"You *slept* with Sylvie?"

All the color drained from Fen's face. "*Dia vhal*. It really is her."

"How sweet," Sylvie cooed. "He remembers."

Rose swallowed a string of curses, fingers tightening around her wineglass. "Yes, she's here, gloating over seducing you."

Fen licked his lips, throat bobbing. "I-it wasn't like that. It was only a one-time thing—I promise."

"Oh, that's hardly fair. I seem to recall it being more than a few rounds."

Rose nearly gagged. "One more word, Sylvie, and I'll gladly leave you as a ghost for all eternity."

"What did she say?" Fen's brow furrowed.

"Far more than I ever needed to know."

His cheeks flushed deeply, and he shoved his mask back into place. It was strange to see him so flustered, like watching a rare comet shoot across the night sky. Though this was hardly as graceful.

After a moment, he cleared his throat. "Well, was she able to shed any light on her—er—situation?"

"No." Rose shot a sharp glance at Sylvie. "Unfortunately for me, she doesn't remember that nearly as well as she remembers the two of you."

"How awful for you, Thenlif." Sylvie rolled her eyes. "Now, if you two are done talking about me like I'm not here, might we get back to Ewan?"

Rose squirmed under her gaze. "Sorry."

"What's she saying?"

"That she'd like us to stop talking about her like she isn't there."

"Well, to me, she isn't." He fidgeted with his mask. "No offense, Sylvie."

"Some taken."

Rose stepped between them. "Actually, Fen, you might be able to help."

His eyes narrowed. "How?"

"We need to talk to Ewan, and I'm guessing they'll be more amenable to you than me." Rose grimaced. More than likely, they wouldn't even speak to her. But Fen could get anyone to talk.

"Ewan?" He frowned. "What do they have to do with any of this?"

"I found a note in Sylvie's room about something called the Order of Salix. Sylvie doesn't remember much, but she's fairly certain Ewan would know more. She thinks it may have something to do with her de—er—disappearance."

"Salix? Never heard of it."

"Nor have I. Which is why we're here."

Fen's eyes slid over her shoulder. "Well, don't look now, but your reason for being here is leaving with their father."

Rose followed his gaze across the dance floor, where Ewan was being dragged away by Imrys. *Wonderful.*

This hardly seemed to deter Sylvie, though, as she perked up beside Rose. "Come on. I want to hear what they're saying."

"Sylvie, wait!"

But Sylvie had already torn off across the room, flitting and weaving through the dancers. With a groan, Rose hiked up the hem of her shimmering gown, nearly getting trampled before she tore out into the corridor.

The silence hit her immediately, almost numbing after the din of the assembly hall. Blinking, she glanced back through the doorway, though it lay dark and empty. Charmed, she was sure—likely to deter students from getting drunk and trying to mingle with the ever-important board members. But the thought was shaken from her head when Fen came stumbling out of the doorway.

"Shh," she hissed.

He frowned. "Where's Sylvie?"

"I don't know, but—"

A slap cut through the still air, cutting her off. "How could you *be* so foolish?"

The deep voice reverberated against the stones. Rose and Fen shared a glance before she stepped forward, inching down the corridor toward it.

"I had to know!" a familiar voice protested. *Ewan.*

Rose peered into the room, dimly lit by a few stray candles, but enough that she could make out Ewan and their father, who towered over them. And Sylvie, who stood in the far corner of the room, her features wrought in something like anguish.

But her eyes remained fixed on Ewan as they cradled their jaw, tears shimmering in their bright blue eyes. Imrys only sneered at them before turning away.

"It was sloppy—*and* a risk." He paced back and forth, thin lines etched deep upon his milky skin. "What if someone saw?"

In this light, he was somehow far more intimidating. Shadows flickered ominously across his sharp features, catching the silver in his hair like stray sparks. His gray eyes were nearly black in the candlelight, burning with cruel disdain as he glowered at his heir.

Ewan straightened, their hand falling away to reveal their raw, swelling cheek. Rose's stomach turned. "No one saw—I was careful."

Saw what? Rose frowned. Were they talking about Sylvie?

"Not careful enough."

"But I—"

"Enough!" Their father rubbed at his brow before sighing deeply. "What's done is done. I will take care of your mess, so long as you promise not to take any further 'initiative' that might put us at risk."

Without another word, Imrys glided from the room. Rose pinned herself against the stone wall, pushing Fen to do the same. After several moments, once his footsteps had faded down the corridor, she peered back into the room.

Ewan simply stood there, shoulders shaking, a lonely figure cast in the dim candlelight. For the briefest moment, Rose almost pitied them. A stinging, off-putting feeling that lingered in her chest—unwanted yet unwavering. Her mother might throw words like blades, but she'd never struck her. Somehow, though, the thought didn't comfort her. Both were meant to hollow out their will, cut them down to keep them small—malleable.

A heavy weight took root in Rose's heart as Sylvie stepped closer. Slowly, silently, she reached for Ewan, but her hand slipped through them like nothing more than smoke.

Suddenly, Rose felt like an intruder. On them, on this quiet, private moment she had no reason to see. She backed away slowly, nudging Fen. But, in the space of a heartbeat, Ewan turned, gliding from the room before she had a chance to duck behind the wall.

Rose's stomach sank as their gazes locked, tear-stained and timid in the shadows. *Shit.* Ewan's eyes widened for a moment before a well-worn mask dropped over their features. Not made of laced fabric, but one she recognized all too well.

She opened her mouth, but nothing came out. Even Fen seemed at a loss, simply staring at their peer like he'd entirely forgotten how to start a conversation. After a moment, Ewan straightened their robes, turning on their heel and taking off down the corridor.

"Wait," Rose called after them. "I need to talk to you!"

"Not now, Thenlif." Their voice was cold as ice.

"It's about Sylvie."

Ewan laughed dryly, still refusing to turn around. "You really don't know when to let something go, do you?"

"And the Order of Salix."

This stopped them in their tracks. Slowly, they turned to face her, fear swimming in their eyes. "Where did you hear that name?"

"You know it, don't you?"

Their gaze darted left and right, as if searching for some shape in the shadows. "Trust me—if you know what's good for you, you'll let this go."

"And if I don't?" She folded her arms over her chest. "Will I disappear like Sylvie?"

Their face went a shade paler, and their throat bobbed. After a moment, they leaned in close, eyes absent of all light.

"You really want to know about the Order?" Their breath brushed against her skin. "Then ask your mother."

17

GOLDEN

ROSE'S head pounded, darkness creeping at the edges of her vision as she struggled to keep her eyes open. The lecture hall held a thick, musty scent as Sylverfir paced before his glimmering map, recounting the disaster that was the First Arbelian War and the influence of spirits on that affair.

She tapped her pen against her sparse notes, fighting back a yawn. She'd barely slept over the rest of the weekend, Ewan's words dancing through her mind like a broken music box, stuck spinning out of tune. What exactly did her mother know about the Order? About all of this, really.

She had already covered up Aveline's death and was well on her way to doing the same with Sylvie's. If the Order really was behind it all, then perhaps she was working with them? It wouldn't surprise Rose much to find her hand in it. Who knew how many skeletons lay buried in her closet. Though most of them weren't up and about haunting her.

Rose ceased her tapping, trying to focus on the lecture. But her thoughts slipped past, like water skimming through her fingers. Spirits didn't spend much time around mortals anymore. No one really knew why—bound to emotions and holding near-godlike power, they'd simply faded away over the centuries, like so much magic before them.

Now, the only spirits left were like Sylvie, lost souls with little aim and far too much time on their hands. Though they too were a thing of the past, mostly vanishing with the ban on necromancy. Rose glanced over to where Sylvie lounged beside her, running her hand through various parts of the wooden bench.

She looked so much like part of the class that it stilled Rose where she sat. A nagging voice at the back of her mind prodded her—some fervent, anxious hope that she had somehow imagined the whole thing. That she would wake up and all this would simply disappear. But she knew it never would. If her mother had taught her anything, it was that hope was a dangerous thing.

"Rose?"

She blinked at Sylverfir, who stared at her expectantly. "I'm sorry, what was the question?"

"Not paying attention, Thenlif?" Sylvie smirked. "Tsk, tsk. What would your mother think?"

Rose resisted the urge to scowl at her, but just barely.

"I asked if anyone could name the Qisan emperor who led the First Arbelian War?"

"Uh, Emperor Altin Trisius I?"

Sylverfir frowned. "No, it was his son Altin Elestius who led the charge."

Rose's cheeks flared. *Of course*—she'd known that. How could she have gotten the wrong Altin?

Sylvie chuckled beside her as Sylverfir went back to his lecture. "How embarrassing—even *I* knew that."

Gritting her teeth, Rose refused to look at Sylvie, burying her head in her notes. The rest of the class passed quickly, but still, Rose's attention was anywhere but on the lecture. When the bell finally rang, she kept her head down, gathering her things and ducking out of the hall before Sylverfir could catch her.

She weaved through the sea of students who dotted the pathways. For once, the air held no threat of rain, and their peers took advantage of the good weather, lounging on the green with their familiars, smoking and laughing. A few even tossed around a ball that seemed adamantly charmed to evade their grasp. Rose dodged it as it went careening past her head, slamming into a first-year instead.

Sylvie trailed along after her, muttering something about how dull the class was, though Rose couldn't be bothered to care. It wasn't until they'd made it back to her dorm that her words actually cut through.

"I wonder if they'll still give me credit for all the time I missed, once I'm back." Sylvie's idle sigh made Rose still as the door clicked shut behind them. "I'm not looking forward to making up all that work."

Once she was back. And what if there was no getting her back? Her stomach twisted at the thought, but she pushed it away.

"Well, I can't see how we're going to do that when you can't remember anything."

Rose turned to her, but Sylvie hardly seemed to be paying attention, flopping onto her bed. She leaned back against the pillows, staring off out the window at some stray point deep within the bleak, gray lines of the forest.

"Then we should talk to your mother."

"No." The word leaped out of her. *Too quick.*

That finally turned Sylvie's head. "Why not? Ewan said she'd know more."

A bitter laugh escaped Rose before she could stop it. "And you think she'll tell *me*? I doubt it."

"Why?"

"Because she doesn't tell me anything."

Sylvie raised an eyebrow. "Really, her golden daughter?"

Golden. Rose swallowed a scoff. Was that how Sylvie saw things? For one bitter moment, a familiar ache wrapped its cruel fist around Rose's heart. Maybe, if she had an ounce of Sylvie's skill with casting, it might have been true.

But as she was? As only herself? Never.

She bit back a sudden wave of tears, blinking quickly as they burned against her eyes. Luckily, Sylvie's gaze had drifted once more, but Rose still turned away. Sucking in sharp, shallow gasps, she willed her pounding heart to slow. She couldn't let Sylvie, of all people, see her like this.

Instead, she turned for something—anything—to draw her thoughts away. To let her fall back into the comfort of cold apathy, no matter how thin of a lie it might be. Swallowing against the corded lump in her throat, Rose's eyes narrowed at her desk. A lonely piece of parchment was tucked beneath her books. Her brow furrowed. She'd never be so careless with her notes.

Stepping toward it, she scanned the harsh, unfamiliar marks. Written in glimmering, oddly shaped letters, she could hardly place the script. But two words etched into the bottom made her mouth go dry.

—The Order

Rose stared at the note for several long seconds, unable to move. Then, slowly, she reached for it. Why would the Order send her anything? Unless …

A wave of nausea washed over her as her fingers brushed the parchment. Swift and staggering, her knees buckled, and a piercing scream ripped through her mind. It was the only sound that slipped between the gnarled trees as they filtered in around her, blocking out even the stars above.

No—the words tangled around her tongue in a broken plea—*please don't.*

But they felt odd, as if they weren't quite her own. Dark auburn curls tumbled over her shoulder, so similar to hers. Yet this was no memory she recognized. A firm hand grabbed her chin, forcing her head up to meet the hollow gaze of a masked face.

You don't belong here. A low voice crept out of it. *You never did.*

"Thenlif?" Warm fingers curled around her wrist, drawing her back to her dorm.

Rose blinked as the trees around her faded into the ivy creeping up her ceiling, the dim light of midday flickering through her window. And Sylvie, standing over her, eyes searching hers and hands cupped gently around Rose's chin.

They sat there for a moment, their gazes locked and Rose's heart pounding in her chest. But then she pulled away, a fierce heat flaring across her cheeks. She could feel Sylvie's eyes upon her as she crossed to her window and threw it open. The fresh air whipped against her skin, a light drizzle falling over her like a fine mist. She breathed in deeply, letting it soothe her.

"You saw something, didn't you?" Sylvie asked finally.

Rose sank back on her heels, leaning her head against the window frame. "I-I don't know. I think it was the Order—some meeting of theirs."

"How?"

"I get … visions." She turned. "Sometimes they're of Aveline, sometimes they're of you. But this one, I think it was me, somehow? I was caught up in an Order meeting and—I don't know. It's like they're getting worse."

"Hauntings don't just get worse." Sylvie moved back to her bed. "Ghosts are static—they don't change, and they certainly don't hand out visions."

"Well, someone forgot to tell Aveline that, I guess."

Though the girl hadn't been present in this one. Rose dug her nail into the soft flesh of her thumb. Like the vision she'd gotten from Sylvie's notes—Aveline had been nowhere in sight.

"I'm serious, Thenlif." Sylvie scowled at her. "If necromancy really is involved, this is like none that I've ever heard of. Ghosts are bound to their summoner—mindless souls in a necromancer's army. This sounds almost more like divining, if anything."

Rose recoiled from the intensity of her gaze. She was right, of course—an unsettling habit of hers these days. Swallowing hard, she moved back to her desk, sinking into her chair.

Divining was old magic—lost to the earliest days of the empire. Well, mostly. Unlike the other forbidden arts, it was weaker now. Where once diviners could walk through time like water, now they could do little more than count the stars and determine fates through the will of old gods. The ban on it was such that their craft was seen more as a relic than genuine magic. Feared still, but holding little actual power. Not like necromancy.

"How do you know so much about it all anyway?" Rose frowned. "You hate magical history."

"I—" Sylvie fidgeted with the ends of her skirt, then stilled. "Ewan's father. He was obsessed with the forbidden arts. He used to go on about it endlessly when we'd visit the family manor. Divining, mainly, but he was interested in necromancy and dreaming too."

Rose's stomach lurched. *Imrys.* Perhaps his obsession had delved into actual practice. Whatever he'd been arguing with Ewan about had certainly unnerved him. Had Ewan threatened to expose him somehow? Though she doubted someone of his standing would be threatened much by the consequences of forbidden magic. Laws were written to uphold the likes of Imrys Elaegius, not tear them down.

"You think he could've had something to do with this?"

"I wouldn't put it past him."

No, Rose had to concede. On that point, they could very much agree. If Sylvie was right, and Imrys was connected to this Order, could it be some ritual of theirs? Old magic cast far from prying eyes—in the depths of the Whispering Woods. But then, why did it seem targeted at her, of all people? Perhaps because she was the only one who lacked the power to stop it?

The thought stung as she reached once more for the note. "Do you know what this is?"

Sylvie frowned as Rose held out the parchment to her. She took it slowly, holding her gaze a moment longer before she scanned the page. "It's familiar, but I couldn't tell you what it says. Besides that it has to do with the Order, obviously."

"Do you think Imrys could have sent it?"

She shook her head. "I doubt it. More likely Ewan did."

"Why Ewan?"

"They knew we were asking about the Order—maybe it's a clue. Maybe we should ask your mother about it."

Rose's nails bit sharp lines into her palms. It seemed to be the path they kept coming back to, but she was loath to take it. "Or they sent it as a warning to stay away."

"You don't"—Sylvie's voice grew small—"you don't think Ewan killed me, do you?"

Rose almost snorted, but the look in Sylvie's eyes was haunted and hollow, and it silenced her in a heartbeat. She forgot sometimes how new this all was for her. Breaking up with Ewan only to wake up and be thrust into investigating her own murder. Who knew what feelings she still held for them. Anger, betrayal—perhaps even love.

Rose's heart swelled with the strangest stirrings of pity. And the faintest sting of envy, but she shoved it aside.

"No." She shook her head. "They might know something about it, but when I told them you were missing, they went looking for you. Why bother if they knew you were dead?"

"To cover their tracks?"

"For whose benefit? There was no one around to witness them save me, and they had no way of knowing I was hiding in your closet."

Sylvie's lips quirked. "You hid in my closet?"

"I—" Rose's cheeks flushed, hot and fierce. That hardly seemed important. "That's not the point."

"Then what is, Thenlif?"

Rose took a deep breath. She knew where they needed to look—where answers truly lay. But they wouldn't come easily.

"We can't just barge in on my mother and demand she tell us everything." She shook her head. "Or Ewan and their father, for that matter. They'll just deny it, unless we have proof."

"So, what do you propose?"

"We need to know what the Order is first. And why they'd even be involved in this." She reached for her bag. "If we can find some sort of record, my mother will have a harder time brushing it off."

Sylvie sighed deeply. "You want to go back to the library, don't you?"

"Not just the library—the Untold Section. You could sneak past the barriers."

"And what? Hopefully find some miraculous tome that answers all our questions? I doubt it."

"It's possible."

"All right. On one condition." Sylvie leaned in close. "When this inevitably fails, we talk to your mother."

Rose exhaled sharply through her nose, the invitation crumbling in her grip. "Fine. But don't say I didn't warn you."

18

A ROSE WITHOUT ITS THORNS

EVENING hung on the tail edge of dusk as Rose left the library, the clouds a pinkish, mottled gray just above the horizon. Her eyes ached and her fingers were nearly raw from all the pages she'd turned, but still she was none the wiser. As she'd known she wouldn't be, somewhere deep down. If any information existed about the Order of Salix, it certainly wasn't in the library. As if someone had gone through and meticulously erased any mention of it.

Rose fidgeted with the waistline of her long woolen skirt. The thought didn't exactly fill her with hope—or put to bed her ideas on the insidious nature of the Order. Still, it had been a long shot, after all. A meager attempt misguided by desperation to avoid where the true answers lay.

"Finally ready to admit this was a waste of time?" Sylvie's voice crashed through her thoughts, making Rose jump.

She leaned idly against the stone wall beside the library doors, a smirk lingering on her lips. Rose glowered at her. Sylvie had disappeared shortly after braving the Untold Section but, given her smug expression, Rose was quite sure she'd spent the last few hours sharpening her "I told you so's."

"No thanks to you."

Sylvie shoved off the wall. "I searched through the Untold Section, like you asked, but that was useless. Then, I watched you fall asleep twice, which was glorious. Then I came out here and overheard some lovely gossip about Arden. Turns out being invisible has its perks."

"Glad you're having fun," Rose scoffed, pushing past her.

"Can we go talk to your mother now?"

Rose swallowed hard. For all the good that would do. At best, her mother would simply ignore any inconvenient question, or else shame her for asking in the first place. At worst …

Well, Rose was quite sure she didn't want to find that out. Besides, she'd already covered up one suspicious death.

"Not yet." Her hand clutched tight around the parchment in her pocket. "I'm going to talk to Sylverfir first. But feel free to stay here and listen to more gossip."

She shoved past Sylvie before she could respond, darting across the colonnade. Rose didn't wait to see if she followed. Didn't care to, really. Though the thought rang hollow in her mind. If she truly didn't care, she wouldn't be here now. She frowned, clutching tighter to her bag.

The lake lay still alongside her, though colorful mummer fish circled in the shallows, snapping at the glowing nightfire moths that dipped low over the surface. Their song floated above the calm waters, luring in the unlucky with its beauty. It had only taken a few students falling prey to their jagged teeth to ward the rest off, but still they sang nightly, ever hopeful. Like everything else at Dunhollow, their beauty lay only skin deep, ever covering their foul nature.

But Rose hardly paid attention to it now, skipping over the wooden footbridge and skirting past the edge of the Whispering Woods. The branches quivered as she brushed against them, hissing with insidious promise. Though nothing so threatening as the shrieks that splintered through the night from further within. She shivered, keeping her gaze firmly on the path ahead.

"Thenlif, wait!" Sylvie's voice carried after her, though there were no thudding footsteps as she chased her down. Rose skidded to a halt as Sylvie planted herself in front of her. "Why Sylverfir?" Rose tried to evade her, but Sylvie was too quick. Finally, she sighed. "He has a masters in ancient languages and magical symbology. He may not know anything about the Order, but he could decipher the note."

"What if he can't figure it out? Will you talk to your mother then?"

"And say what?" She shook her head. "That I'm working with a ghost she doesn't believe exists to uncover some grand conspiracy that the heir of her nemesis claims she might know something about? I'm sure she'd love that."

Sylvie's eyes narrowed. "Is there a reason you don't want to talk to your mother? Something you're not telling me?"

Several reasons. The thought floated through Rose's mind, but she shoved it back. "Like what?"

"Oh, I don't know." Her eyes sparked as she circled around Rose like a cat who had cornered its prey. "You told me you and Fen ran a trace on my blood, but you told him you hadn't mentioned it to your mother yet. Why is that?"

The darkness of the forest behind them muted any color in her eyes, and Rose shivered. They almost held a sunken appearance now. Gaunt, dead, and creeping ever closer.

No. She shook the thought away.

"I—"

Her protest died as Sylvie leaned in. "Did she have something to do with this?"

Rose swallowed hard. Sylvie was so close now. So very close. And so *bright*. She'd have thought a ghost would be cold—lifeless. But she could practically feel Sylvie's annoyance radiating off her in waves of warmth. A soft sensation that tingled against Rose's skin, pulling her in and pushing her away all at once.

Yet, at the moment, all it did was stoke her own frustration, which cracked against the wall she'd so carefully buried it behind. Sylvie really thought she would cover for her mother? That she'd be on her side?

The thought rankled, cutting deep into the scarred parts of Rose's heart. Deeper than she would have liked. After all, what would she do if her mother *did* have some hand in it? Already, she waved away crimes with ease, and Rose had simply watched them disappear with all that remained of her courage. She hadn't stood up to her—hadn't exposed her lies. And a part of her knew she never would. With a scoff, she turned away.

"I don't know, all right?" she snapped. "I doubt directly, but I wouldn't put it past her. I'm quite sure she didn't get where she is today without a few skeletons in her closet."

Sylvie stepped back at that, something dark and dangerous flashing through her eyes. She fell mercifully silent, though the thought pricked Rose with unease. It wasn't like her to be cowed so easily.

"And you really think Sylverfir will help then?" Her eyes flitted over the lake. "Isn't he friends with your mother?"

"He doesn't have to know all the details."

"By the Nine you're stubborn, Thenlif." Sylvie ran a hand through her hair. "Even if he can help, it's already dark—surely his office hours are well past over."

"Yes." Rose squinted at the clock tower looming over the grounds. Just before nine o'clock. *Perfect.* "But we're just in time to catch the tail end of the Chronicler's Conclave."

"Pardon?"

"It's a dinner he hosts midweek." She quickened her pace across the moonlit field to the professors' offices. "More like a study hall, really. We drink, eat dinner, and talk about history and magical theory. I'm surprised you haven't heard of it—it's Sylverfir's worst-kept secret."

Sylvie muttered something Rose didn't quite catch. "So, to find answers about one secret society, you want to go ask another?"

"It's not a secret society. More of a history club."

"A club. And *you're* part of it?"

Rose pursed her lips. It was a fair question, but it still stung coming from Sylvie. In truth, she usually didn't participate much. Not that there was often much to participate *in.* Few students shared her and Sylverfir's passion for history, so most wound up attending to either pine over the professor or pick his brain for their thesis papers.

She clenched her jaw, pulling her jacket tighter against the damp chill in the air. She hadn't thought much of the Chronicler's Conclave since the term started. Avoiding Sylverfir's inquiring gaze in class was one thing, but this had seemed another beast entirely with Aveline's ghost ever over her shoulder. Though Sylvie wasn't much better.

Not that it mattered. Most members probably didn't even realize she wasn't there. Only Fen ever spoke to her, though he usually had to fend off a gaggle of wayward hearts himself.

Cobblestones prodded beneath her soles as she found her way back onto the paved path. Sylverfir's office wasn't far, though a wall of darkness blocked the way. Some intrepid lampposts and a few stray nightfire moths fought against it, but Rose's eyes still skittered through the shadows.

Finally, they came upon the warmth and light of the professors' hall, though Sylvie hardly looked impressed as they ducked through the threshold. Ignoring her, Rose continued on down the corridor, coming to a stop before a familiar door.

Well, familiar in its placement, at least. In appearance, it changed each week to fit whichever theme Sylverfir chose. This time, it seemed to be Arbelian, if the leafy vines were any indication. Sucking in a sharp breath, she raised her fist to knock when the door swung open, revealing a forested foyer and a tall figure.

"Rose—I didn't think you'd make it!" Sylverfir beamed down at her.

His umber skin glowed in the mossy light hanging between the vines, but his smile was somehow brighter. His thin, black braids swung around his waist as he lurched forward and wrapped her in a choking hug. Rose almost laughed as the wool of his ochre sweater tickled her nose, and she burrowed deeper into his shoulder.

Somehow, he always smelled like sinking into a leather chair with a glass of spiced whiskey and a cigar. With everyone else, there was a clear difference between the scent of their magic and whatever perfume they might choose. Some complemented each other, like Fen's caraway and cedarwood fragrance blending in a heady mix with red wine and worn leather. Some were entirely at odds, like Sylvie's, whose perfume of orchid and musk clashed oddly with plum and lilac.

But Sylverfir's melded together in such a way that it was hard to tell where one ended and the other began. If there was truly any difference at all. Perhaps it was because, of all the people in this wretched place, he never wore a mask to hide the worst parts of himself. Every thought, every feeling stitched openly on his sleeve for the world to see.

Rose pulled away from him with a soft sigh. "It's good to see you, Sylverfir."

Something flashed across his gaze, some brief hint of pain that she knew in her heart, though she could hardly bear to say why. For years, he had been just Soren to her. An uncle, a father—she'd never truly had the words. But all that they were to each other was bound up in a single name. One she'd abandoned to chase the favor of others. To be palatable. Pleasing. Though it had never worked.

And now his name hung between them like a broken promise—a reminder of what she'd left behind.

"It's good to see you too," he said finally, tucking a stray strand of auburn hair behind her ear. "I'm afraid you've just missed everyone."

"That's all right." She forced a grin, anything to soothe her fluttering nerves. "I'd rather talk to just you anyway."

Sylvie snorted behind her. "Is this how you keep your good marks then, Thenlif—buttering up the professors with idle flattery?"

Rose's lips pressed in a thin line, and she struggled not to glare at Sylvie. But Sylverfir hardly seemed to notice. Instead, he ushered her through the doorway, still beaming.

"Well, come in, please. Though you'll have to forgive the mess." He took her coat and handed it off to the coat rack, who shook it out as if offended by its dampness. "Can I get you a drink?"

Rose faltered. A drink was the last thing on her mind, though she didn't suppose Sylverfir would take a no easily.

"Let me guess." Sylvie's whisper tickled her ear. "You'll have whatever red wine is on offer, because that's what Fen always drinks, and gods forbid you ever choose something that might suit you instead."

Words caught in Rose's throat. She liked red wine well enough. Not as much as Fen, of course, but she rarely drank on her own anyway. Besides, when had Sylvie become such an expert on her tastes? Flashing a searing glare at Sylvie, she turned back to Sylverfir with a smile.

"What reds do you have?"

"Really, Thenlif?" Sylvie's tone was dry as kindling. "Ask him if he has any port for me while you're at it."

Rose kept her face straight as Sylverfir nodded, gliding back into his office. Slowly, she followed him, careful not to meet Sylvie's eye. Delicate crystal chandeliers cast dancing patterns of light on the walls as she glided under them, and Rose shook her head. For one who rarely had need to cast, nearly everything in Sylverfir's office was positively brimming with magic.

From beckoning couches by the fire to the desk at the far wall made of beautifully carved wood, intricate designs curling around its trim. Some ancient language that held meaning to only Sylverfir's eyes, she was sure. Though it was perhaps the only part of the desk that could be seen beneath the teetering stacks of papers, books, and journals dotted between antique inkwells, a quill pen, and even a well-worn pipe.

Shelves towered on either side of the desk, filled with ancient tomes and old spellbooks. These books did not flutter or fly like the ones in the library, but they did emit a soft glow and seemed to whisper of ancient wisdom and arcane knowledge.

Between the shelves, the walls were adorned with tapestries depicting illustrious moments of history. Each spun in constant motion, the threads charmed to act out scenes from the past. The last queen of Pelanghe facing down the Calamity. The bloody rise of the Qisan empire. The arboreal curses of the Arbelian Wars.

And yet, the warm fire now crackling in the hearth somewhat diminished their severity, accompanied by a few lounging couches atop a plush rug that snored softly. Swirling scents of roasted meat and browned butter turned her gaze to the table at the center of the room, piled with half-empty platters and half-eaten plates left behind.

Sylverfir handed her a glass, following her gaze. "I'm afraid we finished dinner a while ago, but the charm should keep it warm for another hour, if you haven't eaten?"

Remnants of dishes from all over the empire lined the table in an enticing array. Creamy mussel and mushroom pasta from the southern isle of Arbelis, where Sylverfir grew up. Roast duck with a decadent sauce of gooseberries and thyme from the capital of Tol Qilius. Even wine and citrus-soaked fish from the western shores of Ashurd—Fen's home.

Rose's stomach growled, but her nerves were too frayed to keep anything down. She took a long sip of her wine. A robust, rich red—though it did little to take the edge off either her hunger or her nerves.

There was little that could, she supposed. For her, Dunhollow had always been home. She'd been privy to dishes such as these, from the farthest reaches of the empire, but never any of her own. There was no cuisine she reached for in comfort. Nothing that soothed her or reminded her of home. Nothing but this place.

Her jaw tightened. She had family somewhere in the northern reaches of Ir Taril's Outer Isles, she knew, but her mother never spoke of them, and Rose never dared to ask. And so she remained, a tree without its roots. A star without its fire. A rose without its thorns.

Swallowing hard, her eyes darted to Sylvie, who eyed the platters with painful longing. In all their years at each other's throats, she couldn't say she even knew where Sylvie came from. The capital, if her pretension was anything to go by. Besides, it was the only place that still had worshippers of The Nine. Though she doubted Sylvie ran in such plebian circles.

Still, the thought rang hollow in her mind. How could she loathe someone, yet know so little about them? Perhaps that was what hatred was born of, after all—ignorance. Their mutual detestation was made so much easier by the fact that they had rarely spoken to each other. Until now.

"Fen will be sorry he missed you." Sylverfir's voice jarred her from her thoughts, and he gestured for her to sit. "We had a lovely chat about his thesis. Did you know he's trying to create an orb that would channel magic? Wants to make casting more accessible to everyone. Made me miss my alchemy days."

Rose blanched, stumbling back into the couch as the storm-torn orb barreled through her thoughts. *That's* what that was? She held her glass tighter, avoiding Sylvie's gaze, which burned into the back of her head.

"I didn't realize you studied alchemy."

"Oh yes." He grimaced. "It was my major when I was a student here, before I settled on Ancient Linguistics. Safer in the long run."

Sylverfir leaned back with a sigh, his dark eyes dancing in the firelight and an amber glass of whiskey propped against his chest. The plush carpet beneath their chairs nestled around his feet, forming a pair of warm slippers.

"Huh," was the best Rose could manage.

A wry grin tugged at the corner of Sylverfir's lips. "I'm sure you didn't come to chat about my days as a student here—what can I help you with?"

Rose sucked in a short breath, eyes flickering once again to Sylvie before she pulled the crumpled sheet of parchment out of her pocket and slid it across the table. "I was wondering what you might make of this?"

His brow furrowed as he pulled his glasses into place and held the parchment up to the light of the fire. If he recognized it, she could hardly say, for his face held no more clues to his thoughts than

160

a wooden board. But his lips tightened ever so slightly as he set the page back on the table between them.

"I'm not sure." His fingers tapped against it idly. "Where did you get it?"

"I was researching term paper topics and found it in an old book." She shrugged, cheeks flaring. Lying had become second nature to her these days but, around him, it still felt wrong. "I thought perhaps it might be an ancient script, or maybe a code."

Sylverfir sipped at his whiskey. "If it is, it's not one I've ever encountered. Though it could just as easily be nonsense. A prank, perhaps."

Rose frowned. She was certain he'd be more curious about it. This was the same man who'd once spent days trying to decipher a code she'd found in an old textbook, only to later discover it was merely the scribbled notes of a student with particularly atrocious penmanship. Yet now, with a veritable linguistic puzzle plainly before him, he couldn't have been less interested. Her gaze flickered to Sylvie. Perhaps he knew more than he was saying, but what would he have to hide? Unless …

Maybe Sylvie had been right. If her mother knew about the Order, then maybe Sylverfir did too. They'd been friends for years, after all— she doubted there was anyone who knew her mother better.

Before she could ask him anything further, however, a sharp knock rapped against the door. Sylverfir's face fell, his eyes darting to Rose.

"Oh, that might be … hmm."

He leaped from his chair, as Rose and Sylvie shared a sharp glance. "He knows more than he's saying," Sylvie whispered. "I told you he wouldn't help us."

"He might still." Rose shook her head. "He can be rather … verbose after a few glasses of whiskey."

"You want to get a professor drunk and trick him into spilling his secrets?" A slow smirk spread across Sylvie's lips. "My my, Thenlif, I didn't know you had it in you."

Rose almost smiled, until a sharp, familiar voice carried through the foyer. "I just need to speak to you, Soren. It'll only take a moment."

"Araminta, you don't understand—"

Rose swallowed hard as her mother's heels clacked across the room, her cane thudding in tandem. Finally, she came into view, sharp and elegantly mesmerizing as a serpent poised to strike. She stood as if she were waiting for applause, wreathed in an iridescent ebony gown that shimmered in the fire's glow. But her eyes landed on Rose with burning acridity as she came to a halting stop.

"Oh, Rosera. What are you doing here?" Rose's mother loosened her leather gloves, resting her cane against the back of the couch. "I thought your little gathering was long over."

"I stayed late." She lifted her glass with a wan smile as Sylverfir's eyes flitted between them.

Her mother nodded with vague disinterest as she unbuttoned her coat, until her eyes caught upon the parchment, and she stilled. "What's this?"

"Araminta, don't." Sylverfir lurched forward, but it was too late.

Rose's nails carved harsh marks in her palms as her mother snatched it up anyway. "Just a note, Mother," she said.

Her mother's eyes widened as they roved over the odd script, lips pulling in a thin line. Where Sylverfir's face had been cool and impassive, her mother's didn't hide a thing. She knew it. More importantly, she *hated* it. But why? What did it mean?

"Where did you get this?" Her voice was low and cold.

Rose squirmed under her gaze. "I-I told Professor Sylverfir—I found it in an old book. Someone must have left it there."

"Who?"

"If I knew that, I'd hardly be asking about it, would I?"

"Don't get smart with me, Rosera."

"Araminta." Sylverfir placed a soothing hand on her mother's arm. "Don't rile yourself. Like I told Rose, it's probably just some silly prank."

Some unspoken words seemed to pass between them, and her mother's shoulders loosened. Rose's eyes narrowed, flickering to Sylvie, whose brow lay knotted. They were clearly hiding something—and poorly.

Her mother turned back to her. "Who did you speak with before you found this?"

"Fen, mainly … and Ewan."

"Ewan Elaegius? About what?"

Panic crept into her voice, plainly enough that it sent a shiver down Rose's spine. *Interesting.* She took a slow sip of her wine, letting its heady flavor embolden her. Perhaps Sylvie was right. Perhaps this was her best chance to find out just how far her mother's knowledge of this Order extended.

"The Order of Salix," she said finally.

What little color there was to be found in her mother's face drained in an instant. Incredible how one so well versed in politics could wear her thoughts so openly. But useful, for Rose at least.

"How did you hear that name?"

It was such a rare pleasure to see her mother thrown that Rose couldn't help the sly smile that stole across her lips. It wasn't as if she didn't deserve it, after all. Trading in half truths and veiled barbs, perhaps it was only fair she got a taste of her own medicine.

"Oh, here and there, I can't recall."

"This is no jesting matter, Rosera."

"Then what is it?"

"Nothing that concerns you."

"Clearly it does."

"Not anymore." Her pale fingers tightened around the back of Sylverfir's chair. "Stay away from them, Rosera. I mean it."

Rose recoiled. Would it have been so hard for her mother to give a straight answer for once? Or was she so far removed from the truth now that she could no longer even part with it?

Just as with Sylvie's ghost, she hid behind orders and threats and expected Rose to fall into line. But something stopped Rose this time. Some small spark flared to life in her chest, keeping her from simply shrinking away, head bowed.

"Why can't you just tell me what's going on?" She straightened her shoulders. "Would it be so hard to treat me like an adult for once?"

"When you start acting like one, perhaps I will." Her mother's lips thinned, any vestige of warmth receding from her eyes. "Honestly, sometimes I wish you applied the same tenacity to your casting as you do to vexing me. But alas, you were born with only the skill for one."

Fury burgeoned in Rose's chest like a warm flame, but before she could say anything at all, a blast of frost shot across the room, slamming into the window behind her mother's head in icy tendrils.

Rose blinked at her mother. Then at Sylverfir. Then, finally, at Sylvie as the familiar scent of plum and lilac fell over her. But this was mixed with something warmer—something she didn't quite recognize. Rich amber, and something sweet and buttery. Like honey perhaps.

Sylvie dropped Rose's gaze, avoiding it as if it might burn her. Had she cast? But why? And, more importantly, how? Rose's heart pounded against her ribs, the shatter of icy shards ringing through her mind. The last time Sylvie had thrown ice around like that, it had nearly killed Rose. But now, it was almost as if she'd been trying to protect her.

"If that was your way of proving me wrong, Rosera, I'm sure we could have done without the theatrics."

She clenched her fists tight. "You know it wasn't, Mother."

"Then it appears we have a ghost." Her mother gave a hollow smile, waving a hand over the glass to unfreeze it. "Another ghost."

"Araminta"—Sylverfir's voice cut between them, low and cold—"enough."

But it did little to soften the sting of tears against Rose's eyes. She wondered if her mother could even see her as a daughter anymore, or if her shame in Rose's lack of casting drew a shadow over all else. Biting down hard on the inside of her lip, she gave Sylverfir a watery smile.

"It's fine. It's about time she managed a little honesty." Her gaze slid back to her mother, raw and fierce. "All those lies might choke her before her pride does."

Before her mother could fill her ears with more poison, Rose snatched up the note and turned for the door. Yet she faltered at the threshold. Here she was, so desperate for a spark of truth from her mother, all while hiding her own. That it lay against her tongue like a sharpened blade only made it sweeter.

She turned back with a hardened gaze. "While we're being honest, you should know that Fen and I ran a trace on that blood in the library before you cleaned it. It belonged to Sylvie—and someone else."

Her mother's eyes widened. "What?"

"I'm sure the board would love to know how your star caster disappeared from your school after a brutal attack and you did nothing about it."

"Rosera, wait—"

But she turned away. "Have a good night, Mother."

19

NOT ANYMORE

THE silence of Rose's dormitory held little comfort this evening. It clung to her every heartbeat, every stroke of her hairbrush, as she stared numbly at her haggard reflection. Even the gentle glow of candlelight bouncing off her cascade of plants offered no warmth.

She swallowed hard, eyes flickering to the figure lingering over her shoulder. Sylvie said nothing, barely even acknowledging Rose as she brushed some stray, dangling leaves away from her arm. Yet the absence of her words held a weight all of its own, and the silence nearly cracked beneath it.

Rose's throat tightened. Of all the people to witness her mother's outburst, it had to be Sylvie. She'd known it was a bad idea to question her mother, and yet still she'd gone ahead with it. What must Sylvie think of her now?

Her grip on her brush slipped. Hands trembling, she set it aside and sucked in a sharp breath. Tears once again threatened to fall, but she tilted her head, forcing them back. She couldn't stop Sylvie from witnessing the worst of her mother, but she could keep her from seeing the effect she had on Rose. If only just.

After a long moment, Sylvie sighed. "I see now why you're always hiding in the library. I would too, if my mother was like that."

Rose stilled. Something pricked at her heart. Something bitter and mangled recoiled from her pity like a moonweed caught in the sunshine. She gritted her teeth, barbed words twisting around her tongue.

"And yours is much better, I assume?"

"No, she's dead."

Rose's head snapped up. "Oh."

Sylvie's amber eyes danced in the shadows. "You seem surprised."

"I just always thought you were the heir of some illustrious politicians, not—"

"A scholarship orphan?" Sylvie cut across her. "Well, I always thought you were the entitled daughter of the chancellor, so I guess we were both wrong."

Scholarship? She didn't even know Dunhollow did such things—most common casters were only granted entry at lesser universities in the outer provinces. After all, why would the Dunhollow board pay for a student's tuition when they had wealthy parents lining up to buy their heirs' entry? Besides, Sylvie hardly looked like she was struggling, always wearing the latest fashion and that expensive perfume. Rose glanced her up and down in the mirror's reflection, cheeks flaring.

"I—I didn't know Dunhollow did scholarships."

"I'm a rare exception." Sylvie grimaced, setting herself down on the edge of Rose's bed. "Sylverfir caught me casting in a back-alley duel when I was sixteen and convinced your mother I had talent enough to attend. She was keen on the idea, so here I am."

"That doesn't sound like her."

Sylvie snorted, pulling her knees up to her chest. "Yes, well, she also hired a tutor to train me how to act like a noble for two years before I was allowed to enroll. Can't have the elite thinking their heirs are rubbing elbows with common rabble."

"That *does* sound like her."

"I didn't realize she was the same way with you, though. I thought you two were peas in a pod."

Rose barely contained a scathing laugh. "You genuinely thought my mother would be satisfied with a daughter who can't cast? Hardly."

"Well, she spent enough time trying to get me to be as well read as you."

"And she spent the rest of her time trying to make me cast like you." Rose turned to face her. "Honestly, have you forgotten our first year? She forced me into a duel I couldn't win against you, Sylvie. She would've let you impale me if you hadn't made one stupid mistake. What part of that screamed loving, doting mother to you?"

Tears burned at Rose's eyes, and she ducked her head, the years of torment held in a few small words carving into her like knives. How cruel a twist it was that her mother's ideal heir would have been a perfect blend of her and Sylvie, and she had pitted them against each other to make them so. Forced together like pieces of a puzzle that were never meant to fit. She wondered how much of her hatred was based on Sylvie herself, rather than her mother placing her incessantly on a pedestal that Rose could never reach.

"It wasn't a mistake," Sylvie's voice was small—almost timid.

The words echoed in Rose's mind for a moment, jagged and unfamiliar. She lifted her head, slowly. "What?"

"It wasn't a mistake—I threw the match."

Rose stared at her for a long moment, sure she would crack a smile any second. Laugh, gloat, goad her for being so gullible. But there was no deceit in Sylvie's eyes, only concern and some broken, mangled thing Rose had no mind to place now.

"Why would you do that?"

"Because even I could see it wasn't fair." She shook her head. "Gods, Thenlif, I'm not a monster. I didn't want you dead."

That didn't make any sense. Rose swallowed hard. Sylvie had been furious at her loss—had turned everyone in the academy against her in revenge. Hadn't she?

"Then why did you tell everyone my mother had rigged the match?"

"I didn't—they assumed. And I could hardly admit what I'd done. Your mother would've called a rematch, and I didn't think I could protect you again."

Protect her? There was something so aberrant about the idea that it almost felt unreal. Unthinkable, and so far removed from the Sylvie she knew.

Shrewd. Powerful. Ruthless. Everything her mother wanted them both to be. She'd always thought Sylvie filled the role perfectly, but looking at her now ... Rose's stomach flipped. Suddenly, it didn't seem to fit her at all.

She cleared her throat. "So you kept a shred of conscience. Congratulations. I guess that means neither of us lived up to my mother's standards."

"And why should we?" Sylvie got to her feet. "Why even try?"

Rose blinked at her. Tangled words of protest brushed against her lips, but she held them back. She'd imagined it before—leaving Dunhollow and her mother's never-ending expectations behind—but could never truly fathom it.

Even away from these hallowed halls and cloud-torn skies, there would be no escaping her mother. There were parts of Rose wrought by her hand that she would never be free of, even if they lived only within her. Not that Sylvie would understand.

Rose's gaze slid to the window. "We shouldn't. But that doesn't mean we won't."

"So you'll just keep trying to play the perfect daughter, even knowing it will never be enough? Why?"

"What else can I do, Sylvie?" Rose rounded on her, finally daring to meet her gaze. "What else would *you* do? You're a pawn in this game she plays as much as I am."

But the pain dancing through Sylvie's eyes stripped away her anger like a blade peeling back flesh. "Not anymore."

Rose stilled, the weight of her words hanging between them— tenuous as cracked glass. It seemed almost foolish to forget Sylvie sat before her only as a ghost of what she once was. And yet she nearly had.

Somehow, she looked so *alive*. A warm flush still held upon her tawny cheeks, eyes full of spark and passion, even when drowning in misery. It was all Rose could do not to simply stare at her. Would she be so vibrant on the edge of death? Or would she simply fade away from the pain of this world? Perhaps it was a cruelty then, that their fates had not been switched.

"Maybe one day you will be again." Her voice was small when she finally spoke. Shallow and brittle.

"Why would I want to be?" Sylvie's whisper was sharp as steel. "I watched you bury yourself tonight. So far beneath the ground that the truth couldn't even reach you."

"I—"

"Have you even told your mother about Aveline and everything she's done to you?" Sylvie cut across her protest. "About half the things you've seen?"

"No." The truth fell from Rose's lips before she could stop it. But, from Sylvie, she could no longer hide it.

She was silent for a long moment before moving from the foot of Rose's bed. She drew herself closer to Rose, until they were standing nearly chest to chest. Her heart skipped a beat as Sylvie leaned in. Her breath was warm against her skin, even as her words fell upon her like icy shards.

"I had you down as a lot of things, Thenlif, but a coward was never one of them."

Before Rose could respond, Sylvie disappeared, leaving her alone in silence. She sat there for several moments, unmoving, as if all her willpower had been sucked right out of her veins. *She was right.*

The thought left a sour taste on Rose's tongue, and she shook it off. Reaching for her nightgown, she curled herself into her bed, longing to let Sylvie's words simply slip away in the soothing grasp of slumber.

But the scent of her perfume lingered on her sheets, just as her words did on her mind. Rose scoffed, turning on her side. This might be one rare moment without Sylvie nagging at her. She should have been enjoying the small semblance of peace while it lasted, not wallowing it away.

Sighing, she fell into fitful sleep, plagued by dreams infested with shadowed roots crawling up her ankles, pulling her deep into the forest. Somewhere, far off in the distance, Sylvie's voice called to her. Sharp and piercing, it shattered the night air around her, but she could not reach it. Bogged down by the weight ensnaring her, it simply slipped away like so much else, and she gave in to the strangling grip of the wood.

Yet when Rose finally opened her eyes in the dim hours of dawn, it was not Sylvie's soft form that hung beside her bed. Just Aveline's cold, dead eyes, and a shriek that ripped through her very soul.

20

CAIR RIACODLA

THE warmth of the greenhouse sun burned at the back of Rose's neck. Damp soil folded beneath her fingers, digging under her nails as she carefully repotted a shock of blue petals. The classroom was almost eerily quiet. Even with the cheerful buzzing of bees and the soft humming of Briony across the room, there was some hollow tension that pulled at Rose's chest, swallowing up all else.

Her eyes flickered to the empty chair next to her. She hadn't seen Ewan since the night of the board dinner. Or since she'd received that note. Perhaps Sylvie was right, and they *were* involved with her disappearance. Two disappearances, now.

She still hadn't come back. Rose's throat tightened. She'd thought Sylvie would just disappear for a few hours. Maybe clear her head for a bit before returning to sulk and pester her again. And yet it had been nearly a week. Her heart fluttered. Anything could have happened.

It was foolish, perhaps, to be worried about a ghost. *Sylvie's* ghost, out of everyone. After all, what was the worst that *could* happen to her? She should have been overjoyed that Sylvie had finally left her in peace.

But the thought rang hollow, and it did nothing to loosen the noose of dread twisting its way around Rose's heart. Some small part of her had been holding on to the idea that Sylvie was right, she supposed. That she wasn't truly dead.

Yet that seemed almost idealistic now. She sucked in a sharp breath. While they might have had a clue to the Order of Salix's involvement, they still had no idea what it was. Or where Sylvie's body was. Or Aveline's.

The girl's ghost had been missing just as long as Sylvie's. Longer, even. Rose sat up straighter. No, she'd seen her the night Sylvie had left. Her heart sank. But nothing since—same as Sylvie.

She set down her pot, rubbing wearily at her brow. There were secret societies in the empire, of course. Dozens of them. Some even started here in Dunhollow, producing casters of great talent and influence. But, in all her studies of history, she'd never heard of one that could get away with murdering students. Such a thing would cause uproar among the upper echelons of Na Qisan nobility if they thought their heirs were being slaughtered.

Aveline came from wealth, but Sylvie wasn't the heir to any great fortune or title. Rose chewed the inside of her lip. Could anyone else have known that? Ewan and their father, perhaps. If the display at the board dinner was any indication, all they cared about was appearances. Had they found out Sylvie's true background, would that have been enough for them to kill her?

No, that seemed too mundane, somehow. A ritual of some sort seemed more likely—perhaps Sylvie had just been an easy target. And Aveline? Rose's stomach sank. It couldn't be a coincidence that their stories were nearly identical. Both were dating pretentious social climbers and both broke up with them shortly before disappearing. Yet if the Order was as fearsome as her mother claimed, would it really deign to involve itself in petty social dramas? And how did that reckon with forbidden magics? It just didn't make sense.

Unless Sylvie and Aveline had to be silenced. But what secrets would be worth their lives? Rose glanced back to Ewan's empty seat as Briony made her way over to her planter. She needed to find out more. If Sylvie really was gone, then Ewan was her best lead.

"Well done, Rose." Briony peered over her shoulder. Rich scents of damp earth and rain clung to her like a perfume, streaks of dirt staining her cool brown skin. "I thought for sure that iverin stasia was all but dead."

Rose glanced down at the light blue petals, which had regained much of their luster since she had transplanted it two weeks back. "Not quite, Professor. Just dormant."

"Still, it's impressive. None of the others have come back so quickly." She beamed down at Rose, sage curls spilling over her round cheeks. "Oh, that reminds me—I managed to track down a copy of that study I mentioned."

Rose stared at her blankly, racking her brain as the professor handed over a leather dossier. *What study?* "Er—thank you."

"If you do use it for your term paper, I'd be particularly interested in your thoughts on their conclusion," she said, seemingly unfazed by Rose's lack of enthusiasm. "Personally, I think they take too many liberties, and 'Silent Death' is a ridiculous name, but—"

" 'Silent Death'?" Rose's brow creased.

"It's what they took to calling iverin stasia." The professor all but rolled her eyes. "Apparently, between it and the Cair Riacodla incantation, they were able to put patients into such a deep stasis that they had to double-check to make sure they weren't dead."

Rose blanched as the woman chuckled. A state of being so near death as to mimic it? Her mouth went dry.

"Is that use well known, Professor?"

"Not terribly. Like I said, it's only a recent study." She shrugged. "Only those with a passion for herbalism or alchemy might have heard of it."

"And how long would the effect of iverin stasia last?"

"A few hours, I believe, depending on the dosage."

"And if the dosage was given consistently, could it create a prolonged effect?"

Briony frowned. "Planning on using it for something, are you?"

A faint heat crept up Rose's neck, making her collar tight against her skin. "Just curious, I suppose."

"Hmm, well, I look forward to seeing as much thoughtfulness in your analysis of it."

"Y-yes." Rose clutched the dossier. "Of course."

The professor beamed at her brightly before turning for the front of the room, humming as she went. But Rose could only sit there, frozen, fingers sinking into the dirt. Maybe Sylvie *was* right.

If this plant was as powerful as Briony claimed, could someone have used it to keep her and Aveline alive, just an inch away from death? But why? Memories of cloaked, hooded figures danced through Rose's mind, their low chants weaving between gnarled branches. Maybe the Order needed them alive for whatever ritual they were casting. Her heart skipped a beat. Maybe there was still time to save them.

Rose tapped her fingers against the edge of the planter. Glancing around at her classmates, she flipped open the dossier, skimming its contents. It was thicker than most of her textbooks and was crammed full of copies of scribbled notes and observations. The researchers had certainly been thorough. Even she would need time to read through the whole thing.

She traced her fingers along the margins of one set of notes. Scrawled symbols stared up at her—a jumbled mess, but unmistakably alchemical. Advanced too. She frowned, flipping through a few more pages. The dosage equation was also well beyond any novice to herbalism. Whoever had used it must have been a masterful caster. If they'd used it at all.

It was a vain hope, but one she clung to like a lifeline. She slammed the dossier closed as the bell rang and slipped out of the greenhouse. Clutching the dossier tight against her chest, she pulled her scarf closer to her ears. If the spell was that experimental, she knew exactly whom she needed to talk to.

Cold, crisp air bit against Rose's skin, heavy with the threat of snow. Dunhollow village beckoned her over the bridge, twinkling lights and smoking chimneys a cozy offset to the gray skies above. It wasn't even Harvestmas yet—it hardly seemed fair for the weather to have turned so frigid already. Flowers and vines dotted about the village were dying off, chased away by the frigid air and leaving the streets empty of their cheery color.

She shivered, shifting the dossier to her left arm as she reached the pub. This wouldn't have been *her* choice of study venue, but then, she wasn't here for herself.

The bells above the door jingled merrily as she entered, and a blast of warm air enveloped her. Rose flexed her numb fingers before unraveling her scarf from her shoulders. The space wasn't quite as crowded as normal, but it was still quite early, she supposed.

Hollis stood chatting at the bar with some students, though he gave an overenthusiastic wave upon spotting her. A floating phonogram played some soft piano music before the dancing flames of the fire, a gentle melody amid quiet conversations. Breathing in sharply, Rose's stomach growled, for the air swirled with the mouthwatering aromas of baking apple tarts and mulled cider.

She paused, sorely tempted to stop by the bar and order some. But there would be time for that later. Straightening her shoulders, she peered between the students, faces flushed and steam curling around their cheeks, searching for the only one she wanted.

Finally, she spotted Fen in a back booth, bent over scattered papers and glasses fogged up from the steam of his drink. His dark hair sat tousled, pushed all to one side, as if he couldn't stop running his hands through it. Rose grinned, squeezing past the other students to slip into the seat opposite him. He jumped as she slammed her dossier down on the table.

"What do you know about the Cair Riacodla incantation?"

"Well, hello to you too."

"Yes, hello." She pursed her lips. "Have you heard of it?"

Fen set aside his papers, leaning back in the booth. His cream blouse fell loose around his throat, tangling with his long maroon scarf and revealing a glimpse of his tattooed chest. Rose sucked in a breath. He was so effortless in his elegance that he might have stepped out of some advertisement for perfume or fine wine.

"Vaguely." He wiped the fog from his glasses. "It's a medical incantation, right?"

Rose nodded, sliding her dossier toward him. "And did you know it's recently been linked with the iverin stasia plant to produce a prolonged period of near-deathlike unconsciousness?"

"I take it you're going somewhere with this?" Fen took the file, leafing idly through the pages.

"I think that's what happened to Sylvie. And Aveline too."

"What?"

"I thought, at first, that they were tied to necromancy." She wrung her hands. "But maybe they were just aspects of consciousness—some side effect of this incantation. As to why only I can see them, I couldn't say."

Fen stared at her for a long moment. "So, let me get this straight: You think two students were attacked, then secreted away somewhere and subjected to an experimental alchemical formula that brought them so close to death that their consciousnesses were visible only to you? How? And for what reason?"

"I haven't gotten that far yet."

"All right, well, you thought their disappearances were connected to this Order, right? How does that fit in?"

"I haven't figured that out either."

"So, a very fleshed-out theory then, I see." He leaned back in his chair. "And what does Sylvie think of all this?"

"I don't know." Rose thrummed her fingers against the worn, wooden table. "She's missing."

"Missing? How is a ghost missing?"

Rose rubbed the back of her neck. "We had something of a disagreement, and she disappeared ... again. I haven't seen her in a week."

"A *week*?" Fen sat up straighter. "Rose, anything could've happened to her in that time."

"I know that," she snapped. "Why do you think I'm trying to figure this out?"

He sighed, eyeing the dossier again. "And what exactly do you want me to do?"

"Well, I thought maybe you could test out the incantation, see how long it lasts, how viable it is, that sort of thing."

"And who would I be testing this on?"

"Whomever happens to be annoying you?" She shrugged, taking a sip of his cider.

"Sure, help yourself," he muttered wryly. "Anyway, let's say this incantation does work, what does that prove?"

"I don't know, but it would be something, at least." She sighed. "Look, with Sylvie gone, there's no way we can find out what she knew, and Ewan's hardly going to tell me anything. We have to start somewhere—it may as well be here."

Fen grimaced, eyes darting over her shoulder before lighting up. "I wouldn't be so sure."

Rose followed his gaze to the back of the room, where Ewan and Arden stood, locked in what appeared to be some sort of argument. After a moment, Ewan pulled away, swaying dangerously close to the fire.

"Are they drunk? It's barely four o'clock."

"Seems like now would be a great time to get some answers from them?"

"Or get spewed on." Rose scoffed, turning back to face Fen.

"Well, don't look now, but they're coming your way."

Rose stiffened, fingers tightening around Fen's mug. He had to be mistaken. After all, what would Ewan want with *her*? She nearly choked then, when she felt a hand squeeze her shoulder.

"What are you doing?" She yanked away from them, almost pulling Ewan into the booth with her.

But they only stared down at her with a sad smile, tears glistening in their eyes. "You were right. I should have listened to you."

"What are you talking about?"

"I'm sorry. I'm so sorry," they mumbled into their drink. "For all of it."

"I'll go get them some water." Fen scooted out of the booth.

Rose caught his arm. "No, wait. I—"

But she didn't get the chance to finish the thought before a blood-curdling shriek ripped through the air. The whole pub stilled, as if the scream had placed some curse upon them, no one daring to move. Rose glanced at Fen, then at Ewan, both frozen where they stood.

Until another shout went up from just beyond the door, and it was as if a dam had burst. Students scrambled to their feet, hastily pulling their cloaks on before making a mad dash for the door.

Rose leaped up, not even bothering with her coat as she joined the crowd with Fen and Ewan. The cold air hit her like a slap to the face as she stepped out the door, nearly colliding with a tear-stained student. They latched on to Fen, their lips curling around choked sobs.

"What is it?" He took hold of them gently, rubbing their arm. "What's wrong?"

"There's a—a b-body in the river."

"What?" Rose's heart leaped into her throat, pulse pounding in her ears. Once. Twice.

Fen grabbed her arm. "Rose—"

But she shook him off. "What if it's Sylvie?"

"Sylvie?" Ewan slurred the name, eyes darting between the pair of them.

"We don't know that, Rose."

"Who else could it be?"

Pushing past him, she hurtled down the street, ignoring his calls after her. She had to get to the river. She *had* to. If the body belonged to Sylvie, then—

Tears stung her eyes, throat tightening as she stumbled down the hill to the riverbank. Ice-cold air burned in her lungs, chest heaving as she scanned the white-capped water rushing over rocks. Fog hung low over the river, the dim light of dusk all but faded. Yet even that couldn't obscure the twisted, broken form lying upon the shore.

Rose's heart thudded against her ribs. She didn't want to move— didn't want to look. But she had to. Sucking in a sharp breath, she took a step forward. Then another. Close enough to make out matted blond hair clinging to pale skin. She stilled, a wave of nausea roiling over her. It wasn't Sylvie at all.

It was Aveline.

21

WILL TO WILL

FRIGID air curled around Rose's face, biting at her skin as she stood, numb and unmoving. Aveline's eyes stared up at her, as cold and dead as the wind around her. Her peers hung back, muttering among themselves from the safety of the bridge as Rose rushed to the girl's side. Useless prayers fled from her lips for the faintest hint of life. A small breath—a quiet heartbeat. But there was nothing.

Tears spilled down her cheeks, and she sniffled, reaching under Aveline's frozen collar for the lifeless veins at her neck. But the moment her finger brushed against the girl's skin, the world shifted. The river still stretched out before her, and a chilled fog still hung over its waters. But the sky was dark, the stars peeking out from behind intrepid clouds.

Footsteps echoed on slick cobblestones. Slow, at first. Languid. And then faster. Not one set, but two—one fleeing, the other chasing. And then a sickening crack and all the world went dark.

Rose recoiled with a gasp as the vision faded. She stared down at all that remained of the poor girl. But no dark veins lingered on her pale skin now. No milky-white glaze of death covered her blue eyes. She was simply frozen, a glimpse of a life taken too soon, but not yet passed. Almost as if she weren't dead at all. Rose's throat tightened as if a fist had closed around it. *What had happened to her?*

She brushed a stray lock of blond hair from Aveline's cheek, a familiar tingle crawling down her spine. Her presence fell over Rose like a cloak. Not the body before her, but the spirit that had hung on the edges of her mind these past months. She almost didn't want to look, but she owed Aveline that much.

To Rose's shock, it was no longer a gaunt, decaying form that reached for her but a glimmering, faded image of the girl she'd been. Aveline's eyes were clear, hair curling around her shoulders in soft, delicate waves. For the briefest moment, a sad smile spread across her small, pink lips.

Rose frowned. This didn't make any sense. Every vision, every haunting, Aveline had been gripped by the slow decay of death, but now both body and soul were nearly pristine. Had it all been a figment of Rose's fragile mind?

Aveline reached out a hand, almost as if to say some final words. But then she vanished—disappeared into the fog and mist. A breath caught in Rose's chest, light and buoyant. As if some weight had been lifted from her heart. Some part of her, deep down, knew she would never see Aveline again.

"Rose!" A shout carried down the riverbank.

Slowly, numbly, she turned to find Hollis pushing toward her through the crowd of students huddled on the bridge, Fen close on his heels. Hollis's pale skin flushed a deep pink in the cold as he skidded to a stop before her, eyes fixed on Aveline's corpse.

"Dia vhal," Hollis muttered. But then his eyes snapped up, and he held out a warm hand. "Come on, love. There's nothing more you can do for her."

Rose trembled, wet from the stones seeping through the knees of her trousers, soaking her through to the bone. "I—I can't leave her."

It didn't make any sense. What did it matter now that Aveline was gone? But there was a part of Rose that couldn't let her go—not yet.

"Then let me take her." His hand closed around her shoulder. "I'll keep her somewhere safe and warm—I promise."

"Listen to him, Rose." Fen's voice found her upon the frigid air. "Just let her go."

179

She sat there a moment longer, shivering and sobbing as a crowd formed on the bridge above. And then, without thinking, she launched herself at Fen's chest, finding a solid warmth there that she'd long ago lost hope in. And perhaps she didn't deserve it.

"She's gone," she muttered numbly against his heaving chest. "She's really gone."

The warmth of the pub seemed lesser now. Or, if it remained, Rose had all but grown numb to it. Despite the crowd of students who'd taken shelter within, silence hung on the air like a raw, pulsing heartbeat, alive enough that none dared break it.

Blue eyes flashed through Rose's mind. Cold. Dead. *Gone.* And yet, when she'd seen them, her first thought had been relief. A soothing balm to her racing heart that the eyes staring back at her weren't Sylvie's. She shuddered. The thought disgusted her now.

Beside her, Fen sat silently, his hand resting atop hers. Every so often, he gave it a gentle squeeze, but it did nothing to soothe her guilt. All this time she'd spent chasing after Sylvie, she'd almost entirely forgotten about Aveline.

The sallow blue tint of her pale skin hung in the back of Rose's mind. So unlike the decrepit flesh of her ghost, or a corpse long dead. Whatever killed her had done so recently.

Rose clenched her jaw. Had Aveline suffered? Languishing in some torment, perhaps, waiting for someone to come rescue her while the world carried on blissfully without her? Rose swallowed back another wave of tears. Except her.

All these months, she'd seen her. Hanging in every reflection, crying out for help. And what had she done? Cast her away like everyone else, fearing only for herself and her sanity. She could have helped her—could have *saved* her even. Yet all she'd seen was the inconvenience that Aveline had chosen to haunt her, of all people. And now she was gone.

Is that what would happen to Sylvie too? The thought coiled around Rose's heart like a stone fist. Would hers be the next body to wash up?

"Here." Hollis slid two glasses of amber liquid over to her and Fen. "It'll help take the edge off. Can't have been easy stumbling upon that."

Rose nodded her thanks, throwing back the contents of the glass in one sip. She didn't even taste it, merely relishing its burn at the back of her throat. But it did nothing to clear the tangled mess of her mind. She wasn't sure if anything could, now. Still, she was grateful all the same.

Hollis grimaced as she slammed the glass back down on the table, but he refilled it nonetheless. Before Rose could take another sip, however, the doors swung open with a grating creak. She shivered against the blast of cold air as a familiar cane thudded against the wood floor.

Wonderful.

She didn't turn to face her mother—didn't even look up from her glass. She didn't want to know what she'd find lurking in the depths of her eyes. Pity? Guilt? Or only more lies?

She'd known about it all—Sylvie, Aveline, the Order. Yet what had she done to stop any of it? Rose's fingers tightened around the glass. What secrets did she still hide, even now?

"Aramin—er—Chancellor Thenlif." Hollis gave a quick nod. "Thank you for coming."

Rose gritted her teeth. Her mother's presence loomed over her like a shadow, her gaze boring into the back of her head, but she refused to meet it.

"Of course." She stepped toward the bar. "Such a tragedy. Who found the body?"

"Er—a first-year called Aldis, but they're understandably indisposed at the moment. Your daughter identified it, though."

"Rosera?"

Rose bit her lip, sharp words tearing at her tongue, but she swallowed them. Like jagged little razors, they cut all the way down, slicing through her throat and burrowing into the back of her mind. Wincing, she reached for her drink. At least that pain would fade.

After a moment of terse silence, her mother turned back to Hollis. "And where is the body now?"

Hollis glanced between Rose and her mother, his pale skin growing a furious shade of pink. It clashed horribly with the sapphire streaks in his hair, and, for a moment, it was all Rose could do not to laugh. What was she even doing? Sitting here throwing back shots with a fool too fearful of her mother to spit out the truth while a body lay rotting somewhere out in the cold. It was too much.

181

"I moved it into the old shed out back and wrapped it in a shroud. It's not much, but it's the least I could do for the poor kid, left out in the water like that. Horrible."

"You've done plenty, Hollis, thank you." Her mother laid a pale hand on his arm. "It's likely for the best that the body remains there for now, until we can have it examined and then make arrangements for proper rites to be observed."

"Her."

"What?"

Rose lifted her gaze, tears stinging her eyes. But her mother didn't even flinch. She simply stared down at Rose like she was something to be pitied—reviled. Or perhaps just another annoyance to be swept under the rug.

"She was a person." Anger burned beneath Rose's skin, swirling with the headiness of her drink. "Not a body, not an it. Not an inconvenience for you to brush away."

"Rosera, really."

"She had a name—a life. One *you* could've saved."

"Rose." Fen tugged at her arm, but she shrugged him off.

"But you were too busy with what, board dinners? Worrying about the school's reputation? Or maybe just covering up her murder."

Her mother's green eyes widened, painted lips pressing thin. "Rosera, that's enough."

But it wasn't. How could it be? Her heart hammered against her ribs, fueling her fury. And yet, words failed her. What would they do, in the end? She knew well enough by now that hers would never sway her mother. That her mother would never be cowed or cornered by them, because that would require her to care. And that was something she could never do.

Drawing herself up to her full height, Rose met her mother's gaze, refusing to look away this time. They stood like that for a moment—nose to nose, will to will, the room fading around them. And, in the silence, something shifted. Something small, almost imperceptible, that flashed through her mother's eyes before she could stop it.

Fear.

Rose's lips curled in a cruel smile. *Good.* Let her choke on it.

Turning away, she grabbed her coat, sweeping out of the pub before her mother could say another word. Fen called after her, but she didn't stop, didn't wait for him to catch up. There was an ache gnawing at her chest that even he couldn't soothe now.

So, she walked alone, letting the frigid evening air bite into her skin and chase away the warmth of Hollis's liquor. By the time she reached her dorm, her skin was numb—cheeks reddened and eyes heavy from tears held back too long. She leaned against the door, sucking in short, shallow breaths for a moment.

If her mother didn't care to find out what had happened, then Rose would. Whoever killed Aveline had to be behind Sylvie's disappearance too. Whether truly dead, or simply near it, she had to know. She owed Sylvie that much.

Pushing away from the door, she moved to light the candle upon her desk. Its small flame flickered, filling the room with a warm glow. But when she turned to light the lantern hanging over her bed, she froze.

Amber eyes fixed on her in the dim light. Rose gasped. Bold and fierce, they pierced her with an ill-worn familiarity that stopped her in her tracks.

Sylvie.

22

STAY

SYLVIE'S eyes didn't move from her as Rose sucked in short, shallow breaths. *She's back.* The thought rang through her mind. The only worthwhile one amid raucous nonsense. But she couldn't tear her eyes away, and Sylvie didn't seem intent on moving anytime soon, so they both simply stood there, staring.

Sylvie perched upon Rose's bed, locked between the ridiculous array of overhanging plants, her toes skimming the plush rug beneath her. Her sleek hair caught on the same black turtleneck she always wore, her plaid skirt draped gracefully across her knees. Solid and real, if not quite alive. And yet, she was here. The thought filled Rose with unmistakable relief.

For a moment, she didn't even dare to breathe. Her heart fluttered, and then simply stopped, as if all life had left it.

But cold eyes flickered through her mind, pale skin frozen by the river's edge. Bile crept up her throat. She'd thought Sylvie was *dead*. And yet she had the gall to sit there, blinking at her innocently, as if hardly a moment had passed.

The thought coursed through her like a flame, loosening her muscles, burning against her tongue.

"Where have you been?" she blurted out finally.

Sylvie raised a dark eyebrow. "Hello to you too, Thenlif. You look like shit."

"Don't," Rose snapped. "You can't just come back in here after days and pretend like everything is fine."

"Concerned, were you?" Sylvie smirked, looking far too smug for Rose to bear at the moment.

"Of course I was."

The words rolled off her tongue before she could stop them. This, at least, earned a flicker of genuine shock from Sylvie, but Rose's thoughts burned too fiercely now for her to care.

"Oh."

The sound was barely more than a whisper, but it set Rose alight with fury. For Sylvie, for herself—perhaps even just for the unfairness of this whole mess. It trembled beneath her skin with the maddening energy of a storm before it broke upon land. Vibrant—frightening. It was all she could do not to let it swallow her.

"I thought you were *dead*, Sylvie. They dragged Aveline's body out of the river and I—" She faltered, words catching on her breath. After a moment, she exhaled, and when she found her voice again, it was low and smooth, if not quite as forceful as before. "I thought it was you."

All at once, the storm within her dissipated. Lightning and wind rattled about in her thoughts, but nothing of substance kept it from simply wisping away, leaving her hollow. Rose released a breath, slow and shuddering.

To her surprise, Sylvie didn't tease her. Didn't shy away or twist her words. She simply nodded, as if she no longer had the energy for anything else.

"I know."

"You *know*?"

"I saw."

Rose's eyes narrowed as she sank onto the edge of her bed. "How?"

Sylvie didn't speak for a long moment, as if the weight of her thoughts was too much for words. "When I left the other night, I meant to come back, but something ... pulled me away."

"What do you mean?"

185

"Do you remember when you first found me—when I was losing time?"

Rose nodded.

"It was like that." Sylvie's brow furrowed, eyes caught on some stray point like the memory had carried her off. "One minute I was clearing my head on the grounds, the next I was at the edge of the forest, and it felt like something was drawing me in. After that, it was all dark. I could hear voices, feel people moving around even, but my eyes were too heavy to open. Everything was dull and gray, and I—"

Sylvie's voice trembled, then gave out. Sucking in a breath, she leaned back ever so slightly, chin lifting to the overgrown ceiling. To a passing glance, she might have seemed calm, pensive even. But Rose studied her with an eye well trained to find any cracks in her facade.

The subtle tightening of her lips. A weary tilt to her brow. Little fractures in her mask as it threatened to crumble away—weaknesses Rose would have once collected greedily. Yet, to her great surprise, she found she had no stomach for them now.

Sylvie looked so small, tucked up against the pillows. So vulnerable. Every sharp edge and sly word had buried itself away, leaving only a scared, broken girl. Still utterly beautiful, even etched in pain and grief.

For one wild moment, Rose longed to reach for her. To pull her close and brush aside the memories eating away at her. She glanced down at their hands, only a hair's breadth away from each other. And yet it may as well have been a ravine.

Somehow, there was a part of her that knew there would be no coming back from crossing it. This unspoken, mangled thing between them would shatter like cracked glass, and they would both be left scarred by it.

Moving her hand away, Rose swallowed hard, for the thought had left a bitter taste in her mouth. This was *Sylvie*, she reminded herself—not some wounded puppy.

When she spoke again, it nearly made Rose jump. "It was cold, and dark, and I wasn't sure where I was. It smelled like damp stones, and there was this awful, grating, dripping noise. But then I heard your voice, and it was like a dam burst. Suddenly there was light, color—life. I saw you on the riverbank … with Aveline. And after, with your mother. I—I'm sorry."

The word pierced Rose's heart more surely than any blade. Of all people, she never thought she'd hear it fall from Sylvie's lips. Once, the pity pulling at her voice would have wounded her, left her raw and aching. Or her pride, at least.

But it didn't anymore.

Instead, it simply soothed her. Warm and bright, it was clear enough now that she could recognize it for what it was—sympathy. No, even that did not fit. *Empathy.* Simple words to bind them, to let Rose know Sylvie *saw* her. And, in so doing, saw herself too.

"So am I."

Sylvie's brows shot up her forehead. "Why?"

"I—" Rose faltered. *Why, indeed?*

She was the only one who could see Sylvie—who could help her. And yet, just like with Aveline, she'd been so reluctant to lend her aid. She could wrap her inaction in so many pretty reasons, each more compelling than the one before. But she knew, in the deepest parts of her heart, what it truly came down to. *Fear.*

Fear of the law, her mother, even sometimes of her own mind. But she couldn't let it bind her any longer.

"I could have done so much more for you," she said finally. "For both of you. But I won't let you end up like her. I can't. We'll find out what happened to you. I promise."

For a long moment, Sylvie said nothing at all. But then a sad smile spread across her lips, slow and sure. "Thank you, Thenlif." A stray spark danced behind her eyes as her smile faltered and her voice softened. "Rose."

Rose's cheeks flared, and she ducked her head, suddenly unable to hold Sylvie's gaze. Clearing her throat, she turned her attention back to what she'd said before—anything to pull her away from this soft blossoming of unbearable warmth in her chest.

If it was true, then maybe she'd been right. Sylvie wasn't quite dead. But she might be near it. Aveline's body had been almost pristine, so it would track that she too had been held in some sort of stasis all these months. At least, that would be the kinder option. If that was the case, then they might not have much time before Sylvie wound up the same way.

Rose swallowed hard, shaking the thought away. "Have you ever heard of the Cair Riacodla incantation?"

Sylvie blinked. "What does that have to do with anything?"

"Everything, maybe." Rose pursed her lips. "It can be used to keep people in stasis, on the very edge of death. You thought you and Aveline weren't normal ghosts—this could explain why the hauntings are so unusual."

For a moment, she could swear a soft flush stole across Sylvie's cheeks. "And you, uh, think this happened to Aveline too?"

Rose nodded. "Maybe. The room you mentioned—I think I've seen it in one of Aveline's visions. It could be where they're holding you."

"Oh." Sylvie's voice sounded breathless—strained, as if she were fighting the urge to retch. "But then how did Aveline die? Why now, after all this time?"

Rose frowned. She had a point. If Sylvie and Aveline were part of some ritual the Order needed them alive for, why had Aveline turned up dead? And why had her body been abandoned so brazenly for the world to see? There *had* to be something they were missing.

"You're right. It doesn't make sense."

A sly grin broke across Sylvie's face. "Never thought I'd hear you admit that."

"But …"

Her smirk slipped. "And there it is."

"Maybe Aveline's death report will tell us more," Rose continued, ignoring her. "Though I doubt my mother will be keen to share the details. And it likely won't give us anything about where the Order might be holding *you*."

"Do we know that they are?" Sylvie yawned, and then paused.

Rose raised an eyebrow. "Are you … tired?"

"I—I don't know."

Did ghosts even need sleep? Sylvie had never seemed to before—up at all hours, fidgeting with Rose's things in the middle of the night. And yet, when Rose peered closer, circles hung under Sylvie's eyes—dark and heavy. Her heart sank, flashes of Aveline's sunken eyes dancing through her memory. Was this how it started?

"Maybe you should go back to your dorm—"

"No!" The word burst from Sylvie's lips as if it had a life of its own—forceful and fierce.

Rose held her hands up in surrender. "All right."

"Sorry, it's just, if I leave you, I—" She drew her knees up to her chest, her voice soft and small like a child's. "I don't want to be stuck in that place again."

Rose's throat tightened. *No.* She didn't suppose she did. Whatever linked them also bound them. And there was a part of her that didn't want to let Sylvie go either.

"Then stay."

Sylvie's face softened, a shy spark dancing through her eyes as her cheeks flushed. "What, here?"

Heat crept up Rose's neck. She'd made the offer without thought—some instinctive desire to protect Sylvie from the shadows that threatened to swallow her up. But now that the idea lay before them, it set her heart beating faster. The only place for Sylvie to sleep was in her bed. Side by side, all night long. But it was too late to rescind the offer now.

"I mean, sure?" She pulled at her collar, which pressed tight against her flush skin. "Where else would you go?"

It was sound reasoning, but that didn't stop Rose's heart from fluttering in her chest like some erratic caged bird. Sylvie's eyes narrowed as if she could hear it, and the heat beneath her collar grew nearly unbearable.

"As long as you're sure, Thenlif."

Of course she was. She swallowed hard and gave a sharp nod before darting to her dresser. Out of the corner of her eye, she could've sworn a small smile stole across Sylvie's lips, but she didn't dare to look. Grabbing her nightclothes, she hurried into the washroom to change.

The sight that met her in the mirror wasn't kind, but she quickly averted her eyes out of habit, running a comb through her curls and splashing cold water on her face. Eyes fixed firmly on the sink, she blotted the towel over her cheeks and smoothed her night creams and moisturizers across her skin. What was she even *doing*?

Going through her nightly routine as if Sylvie wasn't on the other side of the door, lounging on her bed. Her stomach did a strange sort of flip. But what if Sylvie really was becoming like Aveline? What if she woke in the middle of the night to clouded, dead eyes staring back at her?

A wave of nausea rolled over Rose, and she gripped the edges of the sink, knuckles white. But then she paused, lifting her gaze slowly back to the mirror.

The glass stood utterly still. It didn't shift or waver. It did not move at all, and the only gaunt reflection held within was her own.

Aveline was gone—for good this time. Her milky eyes would no longer hang over her shoulder, her piercing shrieks would no longer haunt her nightmares. She was just gone, with hardly a soul left to mourn her. And what if Sylvie was soon to follow?

Rose sucked in a sharp breath. She had to find out what had happened. If not just for Aveline, then for Sylvie too. To save her from the same slow fate. Tugging her nightclothes into place, she straightened her shoulders and reentered her bedroom.

She'd half expected to be met with some snide remark from Sylvie for her satin sleepwear. Or, at the very least, a mocking glance for the amount of bare skin they showed. But the only sound that greeted her was a soft snoring.

Sylvie's head rested lightly on one of Rose's pillows, her feet tangled around the bedsheets that had been neatly tucked. But she looked at peace, even still dressed in her dark turtleneck and plaid skirt. It was all Rose could do not to stare as she eased into the bed beside her.

Some wild longing took hold in her to stroke Sylvie's cheek. To run her fingers through the soft strands of Sylvie's gossamer hair, or across the gentle curve of her full lips. What would they taste like when the sharpness was gone from her tongue? When all that was left were sweet words and honeyed promises?

Rose's cheeks flushed, and she pulled her hand away. What was she doing—this was *Sylvie*. Crawling under her covers, she firmly shoved all such thoughts to the very back of her mind.

Pulling her duvet up to her ears, Rose settled into her pillows with a soft sigh. Aveline might be gone, but Sylvie was still here. Safe and sound—for now. And, in the morning they would find out who held her. They *had* to.

23

TWO STARS

THE first touch was featherlight. Gentle fingers trailing across the bare stretch of Rose's shoulder, tangling in her curls. The second was firmer: soft kisses brushed against her throat, sending a shiver down her spine. The third was almost feverish as the kisses sank lower. And lower still.

Heat pooled in Rose's stomach, and she groaned as Sylvie's lips brushed against her inner thighs. Tender, tantalizing kisses over delicate flesh that sent a flush creeping across Rose's cheeks. She reached out, longing to wind her fingers through Sylvie's sleek hair, or pull her close—kiss her until the very breath was stolen from her lungs. But they curled only around empty air.

Rose woke with a start. Not to hushed whispers and stolen kisses, though heat still skittered across her skin. Not to quiet birdsongs or the soft patter of rain on old stones, though they echoed in from the window beyond. Rather to an odd scratching sound.

The scribbling of pen over paper—harsh lines scraped deep into the page. Turning her head toward the noise, Rose blinked, blearily making out Sylvie's shape, dull and blurred against the gray skies behind her. Furious heat stole across her cheeks at the sight of her—not at her shoulder, trailing kisses across her bare flesh.

Instead, she was tucked in the window seat, etching away at something in her lap as if the world had ceased to exist around her. Perhaps it had, Rose mused. For this moment, perhaps it was just the two of them lost in this hazy morning, still caught on the edge of slumber.

Breathing in deeply, Sylvie didn't even seem to notice when Rose sat up, peering over her shoulder. Her eyes traced the charcoal lines, cheeks flushing. There was a familiar shape to the drawing, a face she knew well staring back at her as if it were a mirror. *It was her.*

Not drained and dreary as she so often was these days, but vibrant and smiling, curled in the branches of a great tree with a book. Her brow was drawn, and her curls tucked behind her ears, but some charm must have lain over the sketch, for her feet kicked to and fro, her lip caught between her teeth as she flipped through the pages.

A small sigh slipped from Rose's lips before she could stop it. Sylvie jumped and scrambled to cover the drawing, her own cheeks flushing furiously.

"Oh!" Her voice cracked. "I didn't realize you were awake."

For a moment, all Rose could do was smile. It was strange to see Sylvie flustered—so at odds with her elegant facade. Though at least it seemed that she wasn't the only one with tender, longing dreams in the early hours of dawn.

"What were you drawing?"

"Nothing."

Rose ran her hands over her bedsheets, a small frown pulling at her brow. It hadn't looked like nothing. "Where did you find a sketchbook?"

"You had an old one tucked away in your things. It didn't look like you were using it, so I borrowed it."

Sylvie's eyes fell to the floor, and Rose's heart skipped a beat. Perhaps she shouldn't have said anything. Should have let her draw until the dim light of day faded, and they could've curled back into bed. Warm and safe, with the rest of the world tucked away behind her door. Heat crept across Rose's cheeks, words tangling around her tongue when a knock rang through the room.

"Are you expecting someone?" Sylvie asked.

Rose scowled at the door. "No."

It could be Fen, but she couldn't remember the last time he'd actually knocked. Privacy wasn't exactly his strong suit. Swinging her legs over the bed, she pulled a robe over her nightclothes and strode across the room. She'd barely turned the knob when the door flew open, producing none other than Ewan.

Rose stared at them for several long seconds, hazel eyes locked on blue in the silence. A long navy coat hung down to their knees and a white scarf fell from their shoulders, stark against their flushed brown skin. At least this time it looked to be from the wind and not an early bout of drinking.

"Ewan?" Sylvie's voice shook her from her thoughts.

"What are *you* doing here?" Rose finally managed.

"I—" They ran a hand through their gold-streaked hair. "I need to talk to you."

Rose raised an eyebrow, her gaze sliding to Sylvie and back. "Funny, you didn't have much interest in talking before."

"Things are different now."

"Are they?"

Ewan was silent for a long moment, blue eyes piercing as they bore into hers. "Yesterday, you thought the body in the river was Sylvie's, not Aveline's—why?"

Rose scoffed. "I'm surprised you remember yesterday."

"I remember enough." The muscles in their jaw tensed.

"All right." She folded her arms over her chest. "Then what were you apologizing for?"

Ewan recoiled. "What?"

"In the pub, before Aveline's body was found, you said you should've listened to me. About what?"

They stared down at their feet. "That was nothing. Just drunken ramblings."

"They're lying." Sylvie's eyes narrowed. Kicking her feet off the window seat, she glided over to Rose's side.

"Yes, I can tell that much, thanks."

Ewan frowned. "What?"

"Nothing." Rose squirmed under their gaze. "But it was hardly drunken ramblings. You apologized to me. Publicly. Bit out of character, wouldn't you say?"

193

To her surprise, they laughed. She'd never heard the sound before, and it crawled across her skin. "You're the one who chased off down the riverbank in tears over a woman you supposedly hate."

"Tears?" said Sylvie.

Rose cleared her throat. "I wasn't in tears."

"You seemed pretty concerned."

"And you weren't?"

"A bit, sure. But not like you." They shook their head. "The minute they said a body was in the river, you were terrified it was Sylvie. Like you were already expecting the worst."

Rose's eyes narrowed. How could they stand here in front of her like they'd had no hand in this whole mess? Since the day they realized Sylvie was missing, they'd been cagey, elusive. Why should they be at all shocked that Rose was seeking out answers?

"Perhaps it's not so odd that I was expecting it, but rather that you weren't." Rose stepped closer to Ewan. "Sylvie's been missing for weeks, and that wasn't your first thought when a body turned up in the river? Unless you've known all along what happened to her, of course."

"You think *I* had something to do with her disappearance?"

"Didn't you?" said Rose. "Either that or your Order. What did Sylvie do—threaten to expose them? Did they have to silence her?"

"What? No." Ewan shrank back, sucking in a sharp breath. "It's not what you think."

"Then tell me what it is."

"Rose." Sylvie tugged at her arm, but she shook her off.

"I can't." Ewan's voice cracked over the words, their breath growing more ragged as they pressed themselves against the door. "It's safer if you don't know."

"Please," she scoffed. "You don't care about anything or anyone but yourself. Not even Sylvie."

"Rose!" Sylvie stepped between them. "Stop. Just let them breathe."

Rose straightened, her stomach sinking at the way Ewan's chest heaved, their breaths short and shallow. They didn't meet her gaze, their back pressed firmly against the wall, as if bracing for her to strike them. Pity soured on her tongue as memories of their father towering over them flashed through her mind.

Hanging her head, she took a step back. Then another. Until their breathing slowed and their gaze lifted ever so slightly. But their fingers squeezed tightly around the doorknob, as if they might bolt at any moment.

"Tell them I'm here." Sylvie's voice brushed against her ear.

"What? No."

"It'll help … I hope." Sylvie bit her lip. "Tell them I'm sorry, but two stars can never burn in the same orbit."

"What?"

"They'll know what it means."

"Who are you talking to?" Ewan's voice was low and still slightly breathless.

Rose chewed the inside of her lip. Some incessant fear tugged at her chest, an ugly, restless worry. How many unspoken things remained between her and Sylvie? How many untread feelings lay waiting to pull her away from Rose as surely as death itself?

She hated the way her heart fluttered at the thought. Even if they could still save Sylvie, would she run right back to Ewan? Forget whatever soft moments had passed between them in favor of the pairing that offered her safety, power—prestige. All the things that Rose could never give her.

Rose's jaw tightened. It didn't matter.

"I—" She sighed deeply. "Sylvie."

"What?"

"Well, I would have led up to it a bit more than *that*." Sylvie pursed her lips.

"She wants you to know that she's sorry." The words tumbled out of her. "And that two stars can never burn in the same orbit."

All the color drained from Ewan's face, their lips trembling. They stood there a moment, utterly still, as if they'd forgotten how to move. But the spell shattered and they threw open the door, bolting out into the corridor before Rose could stop them.

"Ewan, wait!" she called after them.

But she made no move to follow. Neither, she noted, did Sylvie. Instead, she merely sank onto the bed, staring up at the ceiling.

"What did that mean?" Rose asked finally.

Sylvie sighed. "It's what I said to them when we broke up."

"And you thought that would help?" She raised an eyebrow. But then the meaning of Sylvie's words hit her like a brick. "Wait, you remember?"

"When you were arguing—it's like it knocked something loose."

Rose inched closer. "How much do you remember, then?"

"Enough to know it was Ewan who sent you that note."

"What? How?"

"Because they gave me one just like it that night in the pub." She sat up, finally meeting Rose's gaze. "I think it's why we broke up."

"What is it then?"

"An invitation from the Order."

24

LIKE VULTURES

THE sea of students crowding around the assembly hall made Rose's skin crawl. Their whispers hung on the air—sharp and insidious. They bounced off the soaring ceilings, adorned with ornate moldings and intricate carvings, testaments to the craftsmanship of a bygone era. But there was only one name on everyone's lips. One glaring, empty spot at the front of the room.

Aveline.

It had been months since anyone had even mentioned her, the interest in her disappearance as fleeting as any other piece of idle gossip. But now her death had revived it. Some strange form of life that Aveline herself no longer possessed.

Rose's heart twinged with guilt as she leaned back in her chair. The summons for the assembly had come shortly after Ewan left, with little pretense and even less clarity. But it didn't take a diviner to discern the reason for it. What else could it be?

She glanced over the gathered students, her chest tightening. Some wept quietly, while others just sat in stunned silence. But most chattered away, trading theories and rumors that swirled around the girl's death. Like vultures swarming her corpse—each desperate to pull the best bit of gossip off the bone.

A shudder crept down Rose's spine. Beside her, Sylvie sat in a sort of dazed despondency—eyes fixed unblinkingly at the front of the room. Would they do the same to her one day? If they failed to find her, would her remains become nothing more than fuel for idle tongues?

Shaking the thought away, Rose's gaze drifted around the room. It looked so different from the night of the gala, as if it were another room entirely. Of course, that was the point of it, after all—ever morphing into whatever purpose the academy required of it. Elaborate chandeliers hung from the ceiling, casting a warm and inviting glow over the portraits and plaques upon the walls, paying tribute to Dunhollow's most revered scholars, distinguished alumni, and benefactors.

A grand stage stood at the front of the hall, flanked by sapphire velvet curtains, adorned with the university's crest. She bit back a scoff. Her mother would claim it was a symbol of unity; a reminder to stay strong to the values of Dunhollow in these trying times. But it was little more than a vulgar display of her mother's power as it came under threat.

Now that the matter of Aveline could no longer be ignored, her mother had been forced to leave no stone unturned. Rose was sure that grated at her. For someone who adored the spotlight, her mother always did best in the shadows of subterfuge and guile. If she could not control the story, she wanted no part in it. But now she would have no choice.

A hush fell over the hall as the woman herself swept into the room, wreathed in a black gown and a vague air of grief. But it was a hollow gesture to Rose's eyes, born out of necessity rather than any genuine feeling.

She took to the stage as if the loss were her own, gripping the railing tightly to steady herself as she climbed the low steps. Amazing what a show she could put on when the performance was worth her while.

Clearing her throat, her mother slowly lifted her eyes to gaze out over her audience and gave a watery smile, her bottom lip quivering for added effect. Rose rolled her eyes.

"As I'm sure many of you already know, we're gathered here on this dreadful day to mourn the untimely passing of one of our own. Aveline Goarsbel, taken well before her time."

Her mother bowed her head, allowing a moment of silence to take hold of the room. Some students followed suit, but most just shared glances, a few muffled coughs breaking the quiet hush. Rose fidgeted with her black lace gown.

It seemed wrong, somehow, to mourn the girl now when, for so many months, this was the precise thing she'd wished for. That Aveline might move on and leave her to a fragile peace. But her absence was just as haunting as her presence, a gaping wound Rose could not seem to close.

"What did I miss?" A quiet whisper in her ear made her jump.

Fen peered over her left shoulder, eyes still blurry from sleep and hair slightly disheveled. She shook her head, pulling her satchel off the chair so he could sit.

"Not much." She kept her voice low. "Where have you been?"

"Sleeping," he hissed. "Your mother could've given a bit more warning."

Rose bit her tongue, resisting the urge to remind him that it was nearly noon. Instead, she turned back to her mother, who was wiping a well-timed tear from her pale cheek.

"I know she will be sorely missed, and to give you all time to grieve this awful tragedy, classes will be canceled for the remainder of the week." She stared down at her hands, as if gathering her thoughts. When her gaze lifted again, it was dark and deadly. "Rest assured that while we all feel her loss keenly, the faculty is working in tandem with the capital inquisitors, and we will not rest until we find out why this heinous crime was committed and bring the perpetrator to justice."

Low murmurs broke out across the hall in a hissed cacophony. The capital inquisitors? Well, at least that was something. Provided that her mother treated them to more truth than she had previously. Though the thought of their presence filled Rose with the faintest stirrings of dread.

"Furthermore, in the spirit of transparency, we believe that Aveline may not be the only victim," her mother went on. Rose perked up, her gaze sliding to Sylvie. "Sylven Belliaris has unfortunately also been reported missing. The capital inquisitors have requested we not release any further details, but recommend not traversing campus alone for the time being, and we'll be instituting a curfew of nine o'clock sharp. If you spot any suspicious behavior, please report it to myself or your professors."

199

Of course. Still hiding her failure behind the veil of protocol. Rose's fists clenched in her lap, nails drawing harsh marks against her palms.

"Finally, for any of you who are interested, Professor Troidilis will be hosting sessions to review defensive casting all week."

Was that it—some vague note to be careful and a few casting defense lessons? Rose gritted her teeth. She should have known better than to expect more.

"Thank you all for coming today." Her mother gave another hollow smile. "And remember, if you see anything, please speak up."

The moment she stepped down from the dais, every student in the room was on their feet. The room filled with the steady hum of chatter, the buzz slowly fading as, year by year, they filed out of the hall.

Rose and Fen followed suit, with Sylvie lagging a few paces behind. The steps outside the hall quickly clogged with students, who loitered about chatting, even with the fine mist of rain falling down upon them. Fen cast a glimmering barrier above their heads, taking Rose's hand to pull her through the mess of students.

Hissed whispers and sidelong glances followed them. But Fen only squeezed her hand tighter, pulling her away from the assembly hall and up a footpath to a small alcove. Rose blinked.

It took her a moment to realize where they were. Fen's courtyard, she'd once dubbed it. The only place at Dunhollow he ever sought solitude.

She glanced around at the golden leaves swaying gently in the breeze, nearly hiding the courtyard from view entirely. It was peaceful, she had to admit, with its little garden and moss-laden benches curled around a small pond. But it was so silent.

"So, do we buy her change of heart?" Fen said finally, settling onto one of the benches.

"Please," Rose scoffed. "She doesn't care about Aveline *or* Sylvie. It's just that now she'll have board members asking questions and concerned parents threatening to pull their donations."

"My mothers already sent through a letter this morning." Fen ran a hand through his hair. "They want to bring me home if this doesn't get solved soon."

Rose paused. Perhaps that was a good idea; depending on what they found out about the Order, it could be dangerous. She couldn't let anything happen to him on account of her. Her heart flipped. A selfish, cold part of her wished she could flee too.

"Maybe you should go."

"And miss all the fun?" He winked. "Don't count on it."

"I'm serious, Fen." She rubbed at the sleeve of her blouse. "It could be dangerous."

"Which is exactly why you need me. No offense, but I can't really count on Sylvie to protect you."

"*Fen.*"

"He's right," said Sylvie. "You're not really in any position to fight off an ancient magical society on your own."

"*I* don't matter."

"Yes, you do," Sylvie snapped, at the very same moment that Fen's brow creased.

"You do to me."

Rose recoiled from them both. And what about them? Sylvie hung by a thread already and Fen would follow her into any danger. What would it cost her to get them both out of this safely?

Avoiding their eyes, her gaze flickered through the golden leaves. But they caught on odd shapes, huddled between the columns of the colonnade. Her mother, head bowed low and in stern conference with Sylverfir, Delia and Briony Burroak. *Strange.* She glanced back to the assembly hall, where the other professors herded students toward the main courtyard, offering advice and comfort as they went.

Rose's eyes slid back to her mother's cadre. What was so pressing that they had to discuss it now, out of earshot of the others? Something about Aveline, perhaps?

She darted behind the canopy of leaves, pulling Fen along with her as her mother glanced up. "Sylvie, do you think you could get close enough to hear what they're saying?"

"What?" Her gaze followed Rose's. "Oh, maybe."

Fen peered over her shoulder. "What are you thinking?"

"That my mother might have some news on Aveline's death." She brushed some stray leaves away from her brow. "If we can determine what she had in her system, then maybe we can find out who bought it and trace them back to the Order."

"Worth a shot." Sylvie shrugged.

She turned to leave, but a solid form stepped directly into her path. Sylvie skirted sideways, barely more than a breeze through Arden's shock of red hair. But his pale blue eyes didn't follow her.

Shit.

"Hello, Thenlif." Arden's nasally voice grated at her ears. "I was wondering where you'd run off to hide."

Of all people to run into now. Rose's jaw tightened. Had he been following them? Beside her, Sylvie's lip curled in disgust as Arden sneered down at Rose. Fen, of course, had already pulled a polite smile, stepping up to Rose's side.

"You shouldn't sneak up on people like that, Arden. And all by yourself?" Fen gave a soft *tsk*. "Didn't you hear? It's dangerous to be on your own these days."

"You're one to talk." Arden's lips thinned, glancing Rose up and down. "After her mother's gross negligence in Aveline's case, I can't imagine how you feel safe cavorting with her. Who knows what the two of them might cover up next."

At this, Rose snorted. "You think *I* had something to do with Aveline's death?"

"Oh, it's not just me—the whole school does." He leaned in closer to her. "You know, Aveline's parents are even thinking of suing Dunhollow. On the bright side, if they shut this place down, at least they'll finally get rid of you."

Rose's jaw snapped shut with an audible click. "Really? I'm surprised they don't suspect *you*."

"What?"

Some small voice in the back of her mind urged her to tread carefully. For all that Arden was a fool, he wasn't one to be trifled with lightly. But his audacity bit down to her very bone, and all thought of care or caution fled her.

"Do they know you broke up with their daughter only weeks before she disappeared?" She stepped toward him. "That you did nothing, even when she was reported missing? That your arrogance is only matched by your depravity?"

With a scoff, Arden's eyes flickered to Fen. "Does she always run her mouth like this? Not sure why you put up with it, but I'm sure there must be some other ... benefits to being her only friend."

Fen stilled, the smile slipping from his lips. Gone was any trace of his usual charming facade as he squared his shoulders, drawing himself up to his full, towering height. His dark eyes sparked with flame behind his glasses.

"More than there is to being yours, at least." He tilted his head with a cold smirk. "Your tongue isn't nearly so clever."

Rose grinned as Arden's face flushed, his skin nearly the same color as his hair. What had he hoped to gain in coming here anyway? A confession from her? She doubted it.

No. She studied him as if he were a viper poised to strike. The flush of his freckled cheeks. The malice in his pale eyes. He looked almost unstable, somehow. Like a petulant child on the cusp of a tantrum. And she was perhaps just the easiest target.

Unless .... Had Ewan perhaps told him of their argument this morning—that she was looking into the Order? After all, if Ewan and Sylvie were members, she could bet Arden was too. Perhaps he didn't care about her guilt at all—only tying up loose ends.

"Maybe I'll write to them." Rose gave a small shrug. "Tell them all about you and their daughter. Oh, and your little Order. I'm sure they'd love to know—"

In a heartbeat, Arden's hand curled around her throat, choking the breath out of her. Rose staggered back as lightning sizzled up his arm, inching ever closer to her flesh. "Shut your mouth, Thenlif."

Beside her, Sylvie stiffened. Ice formed around her fists, her magic pulling at the back of Rose's mind. Yet it was Fen who stepped forward, his flames warm and bright against her.

"Let her go, Arden."

But Arden's grip only tightened. Fen was the stronger caster by far, but Arden's pride was boundless. Whatever punishment Fen might bring to bear upon him, he couldn't stand to lose face now. He would squeeze the very life from her—consequences be damned.

Rose's head spun. Memories burned at the back of her mind of Aveline's bloated, rotting fingers curling around her throat. Perhaps Arden had done the very same thing to her.

"Drunk already, Arden?" Ewan's voice cut between them. "You must be, laying hands on the chancellor's daughter so publicly."

Rose blinked. What were *they* doing here?

"And what is our dear chancellor going to do about it?" Arden didn't look away from Rose. "Seems like she has other problems on her hands."

Ewan grabbed his shoulder. "Don't be a fool. Syl is still missing and Aveline just turned up dead—if you run around assaulting people, who do you think the capital inquisitors will investigate first?"

"I'm sure they'll understand."

Rose's pulse pounded in her ears, breath clawing at her throat. But something burgeoned at the back of her mind. Warm and soft, it held her steady, and she latched on to it desperately, pulling herself back from the brink.

"And if they don't?" Ewan's bright blue eyes darted between her and Arden. "Your parents won't bail you out again. Not after the incident in Telemestra."

Finally, Arden looked up. "So, what, you're defending her now?"

"Hardly. But someone has to keep you from digging your own grave." Ewan leaned in closer. "Besides, you wouldn't want my father to hear of this, would you?"

The muscles in Arden's jaw twitched, his hand tightening around Rose's throat for a second longer. But then he released her with a scoff. Rose pitched forward, sucking in shuddering breaths. Fen caught her, his hands warm and soft as he helped her steady herself. Eyes flitting among the three of them, Arden turned, shoved past Ewan, and swept off into the rain without another word.

Rose's throat burned as she swallowed hard. She didn't dare meet Fen's or Sylvie's gazes, but she could almost feel their worry, choking her as surely as Arden's grip. After several long moments, she finally straightened, eyes narrowing at Ewan.

"What are *you* doing here?"

They eyed her a moment before holding up a leather-bound dossier. "We need to talk."

25

THE ARCHIVES

ANCIENT wooden stairs creaked beneath Rose's feet, the dank smell of wet earth and mildew hanging heavy on the air. She swallowed a gag as something sticky dripped onto her shoulder. The archives looked like the kind of place one might expect to find a ghost. Full of cobwebs, old tomes and a fine layer of dust, it was almost like some skeletal ancestor of the library she knew and loved. Rose shuddered as they delved further into their depths.

Why she had agreed to follow Ewan she couldn't say. But some small spark in her heart pushed her forward, some burning hunger for the knowledge they promised.

"Hey." Fen's fingers curled around hers, making her jump in the darkness. "Are you all right?"

"Fine," she muttered, rubbing at her sore throat.

"Rose, please." He pulled her to a stop. "Are you sure?"

His eyes were near black in the darkness of the tunnels, but still they pierced her to the core. Rose ducked her head Of course she wasn't fine. But there was a desperate, restless part of her that begged for action. As if the moment she stopped, she might collapse under the weight of it all.

Her throat throbbed beneath the strain of tears, and she tried to turn away, but Fen didn't let her go. Instead, he cupped his hands around her face, gently stroking away the marks Arden had left with a simple healing incantation. Rose breathed in deeply as the scent of red wine and worn leather washed over her.

Yet it didn't soothe her this time, tugging only at her guilt. Even in this dim light, there was something that flashed in Fen's eyes. Something tender and raw—unnamed and always unspoken between them. Something she couldn't bear to break.

Rose's gaze flashed to Sylvie, but she followed behind Ewan still, seemingly unaware that she and Fen had even stopped. Turning back to Fen, Rose swallowed hard.

"I will be," she said finally. "But we should hear what Ewan has to say."

Whatever lingered in Fen's eyes snuffed out in a moment, falling flat and dull as he stepped back. "Sure." His voice was low and almost hollow. But he recovered quickly. "Do you think they mean to murder us down here?"

Rose shot him a glare. "Not funny, Fen."

Darting through another archway, she joined Ewan and Sylvie before a low table scattered with scrolls and maps. The temperature dropped significantly, and Rose shivered, her breath coming out in small puffs. Honestly, she would hardly have been surprised if they *did* find a skeleton or two down here.

Ewan flicked their wrist, and flames flew forth. Dim, flickering lanterns came alive, casting eerie, dancing shadows on the decaying walls. Towering mahogany shelves, clearly once sturdy and grand, now sagged under the weight of aged tomes and lost history. Cobwebs clung to the corners, as if the spiders had claimed this forgotten realm as their own.

Books and manuscripts, yellowed with age, lined the shelves in scattered disarray. Some volumes were bound in worn leather, their covers bearing cryptic symbols and markings that hinted at arcane knowledge. Parchment scrolls lay unrolled and untouched for some years, if the thick layer of dust covering them was anything to go by.

It was peaceful, in a strange way. Secluded and serene. And almost utterly silent. The stillness was broken only by the staccato of dripping water, as if the hall itself wept for the forgotten stories and lost knowledge that lay within its decaying walls.

"How did you even find this place?" Fen's voice made Rose jump.

She frowned. "More importantly, what are we doing here?"

Ewan turned on them, throat bobbing. "Last time we spoke, you said Sylvie was with you. Is—is she now?"

Rose turned to Sylvie, who nodded slowly, though her eyes didn't quite meet hers. "She's here."

Their chest deflated, shoulders drooping. "Then she's dead?"

"You brought us all the way down here to ask me that?"

"Please, I just need to know."

"Honestly, *I* don't know." Rose sighed. "She seems stuck, somehow—walking the line between life and death."

"Shit," they muttered, running a hand through their short hair. After a moment, they pulled a roll-up from their pocket, lighting it and drawing in deeply. "How? Necromancy?"

Rose almost scoffed. If she knew that, did they really think she'd be here? *They* were the one with connections to the Order. *They* were the one who wanted to talk.

"We should be asking you that. After all, it was *your* Order that attacked her, wasn't it?"

"It's not *my* Order. It's my father's."

That wasn't exactly a denial. Rose's eyes narrowed. They'd dragged them all down into this decrepit crypt—the least they could do was give them some kind of answers.

"And why should we trust a thing out of your mouth? You've been working with your father since this whole mess started."

Ewan waved a hand, lighting an enwebbed set of candles at the center of the table. "How do you figure that?"

"Isn't that what you two were arguing about the night of the gala? He was afraid you'd exposed him somehow. Or *his* Order."

Their eyes darkened. "No, that was when I started to suspect him. I made the mistake of asking too many questions—of searching Sylvie's rooms. He thought my caring was a liability. That I'd bring ... uncomfortable questions upon the Order."

207

"Oh." Rose's heart stirred beneath the sting of pity. But she folded her arms over her chest. "And you're willing to go against him now, what—out of the goodness of your heart?"

"No." Their voice softened, and they held their dossier tighter. "For Sylvie. If my father did anything to her, I'd never … well, I just have to know."

Oh. Rose's chest tightened, and her gaze flickered to Sylvie. Tears welled in her amber eyes, fixed solely on Ewan in a way that twisted at Rose's heart. She hadn't said a word since they showed up. As if Ewan was all she could see. Rose's pulse lurched. Perhaps it was just the lure of finding out what had happened to her? But the thought felt hollow now.

Shoving the feeling aside, Rose turned back to Ewan. "All right then, what *is* the Order?"

They raised an eyebrow. "Sylvie didn't tell you?"

She glanced at Sylvie once again. "Her memory isn't exactly all there at the moment."

Ewan's eyes shifted between her and a bare section of wall behind her. After a moment, Rose realized they were looking for Sylvie. Her heart flipped.

"The Order of Salix has been around nearly as long as the school," they said finally, blowing a puff of foul-smelling smoke across the table. "It was founded by Narissa Salix to cultivate only the best casters. Promising students who could learn from each other and grow in their craft.

"Over time, it was less about skill and more about who you knew. After Narissa died, the masters of the Order began only admitting those students who could offer something to them. Money, power, connections within the empire. The secrecy only made it more elite, more desirable. Until it became the most powerful society on campus—and the most deadly."

"Deadly how?"

"In the same way Dunhollow is." Something flashed behind Ewan's bright blue eyes, dark and dangerous. "It only exists to prove to the world that the empire's spellcasters are the most elite, and it crushes any deemed unworthy of that title. The Order of Salix is the apex of that purpose."

Rose frowned. "Then why have I never heard about it?"

"Because the previous chancellor expunged all records of it, according to my father." They took another long draw from their roll-up.

"Something happened when he was a student—something that ruined the Order. When your mother took over, the ban on the Order remained in place. At least until last year."

Her mother *had* seemed to hate the Order when Rose had brought it up. And she'd certainly always despised Imrys Elaegius. But Rose had assumed that was just a professional vendetta. As head board member, Imrys was always trying to stifle her mother's plans or sabotage her proposals, but maybe there was something more to it.

Still, why would an old school rivalry lead to people dying today? After all, as much as Sylvie used to annoy her, she didn't think she ever could've held on to such hatred for thirty years.

Used to. The thought prodded at the back of her mind. Did she not still?

Had her smile lost its arrogance? Had her sharp tongue grown dull? Rose eyed Sylvie across the table. Perhaps it was just her imagination, but there was a warmth to her now, some small rush of comfort in the scent of her perfume, a longing in her lingering gaze. Like a book worn by fondness, its spine no longer stiff, its pages folded and marred by use.

When had *that* happened? Rose's brow furrowed, the thought curdling like dairy. But memories of Sylvie's phantom kisses flickered through her mind, sending a flush of heat across her cheeks.

"What happened last year?" she asked, turning away from Sylvie.

"The Order was reformed."

"Why?"

Ewan loosened the buttons at their collar. "My father wasn't precisely forthcoming on the matter. From what I gathered, he thought there was power in the timing. It was thirty years to the day that the Order had fallen—some diviner said there was strength in the trinity for rebirth."

So, Sylvie had been right—Imrys had been dabbling in divining. But how did that explain her visions? Or whatever magic made spectres of Sylvie and Aveline?

Fen snorted. "A diviner—really?"

A slow smirk spread across Ewan's lips, their roll-up dangling idly between their fingers. "My father is obsessed with old magic. Ancient artifacts, lost spells, even the forbidden arts. Especially those, really. He thinks it gives him an edge, I imagine."

Rose's jaw clenched. Just as Sylvie had said. Why was it those with the most power who always craved more? Hoarding it away and playing with magic they barely understood, no matter what became of those who had the misfortune of being caught in their path. She shouldn't have been surprised, she supposed. It was exactly the type of thing Dunhollow aimed to breed in its students. Still, the hubris of those with too much money and not enough sense knew no bounds.

"And what does that have to do with Sylvie?"

"Sylvie was an initiate to the Order." Ewan tapped their roll-up at the edge of the table.

A sharp gasp from Sylvie turned Rose's head. "What is it?"

Her eyes were wide, almost frantic. "I remember—Ewan gave me the invitation, but I couldn't go through with it."

"She said she dropped out."

"Yeah." Ewan fixed Rose with a hard stare. "I was her sponsor to join, but the night she disappeared, she backed out—said what she told you about the two stars and just left. When you said she was missing, I went searching in her rooms and saw her notes on the Order, so I figured they had to be involved."

"Just from a note?" said Fen. "Why?"

Ewan pursed their lips, tossing a leather dossier onto the table. "Not just that. Aveline was an initiate too. One of the first, actually, and look how she ended up."

Rose stared at the folder. "Is that—"

"Aveline's death report." They slid it toward her. "Help yourself."

She took it eagerly, flipping through the first few pages. "How did you get it?"

"My father is old friends with the chief examiner, so I requested it on his behalf." They shrugged. "He may be an ass, but he has his uses."

"Does it say if she was drugged?" Sylvie peered over Rose's shoulder.

Rose scanned through the pages. *Cause of death*—it read, *Cardiac arrest.* Then, further down: *Significant traces of sedative build-up, laced with arcane energy—further tests required. Likely that the subject was comatose at time of death, possibly for an extended period.*

"Yes. And there were traces of arcane energy in her system."

"Could be proof of Cair Riacodla then," Fen said. "Alchemy always leaves an arcane trace."

Ewan raised an eyebrow. "What are you talking about?"

Rose glanced between them and Sylvie. "We think that Aveline was kept in a comatose state all this time. Sylvie too."

"*What?*" Ewan choked on a puff of smoke. "So, you think the Order is kidnapping students, putting them in a trance, just to kill them off months later. Why?"

Rose closed the dossier. "You said your father was obsessed with forbidden magics—he didn't happen to mention some arcane necromantic ritual, did he?"

"He didn't pencil anything in on the Order calendar, if that's what you mean." Ewan heaved a sigh. "It could certainly be one of his personal experiments, though."

Rose shuddered. "Still doesn't explain *why*, though. Why them? And why would I be the only one who can see them?"

"What if you're next?" Fen fidgeted with his glasses. "Marked somehow, and Aveline and Sylvie were just warnings all along."

Rose's stomach sank. Perhaps he was right. Aveline had nearly choked the life out of her. What if, all this time, the girl hadn't been a torment but a glimpse into her very future? Icy tendrils of fear snaked through Rose's veins, a chill skittering across her skin.

And Sylvie? Rose glanced over to find her face ashen, her lovely lips parted in a soft gasp. Once, her presence would have been more a terror than even Aveline's ghastly manifestations. But she didn't feel like a warning—neither foul nor fearsome. Not anymore, at least.

"I wouldn't put anything past my father." Ewan's voice jarred Rose from her thoughts. "He'd sacrifice this whole school just for a shred more influence, and Sylvie had powerful casting he'd have loved to siphon. As for you? I don't know, maybe he hopes to hurt your mother?"

Rose's fear soured on her tongue. Well, more the fool him then. Her death would likely be a welcome relief for her mother. Still, to be reduced to little more than a ploy—it stung, like vinegar poured on an open wound. Her life had already been wasted in service of her mother. She couldn't let her death be claimed by her too.

Rose's nails dug into the aging wood of the table, knuckles whitening. "Then how do we prove it was him? He's still holding Sylvie somewhere."

"The Order Guildhall, probably."

"You have a guildhall?"

211

"We're not heathens." They snorted. "It's a huge stone manor on the other end of these tunnels, actually. In the Whispering Woods."

The Whispering Woods? Dark images flickered through Rose's mind. Of scraggly trees and chanting voices. Of dimly lit tunnels and shrinking walls. That could easily be the place she'd seen in her visions.

"Then we need to get in there." She leaned against the table. "Though I doubt your father would let us walk right through the front door."

"Actually, he might." A slow grin spread across Ewan's lips. "I think I have an idea."

26

TO THE MOON

THE start of exam season held a nervous energy that hung heavily over the students of Dunhollow. The library was packed with them, any sense of decorum lost to the bitter stench of desperation. First-years crowded around the front desk, badgering Delia with relentless requests, while second- and third-years battled with misbehaving books and tumultuous tomes. The smell of sweat and fear hung on the air, nearly drowning out the scent of aged books.

Midterms were still two weeks away, but already chaos thrummed through the room like a racing heartbeat. Usually, Rose would have loved the scribblings of frantic pens against parchment. She would have made a sport of it, watching the influx of students to the library, desperately cramming in the knowledge they'd so easily discarded in the first half of the semester.

But now, by a cruel twist of fate, she was one of them, as Sylvie and Aveline had left her precious little time for studying. Or anything, really. It seemed death was all that occupied her now, and the sight of her future filled her with cold, hard dread. If she even made it that far.

"What a mess." Sylvie sighed beside her, eyeing the crowding students with clear disdain.

"It's midterms. Unlike you, some students actually have to study."

"Sounds awful." Sylvie gave a mock shudder. "Why did Ewan want to meet here then? It's packed tighter than a can of sardines."

She wasn't wrong. But Ewan's note had been as elucidating as it was long. A brief "meet me in the library," and little else but a time. Hopefully they had something to show for their grand plan to make up for dragging them here after a week of silence.

Scanning the library, Rose finally spotted their gold-streaked hair at one of the central tables, packed between a gaggle of chattering first-years and a table full of fourth-years, heads all bent low over their texts. Fen sat beside them, poring over a scattering of tomes and what looked to be a few browning maps.

No. Rose frowned as she edged closer. Not maps—schematics. Of the archives, unless she was mistaken.

"Rose!" Fen beamed as he caught sight of her.

"Oh good, you're here." Ewan glanced up as she and Sylvie approached, patting the seat beside them. "Come see."

Rose recoiled. A strange sense of ease held over Ewan, as if they were old friends. As if they hadn't spent the better part of the last three years treating her like a scuff mark on a new pair of loafers. Settling uneasily into the chair beside them, she glanced down at the browned, fading schematics before them, eyes darting to the nearby tables.

"Uh, are you sure this is a conversation you want to have here?"

"I don't just have these schematics lying around my dorm, Thenlif." Their eyes narrowed. There was the bored sense of superiority she was used to. "And you don't know what I had to do to get them, so we'll just have to make do here."

"What about—"

"That creepy corner you and Syl love so much?" They raised an eyebrow, swatting away a book that had dashed over from the table behind them. "Yeah, that's a crime scene now. Or had you forgotten that your mother decided to give a damn?"

Rose clenched her jaw. It was what she'd wanted, wasn't it? But the idea of the capital inquisitors pawing their way through her study nook felt almost violating somehow. That place belonged to her and

Sylvie, if in name only. That was where they'd met, where their rivalry was formed, where Sylvie had been—

The thought made her stomach flip. It was still *theirs*, though. Even if neither of them felt safe there any longer.

"Fine." She cleared her throat. "What did you want to show us?"

"Our way into the Order." They waved their hand over one of the schematics and removed the glamour, exposing a hidden tunnel. "See here? One of the old passageways leads directly to the cellar of the guildhall."

Rose followed their finger along the faded lines of a tunnel. But it didn't lead to a manor—or any structure at all. Just a cluster of trees at the edge of the forest.

"That path goes nowhere."

"I told you, the old chancellor expunged all records of the Order." They shrugged, lowering their voice. "The only reason this survived is because it mentions nothing of the Order by name. But trust me—it's there."

Well, that certainly explained why the library had failed her so utterly when it came to the Order. A sharp trilling made Rose's gaze dart to the front desk, where Delia pressed one of her buzzers.

"Quiet in the library, please," she signed, pointing to a bauble floating beside her.

It flickered haphazardly at eye level with the librarian, beaming brightly to alert Delia each time the din of chatter reached what she might classify as disruptive to the books' delicate sensibilities. Rose straightened. She'd never been shushed in the library before, and a fierce heat stole across her cheeks.

"I thought you said we could go through the front door?" Fen lowered his voice to a whisper.

"*We* can." Ewan gestured between themself and Fen. "This weekend is the equinox, and the Order will gather after Harvestfest to pay homage to the moon. You'll pose as my initiate, Fen, while Sylvie and Rose sneak in through the cellars to poke around."

"You want to split us up?" Rose said. "Absolutely not."

"Well, I can't very well take you as an initiate, can I?" Ewan leaned back in their chair with a creak. "My father has wanted to induct Fen for a while now, though. And that leaves you and Sylvie free to find where he's holding her."

"It will also leave Rose defenseless." Fen frowned, eyeing the schematics. "She can't cast, and neither can Sylvie at the moment. If Rose is your father's next target, I won't just leave her unprotected while we dance around under the full moon upstairs."

"I can sometimes cast," Sylvie protested.

"You cast once," Rose muttered. "And shooting a blast of ice at my mother isn't the same as going up against Ewan's father."

"Who said I wasn't aiming at you?"

"Please," Rose teased, leaning in closer. "You wouldn't dare."

"No." Sylvie's voice softened, her eyes dark and piercing. "I wouldn't."

Heat flared across Rose's cheeks as Sylvie refused to drop her gaze. But it prodded at something deep within her heart. Something barely formed and yet broken, time and time again.

She'd learned long ago to bury it beneath the more palatable guise of guile and dispassion. Easier to pretend she felt nothing at all than to have any feeling used against her, as it so often was here. Only Fen had ever made her feel as if anything beyond apathy was worthwhile.

And yet Sylvie brought it all simmering to the surface as if summoned by her will alone. Sylvie, who hated her guts. Sylvie, who'd made her academic career a living torment. Sylvie, who now stared at Rose like she was the only thing that mattered in the world.

Ewan cleared their throat, and Sylvie finally dropped her gaze. "Whenever you two are through flirting …"

"We're *not* flirting," she and Rose said at the same moment. Though of course, no one could hear Sylvie's protest.

Yet Rose could, all too keenly. The way it rolled off her tongue with such force, the way her lip curled. As if the very idea was an affront to her. Of course, Rose's heart sank. Whatever shreds of warmth had grown between them, it would never be anything more.

When Sylvie was alive and free again, she would leave this all behind in a heartbeat. What else had Rose been expecting? And yet she couldn't deny the way her heart twisted at the thought, a soft heat creeping across her cheeks.

Across the table, Fen raised an eyebrow at her, something faint and fleeting dancing across his gaze—almost crestfallen. But it was gone before it took shape, and he turned back to Ewan.

"Point is, it's too dangerous."

The buzzer trilled again, and Rose flinched, glancing back to Delia and her beaming bauble.

"Quiet!" The librarian's fingers danced over the order. "I won't tell you again."

But Ewan didn't bother lowering their voice. "It's not. My father doesn't think anyone knows about the old tunnels, so he's never bothered warding it, and he'll be too distracted with the ritual upstairs anyway. It's perfect."

"I still don't like it."

Rose frowned. Of course Fen was worried about her, when he was the one who'd be standing in the same room as Imrys. When he was the one who'd be subjected to whatever gruesome ritual the Order had planned. His casting was strong, at least—he could protect himself. Still if anything went wrong ...

She shuddered, unable to bear the thought. Her fingers itched to reach for him, as if she alone might keep him out of harm's way. But then she met Sylvie's eyes, and her stomach sank. She wouldn't fare any better in all this. If her body was being held in the depths of the Order's cellar, how would she feel stumbling upon whatever remained of her?

"What do you think, Sylvie?"

She blinked at Rose for a moment, as if she'd forgotten she could speak. And then she sighed. "It may be our only option."

It was strange the way her heart dropped. As if some persistent hope had finally deflated. But this was a good thing. They would finally catch the Order in the act and expose them. Save Sylvie, even. Yet none of that stopped the gnawing dread that ate away at Rose's mind.

Ewan cleared their throat. "What did she say?"

"She's in."

"Great."

"And what do you think?" said Fen. "The plan puts you in the most danger."

Rose faltered. What did that matter, in the end? "I—"

Before she could answer, a shadow fell over her, dark and looming. She blinked up at Delia, whose eyes burned with a wrath Rose was loath to see.

"Since you three seem to be ignoring my requests, I will have to ask you to leave." The librarian's hands moved with a jagged harshness.

"Sorry, Delia," Rose signed back. "We were just studying."

Delia's eyes fell to the schematics littered across the table, and then widened. Something flashed through them—some spark of fear that set Rose's heart racing. She *knew* them.

"Get out," she signed, her expression cold and hard.

Rose frowned. It wasn't like her to be so harsh. "But, Delia—"

"*Out!*" Her eyes would brook no argument. "Now."

"Yes, of course," Fen signed back. "Our sincerest apologies."

Grabbing hold of Rose, he hauled her to her feet as Ewan scrambled to gather up the schematics. But Delia's glare stopped them in their tracks, and they left them where they lay. Together, they all rushed for the door, like dogs with their tails tucked between their legs, not a word or a whimper uttered among them.

"What was that?" Ewan said finally.

"I've never seen Delia act like that." Fen chimed in. "Even when I returned a book three months late."

"It was the schematics." Rose stared back through the marred glass of the door. "Didn't you see her face? She knew what they were."

Sylvie paled beside her, eyes flickering with untold depths. "But how?"

The thought sank in her like a stone. How indeed? Ewan had said hardly anyone did—unless … perhaps Delia was a member? Who would be able to tell beneath a mask and a cloak? Yet she couldn't quite make the idea fit in her mind.

"She and Sylverfir both knew about the Order and were nervous about me looking into it." She bit down hard on the inside of her lip. "There's only one person they'd both fear enough to keep that secret for."

Fen's dark brow creased. "Rose, you don't really think—"

"Yes, I do," she snapped. "If you can believe Ewan's father is involved in all this, why not my mother? She's the one who covered up Aveline's disappearance and Sylvie's blood. Whatever's happening here, she's at the core of it. And I need to find out why."

27

CLOAK AND MASK

ROSE'S mother's personal chambers were the one place in all of Dunhollow that Rose rarely had cause to visit. She was sure her peers thought otherwise, but she stayed as far from them as she could. Visiting her mother's office was bad enough—and the woman practically lived there anyway. But going to her chambers felt like peeking behind her mother's mask somehow.

Peering into the cold, harsh truth of her soul, as it were. Rose shuddered. It was never a pleasant thing.

"This is a terrible idea," Sylvie whispered in her ear.

As if she didn't know that. But what other choice did they have? Whatever history lay between her mother and the Order, it would be foolish to enter that guildhall without it. Like igniting an alchemical solution without all its ingredients—they would all get burned.

"Yes, thank you," she snapped. "I know."

"Then why are we doing it?"

"Because she knows something about the Order, and I need to know what it is."

Gritting her teeth, Rose inserted her master key into the lock. It felt strange, somehow, using her mother's own key on her door. She doubted that her mother had even spelled the door to keep students out. Only the most foolish of them ever would've dared.

The lock clicked, and the door swung open with a great creak. Rose frowned, taking a timid step into the room. Moonlight filtered through stained-glass windows, casting ethereal hues upon the polished wooden floor. The air was thick with the scent of aged parchment and the faint aroma of forgotten spells. She swallowed hard.

Her mother's door may not have been spelled, but the chambers themselves certainly were. Shimmering wards rippled in the air, distorting the room with disorienting illusions. Intricate webs of magical threads hung from the ceiling, their delicate strands wound to trigger some unseen alarm if disturbed.

Until they flickered—some strain causing the charm to falter. *They weren't real.* Sucking in a sharp breath, Rose ran her hand through one of the spidery tendrils.

"What are you doing?" Sylvie gasped.

But they simply faded away, as fleeting as her mother's love. Rose released the breath coiled in her chest and took a tenuous step forward. Suddenly, the chamber sprang to life, as if the loss of the wards ignited some other errant spell.

Invisible hands turned down the crimson duvet of her mother's mahogany four-poster bed as a fire sparked in the cavernous hearth. The sounds of running water poured out of the washroom on a cloud of lavender-scented steam, while a silver tray floated over to provide her with plush slippers and a glass of whiskey. Rose traded a glance with Sylvie.

It was as if the room was some great machine built to the rigid habits of her mother. But there was little about the space to truly mark it as hers.

A looming wardrobe sat in the far corner of the room, and a desk sat before the window. But no paintings adorned the walls. No tapestries hung between the stones, no vases or photos sat on the mantle. Even the desk was sparsely decorated, though it did, at least, harbor one photograph.

Rose lifted it gently, running a finger over the wooden frame. Two smiling faces beamed back at her, one with familiar dark features, and one with a softer, kinder visage. Just like hers.

Aunt Astoria. A sharp pang lanced through her chest. When had she last seen her mother smile like that? Had she ever? If there was once a more unburdened version of her mother, Rose doubted she had ever known it. Perhaps it died with her sister.

"Thenlif," Sylvie whispered. "We don't have all night."

"Just checking the desk," she hissed, shoving the photograph back in its place. "Keep an eye out for anything Order-related."

"Like what, a cloak or a mask?"

"Maybe."

Her mother could be a member, after all. Though she didn't say so aloud. Instead, she jimmied the drawers of the desk—also unlocked. Probably because they were full only of old pens and scraps of stray paper. Nothing of interest. Rose sighed, sinking into mother's chair.

This was pointless. Whatever secrets her mother had, she hid them well. If they were ever here at all. Leaning back, she stared up at the ceiling, trying to swallow tears that threatened to fall. What was the point of any of this?

Crossing her legs, a curse tore from her lips as her knee slammed into one of the desk drawers—hard. But, when she reached down to cradle her throbbing leg, her knee wasn't anywhere near any of the drawers. *Odd.*

Fumbling in the dim light, Rose ran her fingers over what appeared to be nothing more than air. Yet, while her eyes told her it was empty, her fingers curled around wooden edges. *A hidden drawer.*

She yanked it open, pulling a lone dossier from its depths. Flipping through it, she scanned the pages quickly, which were all too familiar. This was Aveline's death report. Her stomach dropped, for there was one difference. Beneath the coroner's notes about sedatives, her mother had drawn in harsh lines only one name. *Briony?* The swirling letters stared back at her. Her mother couldn't really suspect Briony—could she?

"What did you find?" Sylvie peered over her shoulder.

"It's Aveline's death report. And look—my mother suspected Briony."

"You don't really think—"

She didn't get the chance to finish her thought before footsteps echoed just beyond the door. Rose's heart leaped into her throat, but she froze. She could hide under the desk. *No.* Her mother would see her as soon as she sat down. The wardrobe? She wrinkled her nose. She wasn't keen to repeat that experience.

Her heartbeat pounded in her ears as the latch clicked. Shoving the dossier into the folds of her blazer, she leaped from the desk. But she slammed into its edge, the shatter of glass following behind her. *Shit*.

She stilled, torn by indecision. Until Sylvie's warm hand curled around her wrist and pulled her into the dark corridor to the washroom. She pressed Rose firmly against the shadowed wall, her face mere inches away. In spite of herself, Rose's eyes flew to the soft lines of Sylvie's lips, her pulse quickening at the warmth of her chest pressed tight against her own.

Her heart hammered against her ribs, a dull, aching beat she was almost certain Sylvie could feel. She willed it to quieten, trying to force her gaze away from the soft skin of Sylvie's neck and keep herself from inhaling greedily the intoxicating scent of her perfume. But it was no use.

"Hello?" Her mother's voice carried through the chamber. "Is someone here?"

Shit, shit, shit. This wasn't good. Rose's eyes darted to the bedroom, licking her lips as her mouth went dry. But then she looked back to Sylvie, and all thoughts of her mother fled her head. For the briefest moment, her amber eyes ghosted over Rose's lips, tracing a soft path down her pulsing throat before they flickered back up to her mother.

"Come out, or I promise you will regret it."

Sucking in a breath, Rose moved to step out of the shadows. Perhaps her mother's wrath wouldn't pierce so truly as Sylvie's gaze. But Sylvie held her back, pressing a gentle finger to Rose's lips to silence her as the scent of her casting stole over them. Rose blinked as her form faded into the very wall behind her, just as her mother rounded the corner. Had Sylvie made her *invisible*?

Her head spun, swimming with scents of plum and lilac until her eyes watered and her breath burned in her lungs. But Sylvie didn't even flinch, her eyes blazing like twin flames in the dark. She was so close now. So very close.

Hazy dreams of stolen kisses in the early light of dawn crept unbidden into Rose's mind. The gentle brush of Sylvie's lips against her bare skin as they sank ever lower, stirring her slumbering thoughts. But she was real now.

222

Her touch was both firm and featherlight as she pressed Rose more tightly against the wall, fingertips stilled gently at her thigh. Rose swallowed hard, her pulse throbbing. Desperately, she pushed the thoughts away before she did something foolish that they would both regret.

Finally, Rose's mother's eyes scanned once more over empty air, and she brushed past them, sighing deeply. Not until the washroom door clicked shut behind her did Rose release the breath she'd been holding, sucking in air greedily.

She couldn't stand to be there a moment longer. Not with Sylvie, not with her mother. Not with any of it. Pulling the dossier from her blazer, she tore the page with her mother's notes from the report and tucked the folder back into her desk, refusing to meet Sylvie's gaze before she fled into the cool night air.

28

HARVESTFEST

AUTUMN leaves littered the floor of the main hall, warm scents of apple and cloves swirling in the air. Shouts and laughter carried past on a frigid breeze as the great doors creaked open, and Rose pulled her woolen sweater tighter. It was cold for Harvestfest.

She frowned at the gaggle of students that entered, breathless and laughing. Enchanted scarecrows lined either side of the doors, glaring at all who passed. Woven scarves caught between the scarecrows' claws as the students skirted by, shrieking.

Rose rolled her eyes. Lanterns, adorned with twinkling fairy lights, swayed gently from the ceiling, casting a soft, ethereal glow over the long tables. The gentle melody of a harp sounded from somewhere out of sight, beckoning students to follow its magical notes as the feast before them dragged on.

Ewan stabbed idly at a chicken leg while Sylvie glowered at the surrounding festivities. Sitting together like that, it was almost as if nothing had changed. As if they were still Dunhollow's golden pairing, beautiful and powerful in equal measure. Perfectly made for one another.

A sour feeling took root in Rose's stomach, but she shoved it aside, eyes flickering to Fen instead. Yet even his face held unusual glumness as he sipped his mulled wine. Platters heaped high with autumnal delicacies of all sorts lined the table, but none of their quartet touched the rainbow-colored pastries and sparkling drinks that changed hues with every sip.

"Seems a bit gauche, no?" Sylvie scoffed, eyeing the bubbling cauldrons of mead at the end of each table. "Celebrating not even two weeks after finding a body."

Rose shrugged. "I'm sure my mother will claim you and Aveline would have wanted this."

"Well, up until you found Aveline's body, your mother also would've claimed nothing was wrong." Ewan sighed. "Did you really find nothing else in her office?"

Rose's eyes skirted to Sylvie. Though it had been almost a week since they'd snuck in, the memory of her warmth still pressed against Rose's skin. She swallowed hard. "Just the death report."

"You can't really think Professor Burroak had anything to do with it," said Fen, waving as a few admirers passed by, giggling.

"My mother seems to." Rose shrugged. "And the professor was the one who pointed me in the direction of that study in the first place."

"Hardly damning." Fen pursed his lips. "Unless she was trying to get caught."

Ewan tugged at their long, black robes. "Guilty conscience, you think?"

"Why don't we ask her?" Rose jumped at the sound of Sylvie's voice in her ear.

Following her gaze, it didn't take long to spot Briony's sage hair amid the crowd. She stumbled and weaved through the students, clearly one too many meads in. Rose's heart leaped. Perhaps that made it the perfect time to talk to her.

"C'mon." She got to her feet, pulling her coat over her shoulders.

"What?" Fen spluttered on his wine. "Where?"

Rose wrapped her scarf around her neck. "If I had to guess? The pub."

The Witch's Brew was as bright and cheerful as the main hall had been, except somehow even more packed. Autumn leaves draped over the bar, the air filled with the heady scent of honey and simmering apples.

Pumpkins danced around the counter, and some intrepid students had charmed them with wings, laughing as they whizzed through the air.

A thick crowd blocked the counter, calling out orders and cheers to a haggard-looking Hollis as he ran back and forth. An illusory double of him stood at the other end of the bar, frantically scribbling down orders.

Fen slipped off to brave the crowd for drinks while the rest of them ducked around an intense game of casters' darts and a few mugs of spilled mead. But it didn't take Rose long to spot Briony, swaying on a stool, sage hair askew and cheeks a rosy pink. The professor hiccuped as Rose approached, eyes widening when she caught sight of her.

"Rosera, my goodness," she cooed. "What a beauty you are now. I remember when you were running around this place in diapers."

Rose's cheeks flared as Ewan and Sylvie both snickered. "That was a long time ago, Professor."

"Oh, posh. You can call me Briony here." She patted the stool beside her. "Sit, sit."

A shockingly orange drink sat in front of the professor, bubbling as if it were held over flame, though frozen pumpkins chilled within. Dancing leaves spilled down the sides, almost mesmerizing in a way.

Rose tore her eyes from it with great effort. "Briony, I was wondering if I could ask you something."

"Wassat?"

There was no need for subterfuge now, Rose was sure. The professor could barely see her; Rose doubted she'd remember much in the morning. "On Aveline's death report, it showed she was sedated, possibly with iverin stasia."

"Was she?" The professor's eyes drooped. "My—*hic*—my goodness."

"It also said there were traces of arcane magic, and Fen thinks that's due to alchemy, but I was wondering if you knew of any older spells that may have caused that." She leaned in closer. "Perhaps forbidden magic?"

"Ahh." Briony tapped her nose. "You've always been too bright for your own good. You've been reading up on that study I gave you, hm? Yes, iverin stasia's use in Cair Riacodla was considered by some to delve a little too close to necromancy. Threading that needle all too thinly between life and death. Or undeath. But, not to worry. You can't cast it, so there's no risk."

"That's not what I—"

The words caught on Rose's tongue. Wait—*necromancy?* The thought curdled in the pit of her stomach. She'd been right all along then. Whatever ritual Imrys was casting in his sick obsession was bound to necromancy. Somehow, the thought didn't fill her with any sense of joy or satisfaction.

If she'd been right, then perhaps Fen was too. Perhaps she really was next. Her heart sank, fear coiling in her chest like a ball of lead. *No.* There was still time to stop this. They had to.

"Professor." Rose's voice cracked, and she cleared her throat. "What do you know about the Order of Salix?"

Briony went notably ashen, her throat bobbing. "Why would you ask me that, Astoria?"

"Astoria?"

Her eyes widened. "I'm sorry, you just look so much like—never mind. Forget I said anything."

"But—"

Briony's face went rigid. "Whatever you want to know about the Order, Rose—forget it. The Order, the Starlings, all of it. Some things are better left in the past."

Sliding off the stool, the professor threw back the last of her drink and shoved away from the table. She stumbled, swaying slightly before she righted herself. Sparing one last glance for Rose, she darted off through the sea of bodies.

"Professor, wait!"

But she was already gone, lost to the crowd and the haze of drink. Rose scowled, turning back to the table as Fen approached with three gargantuan mugs.

"Astoria?" asked Ewan.

"My aunt." Rose frowned. "She died before I was born."

Fen thumbed the rim of his glass. "What does she have to do with any of this?"

"I don't know."

"Starlings." Rose jumped at Sylvie's voice. Her brow was creased in a thick knot, eyes fixed on the table. "Ewan's father. I think we had a conversation before I—well. Anyway, he said something to me about the Order."

"You remember something?"

227

"I'm not sure; it's hazy. But I think he'd figured out that I was here on scholarship. He didn't think that was good enough for Ewan and he … he wanted me to rescind my bid to join the Order."

Rose reached for her arm. "Did he threaten you?"

"Who?" Ewan whispered in her ear.

"Shh," she snapped. "Sylvie?"

But her tawny skin had gone a shade paler, full lips pressed thin. "He told me, 'Starlings have never belonged in the Order.'"

They were all silent for a long moment, not a word spoken between them. The festivities carried on around them, shouts and laughter ringing in Rose's ears as their peers drank and danced. But there was a hollow numbness gnawing at her heart.

"What does that even mean?" Rose said finally.

"I don't know." Sylvie shook her head. "But let's hope the Order has more answers."

29

WITHIN THE ORDER

THE silence of the archives ached in Rose's ears. Loose folds of delicate velvet fell around her feet, cloaking her in the quiet embrace of the Order's anonymity. A gift from Ewan that felt as hollow as the fragile peace between them.

A cold white mask lay on the table beside her, features carved in a blank expression. She drew her fingers across it, a shiver building at the edge of her spine. She was no stranger to wearing a mask, but hers was not usually so easily removed. And yet, tonight, it was her only way in. Her only hope of answers.

Sylvie straightened Rose's robes, her fingers lingering a moment too long on the dark fabric. Rose's breath hitched. Sylvie stood so close now. So close that it pulled at something raw and aching in Rose's chest.

"Are you almost ready?" Ewan's voice cut between them.

Rose jumped. They stood in the crumbling archway alongside Fen, both draped in the long robes of the Order. White masks hung around their necks, blank and lifeless, as if they captured the very moment of death.

They almost looked at one with the dark stones around them. How many of the Order's twisted secrets had passed beneath these walls, carved into the very mortar? How many atrocities had the faded cobwebs witnessed? How manymore lay waiting to be uncovered in the forgotten, whispering scrolls? Rose shuddered.

"Er—yeah." She swallowed hard.

"Are you sure this is a good idea?" asked Fen.

"Of course it's not." Rose shrugged. "But what other choice do we have?"

"This is the only way to get to the bottom of the Order's plans." Ewan's eyes darted to some bare corner of the room. "And Sylvie needs us. Right, Syl?"

Rose glanced at Sylvie, but her head was bowed, eyes fixed to the floor. *Odd.* Did she not want them to go? She had seemed strangely reluctant last night at Harvestfest—but why?

Fiercely, desperately, some part of Rose wished they didn't have to. That they could trust her mother to handle this so that no one had to risk anything. But they were here now, and it was too late to turn back. A sharp buzzing from Ewan's pocket made Rose jump.

"We should get going." They handed her a torch, then pressed something small and metallic into her free hand. "My father's office shouldn't be locked, but if it is, I spelled this key to counter his magic."

"You can spell something to a specific caster?"

They shrugged. "Practical magic is my specialty."

Rose frowned. She'd thought their specialty was source magic, same as Sylvie. She wondered if, like her mother, their father would brook no discussion of his heir studying a lesser subject.

"Remember, once you're inside, keep the mask on, and if anyone catches you down there, just pretend to be a lost Order member."

"Yes, I know." Rose nodded, staring at the looming threshold.

"Rose, wait." Fen stepped toward her, holding out a small gadget. "Here."

She turned the small metallic ball over in her hand, running her thumb over the divot at its base. "What is this?"

"A little alchemical trick." He grinned. "If anything goes wrong, press the button, and it'll release a smoke that will buy you time. Just don't breathe it in."

She didn't even want to know what that meant. But the gesture warmed her heart all the same. Reaching for him, she pulled him into a fierce embrace, breathing in the scent of him. It soothed her racing heart, even if only for a moment.

"Thanks, Fen."

He pulled away, pressing a kiss to her forehead. "Just, be careful in there. Please."

"You too."

"Me?" He pulled away with a wry smile. "I'll be fine."

Soft words pushed against her lips, pleas and prayers she would never utter aloud. She could only squeeze his hand, hoping he understood. His mouth quirked as he squeezed back, and she let a small sigh slip from her lungs.

"Come on, you two." Ewan tugged at Fen's arm. "We'll be late if we don't go now. Good luck, Thenlif."

Fen gave a small wave as they disappeared up the steps. "See you on the other side."

A sob nearly choked her, but Rose pushed it back. They didn't have time for that now.

Sylvie reached for her arm. "Are you ready, Thenlif?"

Not really. The truth burgeoned at her lips. How could she be, facing down the threat of the Order on their own? Her nails bit into the soft flesh of her palms. It didn't matter, if that's what it took to get Sylvie back. And to keep herself from ending up the same way.

"Yeah. Let's go get you back."

"Hey." Sylvie pulled her back to face her, cupping a hand around her chin. "It'll be all right."

A soft feeling bloomed in Rose's chest. A small comfort, even in Sylvie's hands. If she had to suffer, at least she did not do so alone. A smirk tugged at the corners of her mouth, wry and lacking all warmth. Misery did love company, after all.

Turning, she held the torch aloft and stepped into the abyss.

The darkness enveloped them in oppressive totality, obscuring all else. Only the torch's flickering glow fought against it, casting eerie shadows on the ancient walls.

Carved from rough-hewn stone, the secret tunnels bore the scars of countless years. Moisture dripped from the ceiling, forming glistening stalactites that shimmered in the torchlight. The air was thick and heavy, carrying the scent of damp earth and musty decay, as if it held the weight of forgotten ages.

Rose's nerves fluttered as she stumbled over the slick, uneven ground beneath them, apprehension drawing her muscles tight. Each step pulled them closer to their mark, like the draw of a bow. Yet she couldn't shake the feeling that they were the target, and the arrow was only awaiting its moment to strike. She shivered against the cold.

The tunnel wound its way through the earth, curving at odd angles and revealing crumbling remains of hidden alcoves. Time had worn away the once-polished stones, leaving behind only the jagged edges of collapsed walls. If she squinted, Rose could just make out the faded lines of ancient inscriptions and symbols carved into the rock, barely discernible now.

Had those come from the Order? Worn instructions left only for their own? Whatever magic they'd once held, it hung by a thread now—a mere tingling against her fingertips, swallowed up by the earth around it.

"Thenlif, wait." Sylvie's voice bounced off the stone. "There's something I need to tell you."

"Can it wait till we're not traversing through this death trap?" Rose grumbled, swinging her torch through more cobwebs.

"No. It can't."

Rose turned with a sigh, drawn by the sharp edges of Sylvie's tone. She wasn't sure what she'd expected to find, but it wasn't Sylvie's gaze boring into hers with a desperate, pained need. She frowned, and it was as if that small gesture broke something within Sylvie. Her shoulders fell, her eyes going flat, and there was something so terrifyingly monstrous in the way the pain leaked away from her face, solidifying in a singularly vacant expression.

"What is it?"

Sylvie's eyes darted away from hers. "If we find my body in there—if we're able to bring me back, I don't want things to change. There's so many things I have to settle with Ewan, but ..."

Rose stilled, her heart sinking. *Oh*. That's what this was about. "Look, Sylvie if you're thinking of getting back together with them, I get it, but I really don't think now is—"

"Getting back together?" Sylvie cut across her. "What are you *talking* about?"

Rose's heart thudded erratically in her chest. "Isn't that what you were going to say?"

"No I—Gods, you're such an idiot sometimes." Sylvie stepped closer with an exasperated sigh. "Ewan and I were never real. I mean, I care about them, sure, but our relationship was for the sake of appearances more than anything. Not like us."

Us. As in …. Heat flooded across Rose's cheeks, her breath quickening as Sylvie took another step closer. And then another still. Until they were nearly chest to chest, nose to nose—breath to breath. *Oh.*

Rose's heart fluttered as Sylvie's fingers caught beneath her chin. She stilled there for a moment, as if waiting for Rose to retreat. But she couldn't—wouldn't. And neither did Sylvie.

Her lips brushed against Rose's, cautious and gentle. But then Rose leaned in, and it was if a flame had burst to life within her. She cupped her hands around Sylvie's jaw, pulling her closer. As if she held her tighter, she somehow might tether her here. To this moment—to life itself.

It seemed an eternity before Sylvie pulled away gently, amber eyes blazing as her fingers threaded through Rose's curls. Fumbling, useless words burgeoned against Rose's tongue but, before she could say anything, her torch sputtered and snuffed out.

"Shit!" She cursed as darkness surrounded them.

Thick, heavy and choking, it closed in all around, pressing at the back of her mind. The sound of dripping water echoed through the tunnel, an eerie symphony that reverberated off the rough walls. A light breeze swept through her hair, carrying soft whispers. As if the tunnel held the memories of those who had traversed its depths long ago, reaching out to draw them further in.

Gaunt faces hid in shadows, racing through Rose's mind in frozen, fractured glimpses. Her chest tightened, breath caught in her throat. The silence was deafening now, ringing numbly in her ears as her knees buckled. They had to get out of here.

"Thenlif?"

Rose's breath shortened, sharp and shallow as it clawed its way from her chest. Head spinning, she fumbled around in the darkness, fingers curling around the jagged edges of stone. Until her foot caught a stray rock and she lurched forward, teetering into the abyss.

"*Rose!*" Sylvie's voice cut through shadow.

Warm fingers curled around Rose's wrist. Sylvie's touch burned like flame, and it lit up the room in such a blaze. The cavern sprawled out in a splintering light, so bright that Rose had to shield her eyes.

Her chest loosened, and her breath came out in a soft "Oh."

Sylvie was beautiful. Luminous against the darkness of the tunnel, she shone like a beacon, but her eyes held Rose's, fierce and raw. Slowly, the light faded to a dim glow, her gaze softening.

"Are you all right?"

"I'm fine."

Sylvie's eyes darkened, but she didn't let go of Rose's hand. They both knew it was a lie, but any words to defend it lay heavy and numb on Rose's tongue. Behind Sylvie loomed a large, half-rotted door, strange symbols carved into its aged wood. The same symbols from the note she'd received. The Order was consistent, if nothing else.

"Come on." Rose's fingers tightened around Sylvie's—a lifeline she refused to release. "Let's just get this over with."

30

INTO DARKNESS

THE cold, dark damp of the tunnels faded away like a nightmare on the edge of dawn as Rose stepped into the Order's basement. She blinked, letting her eyes adjust. But the guildhall was nothing like she had expected. Somehow, she'd imagined it would be like it had been in her visions—dark, dank corridors filled with sickly green light. But it was surprisingly warm and bright.

Built of weathered stone and adorned with intricate carvings, it bore the marks of centuries past. Ivy clung to the walls, as if nature itself had embraced and protected this place from prying eyes.

Rose peered up at the heavy oak beams stretched across the ceiling, embellished with mysterious symbols and protection sigils. Soft candlelight bathed the space in a warm glow, casting shadows that danced across aged tapestries littering the walls. The air was choked with the smell of wet stone, only somewhat covered by a thick, heady incense.

If this was how they'd decorated the cellar, she hated to think how much they'd spent on the upper floors. The dull thud of footsteps creaked above them as Rose crossed over the threshold. She held her breath for a moment, waiting to be struck down or smote, before fitting her mask into place and turning back to Sylvie.

She was almost grateful for the cool ceramic shield as a furious heat crept across her cheeks simply at the sight of Sylvie. For the way she still glowed in the darkness of the tunnel. A radiant star, undimmed by shadow and blood.

Rose bit back a groan—she was being ridiculous. One kiss and already she was a muddled mess before the woman. But they had work to do, and whatever had just happened between her and Sylvie could wait until they were out of this den of evil. Her pulse leaped. When Sylvie was free and alive, they could deal with this strange hunger that had taken root within her, begging to be sated by the soft touch of Sylvie's skin—the warm brush of her lips …

Rose shook her head, cursing under her breath. "Come on, sounds like they've started," she whispered.

"Wonderful," said Sylvie as she ducked through the door. "Where do *we* start?"

Rose glanced down the corridor. It stretched out before them into darkness, sconces flickering feebly between each doorway. There were so many of them. Her stomach sank. It would be near impossible to find Imrys's office before the ceremony was over, unless, by some miracle, he'd put a sign over it.

"I guess we start by seeing which one this key can open." She sighed, then grimaced. "And be careful—we don't know what could be down here."

Like Sylvie's decrepit body, for one. Rose swallowed a wave of nausea, tiptoeing toward the first door to test the key. *Locked.* Frowning, she pressed her ear against the metal surface. But all was quiet within. There was no soft hum of magic, no scent cast upon the air, no insidious whispers pricking at the back of her mind.

She leaned back on her heels, deflated. Somehow, she'd expected something … more. But, as far as she could tell, it was just an ordinary cellar.

"Damn." Sylvie jiggled the handle of another door. "This one is locked too."

Rose shook her head. "If only there was a way we could slip through the door. You know, like a ghost?"

"Oh, right." Sylvie ducked her head, tucking a strand of hair behind her ear. Clearing her throat, she stepped toward the door, only to crash soundly into it. "Shit."

Rose's heart skipped a beat, and for one wild moment she wasn't sure whether to laugh or curse. "What was *that*?"

"I don't know."

Sylvie rubbed gingerly at her brow, then dragged her fingers through her hair. A swift, harsh action, so at odds with the gossamer strands falling around her cheekbones. Rose stood, mesmerized, wondering how they would feel against her skin—tangled between her fingers. But then Sylvie met her gaze with a piercing intensity that shattered any thought about her hair. She cleared her throat.

Turning, she hid her burning cheeks from Sylvie's gaze. But a tremor lurked beneath her skin, as if Sylvie pulled at her blood, her flesh—her very bones. She sucked in a steadying breath before turning back to her.

"Do you feel drawn to any of these doors?"

Sylvie raised a dark eyebrow. "What, like, do I sense my soulless body behind one of them?"

"Yes?"

"No."

Rose sighed. "Then let's keep looking for his office. Maybe he has the keys to other rooms there."

Pushing away from the door, she carried on down the corridor. Thick metal doors hung on either side, splintered by dimly lit sconces; on and on they went, with startling monotony. Any of them could be the study.

"Look," said Sylvie, jabbing her finger toward a door at the end of the corridor.

A soft glow bloomed from the crack underneath it, ebbing and flowing like the dance of flame. A fireplace, perhaps? That had to be the study—what other room would Imrys waste such magic on?

Leaning forward, she traced a hand across the surface. Cold iron greeted her but shifted beneath her touch, swirling into the pattern of a great tree with a small hole carved into its trunk. Sucking in a breath, she slotted Ewan's key into it. *A perfect fit.* With a soft click, its branches tangled up to the doorframe, pulling back from the latch. The door swung ajar, beckoning them in.

Rose faltered. Would some spell ensnare her as soon as she crossed the threshold? Some curse that would strike her down where she stood? Ewan had said the key would counter it, but the air lay still as she stepped through, neither a hint nor a whisper of magic upon it.

A soft sigh bubbled up to her lips—almost a laugh. Between him and her mother, how did either of them ever hope to keep their secrets? The arrogance of those who wielded fear like a weapon, she supposed. They never expected anyone to cross them until it was too late.

This room, at least, looked exactly as she expected. Arched stone ceilings towered up into shadow above them, unreachable even to the glow of the fire that popped away in the hearth. There were no walls, as far as she could see—only bookshelves welded into the stones behind them. Filled with skulls, vials and strange objects floating in murky, viscous liquid, it nearly turned Rose's stomach.

Crystal orbs and star charts littered one of the shelves, tucked between shriveled remains and a dreaming apparatus. She frowned. Could all of this really be down to Imrys's obsession? His vain desire to harness the magics of old for himself leading him to frivolously cast students' lives aside?

"Are you going to stand there gawking all night, Thenlif? Or should we have a look around?"

Rose shook herself out of her daze. "Right."

She crossed to the ornate desk at the center of the room. Neat and tidy, with a truly staggering array of magical artifacts, it almost reminded her a bit of her mother's desk. She supposed, in a way, she and Imrys were two sides of the same coin, though they would both hate the idea.

Rose reached for the nearest drawer, rifling through the papers within. Nothing of note. Just invoices and receipts for his abundant collection.

"What are you doing?" Sylvie whispered.

"Looking for proof, obviously." She leafed through a few stray pages in the corner of the desk. "Maybe he kept a receipt or something in here. Someone had to buy all that sedative."

"You think he'd be that sloppy?"

Rose's hands stilled. "He left a giant bloodstain in the middle of the library, didn't he?"

"Fair point."

"Check the filing cabinet over there." She nodded toward the far end of the room, to the one corner that wasn't occupied by bookshelves. "There might be more in there."

Sylvie rolled her eyes, muttering something under her breath, but did as she was asked. Rose's eyes narrowed at the back of her head.

She should be happy, shouldn't she? That they were here, rummaging through papers and notes rather than being caught out against Imrys himself. So why did she act like looking for the proof to save her was such a chore?

Rose faltered as her fingers caught on something stuck at the back of the drawer. Thicker than the rest of the notes, its edge slipped just out of her grasp. A photograph, by the feel of it. With a firm tug, she pulled it free, a gasp falling from her lips.

Two cold, gray faces stared back at her, one engulfed in charmed flames. But the ink-black hair and bright eyes were unmistakable. Her mother. And beside her, Imrys, cradling her as if she were the most precious thing in the world. Rose traced the outline of her mother's face, hissing as the flames singed her fingers.

They looked so *young*. This had to be decades old, at least. So, why did he still have it, tucked away in the heart of his study? Did his hatred really run so deep?

She leaned against the desk with a small sigh, sliding her thumb against the edge of the photograph. But it split under her grasp, a second photo tumbling onto the desk. This one was of a group, all of them surrounded by flames, like her mother in the first photo. Yet the faces were all still familiar, if far older now. Briony on the right—though her figure was marked by an old name that didn't fit her—then Sylverfir, Delia, Rose's mother, Imrys, Hollis, and, squeezing into the shot on the far left, her aunt.

Astoria looked so young and innocent, arms wrapped around Hollis and beaming cheerfully. This had to be only months before she died. Rose's brow creased, and she flipped the photo over, searching for a date.

But all that greeted her was a neat, sprawling script. *Starlings are pure imitation.* The crimson letters glowed in the light of the fire. Starlings? Her heart lurched.

"Hey, look at this," Sylvie called out, making Rose jump. "It's a list of initiates from thirty years ago—two of them are marked as deceased."

Rose stared at the folder she was waving in the air for a moment before crossing the room. She took the file from Sylvie's hands, scanning the page. *Order of Salix, Members and Initiates of 1889.* Thirty-one years ago. She swallowed hard. Hadn't Ewan said the Order went defunct around that time?

Further down the list, two names jumped out at her, thick lines drawn through them. *Norinne Taldea and Lucinia Voris—Deceased.* Rose's mouth went dry. Numbly, she handed Sylvie the photos, chewing the inside of her lip as she flipped them back and forth.

"Shit, were Imrys and your mother *together*?" Sylvie said finally. "Wait, you don't think …"

"What?"

"What if this isn't the first time this all has happened?" Sylvie thumbed the edge of the photo. "Two students dead then—one and counting now. What if these deaths were why the Order was shut down? Maybe your mother knew too much."

"And, what, Imrys decided to finish what he started thirty years ago?"

"Maybe." Sylvie tugged at the ends of her long hair. "He could be trying to frame your mother for it."

She turned back to the page, scanning it again before she froze. "Shit."

"What?"

She jabbed her finger at the parchment, stabbing a name etched close to the end of the list. *Araminta Thenlif*, it read, *Full member.* Crossed out, but still legible. And then, beside it, a small note in the margin. *Starlings?* Rose's blood ran cold. Her mother had been a member of the Order.

Sylvie gasped, but said nothing. The silence held between them quivered on their breaths, sharp and unstable. Precarious as cracked glass, and it shattered into so many pieces. A muted crash echoed through the halls, reverberating at their feet. She and Sylvie shared a glance, words caught on their tongues. And then, all at once, the lights flickered out, plunging them into darkness.

31

SILENCE OF THE FOREST

IN the seconds following the explosion, only silence filled the air. Then smoke. And, finally, screams. Footsteps thundered overhead—a cacophony of muted cries and coughing carrying down the stairs. Rose stood rooted to the ground, her pulse hammering in her ears.

"Rose?" Sylvie's voice sought her in the darkness. "Are you all right?"

"I-I can't see!" was all she could manage.

Then Sylvie's warm hand curled around hers, the room erupting in a silvery light. Rose's head spun, and her pulse throbbed behind her eyes, but Sylvie's grip held her like a tether. She looked like a spirit of old—ethereal and untouchable. But her eyes were filled with fire.

"Come on." She tugged Rose forward. "We have to go!"

She dug her heels in. "Wait, we haven't found your b—*you* yet!"

"Thenlif, you can't help me if you're dead too. Now come *on.*"

Hesitating a moment longer, Rose finally gave in, letting Sylvie lead her back down the corridor, numbly following behind. Until the door to the tunnel loomed before them, and Rose dug her heels into the stones beneath them.

"No, wait." She yanked Sylvie to a stop. "Upstairs."

"What? No—you'll be caught."

"What about Fen and Ewan?" Rose pulled out of Sylvie's grasp. "We have to make sure they're all right."

Before Sylvie could stop her, Rose tore off back down the corridor, ignoring the cries that carried after her. She had to get to Fen—had to make sure he was safe. Clambering up the stairs, she burst through the cellar door, wincing as the sting of lightning arced across her skin. That must have been the curse Ewan mentioned. But it didn't matter.

Masked faces swarmed around her, their screams and shouts echoing in her ears. Smoke choked the air, burning in her lungs as fleeing initiates shoved past her. Her own mask clung to her skin, but it did nothing to stop the smoke cloying at her nose, tearing through her lungs.

Rose's eyes watered, vision blurring at the edges when a hand curled around hers. Fen? She glanced up hopefully. But it was Sylvie who stared back at her, hazy, like a dream. Still, her heart leaped at the sight of her.

"Close your eyes." She pulled her closer. "The smoke is a poison."

Rose did as she was told, holding tighter to Sylvie's hand. "Can you see Fen? Or Ewan?"

"I can't see anything in here." Sylvie's voice was muffled. "We need to get out to the forest."

Rose let Sylvie draw her forward once more, darting through the sea of bodies. Shoulders rammed into hers, elbows landing hard between her ribs, but still they pushed forward. Her breath coiled in her chest, her head spinning from the lack of air. Until, finally, Rose stumbled over a threshold, the fresh air of the forest hitting her like a wall.

Except it was anything but fresh. Dense and thick, the air hung heavy, as if it had not been broken in centuries. Still, Rose sucked it in greedily. Around them, screams still cleaved the night air, though it was hard to say if they came from fleeing initiates or simply the forest itself.

Rose straightened, finally daring to open her eyes. Above them, the trees loomed like some tapestry of muddled leaves and bristling twigs. They twisted and bent in the moonlight, a fog hanging upon the milky light like smoke. It was peaceful, in some strange way. In the same manner that death was peaceful—the slow decay of the earth reclaiming what belonged to it.

But it shattered in an instant as someone slammed into her back—hard. Rose pitched forward, catching herself in Sylvie's arms as her mask tumbled to the ground. It smashed into pieces over jagged roots. Whatever initiate had collided with her mumbled apologies as they melded back into the sea of bodies, but she could barely hear them.

Sylvie's eyes held her like a spell, her breath soft and warm against Rose's skin, arms tight around her. Her heart stumbled, and then skipped a beat altogether, her mouth dry as parchment. Until Sylvie's gaze flickered over her shoulder, and her face fell.

"Shit."

Rose turned slowly, her heart sinking into the pit of her stomach. There, across the sea of fleeing students, a pair of eyes locked directly on her. Cold and gray, they filled with such malice that it curdled her blood. *Imrys.*

Beside him was Arden, his shock of red hair almost muted in the dim light of the forest. Yet lightning already twisted up his arms, sparking in spidery tendrils and illuminating the rotten lines of his sneer.

Rose didn't protest this time as Sylvie grabbed her hand, dragging her away from the building. They crashed through the trees ahead, their gnarled branches reaching out like skeletal fingers, casting eerie shadows that danced in the dim light. The dense canopy overhead blocked most of the moonlight, enveloping the forest floor in an oppressive darkness that nipped at their heels as they ran.

A stitch prodded at Rose's side, aching between her ribs until, finally, they reached a small clearing. Before she could blink, Sylvie spun her around, shoving her up against the trunk of a tree. A small gasp tore from Rose, and Sylvie held a finger to her lips to silence her. Rose's heart pounded against her ears, almost drowning out all else. *Almost.*

But the air was heavy with faded cries, broken only by the occasional hoot of an owl or the shrieks of the beasts that lurked within these trees. The fog around them fell upon Rose's skin like a sheen of cool sweat, carrying a hint of dampness and decay. Yet no footsteps followed them into the clearing. Sylvie's body pressed tighter against hers—warm and soft, even with the threat of death hanging over them.

Rose's heart leaped, the gentle brush of Sylvie's lips flickering through her memory. The delicate curve of her neck was so close now—it would take no more than a breath of effort to close that distance between them. To trail fervent kisses down her throat and let every promise of danger fade away to the silence of the forest. But she swallowed hard, pushing the thought away.

Pulse racing, Rose counted the seconds as they passed, tracing the paths of the moss clinging to the ancient tree trunks, covering them in a mottled green. Anything to draw her away from the way Sylvie's thigh pressed between hers, her chest pushed up against her own.

The wind whispered through the foliage, carrying with it an unsettling melody that sent a shiver down Rose's spine. But still, nothing. Seconds turned to minutes, which stretched into yawning moments before she finally straightened.

"I don't think he's followed," she whispered against Sylvie's grasp. "Come on, we have to catch up."

"What? Imrys *saw* you." Sylvie stepped away from her. "We should regroup at the archives and wait for Fen and Ewan there."

"We can't just leave them out here."

"No offense, Thenlif, but they're much better equipped to handle themselves than you are. *We* need to get out of here."

"But—"

Sylvie grabbed her hand, sparks dancing behind her eyes. "Listen to me—there are worse things lurking in these woods than Imrys Elaegius. We need to leave before you end up dinner to one of them."

A twig snapped behind them, a sharp puncture to Sylvie's words. Rose turned slowly, eyes darting over the tangle of twisted roots and fallen branches. But there was nothing there. Her breath came out in shallow puffs on the cool night air. Shadows danced around dilapidated tree stumps and mossy fallen logs. If she glanced at them too quickly, they almost seemed to move. But then one turned and lurched toward them.

"Run." Sylvie's voice was low—hard. "Now."

Rose didn't need to be told twice. Launching herself away from the tree, she made it only a few steps before something cracked against the back of her skull. She stumbled, white-hot pain searing through her head. Something warm and wet trickled down the back of her neck, her vision blurring as she reached for it with a trembling hand.

Moonlight glinted off the thick crimson glazing her fingers, and tears burned against her eyes. *Blood.* A soft whimper tangled in her throat as she crawled forward. But her muscles were slow and sluggish, as if somehow removed from the desperate need to move, to flee. To do anything at all.

Dirt curled uselessly beneath her fingers as footsteps grew closer. Worn leather boots crunched through rotting leaves, coming to a stop just under her nose. But Rose didn't have the strength to look up.

An insidious strain of magic raced through her veins. Sharp and greedy, it pulled away at the world around her, until everything grew dark and dull. And then, through the haze, a sharp cry.

"Rose!"

Magic snapped around her, splintering and arcing through the night air. A silvery glow took hold of the forest, rustling through the leaves, ripping through the soil. It slammed into the figure looming over her, a wall of ice rending the forest floor and sinking deep into their flesh with a sickening squelch.

They cried out with a curse, boots stumbling back through the torn earth as the ice snapped. And then they fled. Rose's eyelids drooped, her head dropping into the cool soil beneath. She almost didn't notice the soft scent of the cast falling over her. Plum and lilac, mingling with richly sweet notes of amber and honey.

Though she could hardly bring herself to care now. It was over. At long last, the air grew still, and relief blossomed through her aching chest. But whatever respite she might have found was quickly lost—swallowed up by the stale air and the thick silence of the forest.

32

ABANDONED

SOIL squished under Rose's skin. Cold and wet, it clung to her as her eyes blinked open to the darkness of the forest. Trees towered overhead, sharp and wild, branches tangling around one another in endless discord. She groaned, her head splitting beneath the pain of her wound.

"Rose?" Sylvie knelt beside her. "Hey, stay with me."

Her hands glowed, warmth blossoming at the back of Rose's skull. The pain faded and, slowly, Rose eased herself onto her elbows. Tear tracks glistened on Sylvie's cheeks in the dim moonlight, but she managed a watery smile.

"I've got you."

"Thank you." Rose cast her eyes into the dirt, a fierce heat burgeoning in her chest. "How—how did you manage that?"

All her magic before had been quiet, idle things, barely notable for a caster like Sylvie. But that ice had been a fearsome display. Even alive, she'd rarely seen Sylvie cast like that.

"I-I don't know." She fidgeted with her hands. "I just couldn't let them hurt you."

A million questions tangled around Rose's tongue. "Did you see who it was?"

"No, they were masked, and I—"

A shriek cut through the air, and Sylvie's tawny skin went a shade paler. Her eyes darted over her shoulder, to thundering hoofbeats crashing through the tree line and glowing eyes peering through the leaves. Rose's heart thudded against her ribs, aching and empty—fueled only by fear now.

"Shit." Sylvie scrambled to get Rose on her feet. "Can you run?"

Rose didn't answer, holding fast to Sylvie as she stumbled over tangled roots and loose dirt. Whether or not she could run, her body would not allow her to remain still. It creaked forward, aching and raw, but with only one thought on her mind. *Flee.*

Furious heat coursed through her veins, searing through the weight of her wounds. Though the dense canopy above obscured the moon and the stars, plunging the forest into a pitch-black abyss, she could not stop. Shadows danced and flickered around her, as if reaching out to pull her fleeing form into their depths.

Sharp, shallow breaths burned in her lungs. Branches whipped at her face and arms, leaving stinging marks in their wake. She tried to duck around them, but their insidious grasp snagged at her cloak. The forest was too thick—too cloying. And there would be no escaping it.

The darkness was both friend and foe, offering shelter and peril in the same breath. Rose's eyes strained to pierce the gloom, searching for any sign of a path. But there was nothing before her besides gnarled roots and twisted shadows. Twigs snapped and trees rustled beside her. Whatever chased them grew closer with every breath.

Rose's heart pounded against her ribs, matching the rhythm of her footfalls thudding against the swollen earth. Her legs ached, and her head spun. She could not carry on like this. She wouldn't make it.

A stitch seared against her ribs, and she clutched it tightly, refusing to slow. But her fingers brushed around something else instead, caught in the folds of her robes. *Fen's gift.* Sinking her hand into her pocket, she grasped desperately at the little metallic ball and wrenched it free.

Holding her breath, she found the little divot at its bottom, pressed tight and launched it into the forest behind them. A flash of light danced through the trees. A sharp squeal, the crunch of bone. And then only silence.

But it shattered just as quickly. Footsteps thundered across the damp earth, cracking and crashing through the foliage. They came to a stop mere feet away. All her hair stood on end.

"Rose?" Sylverfir's voice rang in her ears.

"Soren?" Ragged breaths tore from her chest as she blinked up at him, his scarred skin catching odd shapes in the moonlight. "What are you doing here?"

His arms enveloped her in a strong embrace, his voice low and warm in her ear. "I heard the commotion—I came to make sure no one was hurt."

Rose nodded, until the truth of his words sank in, and she froze. How had he heard the commotion? What had he been doing out in the woods in the middle of the night in the first place? She pushed away from him, a soft tremble pulsing through her veins.

A cool shiver ran through her as she glanced him up and down. He was dressed in the robes of the Order, same as her, though he wore no mask. At least, not one so easily removed. Her stomach flipped, roiling beneath a wave of nausea.

"Why was he out here?" Sylvie wheezed, echoing Rose's thoughts.

Before Rose could question him, however, a soft whimper filled her ears. Broken and wounded, it wove sharply through the trees, stirring her muddled heart. *Fen.* Stumbling past Sylverfir, she chased off after the noise.

"Rose, wait!"

But she didn't stop. She couldn't. If he'd been hurt, she'd never forgive herself. Pine needles scratched against her skin, catching in her hair and snapping under her feet.

She came to a halting stop as the ground pitched beneath her, dipping into a shallow ravine that cut across the forest floor like a scar. Perhaps a stream had once run there, but now it was dry and barren, full only of rocks and twigs. And a small form. Huddled in its depths, they were curled in on themselves, but their gold-streaked hair still glinted in the faint moonlight.

"Ewan?" Rose stumbled down the bank of the ravine, falling to her knees at their side. "What happened? Where's Fen?"

"I—" They sucked in a shuddering breath. "We were attacked, and he—"

They lifted a trembling finger, pointing to a dark crevice further down the ravine. Rose's heart leaped into her throat, and she hardly dared look. But Fen was nowhere to be found—the only trace of him left behind was the blood pooling into the earth and a pair of spectacles lying upon it.

Lonely, cracked and utterly abandoned.

She scrambled toward them, heart pounding in her ears. But the moment her fingers curled around them, the forest shifted, a new presence hanging on the air. Lifting her eyes, her heart faltered,and then shattered into a million pieces. There, staring back at her was a pair of warm brown eyes she knew all too well. *Fen.*

His hair was tousled, blood dripping down over his thick brow. But his eyes were still bright, even missing his glasses. Slowly, he reached for her, a sad smile pulling at his full lips. *No.* A breath coiled in her throat. *Not him too.*

The thought seared through her, piercing her heart, aching in her very bones. It tore through her lungs with a wild scream. Anguished and raw, it ripped through the air as she stumbled to her knees. The warmth in her chest became unbearable, racing through her veins like wildfire, until it fled from her with the force of magic that had long sought release.

It burned through the forest, slamming into Ewan and Sylverfir and splintering through Fen's visage. He faded softly away with a sad smile, but it did little to soothe her now. There was nothing left that could.

Until a warm hand curled around hers, holding her steady against the depths of her despair. "I've got you." Sylvie's amber eyes shimmered with tears.

And it was only when they fell that Rose finally let go.

The air cooled around them, silent in the wake of the blast. She reached for Sylvie, stroking her cheek, desperate to reassure her. But as the forest blurred and the world around her faded away, it was not the scent of plum and lilac that greeted her.

It was amber and honey—rich, sweet, and utterly her own. *Her* magic, and only hers.

33

RARE SOURCES

A cloying, acidic scent hung on the air as Rose blinked awake, starched linen folding beneath her fingers. The vaulted ceiling of the infirmary stared down at her, charmed to echo the soothing whir of a forest by night. *The forest*. A sharp pain pierced the back of her head, her skull throbbing with a dull ache. But only one thought seared through her mind. *Fen*.

He was gone. Just like Aveline. Just like *Sylvie*. And it was her fault.

Hot tears leaked down her cheeks at the thought of him out there, alone. Suffering beyond where she could reach him. A sob caught in her throat, but she could not let it escape. Not now. This pain was too great—too terrible. The moment she gave in to it, it would devour her.

She burrowed into her pillows, grateful for the darkness that cloaked her like a shield, broken only by the dim, clouded moonlight that filtered through the large, latticed windows. Glowing vials, bottles, and jars filled with powerful elixirs and potions pulsed in the silence. But otherwise the infirmary was lonely and abandoned. No healers puttered about, and no one else lay condemned to these cots.

No. That wasn't quite true. Rose swallowed a curse as her eyes slid across the aisle to where Ewan lay sleeping, their head bandaged.

Sylvie leaned over them, beautifully unscathed by the events in the Whispering Woods. Her dark hair fell like a sleek curtain over her shoulder, covering her face from view. *Just as well.* The thought sank in Rose like a stone, breath catching in her throat. She wasn't sure she could bear to see it right now.

Sylvie glanced up at her gasp, eyes filled with a cracked, broken sorrow. She took a small step forward but stilled, as if some line marked the ground. Some point of no return that she would not pass. *Could not*—same as Rose.

"I'm sorry." Her whisper filled the silence between them.

The tears stilled on Rose's cheeks. "Don't. Please don't."

She could not bear the grim resolve etched onto Sylvie's features. As if Fen was already gone. As if she would never see him again.

Something flashed across Sylvie's face, but she ducked her head. Sucking in a small breath, she took a step forward. Then another. She stopped at her bedside, and it was only then that Rose noticed the red rims of her eyes, the dried tear tracks spilling down her cheeks.

"Are you all right?" Sylvie said softly.

The weight of more lies twisted around Rose's tongue, but she had no strength to hide behind them now. "No."

With a sigh, Sylvie sank into the chair beside Rose's bed, letting silence fall between them. "You asked once why you and I were linked"—her voice was soft when she finally spoke again—"but when you unleashed your casting, I felt like ... I'm not sure. Like being near you tethered me to life itself."

Rose glanced her over. There *was* something about her now that appeared stronger—brighter. But Rose hadn't cast anything specific. It was just a burst of magic, breaking free after years of being buried deep within parts of her heart that she couldn't even fathom. Wasn't it?

"What do you mean?"

Sylvie bit her lip. "When you think of magic—what are you drawn to?"

Rose blanched. Of all the questions to ask her now. As if she hadn't considered it a thousand times. As if the answer had ever changed.

"Nothing. You know that."

"Please, Rose."

251

There was something in the soft lilt of Sylvie's voice as her name rolled off her tongue. Some earnestness that stilled her aching heart.

She sighed. "Herbalism, I suppose."

"But it's not the charms and incantations of tonics and tinctures, is it?" Sylvie leaned in closer. "It's the feel of roots beneath your fingers—the joy of watching new life sprout from seed to sapling."

"I suppose?" She frowned. "But why does it matter?"

"Because I think you've had magic all along." Her eyes brightened. "I think you can cast source—life source."

"N-no." Rose shook her head. "That's impossible."

"Rare, but not impossible."

"No." Rose swallowed hard. "You're talking about necromancy, Sylvie—it's forbidden."

"And incredibly powerful."

Rose leaned back against her cushions, head spinning. It *couldn't* be. If that were true, then …. Her heart sank. What if the necromancy she'd suspected had never been Imrys, but her own magic, pulling Sylvie and Aveline back from the brink of death? Trapping them in this unliving torment simply because she did not have the skill to set them free. But how could she not have known—not have felt it somehow, even if only deep within?

The thought pulled at her with a strange sort of emptiness. For so long, magic had been all she wanted, yet now that she had it, it had given her nothing but pain. So, what was the point? Of all that longing—all those tears. What purpose did any of it serve when what she craved most lay still beyond her reach?

"Yet you're still a ghost." She frowned. "Fen is still gone."

Sylvie reached for her, fingers curling around her wrist. "But I'm *here*. I have a chance—because of you."

Rose's throat tightened as their gazes met. Sylvie's hands were warm through the thin linen of her shirt, and she wondered briefly, wildly, how they would feel against her bare skin. If there was nothing still standing between them. No death, no rivalry. Just them.

This strange, furious longing that had grown between them twisted through her chest, stealing the very breath from her lungs. Come from somewhere beyond her imagining and with nowhere to go, some part of her knew it could never be. That small tear in her heart stung beneath the thought.

So many wounds she kept buried there—so many scars and scabs that she'd lost count over the years. She stared up into Sylvie's dark eyes, lips trembling with shallow breath. Suddenly, with startling clarity, she knew this wound would never heal—that this aching chasm between them would never close. But she didn't care.

"Sylvie." Her name fell from Rose's lips like a prayer. "Can I—"

"Yes." Her voice was low and fervent—a merciful deity answering her call to worship.

Leaning in, Rose brushed her lips to Sylvie's and ripped her own heart open.

Her mouth was soft and warm—so full of life against her own. Like some current ran between them, both tethering them and shattering them beneath its strength. Sylvie's fingers curled at the back of Rose's neck, coiling in her hair.

She gasped, and Sylvie pulled away, separating them by only a hair's breadth to stare at Rose with wide, desperate eyes. And in that small space between them, nothing had ever seemed more tortuously simple.

Whatever this was—whatever tangled, terrible mess they'd created between them could all be gone tomorrow. But, for now, for this moment, Sylvie was here. She was *real*. And Rose couldn't bring herself to let that go.

Their lips met again, pulsing with a furious heat that threatened to swallow her. She pulled Sylvie closer, tighter, as if she could keep the cloying grasp of death at bay.

But the quiet of their embrace buckled under the weight of a groan, the soft stirring of linen sheets. They broke apart, sharing only the smallest glance before both their gazes slid to Ewan's bed. Another groan fell from them before their eyes fluttered open—and then flickered between them both.

"Sylvie?"

34

IN THE BALANCE

EWAN'S blue eyes fixed on them, unblinking, for several long moments, bright and glassy with tears, their split lips trembled as they sucked in a shuddering breath. They looked fragile as cracked glass, as if the smallest movement might shatter them to pieces.

But Rose's mind raced with desperate questions. Could they really see Sylvie? Heat flared across her cheeks. And see the way she was tangled in Rose's arms? Sylvie's fingers tightened around hers.

"You're here," they managed finally. "You're back?"

"You—" Sylvie's voice broke. "You can see me?"

They gave the smallest nod, their gaze still caught on her. Before Rose could blink, Sylvie darted from her side, throwing her arms around Ewan. A choking, heavy weight took hold of Rose's chest. Whatever Sylvie had said before, she could not help the stinging, subtle pricks of envy that pierced her heart.

"Ewan," she said after a moment, easing herself out of her cot. "What happened to Fen?"

Sylvie turned on her, a frown etched into her dark brow. "Rose, give them a minute."

"No it's okay, I—" Ewan's throat bobbed as they picked at their sheets. "I remember the ritual. We were going through introducing initiates when this explosion ripped through the chamber. There was smoke, but no fire. Everyone ran—there was so much screaming."

Sylvie reached for their hand, squeezing lightly.

"Fen grabbed me and shielded me on the way out." They swallowed hard. "My father was trying to corral everyone, but then we lost track of him, and Fen said to keep running. Neither of us could see anything, but I could hear something—*someone*—following us. I tried to tell Fen, but they hit me over the head and knocked me into the ravine. I think he tried to fight them off, but then everything went quiet. When my vision cleared, all I could find were his glasses."

"And then we found you?"

Ewan nodded.

"Do you think it could've been your father who attacked you?" Rose asked. "He protected you and took Fen?"

"Maybe?" They winced, cradling their head as they frowned. "It's hard to say. We had our masks on, and whatever was in that smoke took our vision. It could've been anyone."

"And Fen may not have been their target," said Sylvie.

"What?" Rose turned on her.

"Think about it—all this time we thought it was the Order that was behind things, right?" She leaned forward on her elbows. "But it's *their* initiates that have gone missing, *their* guild that got attacked. Why would Ewan's father want to destroy his own Order?"

"You think it's someone else?" Ewan lifted the steaming mug of tonic that had been left at their bedside.

"Maybe." Sylvie's gaze darted to Rose, eying her as if she were some fragile, broken thing. "Fen may not have been a real initiate, but someone could have thought he was. Or they were after Ewan. Either way, it seems like whoever is responsible wants to hurt the Order. Maybe they want revenge."

"Who would?"

"My mother," Rose said.

Ewan and Sylvie both fixed her with odd stares, one cast in shock, the other in pity. But she ignored them both. It fit, after all. If Sylvie was right about her magic, then perhaps Rose was never meant to be the next victim of the ritual—Sylvie and Aveline were likely never meant to be around to tell her of it. And her mother certainly never would have counted on her casting.

"Sylvie and I found an initiate list from thirty years ago, and my mother was on it. And we know she hates Ewan's father."

"But we also know she loves this place." Sylvie shook her head. "She wouldn't do anything to jeopardize that."

She was right. Her mother loved Dunhollow more than anything—more even than her. Rose's nails bit into her palms. But she'd also go to great lengths to protect her own reputation.

"If she'd had anything to do with those students dying years ago, then news of that getting out would make her desperate—volatile."

Ewan fidgeted with their sheets. "I know you don't exactly get along with your mother, but she wouldn't risk the academy's reputation, would she? Besides, she has far better ways to get revenge on my father than by murdering her own students."

"You thought your father might be behind this—why not my mother?"

"Because my father *wants* this academy to fail. That's his revenge. To watch everything your mother has built come crumbling down. If your mother was trying to protect herself, she would've just covered it all up, not further threatened her own reputation."

Damn. Rose bit back a curse. They were right. Unless … maybe her mother wasn't acting alone.

Rose's mind drifted back to the photos. Clearly something had happened among their group. She doubted Imrys would bother keeping charred photographs of them tucked away after all this time otherwise. It could be any one of them, born of whatever bad blood had separated them all in the first place.

Though she couldn't really see Delia or Briony thirsting after vengeance. Hollis, too, seemed unlikely. She'd seen the man hold funerals for bees—she doubted he could stomach bludgeoning students. Which left only one person.

"What about Sylverfir?" The words soured on her tongue.

Sylvie frowned. "Why would he want revenge?"

"I don't know." She shook her head. "But I found a photo of my mother and Ewan's father, alongside one with them, Delia, Hollis, Briony and Sylverfir. All of them were scorched—clearly there's a history there."

"Maybe. But, even so, that was decades ago. If he wanted vengeance for something, why now?"

That was the question, wasn't it? This all *had* to be connected somehow, but why wait all these years to act on it? What had changed?

"Because that's when the Order was revived." Ewan set their cup on the table with a dull thud.

Rose glanced up. "What?"

Ewan blinked at her, as if equally surprised they'd spoken. "I mean, that has to be it, right? They were defunct for decades, until last year, when they reemerged, corrupt and insidious as ever."

"And that might have been too much for someone to bear, even after all these years." Sylvie nodded. "Seems plausible, at least."

"Sylverfir was in the woods." Rose frowned. "When we escaped out of the guildhall, he was there."

Ewan and Sylvie shared a glance. "You can't really think he attacked Fen."

"Why not?"

"Because it's Sylverfir." Sylvie sighed. "You're more likely to find him lost in the library than bludgeoning students in the woods."

Rose didn't want to believe it either. That the man who raised her could be capable of something so despicable wrenched her heart in two. But it made sense. A cruel, twisted kind of sense.

"The library *is* where you were attacked."

"That could've been anyone," said Ewan. "Delia runs the library, and you said she was part of this group too, yeah?"

Sylvie leaned against their cot. "And Briony was the one who knew about iverin stasia. Maybe it was her."

"Why not Hollis?" Ewan shrugged. "Aveline was found near the pub."

Rose shook her head. "I can't see any of them doing something like this."

"But Sylverfir you can?"

Rose pursed her lips. Not of his own accord, at least. Whatever his actions, she was sure her mother's hand was behind them. Pulling invisible strings as they all danced to her tune.

But this was more than mere pretension and reputation that she toyed with now. Fen's and Sylvie's lives hung in the balance. Rose couldn't just sit here spinning theories while her mother trod over them to get her way. Not again.

Without another word, she turned for the door. It didn't matter what pain still prodded at her skull. What aches lingered in her very bones. She couldn't stay here. But Sylvie caught her hand, pulling her back.

"Where are you going?"

"Whatever is going on here, my mother is at the heart of it." Rose sucked in a steadying breath. "She owes us some answers."

Sylvie's eyes softened, and she squeezed her hand. "I'll come with you."

"No." The word rushed from her lips, harsh and forceful, even caught on the threat of tears. Then, softer. "No. I need to do this alone."

Whatever lies her mother had spun, whatever cruelty awaited Rose, she could no longer waste time cowering away from it. She had to face it. For Fen. For Sylvie. And for herself too, if she were honest. She needed the truth, even if only this once. She lifted her head, jaw clenched tight. And she would claw it free from her mother's lips, if she had to.

35

STARLINGS ARE PURE IMITATION

ROSE stared up at the doors to her mother's office. So many times before, she'd hesitated before them, approaching only with quiet dread or timid trepidation. But now it was fury that drew her in.

Sharp and jagged, it cut across her heart, tearing through raw wounds and old scars alike. Until, at last, it reached the very core of her—the one tenet by which she'd always lived her life. *Fear.*

It was a brittle thing. Broken and mangled by years of her falling to her knees before it, cowering and retreating each time it reared its ugly head. But not anymore.

With little more than a word, her fear buckled, shattering like glass as she shoved through the doors. Her mother barely glanced up as she entered, magical trinkets whirring around the desk where she sat. But her face betrayed nothing.

No ill thought. No guilt. Not even fear.

"Rosera?" She scribbled her signature onto the parchment before her. "I heard about your escapade in the Whispering Woods. You should still be in the healing hall."

She gasped as Rose ripped the page from her hands. "We need to talk. *Now.*"

Her mother straightened, eyeing Rose as if she were some injured, feral animal. Perhaps she was. Her wounds cut so deep now that she had nothing left to lose. Something in her mother's gaze seemed to recognize that, for she laid her glasses down on the desk and gestured for Rose to sit.

"Very well. About what?"

"I know you were a member of the Order." Rose refused her offer, standing resolutely before the desk. "I know students died back then, that something happened to shut the Order down. I also know that whatever happened then is behind what's happening now. So, tell me what's going on, or I swear, Mother, I will take this all to the board and ruin everything you've ever built."

"Rosera, it's hardly that dramatic."

"Don't lie to me!" Rose slammed her hand onto the desk. But a white glow fled from her palm, the scent of her casting stealing over them as her magic scattered sheaves of parchment across the desk.

Her mother's eyes widened. "Was that—"

"Magic? Yes, Mother." Rose's voice was low and miraculously even, though her shoulders shook with ill-kept fury. "Now, tell me what happened. All of it."

Her mother remained silent, and for a moment Rose thought she might not speak. That the walls would go back up, the mask would fall back in place. But then she sighed, hanging her head.

"I *was* a member of the Order, once."

"I know. I saw your photo with Imrys."

"He recruited me in our third year." She nodded. "We were top students in our respective fields and we thought we'd take over the world one day—that the empire was ours to conquer. We were in love and thought the Order would bring us a glorious future together. But all it did was tear us apart."

Rose blanched. Her mother had been in love with Imrys Elaegius? She'd seen the photo, of course—she should have guessed. But something about the idea just wouldn't sit in her mind, like a puzzle piece set in the wrong place.

"We had a row at the end of our third year." Her mother leaned back in her chair. "Some petty thing about who would lead the Order, perhaps. But,after, he had me kicked out. I lost all my connections, all my hopes for the future, because of his bruised ego. I was furious. So, when my fourth year began, I created my own order."

"The Starlings."

"You seem to know a great deal already. Perhaps I should let you tell this tale."

Rose held her stare. She would not be goaded so easily into that trap, allowing her mother to twist whatever facts she shared. "What happened with the Starlings?"

Her mother's eyes drifted to the fire, wistful and welling with tears. But Rose didn't trust them for a moment. "I found other students the Order had cast aside, or simply those who had no one else. Soren, Briony, Hollis, Delia. And my sister, Astoria. Together, the six of us formed the Starlings, for starlings are a nuisance, and that's precisely what we wanted to be to the Order."

"Why?"

"For revenge. We were young, petty, and thought nothing in the world could touch us. We used to disrupt their meetings, play silly pranks, cast hexes and such on their lodge. Juvenile things, really. Until I took it too far."

"What did you do?"

"I'd heard Imrys was to meet with a prominent diplomat—a promising lead to that bright future we'd both once chased." She bowed her head. "I'd also heard that the diplomat was a stickler for punctuality, so I cast a curse that would make Imrys perpetually late. I thought this would simply ruin his chances—give him a taste of what I'd felt when he dashed my own hopes. But I underestimated him. In his desperation to get there on time, he became reckless and tried crafting a portal, though he didn't yet have the skill, and it backfired horribly.

"It nearly destroyed him, and it killed the two younger Order members he took with him." Her voice wavered—the only sign of weakness in her immaculate mask. "He spent weeks in the infirmary, and people began to whisper that he would never recover. Of course, he did, eventually, but by then, the semester was nearly over. All his plans for the future were put on hold, and he became bitter. Somehow, he figured out I was behind his curse. Or maybe he just assumed. Either way, he set out for revenge."

She got to her feet, straying to the window as if she could walk away from the memory. A thousand questions burned against Rose's tongue, but she held them back. Her mother had been responsible for the deaths of two students—nearly three. And yet she spoke of it with little more gravity than she would the weather. Could she really be so heartless?

After a long moment, her mother finally spoke again. "Just before our graduation, your aunt Astoria planned a trip to the capital to celebrate. I had secured an apprenticeship with one of the most illustrious imperial casters, and she was set to take a role as a professor here. She thought we could have one last weekend where it was just the two of us, before our whole lives changed. But on the way there, our carriage tipped and fell into a ravine. I was lucky—the carriage only crushed my leg. But Astoria ... she was thrown from the carriage and her neck snapped on impact. She died instantly."

"And you think Imrys was responsible?"

"I know he was."

"How?"

"Because as that carriage tipped, and the whole world fell out beneath me, my last thought was not for myself. It wasn't even for my sister. It was that the most curious scent had filled the carriage. Pipeweed and primrose—the exact scent of Imrys's casting. Like I had cursed his trip, he'd done the same to mine, and Astoria paid the price for us both."

Rose kept silent, struck by the mere sight of tears streaming down her mother's cheeks. She thought perhaps it should ignite some pity in her, but it was a hollow feeling. Drawn by the sorrow of her aunt's fate, but not by sympathy for her mother. They had passed that point long ago.

This sincerity was born only out of the same fear she'd wielded against Rose. Fear of the tenuous glass she walked upon finally breaking and taking everything she'd worked for with it. Fear of Rose, for once. But honesty, true honesty, was a stranger her mother would never greet in earnest.

"But what does that have to do with the Order now?" Rose asked finally. "How does that explain what happened to Fen and Sylvie?"

Her mother sucked in a shuddering breath. "Your aunt's death tore a hole in the Starlings. It changed all of us. Confined to the infirmary for months, I lost out on my apprenticeship and resigned myself to taking over Dunhollow one day, as your aunt would have done. Briony and Delia had always planned on seeking their master's degrees here, but they drifted away from the rest of us. Hollis retreated in on himself, giving up an alchemical apprenticeship in the capital to take over his family's pub. And Soren—poor Soren."

"What happened to him?"

"He and your aunt were in love. Everyone thought they would get married one day, and he took her death hardest. When Astoria died, he lost himself in his experiments—he was sure he could bring her back. But death is a threshold not many can cross, and the experiment backfired. Instead of bringing her back, it cursed him with immortal life. After that we all drifted apart."

"But I don't understand—you all stayed. Why?"

"Because a part of us could never leave." Her mother sighed. "In one fateful moment, all of us were inextricably linked to this place. An indelible stain upon our lives that we could not simply wash away."

Rose fell silent for a moment, chewing the inside of her lip. "Would Soren blame Imrys for that?"

"In many ways, I'm sure." Her mother nodded. "If not for Imrys, Astoria might still be with us."

"And ... would he ever seek revenge?"

"By slaughtering students?" Her mother scoffed. "Honestly, Rosera, it's Soren. The man helped change your diapers—do you really think him capable of such a thing?"

"No, but—"

"Whatever is happening here, I can assure you that there's only one person responsible, and that's Imrys Elaegius."

Her words fell away, no more than ashes wisping off the fire. Rose said nothing, eyes still cast on the flickering flames. But, in the deepest part of her heart, she could no longer bring herself to agree.

Finally, she got to her feet. "Well, thank you for your honesty, Mother. It was such a rare treat."

"It was for your own good." Her voice carried over Rose's shoulder, seeping into her skin like venom.

"What?"

"The secrecy." Her mother's green eyes burned bright against the flames, but there was no truth in them now. "I kept it all from you to keep you away from the Order. To keep the past from rearing its ugly head."

Rose's nails cut harsh lines in her palms, her pulse thundering in her ears. "Don't pretend any of this was for me. This was for you—for your gods-damned reputation. Anything to protect that. I just hope that when it all comes crashing down around you, Mother, I'll be there to watch."

36

ASTORIA

SNOW fell softly onto Rose's auburn curls, her breath billowing around her in warm puffs against the frigid air. Her pale skin was raw and pink, but still, she held a bare hand out as snowflakes drifted down upon it.

She'd never seen it snow in Dunhollow before. It rarely got cold enough, for the seasons never changed. But now, it was as if something had thrown that out of balance, sucking all the warmth out of the air.

Perhaps it was Fen. The thought brought tears to her eyes. He'd always been a solitary warmth to these callous, cloying halls. And now he was gone—the world a little colder in his absence.

Rose brushed the tears from her eyes with a sniffle. They would find him. She glanced back toward the professors' hall, watching for any sign of Sylverfir. They *had* to.

Beside her, Sylvie reached out, rubbing Rose's arm almost absently, her eyes never lifting from the book she held. In spite of herself, a slow smile spread across Rose's lips. She couldn't remember the last time she'd seen Sylvie open a book. And it was nice, in a way, to sit here with her, even as the world shattered around them.

They still hadn't spoken since their kiss, and it hung between them like something precious and fragile. Neither of them wanted to be the one to break it, she supposed. Neither of them wanted to admit there was no future for them either. At least, not as they were.

"It says here that necromancers can sometimes be drawn to restless spirits." Sylvie's voice made her jump.

Rose cleared her throat. "Uh-huh."

Eyes darting back to the courtyard, she watched her peers hurry along the frozen paths. Some pulled their coats tight, casting shimmering shields to protect them from the snow. Others embraced the rarity, tossing snowballs at each other and charming snowmen to dance around the frozen green. But no sign of Sylverfir. *Yet.*

She bit the inside of her lip. He should have been here by now—his class started in less than ten minutes. But he had yet to emerge from his quarters, and the seconds ticked by achingly slowly, grating at Rose.

"Most necromancers could only cast shades and ghosts," Sylvie continued. "But the more powerful ones could fully draw souls back from the dead. They abused them terribly, of course. Binding them and forcing them into servitude, but still."

"Very handy."

"Rose, are you even listening?"

"What?" She turned. "Oh, yes. You think I'm incredibly powerful and can fix all this with a wave of my hand. I heard."

"No." Sylvie set the book down between them. "But with practice, you may be able to control it. Keep yourself from attracting ghosts and such things. Or maybe briefly revive people. Who knows what you're really capable of."

Rose swallowed hard. Even with this strange new magic at her fingertips, it wasn't enough. It would *never* be enough.

"And get myself arrested in the process?" She raised an eyebrow. "In case you've forgotten, necromancy isn't legal, Sylvie. And, until a few days ago, we didn't even know I had magic. So, don't get your hopes up."

Her face fell, and Rose's heart flipped. It was the truth, but she hadn't meant to hurt her with it. She reached for her hand when a figure darted past the corner of her eye. *Sylverfir.*

His thin braids were tied in a bun at the top of his head, a burgundy scarf wrapped firmly around his ears as he rushed through the snow. He didn't even spare a glance for her—didn't notice her at all. *Perfect.*

She hopped off the wall. "Come on."

Sylvie's eyes flashed toward Sylverfir's retreating form. "This isn't a good idea, Rose."

"It's fine. He's got a class for the next hour." She pulled her hand back. "Or you can stay here, if you prefer?"

Sylvie picked up the book and hopped off the wall, landing without a sound. "After you ran off to speak to your mother alone? Not a chance."

"I told you everything she said." Rose shrugged as they crossed the courtyard.

No one paid them any notice—no eyes fell upon Sylvie at all. Strange. Only Ewan had thus far been able to see her, but why? Was it some strange trick of her magic? She dodged the outstretched arms of an overly friendly snowman. Perhaps that eruption of it in the Whispering Woods had connected them somehow—allowed them to see what she saw. But then, that meant Sylverfir probably could too.

Sylvie's brow furrowed as Rose opened the door for her. "That's not the point."

The professors' hall was utterly quiet as they entered. She glanced left and right, making sure no other professors were ambling about to stop them before taking to the steps. The hall was smaller than the student dorms, but far grander somehow, with crimson velveteen carpets stretching from one end to the other.

Yet it almost seemed mundane. Most student dorms had magic whizzing left and right, spells backfiring, and potions burning at all hours. But the magic here was quieter, more refined, and the air didn't hold such a cloying scent of petrichor.

A charmed broom swept its way down the corridor, and a fire crackled endlessly in the professors' lounge as they passed. But, otherwise, it was no more magical than Rose's own dorm. Save for the stone stairs, which lurched forward as they stepped onto them, gliding them up to the landing.

Sylverfir's door was worn and familiar ahead of her, and her heart twisted with a strange sense of nostalgia. She didn't need her master key for this one—just three simple knocks. A secret passcode, known only to them. He'd taught her when she was barely up to his knee, but already she'd needed a place to escape from her mother.

She sighed as the door creaked open. His quarters were nothing like his office. More decoration than her mother's chambers, though even smaller somehow. And not nearly as neat. A stray jacket was draped over his desk chair, and a few dying plants littered the windowsill. In spite of herself, Rose reached out, chest swelling when the plants perked up beneath her grasp.

"What are we looking for?" Sylvie cut through her thoughts.

Rose didn't answer at first, crossing instead to the desk at the far wall. It was not as tidy as her mother's either—dozens of papers scattered across it. But it was the lone photograph sitting atop it that drew her in now. The one that had been staring at her for years, blithely giving her every clue she'd needed. Her throat tightened as she reached for it, a small engagement ring rattling around in the frame.

The happy couple ignored the camera, locked in a stolen kiss, forever captured on cold, gray paper. Perhaps the only thing Sylverfir had left of her aunt. She pulled it close.

"This," she whispered, though she wasn't sure why.

"An old photograph?"

"It's my aunt Astoria."

Rose peered at the photo more closely now. She and her aunt had the same round features—the same auburn hair and hazel eyes. It stirred something deep within her, and she ran her finger over the photograph.

But the world lurched. The chambers faded around her, replaced by a dark room, heavy with the stench of smoke. Auburn hair tumbled over her shoulder, her torso faded and caught beneath the grip of some spell. And there, before her, was Sylverfir, eyes hard and weaving the magic that held her.

"Please, don't do this." The whispered plea fell from her lips. "Let me go."

"Rose?" Sylvie's hand curled around her shoulder, jolting her back to the cool glow of Sylverfir's chambers. "Are you all right?"

Rose sucked in a ragged breath, stumbling forward into his desk. The photo fell from her hands with a clatter, knocking into his journal, which tumbled to the floor. Rose steadied herself, cool beads of sweat creeping along her brow.

"Fine," she said finally, bending down to pick up the journal. But her fingers brushed against a scrap of parchment instead.

We need to talk, it read. *Meet at the Witch's Brew tomorrow at one o'clock.* Today's date was scribbled in the top corner, while a looping signature consumed the bottom of the page. *Imrys Elaegius.*

Rose stared at the name a moment longer. "Just fine."

37

BY A THREAD

THE warm steam of Rose's cider curled around her cheeks, tickling her nose. The pub wasn't too busy now, hanging on the tail end of a lunch rush. A few groups of students mingled around the tables and booths, but most still packed the library, she assumed, frantically cramming for midterms.

One student fidgeted in the back booth, dark circles hanging beneath their eyes as a buzzing pen prodded at their ear to keep them awake. The group at the counter crowed loudly over a drunken game of Dead Man's Bluff, the losing cards tearing themselves up in a tizzy. But none seemed to pay them any attention at all. *Good.*

She glanced over at Ewan, who was fiddling with the rim of their cider, while Sylvie stared at the steaming mug longingly. Their table was tucked away from view behind a slow game of Casters' Darts. Hardly ideal, but it gave a perfect view of the door, while also obscuring them. Rose tapped a finger to her mug, nerves fluttering.

"So," said Ewan, "you really think Sylverfir is out to kill my father?"

"Why else would they be meeting?" Rose shrugged. "If he was willing to kill three students just to bring down the Order, why not the man behind my aunt's death?"

"Fair. Still, when we started this, I didn't think we'd be *saving* my father. From Sylverfir, no less."

"If either of them deigns to show up." Rose thrummed her fingers against the table, eyes flickering to the clock above the bar. *They were late.*

"Maybe we should just ask," said Sylvie.

"What?" Ewan shook their head. "No. *You* shouldn't even be here."

Sylvie's gaze darkened, but Rose couldn't help but agree. For the moment, it seemed only Ewan and Rose could see her, but who knew how long that would last? If Sylverfir was behind her attack, then catching sight of her might ruin everything.

"Just Hollis. Maybe they got here earlier than us and he saw."

Rose glowered into her drink. "We got here almost an hour early."

"It's worth a shot."

With a sigh, Rose pushed her chair back, leaving her untouched drink on the table. Ducking past whizzing darts, she leaned over the bar and waved down Hollis.

The burly man turned with a beaming smile. "Rose! Another round of ciders?"

"No, thank you." She propped her elbows up on the counter. "I'm looking for Professor Sylverfir."

"Sylverfir?" The barkeep's brow furrowed. "I haven't seen him since last week."

"He hasn't been in at all today?"

Strange. The note had said one o'clock, and it was going on two now. There was no way he could've snuck by them—unless perhaps the note was a diversion?

"Not that I've seen." Hollis shrugged, wiping down a beer glass. "Why?"

"No reason. He was just supposed to meet—er—someone."

Hollis eyed her strangely. Fair enough. Subterfuge wasn't her strong suit. "He does keep a set of keys for one of the rooms upstairs for meetings and such."

Rose frowned. "Didn't you just say you haven't seen him, though?"

"Well, not in the bar, no." His rugged cheeks flushed an unbecoming shade of pink. "But I'm not always watching the stairs, and we have been a bit swamped with the lunch rush."

Rose glanced around at the crowd of students. That was true enough. Besides, Hollis wasn't exactly the most observant person. He could rattle off the orders of his regulars as easy as breathing, but that seemed to be the only thing his memory was truly dedicated to. And Sylverfir was by far the superior caster—it wouldn't have been hard for him to cast some glamour or charm Hollis into not noticing his presence.

She sighed deeply. "Think I could take a look upstairs?"

"Ah." Hollis's throat bobbed. "The thing is, if he is up there, he'll not want to be disturbed."

"Noted. I'll do my best not to."

"Suit yourself." He shrugged, filling a mug up with a perfect pour of ale. "Room 4, then. Don't say I didn't warn you, though."

Rose let out a heavy sigh as he wandered off. Perhaps the note had been a lie—just an idle bit of misdirection. But why bother? Unless it was planted ... but that could only mean that Sylverfir knew they suspected him. Her heart fluttered. They should check upstairs first— make sure this wasn't all a waste of time.

Returning to the table, she downed her cider in a single gulp, wincing as it scalded her tongue. "Ewan, you should go back to the academy. Maybe they changed their meeting place."

"What?" Their eyebrows shot up. "Why?"

"Because something seems off. Hollis said they might be upstairs but, if not, then it would be less suspicious for you to turn up asking after your father than me."

"Fair point. Still, splitting up doesn't seem smart."

"We'll be fine," said Sylvie. "If we're not back in a few hours, you can send in the capital inquisitors."

They glowered at her. "Don't think I won't."

"Go on." She squeezed their hand. "And be careful."

"Same to you."

A slow grin spread across her lips. "Always."

Giving them both one final glance, Ewan darted out the door. Rose took Sylvie's hand and slipped up the stairs. The din of the pub quietened as they reached the landing. Muted conversations and the muffled clinks of mugs still carried up the steps, but they were softer here, barely audible over the creaking floorboards. She wondered if some spell lay upon it, making the inn upstairs marginally more tenable for travelers.

Scanning the doors, she crept toward the one with a glittering, gilded "4" carved into it. Leaning in close, she listened for any muffled voices or whispers filtering through it. But there was nothing. She frowned. Even if they *were* in there, they'd likely spelled the room with a silencing charm.

She had raised her fist to knock when Sylvie caught it. "Why would you let them know we're here?"

Rose lowered her hand. *Good point.* Nodding, she turned the knob, pushing the door open gently.

But the room was utterly empty as she entered. Cramped but tidy, a canopied four-poster bed took up most of the space. A small dresser was shoved into the far corner, and a few ragged tapestries hung about the walls. But no form or figure lingered within.

"Damn," she muttered. "They're not here."

Sylvie's eyes darted around the space. "We should go back downstairs."

Rose nodded, but the air shifted before her, warping and wavering around a strange form. Fen's eyes stared down at her, bare and raw. And swimming with concern.

"*Run!*" His voice was thin and breathless, as if speaking took all the effort in the world.

Rose's heart lurched, and she reached for him. But it wisped away—shattered as an arm wrapped around her throat. She tried to scream, but a cloth was shoved over her mouth, coarse and smelling of fresh-cut grass and alcohol. Her vision blurred, her lungs burning as her eyelids drooped, darkness welcoming her into its cold embrace.

38

ALL THAT REMAINED

A cold stone floor was the only thing that greeted Rose when she opened her eyes. Beyond that was utter darkness—and a sharp pain shooting through her skull. She groaned, pushing herself up slowly. Dampness and must clung to the stones, wet beneath her fingers. A strange dripping noise grated at her ears and a harsh scent hung on the air, almost like vinegar.

Her stomach churned as her eyes adjusted to a sickly green glow, casting eerie shadows across the stone walls. She *knew* this place. She'd seen it in those rancid visions. This was where Aveline had been held.

"Rose?" Sylvie's voice cut through the shadows. "Are you awake?"

"Sylvie?" Getting slowly to her feet, she brushed damp grit from her clothes. "What's going on?"

"I don't know." Her voice was weak—strained.

A spark of light caught the air, illuminating Sylvie's face in the soft glow of flame. But a scent lingered on the spell that pierced Rose's heart like a blade. Worn leather and red wine. *Fen.*

She turned, heart leaping at the sight of her friend, who stood behind her, fire coiled in the palm of his hand. He looked perfectly unscathed—hair a bit tousled and missing his glasses, perhaps. But, still, here—*alive.*

"Rose." A sad smile split his lips. "Somehow, I knew you'd show up."

He grunted as she slammed into him, but no soft chuckle rumbled through his chest—no warmth enveloped her from the embrace of his arms. A cool grip wrapped itself around her heart, weighted with a truth she could not bear as she pulled back to meet his gaze. His deep brown eyes were soft and kind, as they'd always been, but filled only with sorrow.

"No." Her head pounded, brimming with a thousand piercing thoughts. "You can't be—"

"Not yet." He shook his head. "But it won't be long. For either of us."

Her breath caught in her chest. "I-I don't understand. What's going on?"

Flame pulsed in Fen's palm, arcing out across the room and casting shadows upon aged wooden shelves lined with glowing glass jars. A wave of nausea rolled over her, for they were filled with half-decayed skulls and still-pounding organs.

Cobwebs draped from the corners, their silken strands glistening in the dim light, as if guarding the secrets of this place. Mortars and pestles, alembics, and retorts stood as silent witnesses to whatever sordid experiments were conducted within these walls.

Her eyes flickered to the corner of the room, where an ancient, imposing summoning circle was inscribed upon the floor, its markings weathered but still potent. Atop it sat a tank, its contents held in the sickly green glow that cast its pall upon the room. Strange whispers surrounded it, but they felt stifled and corrupted, like lost souls screaming for release with none to hear their pleas.

Rose glanced back to Fen, hoping for some answer to clear the dread coursing through her. But then he stepped aside and she nearly retched. For there, at the center of the room, lay a thick marble slab, two familiar forms prostrate upon it.

Far from the ghostly forms who watched her, Sylvie's and Fen's bodies were ashen, their skin stained with blood and sweat and their chests rising with shallow breaths. Thick tubes protruded out of them, filled with a pale silvery liquid that echoed in their harshly carved veins.

No. Rose gasped, but her lungs were empty, as if someone had sucked the life out of them. Her knees buckled, and she stumbled forward, dark spots dancing across her vision.

"What have they *done* to you?"

"Rose." Sylvie caught her arm, but her touch was a hollow comfort.

Yet Rose couldn't hold her gaze—could not face the pain she knew would be lurking there. All she could do now was stare at the bodies before her, watching their heartbeats fade with each breath. But it was no longer pain or fear that pulled at her heart—it was fury.

White-hot and seething, it burned through her veins until all else faded away. All that remained was them. Their listless bodies, their lives still hanging by a thread. There was no part of her that didn't want to claw those tubes out of their flesh and jab them straight through the heart of whatever monster had put them there.

But a soft grip drew her to a sharp stop, pulling her hand away from the tube in Fen's right arm. "Rose, don't. They're the only thing keeping us alive."

She blinked up at him, the weight in his gaze quelling her fury in an instant. A sharp pain ripped through her chest, as if the words bore claws aimed straight for her heart. She couldn't lose them—not now. Not after everything.

"There was someone else here." Sylvie traced her fingers along the edges of the marble slab, to an empty space above her own body. "Aveline—if I had to take a guess. This must be how she died."

Rose's eyes followed the outline of the missing shape, bile creeping up her throat. Cold, dead eyes flashed through her memory. Her life drained away from her, and for what? What kind of monster could have done this?

A soft groan stilled her thoughts, her stomach turning as Fen's light scattered over one more prostrate form. *Sylverfir.* A deep gash drew a harsh line across his forehead, blood trickling down his sallow cheeks. What was *he* doing here?

His thin braids clung to the sweat-stained skin around his throat, which bobbed weakly as he groaned again. Rose's heart pounded dully in her chest as she dropped to her knees beside him.

"Sylverfir—Soren, can you hear me?" She gently tapped his cheek until his eyes blinked open.

"Rose?" His voice was dry and scratchy. "You need to get out of here."

"Do you know where we are?"

"No, you can't be here." He lurched forward, pushing her away. "If he comes back, he'll—"

"Who's *he*? Soren, please, just tell me what's going on."

He stared at her a moment longer, blinking rapidly. "My chains, I-I can't cast."

He jangled his bindings, which pulsed with a strange energy. But they were loose, rusted and rotting at their edges. Rose reached for them, straining to pry them apart.

The metal buckled beneath her fingers, but didn't break. "Almost there."

Sylverfir's eyes slipped over Rose's shoulder, dazed and unfocused. "Sylvie?"

"Hello, Professor."

"And Fen? I don't understand."

Rose's jaw tightened, her fingers loosening his chains. The air held heavy with the scent of decay and rot, pricking at the back of her mind. "It's a long story. Now, please, do you remember how you ended up here?"

His brow creased, and he licked his cracked lips. "No, I—there was a note. From Imrys. I thought he wanted to meet after what happened in the woods that night, but when I got here, I ..."

Rose frowned as he trailed off. "But where is *here*?"

Before he could answer, heavy footsteps thudded somewhere outside, and a door swung open with a great bang. Rose blinked, shielding her eyes against the flood of light. But a familiar form took shape in the space between her fingers, a warm smile bearing down on her.

Her heart hammered in her chest, and she slowly lowered her hands. "Hollis?"

39

A LIFE FOR A LIFE

FOR several long moments, all Rose could do was stare. *What was he doing here?* Perhaps Ewan had made good on their promise and sent for help. But then, a dozen capital inquisitors should have been bearing down on them. She shook her head as the door clicked shut behind him. It didn't matter. At the moment, she could've hugged him.

She scrambled to her knees, relief washing over her in trembling waves. "Hollis, quick, help—Sylverfir is hurt."

His magic might not be the strongest, but he was better with healing spells than she was, at least. But his eyes didn't even meet hers, fixing instead on Fen's and Sylvie's waning forms with some strange sense of ... joy? He pushed past Rose, gently examining their bodies upon the slab.

"How is this possible?" he whispered.

Rose frowned. "They've been trapped down here. We need to get them out of here, quickly."

Yet his movements were anything but quick. Slow and methodical, he ran his hands over the tubes and needles that held them, almost as

278

if he were checking them. Why didn't he tear them out or race to find help? But Hollis said nothing at all.

"Rose ..." Sylverfir shook his head weakly. "He won't help."

"What?" Her gaze flickered between them. *No*. That wasn't—it *couldn't* be. Cold, creeping dread coiled in her stomach. "H-how did you know where to find us, Hollis?"

Hollis didn't speak for a long moment, didn't look at her at all. Finally, he hung his head. "I'm sorry. I never wanted you to be a part of this."

Rose's eyes slid from him to Sylvie's and Fen's prostrate forms, and then back again. "No. *No*—tell me it isn't true."

Hollis, who'd always been there with a drink and a sympathetic ear. Who'd saved her countless times from her mother's wrath, given her sanctuary in his pub, and cheered her up with poor jokes. Her *friend*. How could he do any of this?

"I'm sorry," was all he said.

But his apology fell flat against her ears—cold and empty against the raging beat of her heart. *It couldn't be.*

She stumbled back, fingers curling around wet stones as she leaned against the wall for support. "But you weren't in the woods that night. And you were in the pub when Sylvie was attacked. It couldn't have been you."

He grimaced, barely even looking at her as he adjusted the dial of his hideous contraption. "It's easier than you think for a barman to go unnoticed. Casting a few doubles here and there, taking a little too long in the cellars. After all, no one really sees us."

Rose's heart sank as the viscous liquid grew brighter. What was he doing? What was any of this *for*? He didn't sound jaded or drunk on the need for revenge—he sounded desperate, somehow. Almost despondent in his conviction.

Her throat tightened. None of this felt real. "But why?"

"You don't understand. I had to."

"I don't 'understand'?" she hissed. "What exactly is there to understand?"

He reached for her. "Rose, please."

"You *killed* Aveline." She recoiled, pressing herself tighter against the wall. He'd gathered up Aveline's body and had the audacity to call it tragic. Her head spun, tears pricking at her eyes. "You're draining the life from Fen and Sylvie like they're nothing more than blood and bones to be used. And what was I to be, your next victim?"

"Of course not."

"Was the life you've stolen already not enough?" Her chest heaved with ragged breath. "And for what, revenge?"

"Isn't it obvious?" Fen's voice was soft, soothing against the fury that frayed the edges of Rose's mind. "The incantation, that formula—he's using us. Using our lives to fuel another."

Words failed Rose for a moment, the sheer ridiculousness of it stilling her mind. "You stole three lives to save one? Who could be worth that?"

"Oh, Hollis, no." It wasn't Hollis who answered, but Sylverfir. He got slowly to his feet, chains rattling and limbs shaking. "Tell me you didn't—you know the spell is too dangerous."

"What are you talking about?" Rose's eyes darted between them. "Who is he trying to revive?"

"Astoria."

Rose frowned. She'd known whoever was behind this was out for revenge, but this? Her aunt had been dead for decades—how could he hope to save her now?

"She's gone, Hollis." Sylverfir's voice echoed softly through her thoughts. "She can't be saved."

"No, *you* couldn't save her." Hollis's lips curled in a snarl. "But you didn't love her like I did. No one did."

He moved to the back of the room, behind Fen's and Sylvie's bodies, to the large tank. It glowed brightly as he laid a hand upon it, illuminating a small shape caught amid the liquid.

Rose couldn't help the gasp that escaped her, for the face inside was one she knew well. Frozen in old photographs and graying memories. And now in death. Yet she looked so close to life that Rose almost longed to reach for her. To touch a hand to her face and see if she woke.

The thought stirred her. Could it be so simple? Her gaze flickered to the pale, prostate forms. Would her magic allow such a thing?

"Astoria." Her name slipped from Sylverfir's lips, shock and grief warring in his eyes. Until they slid back to Hollis. "What have you done to her?"

"I protected her." He moved in front of the tank, as if he guarded it still. "You let her life slip away like it was nothing and went on living—but I couldn't."

Sylverfir scoffed. "Nothing? I tried *everything*. And now I must suffer eternally without her. So, let her be at peace, please."

"Peace?" Hollis spit out the word, closing the distance between them. "Her killer walks free, her sister practically dances over her grave, living the life she should have had. And you? You've all but forgotten her."

The two men stared each other down, so focused on one another that neither noticed when Rose crept forward. Sylvie was closer to her, one hand lying listless and near enough to touch.

"What are you doing?" Sylvie whispered in her ear.

"Testing your theory."

"What theory?" Fen's brow creased.

"Rose can cast now. Life source."

"*What?*"

Reaching out, Rose touched her fingers to the palm of Sylvie's frozen hand. At first, nothing happened, but then Sylvie linked her hand through hers. The memory of the warmth of her drawing soft lines along Rose's face sent a shiver down her spine. A small glimpse of the life she'd lost—of what they could still have.

Warmth surged out of her fingertips, stealing into Sylvie's palm. For a brief moment, she seemed brighter beside her, her body growing warmer.

Rose's heart leaped, and she pulled her hand away as if she'd been shocked. If she could get her and Fen both awake before Hollis noticed, then they could overpower him. Two of the best casters in their year— he wouldn't stand a chance. But she needed some sort of distraction.

"Fen," she whispered, so quietly even she could barely hear. "I need to distract him—tell me you have something."

In spite of everything, an easy grin spread across his lips. "Right pocket."

She nodded, eyes still fixed on Hollis, as if he were a serpent poised to strike. But Sylverfir had stepped between them, straining against his chains. *Yes.* If she could free him first, he could hold Hollis off long enough for her to wake the others.

Holding her breath in a silent prayer, she dipped her hand into Fen's pocket, fingers curling around three metal balls. *His smoke bombs.* Her heart leaped. When they got out of this, she would never make fun of him for carrying around explosives again.

"Let's say you could bring her back." Sylverfir's voice made her jump, and she nearly dropped the bombs. "That all this works and her body is restored. You think she'd be at peace then? Knowing what you sacrificed to give her life, you think she'd forgive you? She'd hate you for it."

"But she'd be *here*." Pain lanced through Hollis's eyes, and he turned away, just for a moment.

Perfect.

Digging her finger into the divot, Rose pulled back and hurled the bomb across the room. It exploded in a dazzling array of sparks, smoke pouring across the damp stones. It coiled upon the air, choking away the scent of death with an acrid stench of its own. Rose coughed, blinking as her vision blurred.

But she couldn't waste this chance. Stumbling over to Sylverfir, she heaved at his chains, straining against the rusted metal. *Come on.* She groaned as it creaked beneath her. *Almost there.*

"What did you do?" he wheezed in her ear, just as the metal snapped and the chains fell away.

"Just buy me some time—please."

He blinked at her, but she didn't wait for an answer before staggering back over to the slab. Her head spun, and she fought to keep her eyes open, but she *had* to. Fen and Sylvie both reached for her, holding her steady against the encroaching haze.

"What have you done?" Hollis roared through the smoke.

Flames poured across the room, crackling on the air around them, spilling past Rose's ear. But she reached for Sylvie's palm all the same. Her magic warmed the air between them, eking out of her with slow purpose. Sylvie gasped beside her as her form began to fade, her shape weakening as the color in her cheeks returned. But it wasn't enough.

Already her magic faltered—slipping out of Rose's grasp like sand. "*No.* I'm not strong enough."

But then Fen took her other hand, squeezing gently. "Yes, you are. My other pocket—it has my orb. It should help you channel."

Rose's heart leaped as their eyes met, held by a thousand unspoken words. But they shattered in a burst of magic. Rose screamed as an arc of lightning hurtled toward her, but it slammed into a ragged barrier, fizzling into nothing more than scattered light. She blinked at Sylverfir, who smiled weakly as the scent of pipeweed and whiskey stole over her. But his barrier faltered. It wouldn't last long—not in his state.

"Hollis, please." Sylverfir coughed, his barrier wavering. "Astoria wouldn't want this. Just let them go—they're innocent."

Rose winced as the heat of more flames singed her cheek, and she ducked behind the slab for cover. But she couldn't stop. Not now. Pulling her hand from Fen's grasp, she shoved it into his left pocket, fingers skimming over the glassy surface of the orb.

But the moment she touched it, it burned at her like a raw flame. Her magic surged through her, coarse and hot. And so free. It poured into Sylvie, quickening her pulse, breathing life into her lungs. Shards of ice ricocheted off Hollis's barrier, shattering against the ceiling and splintering into Rose's hair. Still, she refused to let go of Sylvie's hand.

"No one is innocent." Hollis's cry came through the haze of smoke. "Not here."

"They don't deserve to *die*."

"Neither did Astoria. She should have *lived*." A sleeping curse slinked through the air. "And you let her die."

"No one *let* her die." Sylverfir shielded Rose as the curse bounded off the barrier. "She just couldn't be saved. It was tragic and senseless and wrong, but this? This won't make it right."

Rose's breath coiled in her chest, cold stone digging into her ribs. Magic burned at the edges of her mind, searing, stretching just beyond the edge of painful. Just a little bit longer, then Sylvie would wake up and she could move on to Fen. They could all walk out of here together. They *had* to.

"Rose." Sylvie pulled at her hand. "Rose, stop. It's taking too much."

"I can get us all out of here, I just need—"

"No, please." Sylvie's form wavered at the edges. "You need to stop."

"I won't." She shook her head. "I can't."

"Please, I—"

But her form wisped away, unspoken words caught forever only in memory. A soft breath carved through her chest, the color returning to her cheeks. And then a heartbeat. Once, twice, it echoed in Rose's ears, and she stilled.

She'd done it. She'd truly done it. Sylvie would be safe—she'd survive. Her eyes flickered to the form still held by the shadows. Now all that was left was Fen.

Her stomach roiled as Sylverfir's barrier waned and then shattered. His knees buckled before he sank to the ground, but Rose no longer had the strength to pull him up again. She didn't have the strength for any of this—not yet. But she had to try all the same, even if the magic tore her apart.

"Rose, no." Fen caught her hand. "Sylvie was right."

But she jerked out of his grasp, reaching for his hand when sickly, spidery tendrils of energy slipped out of the smoke, binding Sylverfir in a web of magical constraints. *No.* Rose's heart lurched. Sylverfir struggled against them, as Hollis stepped forward, eyes rimmed red.

He grabbed Sylverfir gently by the chin, holding him there a moment longer. "I'm sorry, old friend," he whispered before driving a small blade straight through his throat.

For a moment, Sylverfir didn't move—staring wide-eyed at Hollis as he choked on his own blood. Then his eyes rolled back, his body hitting the stones with a dull thud. A scream clawed at Rose's throat, but died on her lips as Hollis turned on her. His eyes flickered between Fen, her, and the gently fading light of her aunt's tomb.

"No," he whispered. Then, louder, *"No!"*

Rose flinched as he stalked toward her, blade dripping with Sylverfir's blood. She couldn't move now; she was so close—so very close. Already, Sylvie's fingers twitched, the color fully returned to her cheeks, while Fen's pulse had quickened. They would live—they'd survive. Even if she wouldn't.

And yet, Hollis didn't raise his blade against her. Instead, he shoved her out of the way, and plunged his blade directly into Fen's heart.

40

LET ME GO

THE blade sank into Fen's listless chest, but it tore through Rose's flesh as if the wound was her own. It drove between his ribs, cracking the bones and burying itself deep within his heart. Fen cried out beside her, but she almost couldn't hear him, her own heart pounding so loudly in her ears it drowned out all else.

Fear didn't bind her now, nor the bitter sting of grief. It was only fury. White-hot and searing, it roared to life within her chest, racing through her veins. And, this time, Rose didn't bury it.

Magic poured out of her in silver flames, ravenous for all in its path, shattering the orb beneath her palm. It slammed into Hollis, throwing him back against the stone walls before he even had the chance to scream. He hit the ground with a sickening thud, her magic eating away at his flesh, burning him away to little more than dust. Every one of his fading heartbeats was bound to her will—ebbing and flowing at her whim as his life fled from him.

For once, she understood the song of magic so many spoke of. Weaving through her, carried on every shred of rage she'd ever buried.

Tangled strings of a haphazard harmony that twisted around her heart, tethering her to Fen. To Sylvie. To life itself. And it was *beautiful*.

But then the song changed—a soft melody of grief against the raging strings of her ire. She reached out, letting it surge into Fen, watching a soft glow build in his cheeks. He wasn't gone—not yet.

"Oh, Hollis," A soft sigh brushed against Rose's ear.

She turned, her magic almost faltering at the sight of the young woman beside her. Like Fen and Sylvie, she was there, but not truly, her brow furrowed as she stared down at Hollis's fallen form. Auburn waves curled around her face, so like Rose's own. But her eyes were rounder, softer. And filled with such sorrow.

"Aunt Astoria?"

"Hello, Rose." Tears welled in her aunt's eyes.

"Are you really here?"

"Only in the same way your friends were." A wan smile pulled at her lips. "Life is a powerful source, and all too dangerous in the wrong hands."

Rose gasped. It was *her*. The woman in the visions—the one haunted in the forest, who'd pleaded with Sylverfir to let her go. The one who'd begged for death. Echoes of her life somehow entwined with Rose's magic.

"I—I'm sorry, I didn't mean to bring you back."

Astoria reached out to stroke her cheek. "Don't apologize—life is best left for the living. Something Hollis forgot long ago. Don't give up yours trying to save what was never meant to be."

Rose followed her gaze to Fen's body, his blood pooling freely on to the table. *Too much.* Rose's magic still raced within her, bubbling under her skin, desperate to seal his wounds.

"No, he's not meant to die. None of this was *meant* to happen."

"Perhaps not, but neither are you," she whispered. "Break my bindings and you'll break Hollis's spell. But it won't save your friend."

With that, she faded. Nothing more than a memory lost. But Fen was still here. Rose's eyes flew to where he stood, shoulders slumped and tears streaming down his cheeks.

"She's right, Rose. I'm dying—you can't give your life for mine."

"No." She shook her head, magic seeping from her in trembling waves. Its light flickered and waned, ebbing beneath her grief. "I can bring you back."

"Rose." His voice was soft, as if miles away. "Look at me. *Look* at me, please."

Pain tore through her mind. Hot and fierce, it raged against her skull, but she swallowed it. Slowly, she lifted her gaze, meeting those eyes she knew so well. Eyes that had given her laughter, comfort. *Love.* But they held only sorrow now.

He reached for her hand. "I can't let you do this."

A soft whimper slipped from her lips. "And I can't let you die."

"I'm already gone."

"No."

She could still do this—could still save him. Like Sylvie, who groaned softly below her. But her head split beneath the strain of her magic, a torrid pain aching in her bones. She shuddered, sinking her head into his chest as he drew her in close, whispered pleas aching on her lips. But then he pulled away, cradling her face gently between his palms.

"It's you." He pressed his lips to her forehead. "It's always been you."

She stared at him a moment longer, so many words tangled between them. But none of them fit, and the moment passed silently into tears.

"No." She choked on a sob. "Please, Fen. Don't do this—don't leave me behind."

"I love you, Rose." He brushed a thumb over her cheek before leaning in to whisper softly in her ear. "So, please, let me go."

As his eyes met hers one final time, the world narrowed around her. Magic waning, she had no strength left to stop him as he placed a hand to her heart, and her casting shattered. The magic wavered and dissipated, leaving the room in utter darkness as Fen's form faded away and his body grew cold and still.

41

SOME DARK REFLECTION

DARKNESS swirled at the edges of Rose's mind. Cold and heavy, it dragged her into its embrace. A ravenous abyss that threatened to swallow her whole. She didn't struggle now— didn't resist at all.

Perhaps it was only fair that death claimed her; its cool grasp would be a welcome reprieve from the pain tearing through her heart. *Fen was gone.* What comfort would she ever find in life?

But then a hand curled around hers. Warm, solid, and so *real*. It held her tight, pulling her back from the edge of the abyss.

"Rose?" The voice was gentle—tender. But soft, as if carried from miles away. "No—stay awake. Please."

Sylvie. Rose tried to open her eyes. To meet that amber gaze she longed for. But she had not the strength to even lift her head. A spark of magic broke through. Hot and fierce, it tore through her chest, shattering the shadow's grasp.

"Don't you dare die on me, Thenlif."

She wanted to reach out, hold her tight. Promise to never leave her side. But the words lay heavy on her tongue, and any promises fell away under the soft lull of slumber.

A soft light burned against Rose's eyelids. With a groan, she rolled onto her side, only to be met with a searing pain. Every muscle in her body ached, her head pounding like it did whenever she let Fen drag her into another bottle of wine. *Fen.* The thought ripped through her heart like a blade.

Tears spilled down her cheeks, landing with a dull finality on the starchy pillowcase beneath her. For every aching pain that pulled at her body, nothing hurt like that. Several long moments crawled by in which she could only weep, curled up in the bed like a small, terrified child.

She wasn't sure how much time passed before she turned, eyes heavy with dried tears as they scanned across the infirmary. She nearly jumped out of her skin then when she caught sight of Sylverfir looming in the doorway, intact and very much alive. Their eyes met before Rose could turn away, and he rushed to her side.

"You're awake!" The flowers he carried tumbled onto the table beside her. "I'll get the healers to bring you some food."

"I don't understand." She sat up slowly. "How are you alive?"

He rubbed the back of his neck, a new, jagged scar curling just under his chin. "Ah, an unfortunate by-product of my curse, I'm afraid. Those rumors about my immortality were never far off. When I woke up, Sylvie and I healed you as best we could before Ewan came barging in with the capital inquisitors."

Rose nodded numbly, her voice taut with tears. "And Fen—is he?"

"He—couldn't be saved." Sylverfir bowed his head. "I'm so sorry, Rose."

It had been foolish to even ask. A desperate, feverish hope against what she already knew to be true. Her throat tightened. "And Hollis?"

Sylverfir's eyes darkened. "Dead. Killed by a blast of life source that the capital inquisitors were happy to chalk up to his own nefarious spell backfiring. Your mother is in Tol Qilius now, smoothing out any dangling inquiries." His eyes flickered to the fallen flowers. "She—er—sent her love."

289

Of course. Protecting Dunhollow's reputation would always take priority for her mother, and even death would not dissuade her from the task. But the thought barely even pierced Rose now.

She sighed deeply, leaning back against her pillows. A distance had grown between her and Sylverfir these past months. His fault or hers, she couldn't really say. But, in that moment, she longed for nothing more than to cross it. To pull him close and weep until all tears subsided. But she didn't.

"How did we get here?" she said finally. "How did any of this happen?"

Sylverfir's face fell, and he sank into the chair at the foot of her bed, rubbing at his beard. "Because I was a fool. I was the first to cast that spell of Hollis's, after your aunt died. But I couldn't bear to use anyone else's life, so I bound it to my own. But life and death are difficult sources, and it backfired. Spectacularly. Still, I should have seen the signs—should've stopped it."

"I think I did." Rose's voice was small, falling from her lips before she could stop it. "See the signs."

"What?"

"When you tried to revive Astoria, she told you to let her go, didn't she?"

"How could you possibly know that?"

"I saw her." She sat up against her starched pillows. "When I connected to Sylvie's and Aveline's souls, I think I let Astoria in too, but only in glimpses. I saw visions of her in the forest with the Order, and then later with you. I think it was her way of warning me—protecting me as best she could."

"Of course she did." Tears welled in his dark eyes. "You remind me so much of her, you know."

"Yes, I saw the photos."

It almost seemed foolish now that she'd once thought it herself in those visions. The benefit of hindsight, she supposed. Or maybe just proof that she did not know herself, even now. Perhaps she was worse than a shade, only a mere echo of a ghost haunting everyone's memory. And maybe that was all she'd ever be, so long as she stayed here.

"No, not that." Sylverfir's voice made her jump. "She too could burn brighter than any sun. But the sun is rarely allowed to shine in Dunhollow. Nothing grows in this place, Rose, it only rots."

Rose frowned. She'd never thought of herself as a sun—perhaps only the pale light of a waning moon. But then she'd rarely had the occasion to see the sun. A strange pain lanced through her heart. *No.* That wasn't quite true. There was one person who'd always brought sunlight to this dreary place.

But she shook her head. She couldn't think about that now. Instead, she forced her mind back to Astoria. She too was burdened by the weight of other people's memories, and each time her story was told, a bit of her changed—a little more was lost.

"My mother said Astoria loved this place—that she planned to teach here."

"Your mother would say that." Sylverfir leaned forward in the chair. "But Astoria never wanted to stay. She agreed to teach here for a few years to appease your grandmother, but after that? She wanted to travel—to tour coastlines and conquer mountains. She wanted to live, and that was stolen from her, just as it was nearly stolen from you."

Rose's gaze fell to her hands. "And instead, Fen paid the price for me."

"Fen made a choice, just as Astoria did. Don't take that away from them."

A terrible choice. Tears spilled down her cheeks. One he'd only had to make because of her. All at once, something within her cracked. Some shard of grief finally shattered, its splintered pieces slicing straight through her heart.

Sobs racked Rose's chest, burning in her aching lungs until it felt as though they might burst. But Sylverfir's arms wrapped around her, warm and steady. As if they might hold the pieces of her broken heart together.

Fen's name alone felt like a shard of jagged glass in her mouth. Losing him tore out a piece of her very soul, but speaking of him was like applying a hot iron to a gaping wound. The pain ran too deep—too fierce. In truth, it was hard to tell where it ended and Rose's heart began, if indeed there was still any difference.

And yet, she couldn't just let him fade away in silent mourning. His sacrifice may only have been for her, but she wouldn't allow it to go unremarked and unremembered. He deserved more than that.

"I don't know how to do this." The whisper fell from her lips as she burrowed deeper into his chest. "How can I go back to classes and casting, when all I see is him? I can't bear anymore ghosts."

Sylverfir's arms tightened around her. "I can't answer that for you. But I do know that you don't have to do it alone." He pulled back, pressing a gentle kiss to her forehead. "Whatever you need, I'm here."

Rose sighed deeply, for she was too tired now for hope. Tired of this place, this grief. She almost wished sleep would find her again. It seemed the only thing capable now of easing the aching pain in her chest. Yet it merely danced at the edge of her thoughts, chased away by the dull thudding of her broken heart.

"Thank you," she managed finally. "But I think I just need rest now."

"Of course. I'll come back later to check on you." He gave her hand a final squeeze before moving toward the doorway. There, he paused, a warm smile spreading across his lips. "Though you may want to hold off on that nap a little longer."

With a wink, he turned and glided out of the room. Rose frowned, staring after him a moment. But then a face peered around the doorway, and any thought of Sylverfir fled out of her mind.

Sylvie.

Her heart fluttered to life in her chest. She looked perfect, as always, but the unfairness of it all didn't prick at her now. As if reading her mind, Sylvie swept into the room with a sly grin, her long houndstooth coat nearly brushing the ground. Dark heels clacked against the stone floor, her tawny cheeks flushed from the cold and framed by soft wisps of hair caught beneath the collar of her coat.

Rose's mouth went dry, heart thudding. She'd always been beautiful, but to see her now so alive was...

Truly, words had never failed her so utterly.

"I—you. You're here."

"Astute as always, Thenlif." She stepped closer to the cot. "Glad to see you awake. You had me worried for a bit there."

Rose fell silent for a moment, picking at the threads of her blanket. Words tangled around her tongue, but none of them quite fitted. What was even left to say between them?

She bit her lip against the sting of tears. "How are you feeling? Being alive again, and all."

"I could ask you the same." Sylvie lowered herself on to the foot of the bed.

"I'm fine."

"Rose ..." Her dark eyes bore into hers, peeling back the lies.

She looked away, hot tears spilling onto her cheeks. "Honestly? None of it quite feels real yet. But I'm glad you're safe. Whatever else, I—I'm glad we got you back."

"I'm sorry about Fen." She squeezed her hand. "I know what he meant to you."

Rose gave her a watery smile. Words failed her, twisting and coiling around her tongue. But Sylvie didn't seem to need them, for she simply sat there, holding her as the tears streamed freely. Somehow, beside her, Rose could almost imagine a day where this pain might fade. Where she could step out of this shadow of grief Fen had left in his wake.

Not now—not today. But someday, she thought, they might find that life together.

42

NOT A CHANCE

THE sky held in a gray silence. Freshly turned earth lay beneath Rose's feet, darkened and damp from the light drizzle of rain and the fall of her own tears. This forgotten courtyard had always been one of Fen's favorite hideaways. The one place in all of Dunhollow he might have ever sought solitude.

She sucked in a sharp breath. His real funeral had been a large affair at his home, full of light and laughter—family and friends. Half the empire had shown up to the memorial festivities afterward. It had made Rose's skin crawl, but Fen would have loved every moment of it.

But now it was just her and Sylvie here in Fen's courtyard. One last goodbye left to say. The small stone stared back at her, Fen's name etched deep into its grooves. She hadn't known what to put beyond that—so many words were left unspoken between them, so many memories she could have named.

It may not have been where his body lay, or where his soul rested. Yet it marked something of him here. All the many parts of him that had lived in this place. His friendships, his studies, his love. He'd never been hers alone in life—he couldn't be in death either.

She sniffed, wiping away a few stray tears as a crumpled letter crinkled in her palm. He was never hers, but this could be. These final words she never got to say, buried deep underneath an empty stone that could never cover all of what he was.

It wasn't enough, but still, it was something.

Squeezing Sylvie's hand, Rose bent down, knees sinking into the damp earth. The soil folded easily beneath her fingers as she tucked the parchment into it before placing her hand gently on the cool stone. One day, she hoped others would come and remember him. That this might be a place of refuge and respite, as he had always been for her.

She lingered there another moment before getting to her feet, letting Sylvie draw her only a short distance away. Her throat tightened as she spread out a woolen blanket on the grass, setting a paper bag atop it.

"You brought it?"

"A bottle of Valé Doir, as requested."

Fresh tears spilled down Rose's cheeks as Sylvie uncorked the bottle of wine. It always was Fen's favorite, and he wouldn't have wanted his death to be a dull affair. She tried her best to muster a genuine smile as Sylvie filled the glasses, but the effort was in vain. Instead, she merely nodded her thanks as Sylvie handed her one of the goblets, crimson wine dancing within.

"To Fen," she whispered.

Their glasses clinked, the wine washing warmly down Rose's throat as a small smile spread sadly across Sylvie's lips.

"Look."

Rose followed her gaze to a small break in the clouds overhead, where one solitary ray of golden sunshine broke through. It stretched down onto them, brushing across Rose's skin with a gentle warmth before fading away. A sad smile pulled at her lips.

Somehow, it almost felt like a goodbye. Like Fen had reached out to squeeze her hand one final time. No matter what Sylverfir said of her, he had been *her* singular light in this place—the one comforting warmth. And now he was gone. Her heart stumbled, breath catching on a choked sob.

Silent tears spilled freely down her cheeks. The sun might always fade in this place, but she wouldn't let his memory slip away so easily. His final gift to her had been life—she would not watch it wither and die like so much else in these hallowed halls.

"Rose?" Sylvie stroked her curls. "Are you all right?"

She leaned back to meet her gaze. The simple answer would have been to lie. To brush away her tears with a scathing laugh and let her mask fall back into place, as she had so many times before. But they were long past simple answers and easy facades now.

"Not today."

She almost wished she could say more, could find words that would soothe her raw and aching heart. But this seemed to be enough for Sylvie, who nodded, bending down to press a gentle kiss to Rose's forehead.

They sat like that awhile longer. To anyone passing, they'd look like nothing more than lovers, entwined in a haze of romantic bliss, lost to a world of their own. Yet, if anyone peered too close, the illusion would quickly shatter, like too much else in this place.

But Rose was past caring now. Sprawled out on the woolen blanket with Sylvie drawing her fingers softly through her curls, she let her tears flow freely, relishing this moment of unguarded peace while she could.

All too soon, the mists would descend, or the rain would fall, and they'd be forced to trade this unmarred silence for crowded halls and false smiles. On and on they would carry, finishing their degrees and suffering in silence, even now that they had each other. This place would never stop taking from them, and they would never stop giving.

What else can we do? she had asked once, though the words rang hollow in her mind. Sylvie hadn't had an answer then, but it seemed almost deceptively simple now. *Anything.*

Doing anything differently would be better than nothing at all. She owed Fen that much—and perhaps herself too.

A soft flutter of wings drew her eyes to the sky before a thick envelope fell into her lap. Rose sat up slowly, turning the paper over in her hands as Sylvie peered over her shoulder.

"What is that?"

"My final results." She ran her thumb over the flap of the envelope, but stilled.

"Well, aren't you going to open it?"

Rose stared at it a moment longer. Once, she'd have torn the envelope apart without a thought. She'd have ravenously counted each mark before cowing Sylvie with her victory. But that all seemed so far away now. With Sylvie lying beside her, warm skin pressed against her own, and amber eyes boring into hers, what use did she have for it?

What meaning did marks hold for spells she would never cast? It had been all she wanted once. But now, with the magic of life burgeoning beneath her fingertips, it just felt empty. She needed something more, something Dunhollow could not give. Sucking in a sharp breath, she finally glanced up, meeting Sylvie's gaze.

"No."

Confusion flashed through her eyes, but only for a moment before shock cut across it. "No?"

"It doesn't matter."

"What?" Sylvie's voice inched up an octave.

In spite of herself, Rose nearly laughed. "It doesn't matter, because I'm going to defer for a semester."

"Defer?" Sylvie's brow creased. "Will your mother allow it?"

"I don't plan to give her much of a choice." Rose pulled at a loose thread in the blanket. She wasn't sure it had ever been done, but it was the least her mother owed her.

"But why?"

She bit her tongue, heart aching for the pain in Sylvie's eyes. It seemed cruel somehow, to leave just when Sylvie had gotten her life back. But staying would be a disservice to them both.

Sylvie needed to reclaim what she'd lost—to rebuild the life that had been taken from her these past few months. But Rose needed to find something she'd never had. And she couldn't do that locked away in the same halls she'd always known, buried beneath familiarity and an empty future only guided by her mother's hand. To live, she needed to leave.

"Because I have to." She squeezed Sylvie's hand. "I spent so long here trying to make myself fit. To mold myself into the perfect student, the perfect caster, the perfect daughter. But none of it was what *I* wanted."

"And leaving is?"

"Not you." The words fell from her lips before she could stop them. "Never you. But I need to do this. To find answers about my casting and, well—maybe myself too."

Because, deep down, there was a part of her that wanted to see, to explore. To go beyond the boundaries of this place and all the horrors it held for her and just never stop. She wanted to see mountains that shattered the sky, oceans that disappeared into the horizon. She wanted to hear a melody of voices meld to her ear and let the wind whip through her hair, if only just to feel something besides this ravenous emptiness in the pit of her stomach.

Sylvie tugged at the ends of her sleeves. "I could go with you."

"And miss another semester?"

"That doesn't matter."

"Yes, it does." Rose stroked a stray strand of hair away from Sylvie's cheek. "To you it does."

She caught her hand. "Not as much as you."

Before she could stop herself, Rose pulled Sylvie close, pressing her lips against hers. They folded beneath her, warm and soft, yet sharp and raw with all the words left unspoken between them. It felt both an eternity and yet far too soon before they broke apart, lips tingling and swollen, and tears drawing tracks down both their cheeks.

"Where will you go?" Sylvie asked finally.

"I'm not sure yet." Rose dried her eyes, leaned back on her hands. "Soren has agreed to go with me. He thinks we should start in the oldest parts of Allian, where necromancy first awoke—that we might find some answers there."

"Oh." Sylvie's face fell. "That's continents away."

Rose's chest tightened, and she stroked Sylvie's cheek with her thumb. "It's not so far that you can't reach me."

"I'll hold you to that, Thenlif." She pulled her into another kiss. "But, before you leave, at least do me one favor."

"What's that?"

"Open your results." Sylvie grinned against her. "If I'm going to complete a semester without you, I need to know what I'm up against."

Rose glanced down at the envelope still clutched between her fingers and smiled. Her thumb grazed over the flap. She could have done her one last kindness, but something stilled her hand.

"And let you win?" Her lips pulled in a wry smile before she turned and hurled the envelope straight into the fountain. "Not a chance."

GLOSSARY OF TERMS

PLACES

Allian (*AH-lee-yahn*) The westernmost of the three continents in the world where Dunhollow exists. Known for its unregulated and powerful magic, it is split up into twenty-two different cohabiting countries across its vast mountains and coastlines, including Etanhe, the birthplace of necromancy.

Ashurd (*Ah-SHERD*) A city at the southwestern tip of the empire. Known as one of the oldest cities in Na Qis, it was the ancient capital of the older Qisan empire and is still a popular destination with the upper echelons of the current empire, thanks to its decadent, ancient architecture and pristine beaches. Also, Fen's home city.

Ir Taril (*EER TAH-rill*) A city/region in the northwestern mountains of Na Qis. Known for both its rugged landscape and its specialty in mental and compulsion magics, it's generally viewed as a less than friendly place by the majority of the empire. However, the imperial family makes great use of the city's skilled compulsionists in their personal court. Rose's family hails from this region.

Isle of Arbelis (*Ahr-BEH-liss*) A forested island off the southeastern coast of the empire. A more recent addition to the empire's ever-growing lands, it's known for its wild grasp of natural magic—particularly pertaining to the forest and the sea. The birthplace of Herbalism and Botany.

Maalstrum Institut (MAHL-strum IHNS-tih-toot) Another magical academy and one of Dunhollow's rivals, commonly referred to simply as Maalstrum. Located in the mountains of Ir Taril, it specializes in mental magics, specifically compulsion.

Na Qis/Na Qisan (Nah KEES/ Nah KEES-awn) The name of both the easternmost continent upon which Dunhollow is located, and the empire that rules it. Meaning "New Qis," it is a continuation of the much smaller Empire of Qis that was brought low centuries before and has now been restyled by its descendants. It covers all corners of the eastern continent and many of its outerlying islands, though it is still expanding. It is well known for its more rigid views of magic and for coveting forms of magic from its conquered territories.

Pellagius of Ilaura (Pell-AH-ghee-us uv Eel-OW-rah) Thought to be one of the earliest settled regions of Allian, Ilaura is an ancient society and one of the first to emerge post-Calamity, built by its survivors. According to history, it was also responsible for bringing magic back into the world.

Pentarchy of Etanhe (Eh-TAHN-heh) The Pentarchy is a coalition of trade cities in the far-western ports of the continent of Allian, while Etanhe is its capital city and the seat of power. Run by a cadre of wealthy merchant families, it is known for being a somewhat lawless place with a long history of piracy and spiritual activity, as well as being the birthplace of necromancy.

Queendom of Pelanghe (Peh-LONG-heh) An ancient queendom, now destroyed, that was located on the western coast of Teonar. According to legend, its last queen was responsible for the Great Calamity, in which she struck down the corrupted old gods, destroyed her city, and became the embodiment of death itself.

Qis/Qisan (Kees/KEES-awn) The original empire that claimed much of the lands around Dunhollow. Much smaller in scope, it spread from the city of Ashurd and reigned for three hundred years before a rebel queen and diviner brought it to its knees in the late sixteenth century (roughly four hundred years ago).

Savoissanta DeVoil (*Sah-vwah-SAHNT-ah duh-VWAHL*) Another magical academy and one of Dunhollow's rivals, commonly referred to simply as DeVoil. Located on the Isle of Arbelis, it specializes in healing magics, namely Botany and Herbalism, and boasts a renowned student hospital.

Telemestra (*Teh-leh-MEH-strah*) A hilly region in central Na Qis known for its vineyards and fine wines.

Teonar (*TEH-oh-nahr*) The southernmost and oldest settled continent in the world. It is widely considered the birthplace of magic, though these days the grand, ancient empires and powerful magics of its western half have largely faded. Its eastern half is ruled by the Southern Trading States, a powerful collection of three countries whose alliance has long fended off the conquering ambitions of Na Qis.

Tol Qilius (*Toll KILL-ee-yus*) The capital of Na Qis. Known for being incredibly opulent, the city seamlessly blends ancient architecture with modern magical advancements. It is both the seat of imperial power and Sylvie's home city.

OTHER TERMS

Cair Riacodla (*Kare Ree-ah-COD-lah*) An incantation that translates to "sleep of death," it is a cutting-edge, dangerous mix of alchemy and herbalism.

Great Calamity/Calamity Though most records of this period are now lost, most remaining ones agree that it was the last great clash between gods and mortals, nearly one thousand years ago, in which those gods were ultimately destroyed. By all accounts, it occurred in the ancient city of Pelanghe and led to its destruction, as well as the very downfall of magic for a time.

Dia vhal (*DEE-yah VAHL*) A common curse that translates to "sacred blood," and can be used to express shock, awe, or anger. Range of intensity includes everything from the relatively inoffensive "oh, damn" to the more vulgar "fuck's sake," depending on the intonation of the swearer.

Edict of Ardalis (*Ar-DAH-liss*) An edict passed about one hundred years before Rose's time that codified in strictest detail the illegality of necromancy alongside dreaming magic and divining, which had unofficially been outlawed centuries earlier.

Iverin stasia (*IH-ver-in STAH-see-yah*) A bright blue plant with sedative properties.

Messere (*Meh-SAIR*) A common honorific and form of address.

(The) Nine The nine gods who founded both the Qisan and Na Qisan empires, according to legend. In the modern day, most within the empire no longer worship them as gods, but rather as folk heroes or powerful casters of old. The old churches and temples to The Nine do, however, still hold some sway in imperial ceremonies and are used by the imperial family to manipulate the lower and middle classes of Na Qisan society, who still largely keep the faith.

Order of Salix (*SAH-licks*) A secretive order founded in the early days of Dunhollow.

Telka (*TELL-kah*) A bitter drink made from the root of the telka plant, that helps increase one's magical reserves. Usually consumed with milk and honey or sweetened cream.

Vaté Doir (*Vah-LEH Dwahr*) Fen's favorite wine, a silky and medium-bodied red with layers of dark fruits complemented by aromas of spice and vanilla leading to a long, honeyed finish.

CAST OF CHARACTERS

Araminta Thenlif (*Ah-rah-MIHN-tah *THEN-leaf*) Thenlif has a harder "th" sound, as in "thin," rather than "then"

Arden Osiander (*AHR-den Oz-YAN-der*)

Astoria Thenlif (*Ah-STOH-ree-yuh THEN-leaf*)

Aveline Goarsbel (*Ah-veh-LEEN GORES-bell*)

Briony Burroak (*BRI-yuh-nee BUR-oak*)

Delia Droosberil (*DEH-lee-yuh DROOS-bare-ill*)

Ewan Elaegius (*YOU-wan Eh-LAY-*ghee-yus*) Elaegius has a harder "g," as in "golly," rather than "gee"

Fenil (Fen) Hathorin (*FEN-ill HAH-*thor-in*) Hathorin has a harder "th" sound, as in "thin," rather than "then"

Imrys Elaegius (*Ihm-REES Eh-LAY-*ghee-yus*)

Hollis Tipill (*HALL-iss TIP-ill*)

Professor Saoloris (*Say-LORE-iss*)

Revan Troidilis (*REH-vahn TROY-dill-iss*)

Rosera (Rose) Thenlif (*ROE-zeh-rah *THEN-leaf*)

Soren Sylverfir (*SORE-en SILL-ver-feer*)

Sylven (Sylvie) Belliaris (*SILL-ven Bell-ee-YAR-iss*)

Printed in the USA
CPSIA information can be obtained
at www.ICGtesting.com
JSHW021437130924
69717JS00001B/1

9 781647 101473